IN HIS COMMAND

IN HIS COMMAND

A Don't Tell Novel

RIE WARREN

New York   Boston

Copyright © 2013 by Rie Warren
Excerpt from *On Her Watch* copyright © 2013 by Rie Warren
Lyric from "These Birds" by Shotgun Tori. Copyright © 2011 by Sheer Music Publishing. Reprinted by permission.

Forever Yours
Hachette Book Group
237 Park Avenue, New York, NY 10017
www.hachettebookgroup.com
www.twitter.com/foreverromance

First Print on Demand Edition: August 2013

Forever Yours is an imprint of Grand Central Publishing.

The Forever Yours name and logo are trademarks of Hachette Book Group, Inc.

The publisher is not responsible for websites (or their content) that are not owned by the publisher.

The Hachette Speakers Bureau provides a wide range of authors for speaking events. To find out more, go to www.hachettespeakersbureau.com or call (866) 376-6591.

ISBN 978-1-4555-7515-2

Acknowledgments

This is such an exciting time and there are so many people to thank for helping me on this massive journey that is the Don't Tell series. My gratitude goes to the team at Grand Central Publishing Forever Yours for their skill and know-how. Latoya Smith, my fabulous editor, is an unbeatable story groomer, guide, and all-around support system.

My crazy band of critique partners are with me from the time I start bouncing around the wildest ideas until the minute I write *The End*. Kat Asimos, Jenna Barton, Nicki Firman, Rowan Moon, Tracey Porcher, Claudia Storheim, and A. D. Wayy are the women I laugh with, rail at, and who rally me when I'm at hair-pulling-out point. My love and appreciation belong to Gillian Littlehale, who reaches across miles of virtual space at least five times a day throughout the entire story process, which goes on long after I've typed *The End*. Many thanks to Ron McAuley, my go-to guy for all things weapons and military tactics.

Last, but most important, I give my thanks and love to my husband, daughters, and my parents. Their support is as invaluable as their understanding is irreplaceable.

IN HIS COMMAND

Chapter One

The song started softly, lilting high notes saturating the air. The pretty tinkling bells—or some such shit—got real dirty real fast, rapidly descending into rough bass that blasted through the soles of my boots, winding up to my balls. The grinding beat joined raunchy flickering strobes, light like the flashes mounted on relic cameras used only by hard-core black-market dealers in explicit art. The kind of camera that once turned on me so long ago I thought I'd put a cap on that crap.

Investing more time in that line of thinking was gonna end in a massive headache and a revisit to heartache. There'd be none of that. Not here. Not now. Not ever.

I focused on the open archways, where the crowd of dancers writhed in sinuous movements. Illicit lovers moaned from shadowy corners and against the massive brick columns of this repurposed sanctuary. Sweat poured from half-naked bodies. *Flash-pound.* Necks thrown back. *Flash-pound.* Hands curling around tits, curving over cocks.

Flash-pound.

My heartbeat.

Shit, with the amount of feedback coming at me, it felt like the Company would find us by the sound waves alone.

I was on leave outside the barricades of Alpha Territory, which was a mighty feat in itself. Definitely not in my barracks, aka my two-roomer with exactly one bed—standard single, two sheets, one flat pillow—a two-burner cooktop, a mini fridge, and a standing-room-only shower. Mildew included.

Twenty-three hundred hours. September 15, 2070. But who the frig cared anymore? The months added up and washed away like so many waste-paper products recycled in the toilet. This day marked my twenty-eighth birthday, and I was celebrating it in the anony-mous arms of the Amphitheater, so called as a dig against the cold, urban Company.

Hell, the Amphitheater was the closest thing I had to a home. The common link I shared with my fellow revelers was that our *perverse, dirty* desires were outlawed. We were shoved so deep un-derground by the new world order, the Amphitheater moved one step ahead of the Company, keeping off the grid, cropping up in the Territory outskirts and occasionally outside. It was a close, closed community—as much as possible given that no personal info was exchanged, no matter how familiar the face.

No tomorrows here, just next time. Unless you got hauled in for homosexual crimes.

Happy fucking birthday to me.

Since I spent most of my time on duty—and in the closet—I needed to throw some enthusiasm into my attitude. Be a peach and all that. Another drink might help me get my chipper on.

The bartender was as round as a cask of contraband hooch her-self, pulling a rare bleak look as she passed me a bottle. "You hear about Jax?"

Jax wasn't the real name of the recently captured lesbian, but one she'd gone by on account of her spirited personality. *Jacked-up Jax.* Bright as a brass button and energetic to boot. A real popular pal with the gals.

"Yeah."

"Her RACE trial, what a goddamn waste of a good woman all because she wasn't a breeder." The barkeep planted her elbows between us, her gray spiked hair leaning left with the suggestion of grief.

Taken into custody for fucking a woman, Jax had gone through enforced rehab, her only way out to perform a straight sex act before the RACE Tribunal. Repopulation and Civilization Enforcement.

Laughs all around.

I nodded over my drink. "At least she went down fighting." She went down because she refused the terms. Now Jax was one of many put in the ground.

"Damn straight…so to speak."

Commiseration came in a shared stare held with painful understanding, not flappy-mouthed conversation. Our bottles clinked, and I exhaled in relief when she buttoned her lip. I was unwilling to discuss anything remotely related to my line of work.

Unlike Jax, we weren't underground this time, and we weren't in a cavernous warehouse; this place was open air, care of the loving touch of whoever had taken TNT to the Civil-War-era church belonging to Old History. Beautiful brick walls were half blasted away so the lamplights and halos shimmered with eerie shadows from the last, aged, live oaks caped in tendrils of Spanish moss.

Arched recesses gave way to mounds of grass—that vibrant green, fragrant left-to-grow stuff not seen inside Alpha Territory walls. The delicate church construction was guarded outside by massive stone mausoleums and great granite gravestones with the names of Wannamaker and Heyward and Rice. On arrival I'd cased the location before stepping one foot inside.

I was horny, not stupid.

Tipping back my beer, I scanned the ruins packed with hot bodies, measuring up possible threats. No such thing as a secure night off in my line of work. My reconnoiter came to a halt when I got a bead on the big blond male quaffing a longneck across from me, his back to a corner, same as mine. His eyes scanned between a couple of the arched openings until our gazes clashed and held.

He was noted from before and very much on my radar. He didn't drop my stare or shift his feet. He had some kind of presence that tipped my guns. Including the one in my pants.

I knocked back my drink and kept my aim on the cocky man rasping two fingers across his lips. His razored hair hung straight past his chin with ends that licked a strong jaw and slanting cheekbones. He was a dirty blond, the dirty was a given from the gimmesome glint of his blue eyes and the flirting line of his full lips. His golden-tipped stubble would leave a good burn on my face, chest, and between my thighs. His shoulders filling the width of the corner he guarded, and every so often his eyes ranged around the place, scoping it out. For security, not sex.

I understood that impulse.

The Purge happened two lifetimes ago, when history was sketchy and intel questionable. Beginning with environmental hazards such as acid rain, global warming, the ice cap melting and ignored by all but the most gung-ho scientists, the Purge slowly steamrolled across the world. Unable to sustain the seven-billion-plus population, our earth finally reached maximum capacity, triggering an environmental downward spiral. The catastrophic earth-wide event was a done deal by 2020. The rest didn't matter all that much to me anyway. What did matter was it left a huge hole in important things like leadership and government, and it did one hell of a number on democracy. The Purge ripped a new asshole right through the hands-holding, back-to-earth, for-the-people ideology of the early twenty-first century.

The Plague that followed later rounded out the destruction detail. I could calculate the damage from that one firsthand. It had cost me my family. My mother, father, and sister. I was still waiting for the next episode to hit.

Shit always comes in threes.

After the Purge, the remaining populace—the refugees—didn't have to wait long for wake-the-hell-up time, except there weren't all that many of them left to wakey-wakey. That's when the Company took control. Fat corporate cats stabilized the crumbling continents by dividing them into identical pie pieces. Their solution? Cultivate the dwindling pop through legalized procreation and industrial division of labor. Democracy gasped its dying breath.

The CO's reach? Worldwide. The number-one wage earner? Reproduction. What would get you a good old-fashioned hanging in the Quadrangle? Homosexuality, and/or any other unapproved sexual activities or proclivities.

Greed and avarice were the new rulers, freedom of worship going the same way as freedom of choice. Whatever, the CO were equal-opportunity ass-maggots.

Who just happened to pay my wage.

For people like me, love was folklore, sexual release fought for, and let's just get rid of that whole cross-your-heart idea of lifelong mates. At least I had my military training, my Corps troops, and my weapons to keep me warm at night.

And this.

Did I say happy fucking birthday to me? Oh yeah.

Add the Class-A asshole at my back doing the breathe-heavy routine—a mere twink compared to the rugged man still watching me—and it was so not party time. Man, I was tired of babysitting.

I didn't have my fatigues on, but I was so fricking fatigued. I did have a Saturday-Night-Special throwaway tucked against the small of my back. There were a lot of things I could do without but a weapon? Call it a security blanket, the only kind I liked tucked against me.

I threatened, "You better back off, pretty boy, before I get trigger happy."

Yeah, I had charming down pat.

I inventoried the hedonistic gasps, moans, music. The more the better, every fetish fulfilled for at least one night. Looking around the destroyed church, I took a little bit of heart that there was worshipping of the sexual kind going on.

My arm brushed against the hand of a woman lying on a bare plank of wood. Her legs were limp, her body relaxed, her neck rolling from side to side as her Dom plinked one more clothespin to the tissue of her breast. Her tits bloomed from the hard wooden fetters. Drugged up on endorphins, the girl didn't move a muscle when his palm meandered under her short skirt and up her thighs until her sudden gasp meant his fingers hit home.

Barkeep served the recognizable mouth breather behind me while he tried to help himself to me. Gripping my beer bottle so tight it was a wonder the glass didn't shatter, I barely moved my lips as I spoke. "Go get yourself another daddy to play with, boy."

As always, the kid had a death wish, because he continued to hang on my back like a damp rag. I ignored him to sweep the scene, stopping at the regulation fucking going on west of me. A top-heavy brunette presented her nipples while she bounced up and down the dick that had escaped the fly of her man's trousers. He clamped over those popped-out buttons like his life depended on it. Probably did.

Her gray spikes perking up with her eyebrows, the barkeep gave a low whistle that sucked in her round rosy cheeks. "Back in the day,

I used to have my pick of the fillies. Nice rack on that one. But she ain't your style."

I confirmed with a nod.

She chortled and bent her head close, mentioning the hanger-on practically drooling down my back. "Neither is he, huh?"

He sure as hell wasn't. Neither was getting flogged, roped up, or—in general—groped. But I did come to get fucked. I simply wanted to find a man, never ask his name, find us a nice private bit of hillside, and make like a jack-off curtain. Get laid. Then get on my way.

That was all the relief I could expect.

The whole hypocrisy thing was carving a canyon straight through my chest. Putting down the few unorganized rebels when I should have been one of 'em. Thing was, my job was the only way to stay out of the breeding program and keep my feet firmly on the ground instead of buried underneath, because no goddamn way would I go before RACE to prove myself a hetero by doing a woman. Just...*no*. Besides, only way to bring the Company down was from the inside. And since that wasn't gonna happen either, I made do with the lose-lose situation.

The swish of a flogger sounded; fat slaps of soft leather landed on flesh. The blindfolded man on the cross shivered; tears of sweat tracked down the indent of his spine, dripping into the cleft of his ass, gorgeous taut globes crisscrossed with pink welts. Thrown into a sharp relief of shadows and light, his muscles bunched and relaxed, bunched and relaxed while his low moan was promptly quieted by the precise smacks of the flogger's handle against his heavy balls. Resuming his strong balletic strokes in a *left, right, left, right* rhythm, every once in a while the Dom dipped to his ear and caressed the heated marks on superior muscle.

Working around the St. Andrew's Cross, another station of wanton worship, I regained the vision I'd lost. Still shouldering up the corner, still on the same beer. Pencil Dick was my steady shadow, but I was so into the other man—hard-core into him—PD and his heavy panting just became more background fuzz.

I was staring at the attractive piece of fuck-me across the way with no subtlety at all when fingers slid over my hips, planted on my crotch, and stroked my big hard one to pole position.

Big Blondie across the way took it all in without a wince.

His blatant disregard combined with the boy's hands on my dick flipped my switch. "Fuck, Leon!"

The insolent bastard pulled me back to his groin. "*Mais*, I never tought I'd hear dem words from you. That an invitation?"

His voice was girlish but his dialect guttural, an accent he put on with the same ease as his inevitable come-ons. The distinct mother tongue a holdover from his ancestors, most of whom had been wiped out during the Purge when it hit the southern deltas of the former United States.

I caught his wrists in one hand, pinning him against a column. "The only invitation you're gonna get is the one to your own funeral. Now, keep your hands off me."

He did that ridiculous bullshit. Dropped his eyelashes, pouted his lips, and nagged like we were the Mr. and Mrs. "*Mais*, I get it. You still hankerin' after dat tall drink of jizz over dere?"

That got my back up. *Hankering?* Not in this lifetime. "Fuck off."

No way was I all het-up because Blondie had made his first appearance in two months. Not that I was counting. As for pining, only one guilty of that was Leon.

"I only see you at the T'eater every month or so. You walk da big walk, but you never let loose."

Again with the whiny wifey routine. I cranked the neck of his shirt in my fist. His eyes were soft, as if he thought I was about to kiss him. I cursed and let him go. "Listen. You're cute but too frigging young for my tastes. And I don't do brunettes." I stalked away, grumbling, "You need to lose the desperate, boy."

At the bar, I made a damn point to stop the massive observation of Captain Cock Hardener in the far corner. So when a voice came across in a deep southern drawl right beside me, I went haywire inside.

"I hate bein' hit on."

I glanced left and confirmed Blondie's stance. Hands loose on his hips, leg cocked, me in his line of fire. This was the man I went home to, fucked my fist to, climaxed long and loud to since I'd first laid eyes on him five months ago. And yeah, even though I'd frequented the Theater a few times since then, the only thing I'd picked up was a beer bottle. I hadn't had a blow job in ages, given head for longer than that, and I'd deflected all the "let's-fuck" invites with the same one-liner I'd just played to Leon: You're not my type.

Jesus. Leon was right. I was pining.

Aaand Blondie hates being hit on. Great. Fucking fantastic, in fact. Guess I wouldn't polish up my smile for him. I took a swill, then went with my usual tight-lipped grimness. "Yeah."

Smooth as bourbon, that was me.

"Can I get you a drink?"

When I turned to him, I caught his suppressed smile. My own was somewhere in the region of my heart, speeding that shit up. "You hitting on me?"

"Yep." His grin widened across the masculine lips I focused on, figuring out how quickly I could get him below me, my dick between those lips until I was rooting against the rooftop of his mouth, aided by what I didn't doubt would be his talented tongue.

My smile spilled out after my, "Okay." *Okay?* What the mother-fuck was that? This wasn't my SOP.

I canned my grin.

We drank, side by side. We watched each other. A spear of long-ing stabbed down my stomach and hit my balls, setting alarm bells off in my brain.

Swiping my hand over my crew cut, I fell back to comfortable ter-ritory. "How do I even know you're legit?"

The man took a moment, his look suspended somewhere below my hips, where all my juice brewed. An eyebrow lifted in direct time with my swift erection. His eyes rose to my mouth before pinpoint-ing on my glare.

His voice was that same deep drawl, combined with the husky tone of hunger. "You always interrogate men tryin' to pick you up?"

"You trying to pick me up or set me up?"

A chuckle jostled those big shoulders. His mutter of, "You've got no idea," was hidden behind a deep draft of his beer.

I made ready to move on, swearing myself to oblivion for even thinking about possibilities beyond my reach. But his fingers on my neck, stroking upward over my throat, held me in a sexual trance I couldn't break.

He was leaner and taller than me, but I could tell his muscles matched mine. And no fucker did that. I would break Leon in two. Not this one. Only...*damn*. He had something I couldn't put my finger on, but I wanted to. And my mouth. Sealing around his cock.

"See that?" He slid behind me, right where I never let anyone stay as long as I could draw a breath or my SIGs.

I steeled my impulse to pat him down—for more than just sidearms—the soft stubble of his cheek gliding against the clean shave of mine. My heart jackhammered; something in my leathers grew steelier than my instincts.

The corner of his lips nearly tasted mine when he spoke. "Over there."

Over there was a table upon which a black-haired woman lay as an all-you-could-eat meal. Her skirt was hiked up to her waist while a lithe little number rolled their breasts together, gyrating their bare pussies in slow undulations. The muscles in her thighs trembled. The moans of the mountee were buried under the all-natural cleft of a voluptuous redhead kneeling in front of her face. Kisses were traded between wet loins and mouths and back again.

I stood my ground when he stepped closer, circling strong arms around my waist, rumbling, "That's nice, isn't it? Reckon if I wanted, I could go on up there, get my cock out, and slide right into one of those warm, wet pussies, starting with that pretty lady on the bottom, get her good and hot first."

Normally the idea of a man on top of a woman hardly got more than a "do what you gotta do, dude" from me, but the idea of him fucking a female rankled me all the way to my nads. My hands clamped over his, ready to tear the teasing asshole off me, but Blondie held tight and continued with the mindfuck that kept me erect and enraged.

"Then I'd slide out and go to work on that sweetie on top. Bang her until the table rocked, and I'd wanna mouthful of the redhead's cunt at the same time."

His harsh, sexual words in that soft accent had my teeth grinding, my muscles locking down, my legs rocking, and my dick ready to rocket off.

"That'd be hot, if I was into it, right?"

"Whatever you say," I growled.

His low chuckle sweeping across my straining neck, he brought me right against him. I felt his raging arousal for the women. He laughed again when I craned away, one step from doing him the favor of dislocating his arms from his shoulder sockets.

"But that's not hot, big man." He shifted, seating himself fully against my ass. "You are."

My head dropped, and I groaned when his lips slid up the back of my neck, brushing into my buzz cut.

He pointed to the centerpiece, the St. Andrew's cross, and dragged his mouth to my ear. "That's what I like."

The scene had varied, same Dom, different play pawn. A regular on the scene, the man must've had one in every pocket of his drawstring leathers. Now he wielded a quirt, and he broke a sweat, as did I.

Yeah, not going there either, so goodbye, sweetheart.

The only torture I dealt in was the kind I doled out, and it wasn't kinky. It was all about getting the canaries to sing. "You into BDSM?"

"I'm talkin' about cock."

Fuck.

"I like the way his sub's gets wider at the base. See that? See how hard he is? Imagine suckin' that down your throat. Nice hook to it, too. *Mmm.*" His fingers triangulating my groin, he asked, "You like to suck cock?"

I was blown away. This shit didn't happen to me. Sure, the "Hit-me-up, big boy" came hot, heavy, and often when I was at the Amphitheater, but my brisk "Go get fucked by a goat" glare took care of that. *I* was the aggressor.

His light finger work remained outside my blast zone. "What I really wanna see is yours."

Well, he could see my cock, suck and get fucked by it, but first, I needed to show him I wasn't some piece of fluff to be toyed with. I was a damn commander, not a cherry. Disengaging from him, I strolled to the Dom, feeling Blondie's bemused stare drilling into my back with every step. I waited for the downstroke of the Dom's whipping arm to have quiet words him.

You wanna be aggressive? Watch this.

I should've been doing more than jacking sub cock, but there weren't a whole lot of other options. Most were paired up, tripled…Fuck, it was an all-out orgy. I certainly wasn't gonna bend Leon over and bang him for Blondie's pleasure. Although, if this was for his pleasure, there were probably better ways to go about it.

Whatever. It wasn't as if we'd traded rings, not even cock rings for that matter.

Given the nod, I dropped to my knees, stroking the rigid length at face level and cupping the sub's sacs. While his master was getting his swing on, I took a double-handed grip on that thick, virile flesh, keeping an eye on Blondie with every upward sweep and swipe across the tumescent cap. Coming down hard and fast, the quirt's lashing clashed with the slow piston of my fists. We stretched the sub to the breaking point of pleasure and pain until sweat dripped, precome curled from his tip in thick teardrops, and his neck pulled back for a silent scream. Another slash, another full-length squeeze up his slick shaft, and the sub lowered his stance, spreading his legs, looking for permission to pour his semen into my palms.

Blondie's eyes lost that hazy, lazy look. They were crystalline, possessing astonishing violence I knew from the occasional view in the mirror. He stormed toward us, fists clenched at his sides. I jerked faster, slipping up and down the rock-hard rod, relishing Blondie's reaction.

He beckoned me away, his features stark. I took my time finishing up by polishing the flat of my palm around and around the dome of the sub's cock. On my feet, I heard the distinct *smack* of cock to stomach followed by the wet suck of a palm to shaft. A fast report of lashes landing on flesh merged into untamed shouts when the sub released his seed all over the ground.

I wiped my hands on my leathers, glad at least the other man's cock hadn't been in my mouth. It would've been disrespectful to Blondie.

Hello, conscience, long time no see.

Stalking past the table of females *in flagrante*, steering away from Leon watching my exit, I motioned Blondie outside with a jerk of my head.

Beyond the escarpment, feathers of a warm breeze blew the steam from my frustrated stomp. A hand on my shoulder clenched and released and Blondie was so close when I spun around, his breath whirled over my forehead, a sweeter warm breeze than the one played by the trees.

He didn't move back; instead he dipped his knees enough so our mouths were level, and his words were hot and pissed off. "You put on that show for me?"

"Nah. Just got tired of talking."

His hands on my hips reeled me in. "How'd you like it if I pulled a stunt like that?"

"I don't know. Did I blink and miss our Joining Ceremony?"

"Damn it!" My mention of the Company-approved marriage act unsettled him for all of a second or two. "Only cock you should be touching is mine."

Double that.

A group of young men and women trudged past. Their uniform was black on black from their hair, kept long and uncut, to their clothing, shabby and unusual. Their heads were down as if in prayer, the murmurs they exchanged too quiet to make out. Worn lace and silks and shawls rustled in their wake like ghosts, leaving me with the bad whiff of Nomad in my nostrils.

With my hand clasped in his, Blondie led me farther away. His steps were precise, his eyes roaming. Mine did the same. The blank, black forest surrounded us, so different from Alpha.

A wooden march led us to a trio of tombstones. With a lowered head, he contemplated the stones whose inscriptions were mostly rubbed out with age and neglect. I made out the first letters of one name: HARM. A fitting warning given the way Blondie's frown drew his fair eyebrows together.

Shaking his head, moving out of the semicircle, he called back, "You like kink?"

"I like sex."

"You get it much?" In the faint glimmer from rigged halo lights, I saw his cheeks flush. "'Cause it looks like you do."

"You digging for illegal activities or offering?"

"I'm askin' you a question. Those lips gonna loosen up for me?"

"No." I was adept at denying myself. I'd done it all my life. All around us Spanish moss clung to the corkscrewing limbs of oaks sprouting with resurrection ferns. There was an old tarmac road parting the ruins from a rare lake whose surface shimmered under the moon. "I'm not answering any questions."

The side of his mouth drawn in, he nodded. "Right. I got it." He backed away, his eyes no longer vigilant but aimed at the ground.

I watched his retreat, powerfully aroused by him, feeling as lonely as I'd ever been. A combo that couldn't be beat.

He jumped at the sound of impact when I brought my fist down hard on my thigh.

"Gonna regret this," I muttered as I walked forward, sweeping my fingers across that strong jaw, rough with golden whiskers, and lifting my mouth.

"Oh Christ." He moaned as my lips fastened on his. Curling his fingers around my ass, he fed from my lips. That was the only way to describe his hunger, our in-and-out lunges chasing the other's tongue.

When my jacket dropped, so did any pretense of being a cold-hearted, coolheaded warrior. I trapped him in my arms as he ran his fingertips around my waist once, twice, before dragging them inside the leather, molding my ass within broad palms.

"Yeah," I rasped, crashing the rigid lengths of our cocks together.

With each roll across each other, he grunted and I moaned, pulling his bottom lip between mine. I shoved my hands into his hair and twisted the lengths between my fingers, angling his head to better fit the way I wanted to kiss him. With nothing but pure greed.

We parted by a paper-thin divide. Our lips plinked, pressed, pursued. *Teased.*

He stroked down my ass, his fingertip circling the star of flesh, pressing and drumming. "You like that, big man?"

My stomach clenched so fucking hard, cramps of lust ran all the way to my cockhead and down to my tightening balls. "Hell, yes."

"*Mmm,* bet you do." He made his way up my chest, tearing into my shirt. "Look at that."

His palms rubbed up and down; then he did the same with his cheek, sending a smattering of kisses and seditious words onto the aroused nubs of my nipples. "Goddamn. You smell like sex, right here. Bet your cock smells even better. I'm gonna get every bit of you wet."

He sucked on my pecs, gnawing away at the hard edges of muscle, meting out sexy punishment on my tight nipples. When he bit the sinews of my ribs and again at my stomach, I pushed him lower.

Working me out of zippers and buttons, he said, "Gonna make you come so hard." He yanked my pants down my thighs, intent on my cock, which was so erect it was swollen at the tip.

A howl of need came from deep within my chest as I threw my head back.

He kneaded my sac and smirked up at me. "Feel good, honey?"

"Yeah," I gasped. "But this'll feel even better."

His face between both my hands, I took him directly to the tip of my dick, letting him get no nearer than a tongue swipe away. Cranking his hair in one hand, I worked my fist up and down my cock, right in front of his face while his tongue lapped my head, capturing the trail of moisture from the slit on top. My teeth gnashed at the torture I inflicted on myself, and I spread my feet to brace myself. I wondered how long it would take him to beg, or if I'd blow my load all over his face first.

In the end, all it took was a wisp of his hot breath over me. I gave in, my muscles shaking. Throbbing in every region of my body, I pushed my pelvis out, brought his head forward, and fucked slowly into his mouth. The softest licks of flat tongue, the deepest suction down his throat. His lips were a strained oval around me, his eyes dark, blue and hooded, hooked on mine. Saliva coated my cock as he sucked me quickly in and out until I was familiar with every surface of his mouth, the stricture of his throat, the pointed pleasure of his tongue.

I stood on the balls of my feet to exploit the downward angle of his throat to a better degree. *Far fucking better.*

Between my meat and his full mouth, his dirty talk did me in when he drew back for a breath, the tease of his tongue touching me as he spoke. "Fuck yeah, honey. Fuck my face. Wanna feel you come in my mouth."

Didn't have to tell me twice. I was used to following orders. I took his head in two hands again. Craning his neck and bending my knees, I sank into his open mouth over and over again until I froze as all the feeling for him—for Blondie—blasted out of me with a roar.

I sawed in and out, and his hands curled over my wet shaft, massaging every ounce of come into his overfull mouth. Shudders racked me in waves, and just when I thought I was done, he furrowed his tongue around my tip, stroked fast, and smiled when another jet pulsed into his mouth.

Falling to the soft cushion of moss on the ground, I pitched him forward on top of me.

Kisses.

Goddamn sleek kisses so deep and intense I sought more. An endless measure of kisses.

I flattened him to his back and got off on the way he spread his arms wide and shifted his groin for my touch. The man I'd wanted for months on end seemed to ache for me as much as I did him. I couldn't keep my hands off beautiful Blondie one second longer, fucking dying to bring every fantasy to life as short harsh breaths cranked from his chest.

With his shirt yanked up and out of the way, I discovered the dense planes of his torso and paps the same dark pink as his mouth, which opened when I traced those nubs with my fingers and then my tongue. The trail from his belly mirrored the dark blond of his hair, a fine tangle all the way to the waist of his trousers. Working his pants over his hips, I found out that line of hair became a clipped curling forest around the base of a cock punching up from a pair of pretty balls, the whole package framed by pelvic cliffs.

My face buried at the base of his thick, blunt-headed cock, I spat on my fingers and strayed to the hot pucker of his ass. With his cock shining from the kiss of my lips and the lap of my tongue, I tucked a finger inside him. Up to one knuckle, moaning over the taste of him inside my mouth when his ass flexed around my fingertip.

I dove lower, licking the area I fingered, adding another. Musky sweetness melted to my mouth until I was tracing a wet path from his ass to the shelf of his cock and back again, always spreading my fingers, thrusting deeper, searching for that ball of tissue hiding high inside.

Blondie's big thighs spread. His back arched, his head tossed, and he sat up so his abs crunched, his fingers pushing inside my mouth alongside his cock until we were both working him hard.

The ground rumbled. Blocks of bricks sheared off, tumbling from church remains. The start of his orgasm shifted the world sideways.

I planted myself on the green ground, getting my knees in, kissing his thighs, and sliding my hands under his ass.

The rumble gathered, shaking the soil.

His shoulders curled off the ground. "You 'bout ready to fuck me?"

"Yeah."

"'Cause I'm tired of the teasin'."

"That so?" I swept my open palms up his muscular ass, backing off when his belly turned tight and his cock fought between us.

The churning ground beneath us soldiered onward.

Soldiered.

"Jesus Christ, tanks!" I whispered harshly, hauling him to his feet as fear ripped through the carnal haze of foreplay.

"This ain't supposed to happen." He zipped up while I shoved his shirt at him.

"No shit." I put my head into *Get-the-fuck-outta-here* mode.

The old tornado siren howled, real alarms ringing with my imagined ones.

A warning to the Amphitheater. Some unlucky fuck was gonna meet dust tonight.

Not me. Not because of him.

If I turned cold while the alarm screamed, he became glacial. His frigid stare hollowed out my gut better than any knife. "You got about one minute."

He knew the drill as well as me: get caught and get shot. Best-case scenario in a situation like this.

I backed to the roadside. "Listen." I hesitated, the incoming tanks roaring closer. "I don't want it to end like this. Come with me." I asked because I'd just been about to ball him. Because I'd always wanted him. Because being alone was my only weakness.

Not like it had been a date or anything, I could add that to the *never-gonna- happen* roster. But I had some damn manners, thank you very much, and I wanted to see the man home and safe.

He remained aloof. "I have my own transport."

"Suit yourself." *Asshole* was implied and correctly inferred when his posture stiffened.

I didn't look back. I sprinted to my bike and gunned it so hard, I took up chunks of turf. I had two seconds to spill across the road ahead of the tanks and down the dirt path that led back thirty kilometers to Alpha Territory. Considering the tornado alarm that had been disabled years ago and whatever had made the Corps come in our direction, I knew shit was up in the city. I'd be briefed by Command soon, and my absence would be viewed as absconding, no matter how goddamn golden my record was.

Suspicion was human nature. The CO banked on it.

Wrapped over my motorcycle, I swayed and rocked with the road.

The night turned cool and sped a few weepies down my cheeks.

That was only the wind at Mach speed, flattening my cheeks.

Not emotion.

Not tonight.

I felt nothing. The wind numbed me. Made me check my emotional gage and compartmentalize Blondie back where he belonged. Names were never shared among us. Only Leon, and that was because he was too happy-go-fucky to know better. I should've checked on him, made sure he got away.

Riding back into Alpha wasn't the breeze it had been getting out.

Jimmying an unguarded gate on the far side of the city from the Quadrangle, I revved down, keeping to alleys, watching as heightened patrol teams took to the streets. My block was in sight when I heard the metallic click of weapons cocking over the low purr of my engine.

"Turn it off. Dismount. Hands in the air." The demand was given in a high-pitched reedy voice.

Oh hell, no. This isn't gonna do.

As I faced the patrolmen, I knew I looked like a menacing motherfucker when I flashed them an evil grin, but they didn't want to mess with me after the night I'd had. On my birthday. After Blondie had blown me off.

Oh, I raised my hands all right, to take off my helmet.

Those two troops weren't from my highly trained squad; that was clear from the newfangled bullshit rapid-blast guns aimed at me—weapons known to seize up in damp weather, but they were flashy and shiny so all the booters wanted them.

It was also clear by the way the rookies looked ready to shit themselves when they recognized me and my fear-inducing scowl.

"Holy hell. Sorry, Commander!" The youth's thin voice turned into a squeak. "We were told to keep an eye out for unusual goings-on. Didn't know it was you. This sector's on lockdown."

"So it is. I was just checking to make sure everything was good. So I suggest you two skedaddle before I report you for compromising your positions."

They hustled away and I called, "Don't make the same mistake twice, boys. Liable to get you court-martialed."

Parking outside my apartment block, I peered around from the slits of my eyes.

Always on guard. Again.

"Fuck this." I punched in my code, crossed the cold lobby, and rode a mirrored elevator eyed with security cameras, cracking my knuckles instead of flipping the bird.

Because I was one of them.

Commander Caspar Cannon of the Elite Tactical Unit, Alpha Territory.

I wanted Blondie.

And now I would never get his name.

Chapter Two

Within the confines of my two-roomer, my all-due-haste receded in favor of licking my wounds. I felt like a pussy for feeling snubbed by Blondie, all because he didn't need a lift home. Truth was, I'd put myself out there for him beyond anything considered smart or reasonable by my own rules of engagement only to get shut down.

Loneliness wasn't an emotion to whine about. It was a way of life.

Checking my tackle, I made sure my balls were swinging and my cock was still attached. *Yep.* At least that was something.

My isolation was compounded by the hair-raising feeling of constant scrutiny combined with the utter CO dependency forced upon all Territory residents. Almost all the roads once webbing outward from this city had been systematically destroyed. What little movement there was among the Territories had to be approved well in advance, and a ticket out was given only for a damn good reason. In the eyes of the Company, there weren't many excuses legitimate enough to warrant leave.

Communications crawled with spyware.

Entertainment meant chaperoned socials or meeting friends for the latest propaganda blockbuster. Not the kind of knees-up I was talking about.

Hookups were damn near impossible and nearly always a bad idea.

The few freedoms to be had were saved for those who worked for the CO and their best little breeder families. The rank and file had something to aspire to, at least, which led them to step *left, right, left, right, left* into the authoritarian ideals.

Independent thinking was discouraged. By discouraged I meant you'd get thirty in lockup for anything unsanctioned. Books, music, art were branded a big bad no-no unless on the list of endorsed materials.

Given my rank, I had a little leeway but not much. Not enough to, say, uproot and leave Alpha. Besides, there wasn't really anyplace else to go.

Guess I'd keep making do with right here and right now.

I was stationed in the epicenter of Alpha Territory, one of four map points in North America, where humankind resided, one of the sixteen divvied out among the other died-out, dried-up land masses across the globe. The rest of the continental United States—the Wilderness—had been left to the primitive Nomads, who protected their land with fierce savagery.

This particular southeastern enclosure of razor-wire barricades, blank-eyed buildings, and budding regeneration became home after I left Basic, my skills needed in subduing any fomenting nonconformists. My intonation didn't fit the southern drawl *hey, y'all* at all. In fact, there wasn't anything smooth about me, care of Corps boot camp, which had beaten all the sweetness out of me. But I wasn't the only one. We were a mashed-up population made of migrants from the Purge.

Delayed waves of death and environmental destruction had annihilated an ever-decreasing circle until the survivors became exiles in the final four Territories of North America. It was the same all across the world, if the rumors could be believed. People were forced closer and closer to the hearts of big business—London, Tokyo, New York…Atlanta—as if willed by the CO itself. Those cities no longer existed, having been swallowed into Delta, Nu, Beta, and Alpha Territories, to name the Big Four.

Each Territory had its own CEO voted in from a pool of Company applicants to convene with the InterNations Ruling Committee. It was a pretty incestuous affair, but they didn't seem to have a problem with that. Especially since it left the general pop with no say over their leaders or laws.

The governance of the Company, including our little piece of paradise, had been welcomed. With parades, promotionals, and cleanups. Followed by raids, rules, and rat-outs.

The business sector of this formerly large city had folded in, conscripting the citizens and reprogramming them. Consumption, consumerism, connubiality, for those who kowtowed of course. Capitalism had a new brand name and an awesome marketing strategy. Unless you were gay.

By the sound of Blondie's accent, he was homegrown, and he sure as hell seemed gay when he was on his knees with my cock down his throat.

Fuck. I need to stop thinking about him.

In my bare-bones apartment, free of curtains, carpets, clutter, and any sense of interior decoration, I figured I had enough time for a shower before my order came to report for duty. Dropping my clothes, I stepped into the shower stall and set that shit to cold. Freezing cold. As cold as Blondie's face when he'd dismissed me.

Still thinking about him.

The arctic trickle didn't help my erection, and since I hadn't turned on my Data-Pak yet, I had some leeway. I went for a jag-off in addition to my rinse-off. Turning the weak jets to steaming hot, I got really warmed up with a lather in my hand, my dick in my fist, and images of Blondie licking his lips before sliding that naughty mouth down my shaft to my balls, coming back up with a curl of his tongue. Figured the sweet bastard knew just how to suck me off. The memories were all the masturbation aid I needed. And more lather to add to the fat drops of preejaculate dotting out and dripping down the tip of my cock.

My hand the most faithful lover I had, I glory-holed my fist, taking it easy on the upswing, loosening over the crown of my head because I liked a damned good tease, and if I was gonna get myself off, it better be worth my effort.

A hand planted on the shower wall, I dropped a pair of fingers to my balls, filled with the image of Blondie's plump lips wrapped around my cock. My stomach muscles tight as a drumhead, my cockhead taut at maximum PSI, I went up on my toes and rammed harder. Gasping, I thrust the hefty handhold of my dick in and out in a pounding rhythm, groaning when my sac banged my knuckles, wishing I had him between my legs, parting my ass with his tongue—

Ripping aside the shower curtain, my hand flew across the scant distance to the back of the commode and came up with my SIG cocked.

Liz.

She grinned at both weapons I hefted, one as rigid as the other. "Thinking about me, Commander Bravado?"

I lowered the muzzle, tempted to shoot between her feet. I shut off the water, not bothering to cover up. Number one: She'd seen it all before in the locker room. Number two: I didn't give a fuck who saw my junk.

I draped a towel around my neck. "How'd you get in?"

"Better question is where the hell you been, and how'd you let me get into this pisshole without tripping your sensors?" She referred to my internal sensors, not a series of security alarms my pisshole definitely didn't possess. I wasn't into the techy bullshit shoved down our throats on a daily basis.

Lounging against the door, Liz had the presence of a sleek, well-oiled Luger, her tall frame coiled like a hairpin trigger. "You left the door unlocked, sir."

Jesus. I never left anything unchecked. Not my surrounds, not my rooms, not my troops.

I covered my lapse with a brusque, "You forget to salute me?"

"Think you're doing enough saluting for both of us."

She was right. There was no willing my hard-on away. But I could ignore it. After painting my cheeks in foam, I started scraping the few hours' growth of dark stubble from my jaw and neck with precise moves. In the mirror, I kept my eyes on the motions of razor blade over soap, softening the turns around my chin, lengthening up the width of my neck.

Possessing no compunction at all—another thing to like about Liz, that and she threw a mean right hook and had sharpshooter aim—she kept up with the observation…on my groin.

"Yep, still hard enough to hang my jacket on."

Her staring had me deflating, finally. I flung a towel around my hips now that my cock wasn't gonna punch right through it and smirked over my shoulder. "Thanks for that."

She slunk to the opposite side of the doorway. "Way to stroke my ego, sir."

"Aw. You wanna get your sissy card stamped?"

While she continued to watch me, she curled her arms around her waist in an uncharacteristic gesture. I glanced back when she said, "My dad used to shave just like you. All routine, efficient, in the same order."

I reached over and clasped her shoulder, just once. Her father, a noted Corps surgeon and geneticist, had died gruesomely at the hands of Nomads during a repair-and-retrieve mission gone wrong in the Wilderness. We didn't talk about it before. And we weren't gonna talk about it now. I could tell by the way she straightened up and pulled her face back together, pressing her fingertips into her hips to steady herself.

I'd joined the Corps because I needed to do some ass kicking after the Plague. When I came of age ten years ago, I was Johnny-on-the-spot with joining up. Who knew I'd have a fucking flair for it, quickly scaling the ranks? The bonus? Because of the lethal nature of the job, we weren't expected to reproduce. Condoms and birth control were doled out in abundance to us, whereas they were ratshack commodities for civilians.

Certain items remained widely available: lube, for instance. Sex toys had been banished unless Company sanctioned and straight-couple orientated. That didn't stop the backstreet hustlers from coming up with their own erotic aids. I had a snug cock sleeve myself, hidden in my closet and used only when my hand became old hat.

Likewise, abortions were illegal backdoor affairs, the stuff wire hanger nightmares were made of. The aftermath of the carnage liberally propagandized during the day-long helpful promotions on the public Data-Pak because planned parenthood was something to aspire to and promiscuity was discouraged. The CO was raising good, wholesome single-family units in *healthy* home environments.

Aside from being a looker, Liz was as asexual as they came, so I figured she hadn't made the Corps her calling to keep the heat off of her own forbidden behaviors. In fact, I didn't know what she got out of it.

A vendetta against the Nomads who'd done the number on her dad, or maybe a genuine belief in Company credo. I didn't ask, she didn't offer, and I didn't care. It was nice to have some camaraderie, and we kept our lips sealed about anything that could get us in trouble.

"What you been up to?" she quizzed me.

"Just a day in the life, Lieutenant."

That earned me a brief chuckle. "Oh yeah? Been a good little drone today, have you? Let me guess." Liz tapped her lips, scanning me head to toe. "Did your time at the clothing factory, but forgot to pick up your own identical uniform, which explains why you're still dressed in a towel. Or maybe you got your hands dirty culturing food and splicing together oh-so-tasty new tidbits for us to gag on?"

I'd gotten my hands dirty all right. Grinning at her, I played along with a wink. "Yep. Joined in with the civvies; wasn't mind-numbing at all."

We made fun of the CO's worker bees, but we knew all about their colorless existence. Food and goods such as electronics, munitions, and a host of other gadgets were churned out from the chain gang. Always just enough and not one bit more.

But what were you gonna do?

Tie up your bootlaces and do your duty no matter how despicable it had become.

At least my daily duties included hitting the gun range with Liz. Drills, raids, and keeping the streets clean of any little hint of revolt added the thrills. My free time was spent working out, working on my bike, and working on the kink in my dick.

"You had your Data-Pak turned off?"

"It's my birthday. I'm on leave."

"You want spankings or to blow out some candles?" She referred to some old notion from a time when birthdays were something to celebrate, winding her hand back to smack my ass.

"How about you get the fuck out?"

"I could, but I won't. You missed the party starter. Where were you? Other than having another mind-blowing date night with your hand?"

As soon as she said party starter, a growl of excitement in her voice, I jerked around. "What?"

"Hand. Cock. Fucking it."

"Liz, what starter? What happened?"

"The rebellion."

"I heard it was a raid."

"Re-bell-ion."

"Rebellion?" Rinsing off the razor blade, I faced her. Liz and I could be twins. Her dark hair was regulation short, spiky as a jack-knife. Her lips full but hard, her eyes a daunting and deadly brown where her pupils bled into the irises. She could have been my sister, but Erica was gone. Liz was my family now. We'd made a pact. Always have the other's back, because this shit could turn ugly in an instant.

Sounded like it just had.

"Confirmed."

"Where'd it start?'

Suddenly, First Lieutenant Liz Grant was all business, just the way I liked her. Twin chrome Desert Eagle .44s were holstered on either hip. She had a hard-on for the classics, same as me. Her light-weight flak jacket buttoned like her lips; she didn't distract with unnecessary gestures.

"Sector Five, water supply shorted, then contaminated." She let loose with a grin and added, "Guess I should've told you as soon as I saw you in the shower."

S-5. I knew it, where the water-purification plant was and where Leon lived with his mother. The four-block neighborhood was a desolate afterthought on the fringes of Alpha. Leon's mom's house always boasted flower boxes filled with bright blooms hanging from the windowsills. I had no idea where she got the seeds, but among the squalor of S-5, her home was the only standout.

I sped to my spartan main room, flicking on the in-house Data-Pak. Broadcasting secure intel channels to Corps and Company execs only, the flat screen dripped a different IV-feed to civilians. Anti-Nomad, antihomo, pro-CO programming with a side of sexual brainwash, such as best timing of the month, basal-body temperatures, optimal sexual positions, all rounded out with scare tactics.

The feed was scientific to a fault, sucking the fun out of fucking, making it more a job than any whoremonger ever had. No wonder needy heteros got a healthy leg-over at the Theater too.

"Isolated?" I asked, skimming the updates.

"Territory wide." She came up beside me, her eyes leaping back and forth in time with mine as I ingested the details. "All the Territories. InterNation insubordination."

Holy fuck. I hardened my expression until my jaw didn't even tic. "We gotta get to Command."

"Affirmative."

"Where are the rebels?"

"Converging on the Quadrangle."

"And the infantry?" I asked.

"Holding pattern."

"Someone's behind this besides plain old rebels."

"Yes, sir."

For half a century, people had been pretty accepting of the regime. It was amazing what you put up with when your basic needs were met after teetering on the brink of extinction.

Noble in the abstract but clumsy as fuck in action, dissent had been fermenting recently. Last time there'd been any excitement had been the surprisingly well-oiled assassination attempt on CEO Cutler eight weeks ago. Backed by my troops, with Liz at my side, I'd busted into his swanky apartment to find him swathed in a towel from the waist down, hand clutched to his neck, and fury mangling his mouth. Of all the goddamned things, he'd been attacked by the stand-in masseur sent to service him. Massage him. Whatever.

No sign of forced entry, no love note from the would-be assassin. No matter how deeply we scoured the streets, we'd met only closed lips and blank looks from our usual cache of canaries.

The only reason he escaped with a nick on his neck instead of bleeding out all over his thick, white carpet was because we'd been tipped off just in time from the head honcho in charge of hack jobs, some CO kid called Rice.

The renegades were becoming more organized, less stupid. This water workup smelled similar to the kill-Cutler attempt, minus fair warning.

Armed, in uniform all the way to the cap sitting on top of her head, Liz was ready to move out. Meanwhile, I stood in nothing more than a towel, rather like Cutler. Called to action, I hauled dark blues up my legs and over my arms. Firearms were the only accessories required. Double cross-chest holsters snuggled my SIG P229s and were joined by a set of matchy-matchy Glock 40s at my hips. A nice even four guns—I was ambidextrous, as I'd been about to demo on my dick—and my pointy friend, a KA-BAR knife, strapped to my thigh, for more delicate work.

When I flicked on my handheld D-P, I got a shock. Hell, I should be used to that; it was only the third pube-curler of the night. I expected to be called into Corps Command along with Liz. Instead I was to be briefed by CEO Cutler.

My first reaction of *so ass-fucked* showed.

Liz scowled. "What?"

"I'm reporting to Company HQ."

She shook her head, turning pale. Nothing good ever came of that place. It was where those in the Corps were sent, at best, for a severe strafing. More likely it was for impersonal interviews of the most personal kind.

"No." Her voice was injected with the correct amount of fear.

"It's standard protocol in this case, remember? Executive roundups and evacs." I reasoned with her and myself.

"Yeah, but—"

"Don't but me, Lieutenant. This is textbook: Maintain order, split the executives, and appoint each of them a handler from the Corps. The only reason Cutler is calling me in is to give me my mission."

Unless he's figured out I'm not just a Corps commander but also an ace cocksucker.

Exiting my apartment building, Liz asked, "You think you're headed to the Outpost?"

"No other explanation."

"That place is bullshit."

The secure regrouping point for Company assets ranked with old-timey tales about a so-called Area 51. It was myth. But right now I wanted to believe in it, especially after I'd let my guard way frigging down at the Amphitheater.

"Let's hope not."

She nodded. "You lead. I'll follow."

"Always," came my gruff reply.

*   *   *

Throttling my bike again, I took a swift jump over a craggy crop of debris. My Harley was one of the last hangers-on. With gas hard to come by, vehicles were few and far between. My bike was fast, loud, obnoxious, and about the only possession I loved, besides my weaponry.

A goddamn rebellion? I couldn't wrap my brain around the idea the rebels had gotten their shit together enough to pull something of this magnitude off, InterNations wide. It lent a heady taste to my lips, lips I still wanted wrapped around Blondie's cock.

I had zero time to savor either off-limits flavor because shit went from bad to FUBAR the closer we got to the Quadrangle.

Usually a trip like this would be almost scenic, if you considered pockets of poverty overshadowed by the supershine of money to be something you wanted to take a picture of with your multifunctional D-P. The straight gridded roads were glossed to a high polish nearing City Center, care of the litter-uppers. On any given day—in the event of heavy foot traffic, since most citizens couldn't afford a car—I simply gunned onto the sidewalks, because I liked to raise a little hell once in a while.

At this time of night, dawn approaching, the roads were supposed to be quiet due to the mandatory curfew. The Company was really into oppression for our own good like that, because that scary boogeyman of sexual liberation was most likely to spread after dark.

Tonight was a different story, one quickly progressing to Armageddon proportions. The blare of sirens added to the violent commotion. This was a vastly different scene from the one I'd returned to an hour earlier.

The sector flew past, my head whipping left, right, and to my rear to check Liz's position on my tail, dodging fast on her dead black bike. Each block in more disarray than the one before. Coming from S-4 and S-5 at the back of us, columns of belching black smoke rose, chimneys taken to the sky, buildings licked by fire as revolt became hell on earth.

Sector Two, where I lived, butted against S-1, home to central operations and all it entailed. The roads narrowed for basic herding tactics and the utilitarian housing became subsidized businesses rising in needlelike buildings with sleek reflective surfaces and tiny slits for windows, manufacturing shit most citizens didn't need, couldn't afford, but longed to buy. Looming sky-high condos soared into the air, lording it over the gen pop with their expensive expanses of terraces complete with plants and outdoor lounging furniture. Housing for Company hotshots.

Here, in the heart of Alpha, chaos swarmed, the CO cannibalized by its own children raised to kneel at its despotic altar. I planted a blank look on my face instead of shouting out the cheers bubbling up the back of my throat.

As always in City Center, there were more patrols—had to keep the assholes safe, after all—more cameras perched on building corners. The once-thriving metropolis consisting of over 155,000 square kilometers had been reduced to an area of 16,000 kilometers over the past half century. Easier access to resources for the scaled-down population, the Company claimed. The reality? It all came down to controlling the animals in the zoo.

Worst-case scenario happened side by side in the seething, writhing mass of bodies from which screams rose, blood gushed, and bullets whistled. I hunkered over my motorcycle and trammeled through the flailing bodies, spinning off groups of Nomads going at it beside homegrown rebels, both factions giving as good as they got to Corps troops.

I homed in on the wild Nomads. Hefting bows, axes, sharpened farming implements, they put the archaic tools to good use, hacking, sawing, and garroting. Their homespun clothes covered in patchworks of foraged armor, their hair longer, they looked exactly like the brutal barbarians they were rumored to be.

They'd breached the gate or been let in.

Beside me, the sound of flesh meeting flesh made a pulpy squelch. Blood cascaded across my arm. A kick and a crunch, the shrieking rebel's foot dangled like a chew toy from the string of his ankle tendon. Staring ahead, I revved through the fallen bodies and the pound of boots as more troops infiltrated the area.

By the time we reached the Quad, the fog of smoke bombs ghosted across a pink-tinged dawn. And I was barely holding in my shakes to go back to the fray, join the agitators.

Dismounting, I caught Liz's eye as she headed in the opposite direction. She stopped, giving me a full salute, fucking finally. The smirk on her mouth faded before it reached her eyes.

I went due north to the Company headquarters, the government seat. To my left stood Corps Command; to the right was the hospital now on five-alarm status, casualties from all quarters being wheeled in, and squat at my flank was the Tribunal. Court and prison and where RACE executed gays in inglorious numbers. The three-meter-tall walls surrounding the whole of the Quad kept the dissenters at bay.

For the time being.

I waited while the prestigious doors of HQ opened after my retinal scan. At the desk, I stated, "Commander Cannon for CEO Cutler."

An extra iris imprint, a D-P check, and I put my weapons on safety before heading to the bank of elevators in the black marble hall that swallowed the sounds of my boots and spat them back at me.

The elevator whizzed from the lobby to fifty-five in the blink of an eye, depositing me onto a plush carpet that hushed my footsteps. I didn't have far to go; the fifty-fifth belonged solely to Cutler. I smelled like smoke, tasted blood in my mouth, and still heard the groans from outside, embedded in my think tank.

Walking into the well-appointed office, I came face-to-face with…Blondie.

Jesus Christ.

This was an oh-shit moment of the highest magnitude, and I almost gagged on the hunky-dory I'd told Liz earlier about this meeting.

Except this version of Blondie didn't resemble a snitch. Not at all. His sleepy blue eyes were sharp. Angular jaw clean of sun-hued stubble. His hair was pulled back, revealing a little bit of hotness I'd missed before. Buzzed with a number-two razor guard, his hair was close on the sides of his head in two wide swaths, with that long, grade-A Mohawk pulled back in a ponytail. Add the double-helix piercing through the cartilage of his ear and he was straight-up sex, modeling a suit that probably cost as much as filling my tank for five months.

Shock? More like shell shock at this point. Blondie knew I was gay, yet he was a Company exec or else he wouldn't be here. I was his butt boy in the worst possible way.

When I squinted at him, he gave nothing up. Neither did I. I had shit on this newly minted man too.

Double fucking jeopardy, jackass.

Chapter Three

My nerves steely as ever, I turned to CEO Cutler. Last time I'd seen him, he hadn't been all that pleased with my performance, but apart from hanging any old culprit for a crime not committed, there wasn't a whole hell of a lot I could have done.

And now this.

Cutler had the appearance of a bald eagle from his white crested hair to his regal nose and strong, streamlined torso. He exemplified the same predatory aura too, at least when he was dressed in more than a towel. The birds were extinct now, but I'd seen one a long time ago back in Epsilon. My pop had pointed it out, explaining the majestic American symbolism of the eagle.

Cutler missed the majesty part by the cruel curl of his lips.

Making with the howdy-do, he scrutinized the tension televised between me and Blondie. "Commander Cannon, welcome."

I managed some sort of response.

"This is Mr. Rice. Head of technological acquisitions."

Mr. Rice. The hacker with the all-the-best gen. The hunk who'd sucked my cock.

Major Head Fuck, more like.

I figured I had a couple minutes' reprieve before being fisticuffed, face-punched, and hauled over to the Tribunal, so I put on the dog-and-pony show.

Taking a seat, Blondie Rice watched the proceedings with as much interest as choosing a new tie from a rack of hundreds.

"We're under attack."

"Yes, sir." *State the obvious, why don't you?* "What do they want?"

"Freedom, I presume." Cutler sneered.

Can't allow that, can we?

He clasped his hands behind his back. "That's neither here nor there. The ingrates will be dealt with. You've got something else to worry about, Commander. Assuming you're ready to prove yourself after the last cock-up?"

From the cushy lounge, Blondie's eyebrow rose.

Cock-up. I'll give him one if he doesn't watch it.

"At your service, sir."

"You know the strategy, then."

"Top Corps to escort Company execs to the Outpost."

"Exactly." Cutler took a seat, leaving me standing. I widened my stance and considered discreetly fingering my guns off safety, just in case.

"You are charged with the safety of Mr. Rice. Escort him to the Outpost and I'll wipe the gigs off your record. Shouldn't take more than four weeks to reach it. You can keep your head on straight that long, can't you?"

Which one?

"Yes, sir."

He went on about the Outpost, aka the Brier, the legendary place that didn't exist. Unless you were top-level clearance, apparently. All I could make out through the droning anxiety deafening me was that it had been a bunker built when the defunct United States was embroiled in a Cold War.

Things were about to heat up.

Blondie relaxed like he was prepping for a vacation while the details were hashed out about how I was going to guide him. Alone. He even stretched out on top of the sofa and linked his hands behind his head so his shirt and jacket strained over his chest.

This smelled like a case of crotch rot and total setup. In fact, the whole situation was ludicrous, including the one rising in my pants because being pissed off made me horny, obviously, and he wasn't helping with that highly unprofessional slow lip lick of his.

As if I didn't have enough worries, I planted my size-fourteen boot in it. "With all due respect, this mission is bogus. I have command of my infantry. Here."

"Are you implying you have no faith in your second, Lieutenant Grant?"

Right. The motherfucker made it look like I questioned Liz, putting her in jeopardy. "No, sir. She is completely capable of leading our company."

"Then you will complete your assignment to rendezvous at the Outpost where the leaders are convening to regain control of the Territories. Meanwhile, the remaining infantry will quell the uprising...or level the city."

Did I say mother fuck?

"I'll leave you to formulate plans. Make full use of the maps." Cutler rose to his feet, gripping my hand. "Your transport will be readied by twelve hundred tomorrow."

I thrust my contaminated palm into my pocket when he sent back, "I trust you'll be fully armed, Commander."

He had no idea.

The door closed behind him.

I pulled out maps, pinning the location of the place. Isolated, its position couldn't have been worse. What should've been a straight two-week shot north looked like a freaking mine had exploded all over the landscape. Checking measurements, I reckoned hundreds of meters of inhospitable vegetation in every direction stood between me and the Brier. What an apt name.

After adjusting the guidance system on my D-P, I approached the slit of a window overlooking the Quad walls and wished I hadn't. Reeling back from the volcanic fountains of artillery, smoke, and fire outside, I hit a solid wall of male body. Blondie's scent drifted over me.

"Not gonna talk to me, then?"

I swiveled around. "Not into chitchat."

"You were pretty chatty a few hours ago." A lean smile pursing his cocksucking lips, he looked me over. "Four weeks is a long time, you know?" He'd dropped his Company-composed veneer, becoming the fantasy man I'd fist-banged in my shower.

"Got nothing to say to you."

His hands whispered to my shoulders, sending thrills through my body. "Had a lot to tell me earlier, Cannon." He tugged my earlobe, his teeth biting, his lips healing.

"Is this foreplay or foul play?"

"Gettin' to ya, am I?"

Peering at the high corners of the room where I guessed one, if not two or three, recording devices spied on us, I hissed, "Why don't you keep your hands to yourself. Eyes and ears, asshole."

"Got the cameras on loop." His fingertips brushed the back of my neck.

I shoved him off. "You're a cunt's hair from getting your head shot off—"

"Don't I know it." He watched the crotch of my fatigues stretch to obscene proportions.

"The head on top of your neck, Rice."

"How about a name?"

"Commander Cannon."

He cajoled, "Given name?"

"Caspar."

"Commander Caspar Cannon." The way he said it made me want to throw him over the desk, rip his pants off, and sink into that rosy bud of his. Immediately.

He knew it too.

"A soldier."

"Correct."

His prowl toward me had my breath trapped in my windpipe, my mind scrambling for even footing.

I did not fucking swoon.

I crossed my arms over my chest, ignoring the fatal thud of my heart. "You gonna capitulate? Because I'm not calling you 'sir.'"

"That so?" His fingertips brushed across my belt, then tugged me closer.

Walking my fingers down his tie, his shirt buttons, his jacket, I found his cock, and he was impossibly hard. "Affirmative."

I palmed him with rough strokes, the feel of him so fulfilling in my hand, no matter how damned I was for giving in.

When he sighed against my shoulder, "Nathaniel Rice," I relinquished him.

Now I had a name, one I could curse at will, sparing a few choice swears for myself. "Landowner."

"Yeah."

Great. His surname denotes him as a spoiled, living-the-high-life Company exec from a privileged background.

The reports and maps gathered up, I not-so-gently knocked past him.

Calculation quirked the side of his mouth. "You're wonderin' if this is the real me. Or am I the man who had your delicious cock down my throat"—he stopped to look at his heavy gold watch—"four hours ago."

"I'm wondering how long I have to deal with this bullshit before I can brief my troops. Oh, and I gotta feed my goldfish. Let's get this straight, Blondie—"

"Blondie?"

"That's an insult, not a pet name."

His eyebrow arched.

"You're an assignment, not an assignation. Soon as I get your pretty-boy ass through the Wilderness and deliver you to the Outpost, you're no more than a stain to spit shine off my boots."

He slinked forward, invading my space. I feinted left and he blocked me with his forearm to the wall, backing me into a corner. That shit made my blood boil. I could chop my hand down, probably break a bone or two in the process. I was contemplating the smarts of that move when the bastard brought his palm to my neck, his fingers dipping in to the throbbing pulse, measuring how much he affected me.

"Yeah. What if I'm on the Executive Committee, huh, Caspar? You wanna know if I was takin' names and faces at the Amphitheater? That's what got your heart pounding?"

"You got it. Congrats. You win a furlough with me."

"Maybe you're still thinkin' about how much you want to slide that gorgeous cock of yours into my ass?" He lifted his hands, halting when he realized his hair was tethered back. He settled for pulling the ends of his ponytail, the one I wanted coiled around my fist when I yanked his head back for my kiss while I fucked him slow and deep from behind.

"Or maybe you wanna rush off to report me."

I sent him an evil grin. "Thought had crossed my mind."

"Good. Don't trust anyone."

"Double that."

Mutual distrust, a nice little bed warmer.

He had me turtle-up. My hard shell cracked when I thought about his words, his mouth, his tongue. I cranked down on those memories, filed 'em away in a lockbox stored in a safe, hidden inside meter-thick vault walls.

"You're gonna need to spiff down before I take you anywhere," I said.

His smile broadcast across his face, playing up some serious dimples. Bet he had a matched pair on his ass. That smile made a massive misinterpretation of my words, filling me with a *before I take you out on a date* kind of vibe.

I headed out in front of Blondie because (a) it was impossible to hide my hard-on and (b) having a front-row view of his ass in those perfectly tailored slacks wouldn't help. At fucking all.

Great way to inaugurate the rebellion. Getting screwed from the inside out.

Not if I turn him in first.

I clicked right, toward Corps Command.

A hand clasped my shoulder, making me blow my wad because one more suggestive comment in his southern *c'mon, boy* voice, I was gonna fuck him until he couldn't walk anymore, or I was gonna pull my Glock out and—

Jesus Goddamn Christ. I saw why Blondie had stopped me. Dead in front of me stood Leon.

Stood was a poor choice of words, but it was Leon all right. Looking one hundred and eighty degrees different from the last time I'd seen him.

Held up between two military police, his hands were cuffed behind him, his shoulder stretched back. His face was a mass of swollen tissue in shades of purple with ugly greenish yellow mixed in, a thread of bloodied spit dangling from his lips. His mesh vest was torn to shreds, revealing slender muscles bruised by fists and metal-capped boots.

When I marched up to the troopers dragging his floppy body by the elbows, Blondie kept pace.

The traitor better not mess with my operations.

I addressed the grunt closest to me. "Where are you taking this man?"

At the sound of my voice, Leon drew his head up. His hair hung in sweaty clumps over his eyes, but he recognized me—the little shit had had his hands on my crotch only a few hours earlier. More cunning than I suspected, he maintained the same blank look Blondie and I adopted, with a hate-filled sneer for added emphasis.

MP Coombes had a face like the sole of a boot and about as much charm. He and his hard-liner cohort were the opposite of the recruits I'd sent ass-backward at the never-ending beginning of this night.

"He's not a man; he's a faggot," Coombes spat.

Being a ruthless bully, he grabbed Leon's chin, digging his fingertips into one of the fresh cuts. Leon didn't flinch when he jeered, "Ain't you, boy? Like it up the ass. Fuckin' dog. The queer's implicated in the rebellion. Arrested him at that gay rave, the Amphitheater. All dolled up, wasn't he, Jenoah?"

The Jenoah in question was a bleak-featured bitch with eyes that held all the emotion of steaming shitholes in snow, except now there was a sick gleam to them, because she'd caught one of us.

Landing a blow on Leon's cheek, she agreed. "Sure was. Had to mess up that pretty face. The body too. Unnatural is what this shitpacker is. Bet he won't get much action anymore." She beamed at me, her superior, expecting a reward.

Taking very deep breaths, I barely held in my hotheaded temper.

"MOVE OUT!" A fresh wave of troopers deployed to the left of us, reminding me there was a lot more going down than just Leon, but he took top spec in my mind. Damned if I was going to let another good man end up with a rope around his throat.

"He's headed for the stockades for now," added Coombes.

"Under whose orders?" My hands curled into fists, ready to do something seriously stupid. Blondie touched my shoulder, murmuring something too soft to hear, but his light assurance delivered instant calm.

"The XO."

No way around that.

Leon's eyes stopped spinning long enough to pierce me. "What you be lookin' at, Corps cunt?" His insult came out gargled with fresh blood.

That earned him another ball-kick before they hauled him away.

His barb salted the open wounds from the entire messed-up night. There was only one way to deal with the duality of what I was—cut out all the emotion from my life.

Another blast shook the ground. That would be the electrics grid shorting out.

Blondie staggered into me with the earthquake hilling under our feet. For a second, I let myself be the fulcrum to his body.

My D-P went off. I barely heard it through his low words, the rat-tat of gunfire, and the buzz of generators starting from scratch, relighting the Quad first and then *hum-hum-humming* halos outside the compound. Their weak illumination joined the rising sun barely visible through black entrails of fire and the rain of fat ashes.

Leon was at the doors of the Tribunal.

The acrid smoke choked me, stung my eyes.

When Blondie said something about seeing what he could do for my moony-eyed boy, I figured my ears were still tinny from the explosions until he clasped my hand, holding it firm and tight and letting go to say, "I know you feel responsible for him. Not sure why."

A grin pushed up my lips. "Me neither."

"Should count him as competition and call myself lucky he's off your grid."

"Leon isn't even in the running."

The smirk. The wink.

My error.

"I'll get him off the stockades, see about delaying the Tribunal. They'll have more important things to deal with than your Leon."

My Leon.

Those words rang a hollow tune inside my heart. I had a wish, a dead plant, and no relatives. I didn't belong to anyone and for damn sure I didn't possess Leon, Blondie, or any other man. I wheeled left. All thoughts, all memories, all wants that were not gonna happen got stuffed into the Happily Never After crypt. "Pick you up in six," was my curt goodbye.

I didn't have to look back to know his hands were on his hips, his cheek curved upward, his eyes merry over my words. This was exactly the weak in-love stuff I steered clear of. Men like him. Guys who slashed into my heart with their free-and-easy grins, until those grins were ground out of them right in front of me.

Maybe I preferred the anonymity blessed unto us by the Company. Whatever. I shoved it all into the lockbox, inside the vault of my memories, contained behind a reinforced entrance, then strode to the indestructible doors of Command. After a thumbprint and a retinal scan, I was in.

Making my way through Central Command, I might have been a

little shaken by the night's events—with Leon the unpopped cherry on top—but I wasn't gonna show it.

The room I entered was a sight for sore eyes. Guess I got my sense of decorating from the Corps, because the bland gray walls finally settled my balls. One long table glowed from the multifaced D-P vomiting streams of information from its center. A cold, concrete room, the only color in it came from the rows of Territory flags, sixteen identical sentinels stationed against the walls. *Regeneration. Veneration. Salvation.* The standard salvo was printed in blue across thick bars of gold. Stars and stripes rebranded to bars and strips.

The Roman numerals on each was the only bit of individuality allowed, denoting the separate Territories. Repetition was crammed up our asses until it was ingrained in our brains.

The air vents stalled as generators went to work on the most important electrics—halos, security, data banks—leaving the banners hanging like limp prisoners from their posts. Liz stood between two of the flags, their edges caressing her shoulders. Her posture was precise whereas they drooped in defeat. Only her slow popping of knuckles from one finger to the next gave away her worry.

"Give it to me, sir."

I joked, "Like this? Here? Goddamn, I thought you women were into the romancing."

Her short dark hair created a sharp cap on her head, the sharpness reflected in her narrow eyes. She didn't crack a smile. "Our troops are suited up, awaiting your orders."

"Change of plans."

Pushing off the wall, her chin jerked up. "What's our detail?"

I clasped one hand at the back of my neck. "*My* detail."

Other than the visible gulp in her throat, she showed no reaction. *That's my girl.* "You're going outside."

"Affirmative. Personal escort to the head of technological acquisitions."

"This Head-of got a name?"

"Yeah... Asshole."

That won me a short-lived snort.

She didn't fidget or fight when I brought her to me, folding her inside my arms. She grabbed my shoulders and held on, too.

Fucking hugging and hand-holding.

"You know what you're doing?"

"Always."

She cupped my chin, brought it to her shoulder, whispering into my ear, "I know you're different."

My arms dropped and my head shot up. Shock was replaced by sternness when I said, "You're in charge now."

"Commander—"

"Clear the streets of Nomads and rebels, enforce the curfew, and evacuate the civilians to Beta Territory. They're more capable of handling this blitz. They're bigger, with better resources."

"Cannon—"

"Restore order, Liz."

"Is that really what you want?"

"I have no opinion." Because the other one would put her in danger, and there'd be a great big grave with my name on it.

She tugged down the sleeves of her jacket. "Caspar, you better stay on your game out there."

"I'm always on point, Lieutenant." I drew a line in the sand, using her title instead of her name.

"Right." She drew herself up.

"Got my six?"

"Always."

"Liz..."

"Don't say it, Commander." She pivoted on her heel and aimed straight ahead. "Don't send me off with some bullshit story."

She didn't think I was returning any more than I did. I performed an internal check, and yep, that notion hurt. Not enough to let her know though. I winked and gave her an easy smile. "Don't say what? That you better keep this place tight until I get back?"

"You're such a dickhead…sir."

"Just don't go soft on me."

Grabbing her crotch, she grinned. "Not possible."

"I've got my D-P, so we'll be in touch. And you've got your orders." I spoke through a throat working overtime. "You take care."

Blinking rapidly, she saluted and marched from the room without a backward glance. Palms down on the table, I rolled my neck a few times, loosening that shit up. Sucked in a couple deep breaths and let 'em out slow.

Fucking errand boy. I wasn't gonna fall apart over this situation. I took a moment to inventory my arsenal and nodded. *So be it.* If this was my mission, I was gonna be the best damn errand boy money couldn't buy. Make sure no harm came to Blondie unless the blow was personally delivered by me.

I allowed myself a nasty grin at that thought before striding outside.

*   *   *

I had some details to square away, and sleep ranked low on my things-to-do-before-I-got-fucked list. My remaining time in Alpha also didn't include being pussy-whipped about Blondie or wondering whether he would bring me flowers. Oh, and that goldfish I had to feed? Little turd went belly-up the week after Liz gave it to me. Surely had something to do with it being one of the pet clones the

RACE team worked on in their spare let's-fuck-with-nature time, not the fact I knew nothing from nurture.

My things-to-do were nothing compared to the Company's. The initial catastrophe dropped the orderly CO into chaos, and I would have liked that if it wasn't so damned detrimental to the people.

The smoke from the S-5 blazes had some serious hang time, swathing the area in great gray clouds. On my way into the sector, the water plant was cordoned off and more suits swarmed around, but this time the suits were less business attire and more neon, neoprene outer-body shells to protect against possible contamination.

With most of the rebel action taking place near City Center, civilians in this area were contained and housebound. I hoped to get a private moment with Mrs. Cheramie. The least I could do was let her know her son was alive, if not exactly safe.

Stripping off my helmet, I leaned my bike on the kickstand. The square plots of weeds that passed for lawns in S-5 were scorched, but those pretty red flowers blossomed brighter than fire in the early morning's haze. I bounded up the crumbling stone steps toward the door, which hadn't ever hung straight from its jamb.

Before I could knock, the door swung wide. Close up, Mrs. Cheramie was younger than I'd thought, making me realize her son had been born when she was barely legal. She had the long wild hair of a Nomad—loose, sun-catching waves. A small slight to the Company. There was a little rebel in everyone.

"You be here about Leon."

A painful twist of guilt knotted my stomach. I should never have left the kid alone at the Amphitheater. Holding her strong summery green gaze, I told her, "I'm Commander Cannon, ma'am. Leon's been taken into custody."

Mrs. Cheramie stepped back, inviting me inside. "He be mentionin' you." Her voice richer than her son's, she growled out the words in a thick accent.

I must've looked panicked, because she hastened to reassure me while she ushered me through the doorway. "Only dat he respec' you, Commander."

"Caspar, if you please, ma'am."

She beckoned down a hall lit by candles, overwhelming in its colorful scavenged disorder from patterns of dried flowers forming makeshift wallpaper to beads shimmering from lamp shades.

There was a reason I hated untidiness like this. Climbing with shelves of books that were surely restricted and jars of this and that, the hall sent me into a claustrophobic nightmare of memories. It put me in mind of a place I'd once considered my second home, small rooms overflowing with similar types of shit that had pissed me off on the one hand and become loveable on the other.

Since I couldn't control my desires, I maintained brisk control of my area. My small rooms were devoid of visual interest so no re-membrances could sneak up and fill me with unattainable ideas of what-if.

Running my fingertip down a crack in the wall that zigzagged from ceiling to floor, I couldn't see how I was gonna maintain my distance from Blondie for four weeks. He represented the whole big ball of what-if, bringing it together in one sexy, strong, eager package.

When Mrs. Cheramie called over her shoulder, "Dem put da fah-yuh out; let's do da same, boy," she threw me back to a different era.

Boy. Mom used to call me that when she was pissed off.

In our family, Erica had been the tearaway, but as the oldest I was always the one facing the *boy* charges. I'd been well aware something was wrong with me that I couldn't get over with a quick fix, so I'd tried to fit in any way I could, unlike my sister. There wasn't much trouble to get into up in Epsilon, but she sure made a point of sniffing that stuff out. I could never talk her out of her harebrained ideas and I couldn't let her go alone, so I ended up shadowing her.

That last time, she'd wanted to see the ocean. "C'mon, Cas! It's what? A four-hour hike? We leave at sunrise, return at dusk. We can do it."

I'd been sixteen to her fourteen. I'd never been a pushover, but give me those big brown eyes and the pout from Sis's mouth and I was much more moldable than now.

Escape was easier back then, some saved-up scrip in the right hands bought a day of liberation. It had been August, a hot one. During our hike, I'd marveled at the massive trees with Erica making fun of me in her free-wheeling way, nothing I'd ever take slight to. When we'd finally hit sand, we'd thrown off our clothes down to underpants and T-shirts, racing each other into the wild surf.

She'd hooked her fingers behind her ears, shoving her tongue out, taunting, "Scared to go deeper, Cas?"

Diving into the cold water, the effervescent bubbles coating my skin, I'd grabbed her ankles and dragged her down. I'd come up triumphant while she rose to the surface like a spitting cat, shaking out her hair.

"Ass."

"Pain in the," I'd replied with my teenager's insult.

Salt. That's what I remembered. That frothy water had tasted like salt on my lips. The ocean pounded so hard, knocking us back only to have us come up from the depths sputtering, laughing.

The northern ocean had been limitless, the sun glorious, the day unmatched.

We hadn't made it back before sundown. Worn out from the surf, Erica dragged ass until I'd hefted her across my back, carrying her through the dense Wilderness. There was no scrubbing away our sunburns or the smell of sea water; the foreign air clung to us. There was no excusing the demerits on our records for a day missed from the institute.

Once home, Erica was sent to her room, leaving me to face our mom. Already she was shorter than me, but she was still capable of inspiring fear. Anxiety had gnawed a hole in my stomach.

Looking up at me, brow furrowed, eyes wide, she'd whispered, "Damn it, boy!"

She'd backed away from the windows, making me follow her into the kitchen, where everything was labeled, organized, shipshape. Chair legs scratching against the floor, she pushed the four matching seats tableside and smoothed the napkins laid out for breakfast in the morning. Her lips trembling, she'd shut the curtains with quick yanks, though not before I saw her peeking outside.

Tears had spilled from her eyes, fear fading to relief. "Get over here."

She'd embraced me while I listened to the catch in her voice whispered against the new stubble on my cheek. "You know we do everything we can to keep you safe. But when you disobey the rules, Cas…"

She hadn't finished her sentence.

It was already fully loaded.

When I disobeyed, people—my family—got hurt.

There was only one time I'd told Erica no and I'd regretted it ever since.

Trying to hide away my reopened wounds from the past, I double-timed it into Mrs. Cheramie's kitchen, hitting the top of my head on some hanging gewgaw.

I rubbed my skull and glared at the decorative eyesore. "Could use a top-up, ma'am."

She scooted me to the side, rising on tiptoes to stop the clash of the mobile I'd swung into motion. "Shoosh, *grand beede*! *Gar ici*, dat be from my *mamère*. Dem shells seen da best and worst of it. From da Grand Isle."

"Grand beede?" I sloped across the floor, measuring out the small space with my paces until I found a homey corner with a view of everything.

"Big clumsy man."

I went red in the face. "My apologies, ma'am."

Waving my courtesy aside, she picked up a bottle of liquor from the counter overrun by tiny plant pots and mugs whose glaze was cracked, half their handles chipped away.

"You take your libation here, you call me Evangeline." She swirled the bottle, its potent fumes lifting between us. "Don' be reportin' me?"

"No, ma'am, Evangeline."

She moved with the same slinky grace as her son, from cupboard to cups to table. She clinked my glass. *"Que le bon Dieu vous benit."*

The alcohol burned my throat, warmed my insides. Just the kick starter I needed. When I set the glass down, I was tempted to swirl it, or jitter my thigh, talk some crap. Helpless in this situation, all I could do was tell her the truth about what had happened to Leon.

"My Leon's *mal pris*?" She rubbed her hands over the scarred tabletop, resting her fingers near the tips of mine. "Tell me da trut'."

She earned my admiration with her straight-shooter talk. "It doesn't look good. He was caught at the Amphitheater. They're charging him with being an instigator in the rebellion."

She used her shirtsleeve to dab her eyes. "He got the gumbo, dat boy, but he don't mean to make the *misère*, eh, Cazpar?"

"I'd like to tell you I'll do what I can for him."

A wry smile flew over her lips. *"Mais*, you can't."

"No, ma'am."

She nodded. "Dat I know, *cher*."

Christ. Her maternal acceptance wrapped around me like the soft blankets neatly folded at the top of my closet, the ones I never let myself use.

She patted my hand. "It's g'on be okay."

This was too close to home, hearth…heartbreak. Thinking, *It won't be okay*, I got to my feet and left her to believe whatever the hell she needed to.

"You should leave soon with the evac. Find First Lieutenant Grant and follow her orders."

She was right behind me, with her riotous hair and willfulness. "He be wily, dat boy. Don' you be worryin' about him none."

There is one other thing I can do.

I brought the keys to my bike and the helmet to her. "When Leon makes it out"—my voice got real low—"tell him to take care of my motorcycle for me." As if by giving him my touchstone, fate would have no choice but to bring him home.

I took off on foot. The riots might not have reached S-5, but shit was alive and well near my building. A skinny rebel bent toward the door of the building, trying to jimmy the keypad. Grabbing him by the scruff of his neck, I hauled him up to meet my fist, splitting four knuckles against his teeth. He didn't have much to say after that, collapsing in an unconscious pile at my feet.

Then I got really pissed when the message end of a gun muzzle nuzzled up to my ribs. I rolled out from the rebel and took his feet with me, catching his gun when he hit pavement. Swiveling it through my fingers, I took aim dead center on his forehead.

Except it wasn't a male.

Fear widening the female's eyes until the irises were surrounded by dinner plates of white, she scrambled back. She searched for a weapon and came up with a jagged hunk of brick.

"Drop it," I barked.

Instead of taking my advice, she leaped to her feet. She was an agile thing with too much courage for her own good. I counted to five, watching her hesitate and scan the area for an escape route before her resolve firmed. She lifted her arm, preparing to launch the brick at my skull.

I never liked to use weapons on women, but I was forced to cock the gun as I spoke through gritted teeth. If one of us had to die this morning, it would not be me. "I said *drop it.*"

Chapter Four

Ignoring my order, the woman hurled the brick at me. It headed for impact with my face, flying on a fast trajectory until I fired the gun. The brick burst into dust when the bullet hit it midflight

"Get the fuck outta here, or you're next."

She grabbed the arm of a fellow rebel coming to her rescue and took off in the opposite direction. More fighting coming every which way, I ducked inside my building, taking the stairs to my rooms. I wasn't one to hightail it from a brawl, but I needed a few minutes of downtime to make sure I didn't flake out when I came face-to-face with Blondie again.

The hollowness in my heart reverberated in my gut. At least this was one need I could take care of on my own, because I damn sure wasn't going to the Corps mess hall for my grub. I fried up some nondescript meat with a couple slices of bread, grabbed an apple that was only half mushy, and found a corner of the counter to eat at.

Throwing the frying pan-cum-plate into the sink, I washed my hands and air dried. A look in the fridge that was no bigger than an old-fashioned cooler and I hit pay dirt. Beer. *Fuck yeah.* I had two hours before rendezvous time, and I needed something, even if it was just one damn drink, to loosen the nut-fuck in my head. I slid onto my cot, back against the cool wall, took a long pull, and shut my eyes. I made a mental list of things not to think about. Liz. Leon. Blondie.

I drank some more, slipping down the wall, and considered the trek ahead. Our destination was almost due north, eight hundred kilometers. Given the fact much of the Wilderness was impassible after the obliteration of the Purge and the subsequent invasion of nature, our route wasn't a straight shot. It bent west, dipped south, eased northeast, and would bring us to the Outpost bunker in approximately one month, on foot once the Land Cruiser ran out of gas. Seeing as there weren't any refueling stations on the way.

Four weeks to keep my hands off Blondie when I could hardly keep my mind off him. Four weeks to guard him, keep him safe from Nomads. *Four weeks to figure out how badly he's gonna screw me.*

I backed right up to the Nomads, stunned some of them had broken into Alpha to team up with the rebels. They were a winning combo, packing a wallop against Corps troops so far since they were still on the loose in the streets.

The Nomads were a crude breed one step above animals. They originated from settlers who'd been prepared for the end of days and preferred to stick it out with Mother Nature rather than fall in line with the Company. Left to their own devices for fifty years, they'd fallen back to a way of life called basic at best, downright undeveloped at worst.

There was talk about exiles sent outside Territory walls being sacrificed to a malevolent earth goddess. There were also rumors that Nomad communes were free-thinking, well-established colonies and escapees were welcomed with open arms.

I was more likely to believe they were violent mongrels in need of training.

Since they didn't subjugate themselves to CO authority, they were classified as the enemy, and the war in the Wilderness was always raging. I'd been on the front lines against them before, so I had firsthand experience with their guerilla tactics, which amounted to ambushes and dirty fighting. They were savages whose people were to be put down. That pretty much summed them up per the publicity, and this was one time I thought the CO got it right.

Plan A had always been to keep myself alive, get my kicks off when I could. Keep an eye on Liz and my troops. Hell, I was all about order, structure, and rules. In that one way, I had something in common with the Company ethos, but now I wasn't so sure this keeping-the-peace plan was worth the sacrifice of my soul.

I must've fallen asleep because I snapped alert fifteen minutes later to the building shaking in its foundations. Checking outside, I got confirmation of the scatter bomb just let off. I was fresh as a fucking bunny and grateful I'd dozed off during my woe-is-me moment. It was the perfect time for a getaway.

My booted feet hit the floor, and I found my backpack in the closet. Time for rations and munitions. I wasn't so much into food as getting my fight on. My SIGS, my Glocks, and for the really good times, I was bringing along a modified M4. A piece of perfection with its shortened barrel, collapsible stock, and full auto capabilities, it was the badass big brother to my others. Adding my KA-BAR for a little carving practice, I completed my armaments with a pair of pretty polished brass knuckles I'd gotten off a dealer.

My D-P with downloaded maps, sat reception strong. I input Blondie's contact information, made sure Liz had checked in, and zoomed in on Mrs. Cheramie's house just to see those flowers, and my bike, one more time.

Pulling my fingers over my jaw, I glanced at the stand beside the cot. *Do not even go there.* The box was three quarters full, the bottle brand new. Cock covers and glide. My fingers balled into fists. Reaching for the fuck supplies, I stowed them at the bottom of my pack, out of sight. This kind of wishful thinking was gonna get me compromised or killed.

There was no time for a jerk-off session, although that might have been a mistake. The mere idea of weeks alone with Blondie was enough to start up my hard-on. His soft wet tongue, the scrape of his stubble burning my stomach before he looked up and pointed his tongue into the dripping slit of my cock. I should have fucked him, gotten the forbidden fruit out of my system. I wished for a moment I had a damn dog or, hell, even robo-fish to complain to. Something alive but mute, who would listen to me but never tell a soul.

Yeah, sissy pants, time to shove out of this shithole.

I scoped the surrounds outside, glad to see the scatter bomb had done its job. It was still eerily quiet and gloomy as fuck. Nevertheless, on the way to S-1, fire escapes were my friends. Back alleys too. The new mountains of rubble made excellent leaping-off points so long as I didn't consider the mangled body parts and brain matter decorating the whole mess.

Nearing the Quad, things got a little dicey. The explosions continued, but they were littered with resounding silence. I kept a close eye on the rebels being strong-armed to the tarmac. I made sure to circle around the infantry caught up in one massive wave of Nomads pressing to get into the Quad.

At Commissions, I picked up the Land Cruiser. A quick survey found gasoline cans lined up in the back to augment the hydra-charger and see us a little farther down the road. Jumping into the driver's seat, I sneered at the preprogrammed D-P guidance system and coms link. This tin can was gonna be recycling material in roughly seven days.

Chauffeuring to Rice's digs, I leaped the sandbags surrounding the obelisk tower of glittering glass. The elevator was on standby, so I took the stairs two at a time for fifteen floors; then I leaned against the buzzer and waited.

The door opened and I swung inside as if I owned the place. It was plush with furnishings, paintings, and mirrors. He even had fresh flowers, a vase of glossy white blooms unfurling on a stand next to me. I bent over to sniff the soft lemony scent, jumping back at Blondie's admonishment. "You're impatient."

"What? No servants?"

He sent his tongue along his bottom lip. "Just me."

"Hmph."

"But c'mon in. You want a drink?"

Damn southerners and their bullshit charm.

"I wanna bug-out before this whole fricking place implodes." I wouldn't have minded a minute or two to turn the place upside down and find out all his secrets.

"That right?"

"Yep."

Then I did the dumbass thing and checked him out. He was in drab cammies accentuating his built body and dark blond hair, which slanted down to his chin. Blondie was armed with a good-looking Glock 5 on his right hip and a sheath showing a well-used knife grip. Dressed down and well armed, he sported my favorite look in a man.

Turn it off, Cannon. End-of-world crisis, so cuff your crap and get your guard up.

Blondie caught me lingering over his hair and holsters. "Weapons make you hot?"

I grunted in approval, grabbed one of his knapsacks, and headed to the hallway.

"Always did want a male escort." He hefted the last two back-packs with no visible strain.

That made me hot too.

I gritted my teeth. "Bet you got enough Company scrip if that's all you wanted. Be a much easier way to get laid than this head trip."

He came back with a quiet murmur that rocked me sideways. "What if I just want you?"

My stomach lurched with something deeper than hunger and so long unsatisfied, a piercing pain and pleasurable rush collided inside me. I pounded down the stairwell ahead of him. "You've packed heavy."

"Well, I'm sure I'll lose something along the way." He winked.

Cursing, I pushed outside and came to a complete stop. Apart from a few stragglers, the street was dead. "Where the hell is every-one?"

"Tryin' to get out."

A pair of wounded rebels rounded the corner, their wobbly walk turning into an all-out run in our direction. I dropped the bag and took out my gun. Only Blondie's hand on my wrist stopped me from doing the deed this time.

He waved something in their faces. His keycard. "Take it. Sell the stuff; eat the food—just get off the streets while y'all can."

Wary gray eyes narrowed in a soot-covered face. The man snatched the card and spat a filthy stream of juice toward Blondie's face. They backed into the building, their eyes on us the entire time.

While I wondered at his game, he wiped his face, stowed his shit, and made for the driver's seat. "Gonna get in?"

"Roger that." I leaped across the hood. "But I'm not taking the passenger side."

My trigger ready to fire off, I jammed my hips against his until he hit the door.

Blondie rotated his groin against mine. "You want to drive, I take it."

I put my hand next to his shoulder on the door frame, not touching, but real close. "Look, Blondie. I'm not asking you to bottom, just to fucking navigate."

His laughter tapped down to my belly and he slid inside, hopping his ass over the console to the passenger side. Maybe he was undercover. Maybe he was a fake. Maybe he was gonna be the cause of my death. Didn't matter. For once a warm fire was lit inside me, all because I'd made him laugh.

It took only a mile to erase all the happy I was feeling. A pack of bewildered civilians were being herded away from the gates, looking around with wide eyes and the confusion of children when their world dissolved. Because it had. With no solution to the water problem, the situation was gonna get even uglier. Sewage would back up, bacteria would breed, and illness would spread. The civilians could forget about plain old dying of thirst.

As we approached the monstrous gates decked out with sniper towers and rows upon rows of razor wire, hundreds more milled around the hot zone. We were recognized by the mixed bag of mobbers, one shout becoming a loud chorus from an army of angry residents bearing down on us. Marauders swarmed the Land Cruiser, rocking it from side to side.

"It's the commander!"

"And that CEO boy. Rice! Rice!"

I eased my foot on the gas, maneuvering through the melee until the back window was smashed out, showering glass inside. It snipped my face, neck, and hands as I went for my rifle. Taking out my window, I used the M4 to butt the face directly beside me, then the next and the next.

Blondie was hanging half outside his window, firing into the air.

A young mother ran through the path I'd cleared beside the vehicle, tears tracking down her dirty face, the baby in her arms squalling.

She pushed the bundle toward me, screaming, "Take him. Take my Wyatt!"

"Ma'am." I laid the rifle aside, holding up empty hands. "I can't do that."

"We'll die in here. Take my boy!"

"It's not safe out there either."

Blondie dropped inside to urge, "Drive, Cannon," his face hard, voice emotionless.

Sending the Cruiser forward, I checked the mirror, then wished I hadn't. Clutching the baby, the woman stumbled to her knees behind us, care of a soldier's fist to her face.

"Fuck this," I growled, ready to go back for her.

Just then, the tide of renegades turned. All the terror, all the vindictiveness the renegades had unleashed on us was directed on the slap-happy soldier.

I hit the gas hard, slamming us forward. Troops formed a human barrier between us and any other would-be evacuees while the thick fortress of Alpha Territory peeled back like the lid of a can, opening to the Wilderness.

In the rearview, I saw the razed city and watched mortars light the sky. White knuckling the steering wheel, I gunned over the iron grid and kept going.

No more looking back.

At times like this, I was usually flying solo or with Liz. We didn't so much talk it out as trudge through it. I didn't know what to make of Blondie, but I knew one thing. "That's wrong, man. What they're doing, what we're part of, it's not right."

Beside me, he shielded his eyes. "I know."

His elbow was on the armrest, his hand laid almost on top of mine as I handled the gearshift. A pothole in the dirt road jostled him sideways, against my arm. I wanted to pull him closer. He righted himself to the opposite side of his seat, forming the division I should have. He'd felt good during that brief contact. It would've been natural to stretch my arm across his shoulders.

No matter how much I wanted the fleeting feeling of belonging with someone, especially after what had just gone down, I didn't move a single muscle toward him.

Eventually, after watching me for an hour's worth of dusty miles, he sent me a slight smile. "So, that it? You gonna be the strong silent type the rest of the way?"

It wasn't much, but it was enough to make me take my eyes off the track to tease, "Well, I'm not sucking your cock again, if that's what you're after."

The sudden quirk of his lips said, *We'll just see about that.* And then his smile grew when he joked, "Jesus, Caspar. I'm not askin' you to top me, just to talk."

*   *   *

The hot sun had fallen behind the trees by the time we called it a day, settling into a hollow of soft moss with tufts of green grass, surrounded by a ring of old-growth pines. A clear stream gurgled like the water pipes of my single shower, and beside it a mound of purple-blue wildflowers nodded their starry heads. They were the same shade of blue as Blondie's eyes. I bent to one knee, lifting a blossom to my nose. *Fresh, fragrant.* I shut my eyes to savor the clean scent.

When I opened them, he was staring at me. My cheeks warmed, and for once I wished I'd grown a beard to hide the pink stain on my face.

"You just gonna stand there, Company Man? Or help me set up camp?"

His eyes narrowed in challenge. "You're gonna keep pretending nothin' affects you, big man?"

"Fuck you." I stormed to the Land Cruiser, kicking the crust of mud from a tire.

Beside me, he reached into the back of the vehicle, pulling out supplies. "Gladly take you up on that offer, but I usually like to have a decent conversation with my lovers first."

"Guess you're out of luck. I don't do idle chitchat." *Should have remembered that when I opened my big mouth earlier.*

Busy unpacking the essentials for the night, my mind back-tracked to the day's journey. It was a good thing we had fresh water to clean up with, after Blondie's antics once he took over driving. With him at the wheel, I'd been vigilant. The rebellion was contained within the environs of Alpha—the insurgents concentrating on seats of power—leaving me on the lookout for possible Nomad tangos. I'd been heedful of the unrecognizable landscape and more than a little fixated on Blondie.

He'd draped a wrist over the wheel, and a whistle, of all the god-damn things, had parted his lips. *How the hell can he be so relaxed?* He'd dropped his CO makeover the same way he'd switched his package-hugging suit for ass-cupping camos.

After the Purge, the roads had been blown up, making any to-and-fro almost impossible. The Cruiser's struts bounced over ruts in the nearly invisible dirt track, getting a good workout. I was getting a workout, too, restraining my eyes from his thighs shifting with every press of clutch and gas, biting back my moan as the scorching sun sent a trickle of sweat from his temple to jaw and down the ropes of his neck.

Performing an all-points check, I'd pressed my foot down to the running board, hoping to hit an imaginary brake. "You're not driving through that."

That was a wide well of brackish water, scummy with a yellow sheen on top.

"The great Commander Cannon scared of a bog? Ain't gonna hurt you none. I've done it before." He gave me a sideways glance and a halfway smile.

It wasn't a bog. It was a damn swamp, and we had no idea how deep it ran. In no mood to lose our transport on the first day out, I glared at him. "You're fucking crazy."

"Maybe. But this is gonna be fun. I promise you."

He'd motored right into the swamp, shouting a whoop-holler when mud cascaded in thick fountains on either side of us. The Land Cruiser stuttered, and he'd eased it smoothly out of the suction, slicing left and right. His boyish delight pressed a dimple into his cheek. By the time we'd reached the other side, I was grinning, he was laughing, and the commissary vehicle was coated in the same oily muck splattered up our arms to our faces.

Bumping along, sun drying, I'd asked, "You've been outside Alpha before?"

"'Course I have. You know that." His wicked look seared through me, tightening my groin.

I'd brushed away immediate hunger, hulking against the door. "Not talkin' about the Theater, Blondie."

"I have a name, y' know."

Yeah, Nathaniel. It's etched on my brain. The first time I said it was gonna be when I slid inside that perfect ass of his. "I meant, have you been out here for official business...or family?"

His mercurial face closed up shop. That's why I had one expression in my repertoire. The fuck-you look.

He'd stopped the vehicle to face me. "Yeah, I got family. And yes, I been out here before."

Bounties were paid for gays turned in, a new kind of headhunter for Team RACE. I'd met his eyes. "I still think you're screwing with me."

"Do you? Maybe I'm just more adept at hidin' what I am; I've been indoctrinated and brought up in the Company way, after all. Now, you? You show your desire every time you look at me, Caspar. Don't believe for a second I don't see it." He'd leaned in, whispering, "Don't think for a moment I don't want you on top of me, inside of me."

I inhaled at the implication when he added, "I wanna fuck you, too."

"You're playing me."

The snap of my fatigues came loose under his fingers. "I want to." His face was carved with sharp longing. His mouth slipping across my stomach had my cock fueled for a fuck. "I did take notes on you. Not for work, but for pleasure."

No matter how much I shouldn't believe him, the pressure of his lips, the sound of his voice, damn near hypnotized me. He was pulling all my strings, pulling them taut until I was stretched by desire.

Toying with the shelf of my cockhead still battened down inside my pants, his breathy words bathed my hips and wetted the line of hair bisecting my abdomen. "I saw you five months ago. That twink was all over you." His hands ran below to my ass, pulling me up. "Leon."

The material covering my erection tugged into his mouth, he'd snarled, "I wanted to punch that boy in the face when he dared call you *cher*. I've been poundin' my fist in time to your name all this time. I don't want anyone else touchin' you."

I'd seized him by his hair, hauling him up to my face. "Get off me."

"You're a big guy. Make me." Blondie smiled when I smoothed the knots of hair I'd made at the nape of his neck instead of pushing him away. "You don't trust me."

Arching into his hips, I'd aligned our stiff cocks. "Not one bit."

Except he wasn't the only one who'd wanted for months. Bet my palm was more chafed than Blondie's, all because of a hundred filthy fantasies starring him. This was a take-what-you-could-get kind of world for gays, then make a quick getaway. There was no getting away this time and maybe I didn't want there to be. Besides, I could always fuck Blondie with a capital F, after I fucked him, of course.

His lips had touched my ear. "You think you're always in charge. I pursued you. I knew who and what you were the first time I saw you at the Theater. Think I didn't notice you swaggerin' around the Quad?" He bit the tendon linking my shoulder to my neck, causing a thrill to race down my body. "Yeah, I watched you. I followed you to the Amphitheater. I almost came in my pants when I got your voice over the D-P, that night I warned y'all about the attempt on Cutler's life. I've wanted you for such a damn long time." Moving his lips back to my ear, he rasped, "I requested you as my escort."

"Bullshit." I was knotted up inside, trying to maintain my bluff, but desire was getting a good stranglehold on disbelief.

"Bullshit, huh?" He'd held my thighs in a hard grip. "Think about this. I've had ample opportunity. I had the evidence of what you are in my mouth last night. Why haven't I turned you in already, collected my bonus?"

"To lull me into a false sense of security before you knife me in the back."

"So damn pigheaded. I've studied you, not to report you, Caspar, but because I want a relationship with you."

The stranglehold was cutting off my oxygen, which I deemed the only way to make sense of the fact I was considering his words at all. *Studied me.* Sure as fuck I'd made a point of watching him too. As for a relationship, well shit. That kind of thinking was just pipe dreams easily blown up by pipe bombs. I should know. My personal life was even more high risk than my job. Yet here I was, with Blondie in my lap, my heart rate rocketing because of his proximity. His confessions. His sensual overload doing a number on all my well-laid suspicions.

Hitting back with the truth of our fragged situation, I said, "You realize what kind of fucked-up antifaggot society we live in, right? You understand we both work on the side that will always keep us apart?"

I'd expected him to push away, but he just stared at me, his broad palms running up and down my thighs until my muscles bucked in time with my throbbing dick. Until I said, "Studied me, have you?" Jerking my chin, I asked, "Learn anything useful?"

His full lower lip between his teeth, his look smoldered along my body, but the words that left that lush mouth made my chest bounce in laughter, *the fucker.* "Yeah. You don't really have a goldfish."

I peeled his hands off my lap. "I'm not gonna get caught."

"Neither am I." He scooted back to the driver's seat. "You're detrimental to my plan, you know?"

"Ditto." I'd curled my fingers over the armrest to keep myself completely away from him as my heart got sucked into my gut. "What if I call you Major Head Fuck from now on?"

He'd gnawed on a downturned corner of his mouth before turning his face out the window. "I'd sure prefer it if you called me Nathaniel, but Blondie's good too."

Remembering the important shit, I'd looked dead ahead into the forest. Assignment, delivery, good riddance. Not get my jock off.

He'd interpreted my body language correctly. "How can I get to you?"

"You can't. No one can." *Not anymore.*

"You're gonna lie about this?" He drew me to him, a hand cupping my shoulder.

Betraying my own need, I went willingly. He'd hesitated when our lips were so close I could make out the tip of his tongue waiting inside his parted mouth. We'd leaned toward each other at the same time, joining in a furious tangle of tongues, wet lips, and widened mouths to suck it all in. When I'd strained to connect our bodies, he broke away.

I struggled to breathe, fisting my hands on the seat between us.

"You gonna lie about what we have?" His voice was hoarse.

I pushed off the seat to my side of the vehicle. "It's only because there's no one else."

His face bleak with emotion, he'd assured me, "It doesn't matter where I am, or who I'm with… *God, Caspar.* I've dreamed about being with you."

The rest of the ride had been uncomfortable, culminating in him catching me sniffing fucking flowers.

Just a day in the life.

I washed the memories from my mind and the mud from my face, dipping my head underwater, cooling off. When my ears cleared, I heard him whistling again. Music was a major illegal item. Proven to incite riots, the airwaves were filled with the Company's monotonous propaganda pipeline. The only time I heard tunes was at the Theater, heavy thumping bass with no lyrics. Mostly it was a luxury I didn't miss, along with everything but the most basic amenities, yet listening to Blondie was strangely soothing.

Wiping my chest with my shirt, I knew it was a sound I'd yearn for when this was all over. "What's that song?"

"My momma had this device called an MP3 filled with songs from back in the day. She hung on to it like a lifeline and hid it whenever we had Company *company*." He winked. "She used to curse that thing out. It was so old, it was pre-Purge. It couldn't hold a charge half the time. Once I started gettin' good with wires, I made all sorts of peripherals for it. Man, could she dance, too. Cut a rug—that was the term she used." He peered up at the sky with a grin parting his lips. "She had a thing for this one singer, name of Van Morrison. Song's called 'Brown Eyed Girl.'"

I joined him, and we passed poles through the open-sided tent's loops, another throwback instead of the pump-up pup tents the Corps used on excursions.

"Well, your eyes are blue."

He smiled over at me. "Didn't think you noticed."

Oh, I noticed and have been polarized by the first bit of blue matching your eyes that nature provided. I glanced at that clump of flowers, glad they couldn't tell on me. "Yeah, well, blue is blue."

"That's right." In a couple steps, he was in front of me. His extra two inches in height made me knock my head back to see just how blue his irises were. "My momma used to sing it, but not about me. She knew my type of man. She'd say you were just the right amount of dark *sugah* I needed. That sleek black brush cut, those big muscles. Those dark brown eyes with little flecks of gold when you grin, that darken when you're worried."

I pushed through his seduction with a forced laugh. "Too bad the song's 'Brown Eyed Girl,' not guy."

"I can improvise." He shrugged.

I wanted to make a smartass remark about him being a momma's boy, but I couldn't do that. Not when I had my own demons, in quadruple form. "Where is she now, your mother?"

"She's safe."

"Anyone else?"

"Yeah."

I swallowed fast and let it fly. "A lover?"

Raising his hands, he held his hair back, his gaze hitting mine. "No lover, Caspar."

I cleared my throat of the way it tightened to think he was available. "Think we oughtta get our shit sorted for the night?"

"You askin' me on a date?"

"Nah, I'm telling you to haul ass before we go darkout."

His chuckle was broken up with a murmured, "Wouldn't mind fumblin' in the dark with you."

We worked side by side, and I was surprised by his speed and agility. His methodical motions matched mine as we laid a boundary of dry twigs and wrangled the night's rations inside the circle we'd booby-trapped.

While Blondie started the fire, I watched his hands. It was almost dark and I was unseen in the shadow of the trees. "Had you pegged for a suit," I called as I stepped into the clearing.

Crouched low, he looked up. He brushed that dirty-blond hair from his face, leaving a trail of soot on his cheek. "Had you pegged for a succinct sonuvabitch. Guess I win."

I handed him the warm furred rabbit I'd snared. Scrutinizing his slick skinning of the animal, I was closer to flirting than I'd ever dared. "A *stiff* suit."

His hands halted. "Caspar?"

Chapter Five

Keep going. I like a man who knows how to handle a knife." I could have crowed at the way his hands shook. Instead, I steadied his wrist inside my fingers, then traced his forearm over the hill of his biceps to his shoulder.

The sticky blood made the knife slip, and he let out a gritty laugh. "You're makin' me fuck this up."

"I'll leave you to it."

"No, don't."

Determined, he bared meat from fur, halting when I drove my fingers into his hair. It filtered through my fingers until I tugged his head to the side, baring his neck. I licked a line to his Adam's apple and rubbed my cheek up and down his throat. "I'm hungry, Blondie. Gonna feed me sometime tonight?"

"Ye-e-es."

I liked his breathy exhalation more than I should have. "Go on then." I bit his jaw, right on the hard edge, laughing when he leaped forward. *Perfect for a smack on the ass.* I hauled back and slapped, chuckling over the control I had of him. Squeezing that tight butt, I eased the sting. "Think I better leave you to it."

As I sauntered to the tent, I heard him say, "I'm not just a Company suit. I'm a survivor."

That makes two of us.

Unceremoniously digging through his gear, I found his secret stash. "A survivor who brings a seventy-five-year-old bottle of bourbon on a Wilderness trek?"

"A man must drink."

Placing the heavy bottle aside, I rummaged further.

"You happen to find the cigars?"

My fingers ran over something familiar. I bent forward, exploring what I'd found.

Blondie spoke real softly. "Find somethin' else, big man? You're not the only one who has plans."

The foil of condom wrappers crinkled as I whipped toward him. Through a hot blush and the fierce rush of arousal, I willed my voice to be steady. "Like what? You plan on deep-throating one of these?" I held up a cigar.

His low laughter bounced off the trees while he went back to work. After he'd cooked and I'd been cooked in my skin—watching his hands in action, his wide wrists turning, his forearms flexing—he commanded, "Take a seat."

I grabbed a piece of ground beside him, and he arranged a plate in front of me. "Eat."

"What the hell's that?" I pointed at my plate, circled by a real glass, authentic silverware, and a cloth napkin. The man traveled like a pasha, used to his luxuries and gadgets.

"Rabbit. You caught it. I cooked it."

"What's on it?"

"Spices."

"Spices?"

"Flavor. Stop being so goddamn ornery." He held a chunk between his fingers, offering it to me. "Open up. It ain't gonna kill you."

He guided the juicy meat inside my mouth, his fingers lingering. I lapped all around his roughened fingertips, shooting a look to his lips, watching his tongue stroll out to make them slick and wet.

"Goddamn. You are a sexy man, Caspar." He smeared the grease over my lips and licked it off before giving me another bite.

The food was delicious. A hundred times better than the fried bread and mashed-up meat I was used to.

"You gonna feed me now?"

My eyes shot from his mouth to his eyes and back again. "Don't think so."

He spoke with a lover's low, slumberous voice. "C'mon, Caspar. I know you're no monk. What you did to me last night, the way your body's reacting to me right now. You like sucking my fingers, I think almost as much as sucking my cock. So gimme somethin' to eat. I'm starving."

"You're a persuasive motherfucker." I held a bite above his lips, keeping it just out of reach when he stretched up.

He panted, "So I've been told," before he caught the piece between his teeth, taking my fingertip inside for a hot swirl of his tongue.

My breath came so hard, it felt like my chest was gonna rip out of my shirt. Once he swallowed, I followed in with my lips, brushing them back and forth over his. His mouth parted with a deep moan, and he touched the tip of his tongue to mine before pulling back so only our wet lips clung to each other, exploring.

This wasn't the fast have-to-fuck kiss we'd shared before. The kind necessary when capture loomed in the background. It was something a hell of a lot deeper and a lot more fucking scary.

His forehead tipped against mine when our mouths separated. "Best kiss I've ever had."

I could only gulp, waiting for my pounding heart to calm the fuck down. I backed up to a tree and cracked my knuckles in Liz fashion, staring up through the canopy of leaves. I used to have my head screwed on so tight there was a roadblock going in both directions. No entry. No exit. My shit had been stirred up by seeing Leon strung up. It'd gotten another good shakedown at Mrs. Cheramie's house, creating a damn hole through which memories continued to bum-rush me.

Add our tender kiss and something else was opening. For once it wasn't a scarred old battle wound. I worked my shoulders against the rough bark. "I can't remember the last time I shared a meal with someone. Sitting down and making small talk." At Blondie's huff of laughter, I looked over. "Yeah, I know. Not a big talker, am I?"

Man, sometimes he made me feel so easy, and he could turn me on like no other, with just a look or a quirk of those sensual lips. I caught his smile across the fire and stretched out my legs, placing my hands behind my head. "Sharing food, you know?"

He nodded, stirring the fire with a twig.

"I guess the whole sit-down dinner idea went out the window with the Plague when I was a teenager, up in Epsilon." *That was before things went bad.* "I should've figured something just as disastrous would come after the Purge."

"What'd you hear about the Purge?" Blondie tossed the stick aside and leaned forward.

"Hell, probably the same as you, being a second-generation kid. There was never much in the CO-authorized history books at the institute where I went to school. Most of what we learned was a life lesson in why we had to trust that the Company had our best interests at heart."

His smile wry, he asked, "You got the whole *The world's resources were tapped to extinction level by your predecessors* spiel too, huh?"

I'd gotten that and more, although I didn't know how much was the truth and how much was Company spin. We were told water had become the new oil, a shortage that leveled humanity with schools of fish dying as the shorelines shrank. Birds dropped from the sky in flocks, and crops were blighted by bio-diseases created by man and gone rogue. By 2020, billions of people were dead.

"Oh yeah. What they really meant to say was our ancestors left us with the fuck-end of the bill." I rephrased the CO's maxim to my liking.

"You've got a way with words I'm sure they didn't teach you at the institute." He chuckled.

The Purge led to civil and cross-country warfare among the survivors and caused famine, disease, and drought. "You ever hear this one? *The survivors needed a good strong hand, leadership, guidance,*" I intoned. "What the Company really meant to say was they needed a good swift kick in the nuts."

Blondie's grin smothered, he said, "We really shouldn't laugh about it."

"I know. There's not a whole hell of a lot to laugh about anymore, is there?" We both went quiet.

Blondie made his way closer. He sat across from me with his back to the fire, the orange light drawing sparkling fingers along his hair. "What about the Plague?"

I could've shut down, probably should have. But coulda and shoulda were little bastards that skedaddled into the underbrush along with my tendency to keep my trap shut.

The Purge was Old History, but the Plague was an epidemic I'd lived through. I raised my knees, settling a final barrier between us.

"What a heartless bitch, that plague was. Know what I mean?" I asked.

"What happened, Caspar?"

I tufted my fingers against the soft moss. "I used to be a real good boy, taking to the policies the way I was supposed to 'cause structure grounded me. Guess that makes me pretty fucked up, huh?"

"Nah, I can see the two sides to you." He scooted closer, the toes of his boots resting against mine.

I tried to inch backward, only that goddamn tree blocked my retreat. "A good boy, that was Caspar Cannon. Making stellar marks at the conformists' institutes. Our parents were pretty damn proud of me and Erica, the perfect Territorian youths."

"Erica?"

I rubbed the moss hard enough to expose the soil underneath. "My sister." The words tumbled out. "I hit my teens, and right about when I was supposed to be looking for my lifelong female mate, I figured out girls didn't cut it for me. Tits were just completely fucking surplus to requirements."

Blondie chuckled, running his palm up my calf.

I smiled at him, shook my head a little. "Yeah. I liked hard bodies, lean hips, and big shoulders. We both know the problem with that. Tolerance wasn't taught in any household. Homosexuals were bad people, criminals whispered about, blamed as freaks deserving every punishment they got."

"I wish like hell you hadn't gone through that, honey." His hand made another foray over my leg, the heat generated from his touch gentling my anger.

"I'd been a pretty popular guy, probably an arrogant prick too. A shining example of CO values in a strong young man with a bright future in the Company's higher reaches.

"The more I got all hotted up over men instead of women, the less my hotshot future seemed possible. Nothing I could do about that." I met his eyes, knowing my pain showed.

Quiet, so quiet and calm, Blondie moved beside me, where he could wrestle my fingers free from clumps of moss and twine ours together. It stole my breath the way this man could reassure me with a touch, or make my body ache with his kiss.

"I ditched my friends. I didn't want to implicate anyone because I was a dirty, wrong homo. There wasn't much I could do about my family though. That's brutal, being ashamed all the time. The understanding I'd never fit the square peg the Company Constitution had custom-made for a man of my talents. Worrying any little lingering look might get your family fucked."

Another one of his tugs on my fingers held me in this place under the stars instead of letting me slip all the way back into those shitty final years in Epsilon. "Nightmares about my own Marriage Testimonial used to make me scream awake. That wedding-night performance between husband and wife—first fucking observed by a select few—including one or two representatives from the RACE Executive Committee. Before I knew what it all meant, I used to joke about it with my friends: doing the Marriage Testes in front of the Execution Committee."

"Jesus Christ." Blondie's expression was as stark as I felt.

I tried to pull my hand from his. "You'd know all about it, right? The Testimonial? Just the CO keeping shit legit and aboveboard."

He shook his head. "We had our own particular traditions, not that one though."

"Just an extra-special bonus for us up in Epsilon, I guess." My grin fell flat, and I still wanted my damn hand back from his. "I don't like talking about this."

"I know."

"I don't even know why I'm telling this to you, of all people."

His lower lip made a downward curve. "I know."

"That's it? That's all you got to say?" I couldn't believe he wasn't trying to wriggle more secrets from me.

"No, that ain't it. I wanna know everything. I'm interested in you, not for a fast fling, not to turn you in."

I regarded him with wariness weighing me down. "Then why?"

His arm slowly curling over my shoulders, the hush of his words made a direct hit with my heart. "I wanna take some of your pain away."

I blew out a long breath. "My little sis, Erica, was only two years younger than me, which was perfect timing for siblings in the Territories. She was so goddamn intuitive. Well, they all knew, but she was the only one who talked about it, about how I was…different. Mom and Pop encouraged me to join the Corps since it'd be some kind of safety net. But Erica." I laughed. "Oh, man. She was such a shit-stirrer. Always pushing me to go outside, to live with the Nomads. She was the daydreamer. I was the 'yes' guy, except for that one damn thing I couldn't control."

Go on, Cas. You can make it out there. I'll come with you. Mom and Pop only want you to be safe, y' know? I could still hear her excited whispers.

"I couldn't leave them any more than I could drag her along on some freaking soul-searching quest that would end in the hands of savages. I figured I'd do the Corps thing, or I don't know…one day get turned in. Always the yes man, but that one time I'd told her no.

"She stood up for me, and I was supposed to be her strong, older brother, but I wasn't strong enough to keep the Plague away."

His hands roved down my arms, pulling my fingers from their knuckle-white clasp on my knees, joining them back with his. "Caspar…"

I pressed on, doing a lot of blinking. "Your lot called it the Gay

Plague. Thing is, I don't recall it hitting the homosexuals that hard. It was the moms and dads, the children. My sister. I was seventeen that summer."

"I was fourteen."

"You sure shot up the ranks fast."

"So did you."

I caught him in the crosshairs of my glare. "That CO spin of yours worked well, didn't it, Blondie? Took the civilians' minds off the fact whole families were obliterated by the gut-rot eating their intestines and pulverizing their organs, spreading with airborne toxicity. That pandemic wasn't a sexually transmitted disease. There's just no way. Erica was only a kid!"

My voice cracking, I took a hard tug of air. "She was a good girl, goddamn it. After Mom and Dad died, when I had to leave their bodies outside wrapped in bedsheets to be picked up by the bod squad, I went back inside. To Erica's bedroom. I held her all night, her sweat soaking through my clothes. I fucking prayed, man. I would do anything, I'd fake being straight. Just let my sis live. Did they? *Did you?*"

Blondie didn't flinch, and he wasn't holding back the tears either.

I wiped my nose on my sleeve and pinched my wet eyes shut. "That night, she was unconscious but still crying. Her body seizing in pain, her face screwed up, so small. The kicker was when blood started running from her ears. Where was the Company then? Where was the FUCKING CURE?"

I could barely make the words come out. "Erica died at exactly 17:39 on August sixth, 2059. I will never forget that, because for the last two hours of her life I held her through the seizures, watching the minutes on the D-P count up with every glug of her lungs, wishing her breaths would speed up in time with the clock instead of slowing down.

"I couldn't put her on the doorstep to be carted away. I washed her up, and…I sang to her. I don't know what it was, some tuneless crap probably. I put her in her favorite outfit, not that there was much to choose from. I kissed her, right below the little peak of hair she'd always complained about, where I used to flick her forehead when she pissed me off, and her hair was shiny, brushed the way she liked."

My fists punched the ground. My head hanging, I rasped, "I tore apart the shed, used the planks to make a coffin. Probably wasn't pretty. I put a locket around her neck that held a tiny picture of all of us, and I buried her.

"I buried my little sister."

Using my shirt to wipe my face, I sat back, facing the sky again. At least the stars were visible out here. Erica had been right. I did like the Wilderness. It was better than the stomach full of hurt and my heart overflowing with grief. At least there was a sky and trees and flowers.

"Then I joined the Corps. End of story."

"Why do I get the feelin' there's more to it than that?" He huddled next to me, running one firm hand up and down my arm.

"Well, that's all you're getting from me." I pretended to yawn and stretched out, knocking his hand away in the process. "Never knew how tired spilling my guts'd make me."

"You get used to it."

"I'll make a note not to." I unrolled a blanket and lay down, flat on my back.

He took the hint and retreated to the tent, where he tacked down the sides. "Why don't you come in here?"

"Used to roughing it."

"Just because you're used to it doesn't mean you have to."

"Yeah, it does." Because my lack of creature comforts was my own personal torture device, like the horsehair shirts I'd read about once. My reminder I was a hypocrite, doing the Company's dirty work when every part of me was disgusted by them.

Still, my fucking motormouth decided it wasn't time to turn in. "Erica always thought there was something better. I couldn't afford to think that way."

Stepping around the hot coals of the fire, Blondie stood over me with his hands on his hips. "Maybe you can."

I rolled onto my side, lifting my head to meet his gaze. "You suggesting you're that something?"

"That's exactly what I'm suggestin'." He was defiant. There was no smile to relieve the seriousness on his face. His dimples had been MIA all night long, and I wondered if I'd ever see them again. "I've been beaten by the same stick, you know? Guess I'm just an idealist."

He turned back to the tent with a shrug, leaving me with a few words that were nothing near the good night I wanted to hear. "But I understand where you're comin' from."

Where I was coming from wasn't a place I wanted to revisit. This thing unfolding inside me was taking up a lot of space. It felt like hope, hope I hadn't tasted in a long time, and I wasn't willing to give that up yet. Leaping to my feet, I followed him into the tent. His shirt was halfway over his head, his back to me.

Perfect.

I ran one knuckle down his spine, watching chills rise and collide along his sides. His motions halted with his head still stuck inside the shirt.

I peeled it all the way off, his jaw captured in my hand while I brushed his ear with my lips. "I'm looking for something better tonight."

Shudders coursed from his shoulders to those lean hips I was growing to love. I spun him around and yanked his pants lower until a peek of pubes and the cliffs of muscle showed.

With my forearms grasped in his hands, he drove his tongue along my collarbone. "That's right, big man. Take what you need."

Shoving him on top of a sumptuous bed of blankets he'd arranged inside the tent, I towered over him. "You sure you know what you're saying?"

His wink set off the crinkly corners of his eyes. "Sure as I am of anything."

I toed off my boots, staring at his mouthwatering torso, the sloping pads of his pecs. "That's not real reassuring."

"Fuck reassuring. Take those pants off and get down here, honey." He grinned.

Mmm. Hello, dimples. I've been waiting for you.

I knew when I broke the rules people got hurt. Well, there was no one left to hurt out here but me...and him. What the hell else did I have to live for? Maybe the Corps was a bust and this mission was a trap. Maybe I'd never been allowed to have what I wanted. That was gonna change now.

Then he arched in such a sinuous way that my mind was totally made up. My fatigues quickly shed, I kicked his legs wide. I tore through the button and zipper of his pants, bringing his cock into my hand. *Fuck, he was gorgeous.* His penis was a thick solid length drizzled in precome. His body shifted and bucked in time with my caresses as I stroked him in and out of my fist.

I felt the beat of his dick under my lips when I sent slow wet kisses up and down his shaft, nibbling the thick veins, lapping at the soft triangle of skin under the head until his thighs jerked beneath my hands. His cock batted my abdomen when I stalked higher, biting and bruising his nipples with hard pinches. And true to form, Blondie was a talker.

"Fuck, yes," he hissed. Hiking up his hips, he hit his cock to mine, letting out a dirty laugh when I moaned. "Like that, big man? Like to feel my cock sliding against yours?"

I mashed my mouth to his, planting my hands beside his head as I rose. I brushed his hair aside and sampled his earlobe. "You're damned right I like it. What about this?"

I slid our throbbing weights together, propelling him up while I fucked down until we made a magnificent rhythm of balls slapping, cockheads tapping, hands kneading. His ass in my hands, I sat back on my heels, our shafts sliding and grinding together.

"Look at that," he gasped, lunging his hips.

I slapped my hand down on his abs, controlling him. "You wanna come?"

"Yes!"

Our cocks crushed between our stomachs, I let go to the hungry rush ricocheting inside me. I spread his thighs so I could get right between them, nipping his lips, sucking his tongue into my mouth.

Blondie lent a slick hand to my balls. "I'm gonna suck you so good down here; have these plums inside my mouth until you come right down my throat."

Thrown into ecstasy, I yelled, "*Ahhh*, yes, baby!" Lightning raced down my spine and up through the tip of my cock, and I jetted come up his chest, jerking like a puppet on the strained strings of my orgasm.

Choking on groans I couldn't contain, I tore my fist up and down his dick, watching his pulse kick, his blood race, his face cave in as his muscles screamed for release.

Knocking his knees farther apart, I brought a fingertip damp with my seed to his lips. "Taste this while I drink you."

I swooped over his cock, taking it down until all his long dense arousal was beating against the back of my throat and his sacs rested under my chin. Then I lashed low upon his delicious testicles with my tongue. His cry billowed out the same as his come did, unending satisfaction rending the night, rippling in a warm gush down my throat.

I gathered him in my arms. A job-well-done grin spilling from my lips, I nuzzled the shaved side of his hair. "Next time, you're gonna come same time I do."

His stomach jumped under my hand. "That an order, Commander?"

"Get used to it, Blondie."

*   *   *

The hell is that earsplitting noise?

Completely awake in .5 seconds, I cocked my Glock, confused by the sounds of shrieking all around me. Looking left, out the open sides of the tent, I saw them. Swarms of screeching low-fliers. Aiming, I was ready to take the closest one out when I shook from my disorientation. *Birds.* Dozens of birds. More than I'd ever seen congregated in one place. Not swarms, but flocks. Brightly colored, red, sky blue, glistening brown sleek bodies, acrobats of the air, swooping on spread wings, singing to one another.

Wild and natural, birds didn't stray into the barren compounds of the Territories, not in this number, not enough to wake me up with their trilling song. For that matter, I never needed a wake-up call. I was used to doze-time, not deep sleep. I'd slept right through daybreak. Lowering my sidearm, I lay down, stretching from the tips of my fingers to the soles of my feet. *Huh.* I felt relaxed, replete.

Fuck it. After last night with Blondie, I was smug as hell.

Blondie. Obviously my inner guard dog was making big old puppy eyes at the man, trusting him enough to let my back down.

Make that surprise number whatever, but who was counting anymore?

I didn't see him when I rolled over. Good thing, considering I'd almost gone ballistic on a pack of vociferous, oh-so-scary feathered friends. What I came face-to-face with was flowers, of all the goddamn things. A bundle of those blue ones from down by the creek were right next to me, where Blondie had slept in my arms.

A token from Mother Nature I'd been starved of in Alpha.

"Mornin."

His husky whisper punched me up straight, the delicate blooms all but strangled in my big fist. His hair was wet and loose, his eyes so frigging soft. In his hands he carried a couple plates of food. Shit that smelled heavenly.

My voice was rusty from disuse when I returned, "Morning."

Nodding at my hand, he smiled. "They're called forget-me-nots."

Of-fucking-course they are.

Chapter Six

Figured it wasn't bullets that got me into trouble. No, it was those forget-me-nots. When Blondie wasn't looking, I'd flattened them between the soles of my spare boots after carefully wrapping them in one of his fancy napkins.

Jesus.

I spent a lot of time thinking about that damn dog I didn't own, and how if I did, I wouldn't have spewed all that truth about my mom and pop and Erica. Then again, I wouldn't have woken with Blondie's pillow held to my chest and the singsong of birds—cardinals, he called the scarlet-feathered ones—instead of the usual fugue of my nightmares.

I was supposed to regret having laid all my pain out in the open for Blondie to witness, but I didn't. It'd been a long time since I'd spoken about my sister and then only with Liz because the woman knew how to keep a secret. It was those rare moments that had cemented our friendship, along with our daily target practice sessions.

We'd sat side by side on the cross-country route from Epsilon to Alpha, when I'd started out at the bottom of the Corps food chain, sharing a hard bench under a canvas awning. We'd both ignored the jokes of the other recruits and the jostles of the road.

One day we planted asses outside on a pit stop, raking the stench of body odor from our noses and stretching the cramps of enclosure from our muscles, when she said, "Penned up again, huh?"

Chewing on a piece of grass, I'd looked at her short cap of hair and shrewd eyes. "Yup."

"You don't say much."

"Neither do you."

She held her fist up for a bump. I hit it hard, waiting for her to wince. She blew across her knuckles. "Don't hold back or anything."

"Not a problem."

The clouds wandering across a limitless sky had put me back on the shore of the northern ocean with my sis when Liz mentioned, "Never thought this was for me, but my dad got offed by Nomads and my mom went suicide right after. I ended up an instant orphan. The Corps gotta be some kind of family, right?"

I'd repeated the Company credo by heart. *"Regeneration, Veneration, Salvation."*

"You believe that?"

"What's not to like about a perfectly tight slogo?" I grinned.

She'd looked at a group of Corpsmen with their jocks out, seeing who could hit a seed head with piss, but she was paying real close attention to me. "What's your story?"

"Same as you. Nothing else for me. No other redemption in this world."

Liz was my junior, tight in her aim, ready for a fight, relentless when needed and not just a hard-core grunt. When I gave the bad news to a civilian family, she did the cleanup. I'd seen her comfort everyone from rebels to lifers in the Corps.

She'd consoled me too. Not in a *let's-exchange-spit* way and not in a girly *gotta-have-you* way either. The best thing about that woman was her heart, and she didn't show that to anyone. Liz kept her feelings tucked away, but even out of sight they ran deep. It came out in actions, not emotions.

The time she gave me robo-fish was the first time I stepped into her apartment, following a trail of feminine perfume through stark hallways as bleak as my place until I reached her bedroom. Brightly colored with worldly comforts, some of which were smuggled items, her room was a hidden haven full of pillows and lit candles, artwork hanging on every wall. She'd backed me out, shutting the door behind us. "Pretend you never saw that."

That was our motto, right?

Three days after the forget-me-not fiasco, driving farther into the Wilderness, I still hadn't received any coms from Liz.

Blondie must've been inside my head, a space already crammed with too many people. "You're worried."

I composed my face, becoming a blank image. "Better?"

"No." Touching the corner of my mouth, he drawled, "What are ya' thinkin' about?"

I placed his hand back where it belonged, on his side of the Cruiser. "How about all those people we left to rot back in Alpha, for starters?"

"I wouldn't worry about them." He kept his eyes on the unfriendly woods we slowly drove through, tree limbs and leaves slapping the windshield.

"The fuck's that mean? They have no water!" I hit the brakes and turned to him. "You don't give a shit about the casualties of this war, do you?"

Dragging his eyes back to me, he snapped his teeth together, the muscle in his jaw bulging. "You think I'm nothin' but a monster anyway."

"Moot fucking point." My finger stabbed his chest with every word. Damn right I did. Part of me did. Sometimes. But, Christ, I was the same as him, working to keep a repressive regime in power. Even out here, I was proving myself to be a grade-A hypocrite and a dickhead to boot.

I pushed the driver's seat back another hitch, glaring ahead.

"Fine. Believe what you gotta. But don't think you can keep getting away with playin' me two ways. You want me; you hate me. And I'm the one head fuckin' you?" His arms crossed over his chest presented me with a stalemate.

He was turning me inside out. A roiling knot invaded my gut. "Liz. She's the one I'm worrying about most."

He braved a tentative touch to the back of my hand. "Your second?"

"She's not just my second, and I'm not talking about her."

A flicker of hurt dimmed his eyes and pressed his mouth closed. He snatched his hand back.

"What? No snappy comeback?"

His answer was low. "Not this time, Commander."

Fuck. I hate this. This...this...feeling bullshit. At the start of the journey, I'd had no reason to apologize to him. There'd been nothing between us, except that very first top-mark blow job after months of wanting. Now there were names, nicknames, hell, sometimes there were even endearments when we were bedding down for the night. This shit scared me.

I drove; he sat.

I sulked; he moved next to me until our forearms rubbed. I clasped his hand in mine, making sure to slide my fingers all the way between his, rubbing the hill of his palm just the way he liked it.

I relaxed into the ride the very moment he started to whistle, tapping his heavy signet ring in time on the armrest.

During the day, I tried to maintain my distance as the kilometers from Alpha grew. The bogs became bayous. Through low-lying ground, the jumble of tree roots, the sharp smell of soil and slow-moving water, we pushed farther into no-man's-land.

Nomads' land, to be very fucking precise.

When the way became impenetrable, Blondie would jump out to cut through the clog of prickles and brambles, slashing at interlocking tree limbs that looked like they'd been hugging one another for a century or more. He always found the route, always on the other side of some wild scree.

The first time he'd ambled to the back and pulled out his badass machete, I almost jumped him on the hood of the truck. It was one hell of a weapon, wielded by one hell of a man.

I'd waited until we set up camp that night to pounce on him.

My latest battle had nothing to do with the Company, the rebels, or any other faction. It was out-and-out warfare between my head and my heart. Keeping it cool during daylight, versus nighttime, when I unleashed my passion for him.

So far our nighttime escapades outranked everything else. Sundown found us scrambling, desperately tearing at clothes, gasping, grunting, lunging, coming. Committing every single Company sexual crime except outright fucking, because I was saving myself for marriage apparently. Though, knowing he'd lusted after me for months made it damn near impossible to shut down the sheer intensity of desire I felt for him. Add in our solo vacation from rules, I was determined to make full use of our downtime.

Turned out the Wilderness was a lot more hostile than me.

Blondie stood on a shallow bank on the fifth night. In the dim lighting, I saw he'd tossed off his boots and socks, working his toes into the cool mud. His shirt was sent the same way as his footwear, his fatigues slung low so his skintight white briefs caught on the rounds of his ass. Shoulders curling inward, his arms worked, and he sighed.

He'd pushed his pants below his cock. He was getting himself off. *Fuck.*

I left the fireside, stalking beside him. He was bathed by the orange glow of the moon, his erection strapped to his abdomen, the veins a highway to the darker head.

Releasing his bottom lip from his teeth, he glanced at me with half-mast eyes. "No baths tonight."

"I'll clean you up."

"Yeah?"

"Absolutely." My voice lowered, my cock was turgid. I needed to get my hands and mouth on him pronto. Starting with firm laps all down his torso, I kissed his nipples until they puckered tight and hot for a nibble of my teeth.

"Sweet hell, yes, honey," he whispered.

My fingers took over the torture of flicking and twisting the satiny nubs until his hips rolled and his head kicked back. I tickled his sinewy sides with my tongue, then wet the soft curls that sliced through his rippling abs, following to the money spot where his glorious cock grew from a base of dark blond hair. I bit near the top of his dick, right on the spot he was widest. If he was ever inside me, *Jesus*, he'd stretch me more than any man ever had.

"*Ahh*, fuck yeah. Your mouth is so hot. Suck me. Suck me hard." His head was thrown back, but his eyes focused on me.

My palm slid up the velvety weight and all his veins throbbed. Trapping him against his stomach, I soothed, *"Shhh,"* before taking one ball into my mouth.

"Oh yeah!" Thighs trembling under my hand, he chanted, "Yeah, baby, yeah. That's better… That's…"

He lost his voice when I moved my head further between his

legs, my short hair rubbing the root of his cock. I lapped and licked and suckled his other sac until they were both shiny pieces of fruit I rolled inside my fingers. When I let his cock go, it stood in a broad arch, distended, glistening, moving in a tempting dance.

Blondie's hands found my face, pulling me away. Looking down over his rugged body, his breath chugging, he said all breathless and sexy. "I need to be in your mouth."

"Not yet." I slapped his ass with a smart blow, smiling when he hissed and a droplet of precome drizzled from the tiny lips of his dick's slit.

Now that, I was having. I scooped it onto the tip of my tongue, roughly turned him around, and went to work on all those bundles of muscles of his back. He flexed and groaned and swayed into my fingers, my mouth, crying out when I hit the sensitive joints of his spine. My forefinger trailed the line of sweat trickling down to his ass. Those goddamn beautiful globes fit into my hands, and sure enough the twin dimples at the base of his back were just begging for my tongue. Diving in to lap and lick, I gripped his crescent-shaped buttocks hard.

He reared away on a moan and thrust back with a guttural, "*Oooh*, your hands, man."

I swatted him again, and he shivered. I made wet paths all over his rear until I reached the sweet divide. His ass was so fucking tight, I had to squeeze my tongue into that steamy clasp, and that was exactly where I wanted my cock the next time I came.

"*Mmm.*" I hummed when the tip of my tongue traced the warm line that led to his gorgeous pink bud. I didn't use my hands to spread him, enjoying the way his ass clutched my tongue, grinning when he swiveled his hips to get me deeper.

His hands fell to his cock. I captured his wrists and cuffed them behind his back. With one, two, and three stabs against his starred flesh—reveling in the taste of man and musk, sweet and dark—I ordered, "You. Don't. Touch."

His fingers curled, his hips wiggled, and he gasped when my stiffened tongue dove inside. "Then you better, 'cause I need to come, Caspar."

Removing my face from the sexy heaven of his ass, I swiveled him around. "Then you better ask me politely."

He stole his dick across my cheek, down my chin, up my throat. I strained backward. His hands quivered before he yanked me to his balls, but I held off, lashing a quick spiral of my tongue to the throbbing length. For damn sure I wasn't gonna suck anything until he said please in that low southern drawl.

"I could just fuck my hand."

I leaned back. "Go for it."

His fist around his dick, he pleaded in a husky tone, "Fuck. Please, Caspar, you're killin' me."

My hand wrapped around his, I took his long, leaking shaft into my mouth, tonguing under his deep red head, closing my lips around him, pushing my throat down until he pulsed all the way inside.

He shouted to the stars, widening his stance. I slurped back, leaving a wash of saliva all down his cock, laughing when he grunted, "More."

I opened my mouth, watching his face collapse in pained arousal when he pushed himself inside. "When are you gonna fuck me, big man?"

My face was turned to the side, the heat of his cockhead stretching my cheek in a manly caress. Fingers tenderizing his ass, slipping down and in, I let go with a rough pinch. "You're not ready for me."

"The hell I ain't." Pushing onto my fingertip until it squeezed inside him, he pitched forward, catching himself on my shoulders.

My finger plunged inside that clenching passage, my throat impaled by him. It took only one more deep suck before he blasted inside my mouth. His fingers convulsed in my hair as his ejaculate washed down my throat.

With a final press, his muscles released, and his mouth opened on a shout. "Yes, Caspar! Swallow it."

I rose to my feet and kissed his plump lips, stroking my tongue inside, thrusting my hips when he bit the tip and soothed it gently. I burned my mouth against the whiskers on his chin, kissed his dimples, and put my cheek to the soft razor-shorn side of his hair, holding the longer strands in my hand.

I admitted against his ear, "I'm not ready to fuck you."

My shirt shredded in his fists, he shoved my pants aside, running the pads of his fingertips from my scalp to my ass and back up again.

He turned his head and took my lips. "What do you need, honey?"

Slamming my eyes shut over his endearment, I croaked, "Go to the truck and bend over for me."

His pupils dilated, he flushed.

"Now," I demanded.

I took zero time following him as he bent over, as I'd ordered. *I could get used to this.*

Just once, I swiped my hands down his back, raising goose bumps.

Braced on his arms, all his muscle showed: his big biceps, his flexed forearms, the fan of sinew spreading from his spine. "Very nice, lover."

He sucked in a breath and arched his back.

"Even better." I stepped into the lee of his legs until my cock pointed skyward against his ass. "Not gonna fuck you yet, but here's an idea about what it'll be like when I do."

I nipped the nape of his neck and parted his ass cheeks. When I slowly let them go, his rear hugged my dick. I was so swollen, a glaze of release made his cushioned home slick for my taking. From the balls of my feet to my thighs, I rammed between his tight, clenched ass over and over again. "But you're gonna be good and wait, aren't you?"

"Yeah. *Yes!*"

Fuck, he was hard again. The pump of his hips backward and forward timed with mine; his hand was at work down in front. Our sacs slapped loudly while my dick sawed up and down, and my head was so sensitive, it was gushing more come every time I crested between the hot domes of his ass, never penetrating.

"Good. Now I'm gonna come all over this ass." I grasped his hips, hauling him with me until I balanced both of us on my thighs, gritting out, *"Aw fuck!"* I exploded in a pounding rhythm, sandwiched against his ass.

Each furious lash of come made me groan and made Blondie jerk. Placing my palm on his back as his body seized in another climax, I lowered his chest to the truck, coating him in another white whip.

Then I covered him with my body, the hot wetness clinging between us, running down his ass to my cock. His skin was warm from my slaps, his back sticky from me.

My mark was all over him.

I loved that.

It took a good few minutes to come around from seeing stars to seeing the actual stars, bright in the black sky above us. It sounded so quiet after our shouts and gasps and yells. Quiet, like a big blanket had fallen over us.

We heaped together and I groaned, "I'm fucking wiped."

"*Mmm*, me too, big man. You just…" He rubbed his face over my hair, whispering, "That was amazin'."

All my damn muscles relaxed from the day's rage against myself, and I smiled. "Yep." Steadying myself, I hefted Blondie into my arms, carrying him toward the tent.

"The hell, Caspar?"

"Figured it's the considerate thing to do, since you let me come all over your backside. And I'm just letting you recover so you've got enough energy to bring me some food later."

That was partly true. The man built up an appetite in me for something bigger than sex or food. It made me want to take care of him, too.

*   *   *

For a few more days, it was all birds and flowers and fucking, but not exactly.

Fucking with my mental gear. *Most definitely.*

We'd completed the southern route and now headed northeast into a place that used to be called Tennessee. Distant mountains marched one behind the other in a bleary blue terrain. *Mountains*, just in time for hoofing it. The upcoming weeks of physical exertion better take me out of my head space, because it was getting crammed in there.

The day we ran out of gas was the day I got my ass handed to me. We were reconfiguring our supplies for the on-foot portion of our trek when Liz's com came in.

Throwing down the duffels, I punched the buttons on my D-P. "Liz? Liz!"

She came across in full static. "Commander, do you copy?"

"Status, Lieutenant?"

"Can't…hear. Rebellion has gone…Revolution level."

I cupped the D-P to my ear, reeling when the crack of gunfire sizzled across our transmission. "Fuck! Liz?"

She suddenly came over clear-voiced. "Sir. The attack on the water supply in Sector Five was replicated internationally in all sixteen Territories. It was internally synchronized by digital remote."

I narrowed my eyes at Blondie, the head of technological acquisitions. This intel wasn't simply Nomad plus rebel work. *Right.*

"Dire all-Territories-wide situation taking place, Commander. Gotta embrace the suck."

I didn't like the sound of that, her having to make the best of a shitty situation. "What are your orders?"

"Continue to Beta with evacuees, but they're in trouble too, sir."

"Keep the civilians safe." I hoped Leon and his mother were with them. "Defy the chain of command if you have to."

An electronic squeal shorted her words. "Contaminant…chemical released…a hoax."

"What?" I shoved a finger into my ear, deafening the buzz of daytime's loud insects.

"Forty-eight hours after…" Shouts crackled across the squawk box. "Water clean. Enough time for CO control to slip. *SHIT!*"

Holy shit. "Lieutenant, *alpha23bravo06SITREP.*"

"That was a close one. Almost got me by a cunt-hair."

I couldn't even manage a chuckle, seeing her curled in a ball, examining the crosshairs of her scope, not her crotch.

"Sabotage. A flash point. Some fucker out there's a real smartass. Manipulating the control of essentials to create chaos."

A screaming whistle made me drop the D-P. When I picked it back up, she was speaking in chopped-up sentences again. "Need to…tell…my dad…the Nomads—"

Hunkering on my heels, I pressed my head to the hot metal door of the Cruiser. "Liz, you get hit?"

There was no smart-mouthed retort. Static followed the silence.

I lost her. I bent over and breathed heavy. In, out. In and out. I stowed my D-P in my pocket, straightened up, and went back to work stripping the Land Cruiser.

When I raised the hood, disconnecting wires and leads, planning on putting a bullet in the head gasket, Blondie lifted my finger from the trigger. "You don't want to do that."

"I need to shoot something. So, the Cruiser or you?"

He turned his back, a tall blank emblem as I recocked and fired.

All afternoon, we wound through foothills picking our way though untrammeled brush and brambles, and I thought about Liz.

After we set up camp in a forest glen, Blondie went off on his own, equipped with his portable sat system, the sophisticated Company version of the D-P. *Confusing SOB.* It was probably a good thing he left me alone because I was a grouchy motherfucker and I still wanted target practice on something or someone.

I grabbed the ax from the loop on my backpack, laid it across my shoulder, and tromped into the woods in the opposite direction. Bastard might have made it his life's work to spy on me, but I had better things to do, like taking something down, building up a sweat, and backing away from the precipice I'd been teetering over since Liz's coms cut out.

I picked the biggest tree I could find and gave a few practice swings. Pressing the blade into the bark, I tested my aim, swung back and...stopped. I placed my forehead against the papery white bark before backing off. I was still gonna chop some damn wood, just not that particular tree; thing was too noble. With its fragrant bark curling back, the pink undersides were too close to the color of Blondie's goddamn lips.

Fucking ridiculous, sparing a tree because it reminds me of him.

I toed up to a maple and sliced into it before I could notice the way the leaves had turned from deep green to the same red as the head of Blondie's... *Yeah. Not thinking about his cock, either.*

Ripping off my sweat-soaked shirt, I hacked over and over again. Wood chips a maelstrom of grenades raining over me, I watched the trunk weave left with every huge blow.

Yelling, "Timber!" just because my pop had told me about that tradition once, I gave a satisfied laugh when the behemoth wavered to the left, suspended for a few seconds at an impossible angle, then crashed to the forest floor with ground-shaking vibrations.

For the next hour, I chopped wood until I had to wipe the perspiration from my eyes and use my shirt to dry my stomach. The scent of sweet sap filled the air, instead of me being the sap for a change. I humped the loads of wood camp side and was busy stacking it all neat and tidy, orderly, the way I liked shit, when Major Head Fuck ambled into the clearing, hitting me with another slug of mistrust. He'd been gone for more than two hours, no doubt reporting to the CO, quite possibly about my sexual deviancy.

Exhaling with finality, I slammed the ax head into my chopping block one last time, raising my arm to wipe my forehead. He leaned down, inspecting my afternoon's work; then he swerved over to gather a bead of sweat from my shoulder with his tongue.

My nostrils flared, my fingers curled, and I fought to hold my neck steady rather than tilt it sideways, offering my throat for his kisses.

He tapped the teasing curve of his bottom lip and arched an eyebrow. "If you needed a workout, you could've waited for me."

"Fuck you," I growled.

His other eyebrow shot up in surprise. "That's what I meant."

That response raised my temperature another notch. "Where the hell were you?"

"Had some business to take care of." His loose grin aimed at my groin tightened my nut when he said, "See you do too."

No brainer. Soon as I saw Blondie, I busted a boner no matter the circumstances.

"You get a report on the rebellion?" I ignored the blatant situation in my pants.

One eyebrow remained high in a silent question, which went something like, *What's your fuckin' problem this time?* "Sure, what I'm entitled to. Goes along the lines of what your lieutenant told you." He shrugged. "The rebels are in league with Nomads, and they've amassed international unity in high proportions. And, of course, the upgrade to Revolution."

"Why don't you look worried?"

"Why do you look like you wanna shoot me?"

"Probably the same reason as always. I don't fucking trust you, Company Man," I sneered. "Every time you traipse off into the trees to hit your knees with InterNations cock shoved down your throat, I sit here and think about all the traitorous tidbits you're describing to your CEO."

The cunt-ass Cutler in question still held a black ball against me because he'd been dumb enough to get caught with his pants down while his assailant slipped past my troops.

His tone turned brittle. "How about we fight it out and get it over with." Dropping his shirt, he raised his fists.

"Give you more ammo by assaulting a Company executive? Don't think so." I couldn't look at him when I quietly admitted, "Besides, I've gone down heartbreak road before, and I don't plan on a return trip. So you do what you gotta do. Hit me; turn me in. It doesn't matter. I'm done."

He came at me, his hands raised, only to take my face between them. At my reactionary flinch, he inched away, whispering, "Damn it, man. You still think I'm gonna work you over?"

"Second nature."

Dejection sank his shoulder. "Will you ever believe me?"

"Your kind isn't in good standing. Once you're Company, you're a lifer. Just like your children will be after you, and on and on. You were born to it."

My harsh words had the desired effect. He retreated a couple steps, saying, "You're a goddamn hypocrite, you know that?"

Blondie was right, and it was better that he believed I was an asshole rather than good relationship material, so I swallowed down the truth of his words without even trying to dispute them. After a few moments of nodding, he lifted eyes that were resolved. "It was your birthday that night at the Amphitheater."

There was no one to remember it anymore except Liz, not since the Plague had taken my family. "That's right. You've seen my file."

"What did you wish for that night?" Blondie asked.

"Huh?"

"You haven't heard of it?"

"Birthday wishes?" I'd heard of the odd cake, a lighthearted spanking to toll every year. Those were nice dreams but nothing like what I'd experienced. And I had no recollection of this wishes bullshit.

"In the old days, they used to blow out candles on their cake. One for every year. Makin' a silent wish, and if all the candles went out, it was said their wish would be granted. You don't know this?"

I lined up the shelves of wood. "Nah. We had a real special tradition in Epsilon; maybe you haven't heard of this one. We presented ourselves to the Tribunal for a nice committee viewing, just to see how we were coming along year after year. Questions were asked and answers recorded to measure intellectual aptitude; physical trials were performed so our future work roles within the Territory could be identified and redefined. In later years, we got to answer a battery of questions based on sexual orientation."

Blondie's face flushed with anger. "That doesn't happen in Alpha."

"Seems Epsilon was full of fun surprises. Anyway, I had a cake once. It was an experience I don't want to repeat." I smiled at the memory. "Sis baked it. Let me put it this way: I'm a better cook than she is. Than she *was*."

He stroked the back of my hand. "If you'd had a wish that night, what would it have been?"

I turned my palm over, joining our fingers. I went balls to the walls. "You. I would've wished for you."

"Same thing I wanted."

"Blondie—"

His fingertips dusted across my mouth. My breath stuttered when he said, "I can give you me."

I started to step away, but he encircled my hips. "I know you can't trust me, Caspar."

That statement was so loaded, it made my head spin as much as his slow caress over my abdomen. *Can't*, because he truly was untrustworthy? *Can't*, because he finally understood my hard limits? Or why not both reasons, for bonus points? I saw one truth through it all when I delved into his eyes. He was sad that I would never trust him.

"Yeah, I get it," he said. "And I'll take what I can get. But understand this, big man. I want more. I want all of you."

Before I could retreat, he tilted his head and let loose with that sensual, breathy drawl. "Lemme love you tonight."

I swallowed when his lips dragged down my neck. "Okay."

"Good." He sauntered to the tent and back to me, a small cloth bag in one hand. He pulled me after him. "Wanna show you something I found earlier. You'll like it."

"Ah, but will I love it?"

With a rumble of laughter, he towed me to his side, joining our hands. The fat silvery band on his forefinger dug into my flesh the way I liked it.

The sun had fallen away, leaving room for a bright full moon chased by wraithlike clouds to light our short hike. The day's warmth still lingered, and I imagined this might be our last temperate evening with the directional change of our journey.

The night filled out with the low hum of creatures, insects, and nocturnal scavengers. Wings flapped overhead, and I looked up in time to see a large snowy white and auburn speckled bird with no neck at all, propelling loftily along, adding its own song with an echoing, *"Hoot-hoot, hoot-hoot."*

"Barn owl," Blondie said.

Barn owl. I'd have to add that one to my D-P. I'd kept track of all the animals and plants we'd come across. While the resonant *hoot-hoot, hoot-hoot* faded, a new noise hit my ears. A wet splashing pattern like heavy rain, but there wasn't a rain cloud in sight. "What's that?"

"C'mon." He hurried us toward the rushing sound.

Around a bend, I stopped dead in my tracks. In awe of the curtain of water falling from a cliff of rocks four meters above, I murmured, "That's a—"

"Waterfall, yeah." Hopping onto a rock, he held his hand under the cascade, then flicked it toward me.

"Never seen one in real life." The noise had amplified to a deafening thunder at our approach.

"Not too many around, least not that you can get to anymore."

The water dripped down my face. *So clean.* I'd never witnessed this wonder of nature before. I couldn't take my eyes off the waterfall or the man beside it.

His voice so rich, I heard him above the pounding water. "I know how much you like fresh water."

My lips split for a grin. "Yeah, this sure makes a change from my shitty little shower back in Alpha with that trickle of reprocessed liquid." He'd been paying such close attention to me out here. The flowers and now this. My heart sped up. Instead of worrying me at being so intimately watched, he aroused me, attracted me more than ever before.

I couldn't get my clothes off fast enough. We both laughed when I fell smack on my ass, trying to unlace my boots.

At my feet, he took over. "Let me."

"Okay. But hurry up. I need to get in there, man."

Dimples plugged into his cheeks when he smiled up at me. "I can see that."

I groaned, stepping into the pool. The falling water flicked my calves with fizzy coolness. I wanted to feel that effervescence on my cock. Over my shoulder, Blondie was shedding his pants as hastily as I had, and the heated look in his eyes reminded me of the night I'd bathed him with my tongue. Memories made my spine tingle, my cock stretch all the way up to my belly button and beyond. I held my hand out to him, helping him in, backing us up until the water reached my hips and we stood directly under the rapid flow.

He was so hot and hard against me. There was nothing like the muscles on a man's body. Settling my cock beside his so our wet rubbing made my tip pulse and my ass pucker, I grabbed his hair in a sleek ponytail and slanted my lips to his. Tongues coiled and teeth clashed, mouths pulled and suckled during our hungry kiss. He slowed me with his hands low on my pelvis, undulating against me to some earthly tune that made my blood race with fever to suck him, fist him, fuck him wild.

I reached for the long hot pole of his cock, and he nudged me aside. "No. I said let me love you."

My lips at the corner of his mouth, I growled, "Get on with it."

"You are so impatient." He reached back, coming up with that small bag he'd brought, and emptied the contents. He held out a bar of spicy scented soap. I'd never wanted to be cleaned up so much in my life.

His hands looped along my shoulders, spreading a lather that floated over my chest and joined the water's jets as they brushed around my cock. He got behind me, and this time I didn't mind at all. Fingers digging in, surrounding me in his brusque caresses and the same scent that clung to him all day long, he dipped both hands to my ass, two soapy fingertips sliding inside me.

His delicious whispers set me off. "So fucking tight, honey. Your ass is gorgeous. Can't wait to fuck it."

A frigging whimper escaped my throat at the thought of him lowering over my back, spreading my ass with his palms, and smoothly working his cock inside me. *Fuck.* I didn't let anyone top me—hadn't for a long time—but I'd let Blondie. *Nathaniel.*

He kissed and lathered and teased all over my armpits, my ribs, my groin, stopping just short of my dick. When he grasped me in both soapy hands, my eyes slammed shut and my breath flew out as I held back my orgasm.

"Love how hard you get for me, honey. This big cock for me?"

God-fucking-damn. "Yes!"

"Hmm." He applied more pressure, frothing me inside fists, tightening when he got to the dark engorged head to twist, let go, and start back again at the bottom.

The waterfall aimed acute points at my dick, hitting me with a one-two punch that had me on the edge, on my tiptoes, my back arched and my neck thrown back.

The eroticism of what we were doing drove a scorching dagger into the pit of my belly. Caressed by the water, held over a cliff by Blondie's sure, smooth motions, I mashed his hair in my hands, garbling such fucking nonsense I had no idea what I was saying anymore.

His lips moving down the line of my abs, his husky laughter made me moan. "You love this, don't you? You're such a sensualist; aren't you, honey?"

I shook when he finally sank his lush lips over the head of my dick, his tongue so damn talented as it swiped and swirled, teasing out the most sensitive flesh of my rock-hard cock.

Bracing my hands on the outcropping behind me, I gasped. "Sensualist?" He made me feel naive, almost young. I hadn't felt that way in years.

He hummed, popping off the dripping head of my shaft just as I was ready to fire off. He applied more masterful tongue work up and down the stiff sides of my cock until I jerked uncontrollably from head to toe. "Pleasure from touch."

He took me all the way down his throat and my head fell back. As he pulled off, the insides of his lips released my head with an obscene kiss. "Pleasure from sounds. You like how much I love suckin' your sexy cock, don't you?" Blondie pursed his lips over the broad tip, created a tight seal, and hummed into me.

"*Oh fuck.*"

"Pleasure from taste." He kneeled up, stroking his length for a dab of precome. He held it out on his fingertip. I sucked that honey, devouring his finger like it was his cock.

I was near demented with the need to come. "Yes, I love it. *More.*"

His chuckle went straight to my balls when he made love to my cock again, his hands ranging around my thighs and onto my ass for a rough handhold. "You're so damn beautiful, Caspar."

Savage, I yanked him away. "I want you to come with me." I brought him to his feet, steadied him inside my embrace, and kissed his mouth until he broke away to watch the glide of our wet cocks massaging together between our stomachs.

"Fucking gorgeous." I moaned.

I moaned even louder when his hand, soaped once more, joined us inside his fist. *"Ahh."*

"Jesus. *Jesus.* Caspar."

Hearing the slap of our balls banging as we stroked was a goddamn barrage of sensation, I couldn't hold off any longer. It grew from the low of my back, twisted my nuts high, and set off a blast that made me yell.

His cock jerked beside mine. Through the overspill of come, he kept hold of us, kept me on my feet.

The water washed away our semen and we were left under that free-flowing stream, hugging each other.

Later, in our bed of soft blankets over hard ground, he whispered with a kiss, "You believe me now?"

*   *   *

Three nights later, I woke to a brisk chill. It was colder now that we'd forged into the mountains. The frosty air didn't make a dent inside our nest of arms and legs. *Body heat, mmm.* Cuddling closer to Blondie, I relished the rush of arousal racing down my body.

We weren't fucking yet, but we weren't fucking with each other anymore either. There were too many cards on the table for me to keep a poker face. Not that I knew the game. Gambling was another strictly off-limits pastime, though I'd heard about the shakedown artists.

A branch creaked. Then another.

Dry tinder broke to the left of our tent. I sat up, hushing Blondie when he sat upright beside me. Cocking my head, I heard the telltale snap of another twig and the almost imperceptible crunch of hoar-frost underfoot.

I won't let another get captured, not on my watch. Instinct kicking in, I leaped to my feet, grabbing the SIG under my pillow and the one on top of my backpack. I had a few seconds to wish I'd gone to bed fully clothed instead of bare-assed, because then I'd have my knife too.

Thinking was overrated.

Breaking free of the tent, I caught wind of them before I saw them. They'd covered their scent with the musky oil of the deer I'd watched earlier in the day. *Clever fucking Nomads.*

There were six, camouflaged to such perfection I was able to count them only when they moved, showing their positions. True hunters, they hid among the trees, stealing closer and closer.

I circled; they encircled me.

The moon's light glinted off a metal edge. *Knives.*

Feeling Blondie behind me, I hissed, "Get back inside. Now."

He stood his ground, armed like me. "Not happenin'."

"You're wasting my time. Retreat!"

They darted nearer. *Protect this man.* Recognizing the stubborn jut of his chin, I did the necessary thing. My elbow sent back in a high jab, the blow with his cheek shuddering along my arm. I almost dropped my gun, but Blondie dropped first, unconscious.

This was a threat I knew how to neutralize…hostiles.

They came at me in twos, long-haired Wilderness dwellers, one leading and one flanking.

Good tactics.

The closest pair met my fist in the solar plexus and my heel in the sternum, dropping like the forbidden dominoes Erica and I had played on summer nights.

The second duo learned fast; they were at my rear before I'd flattened the first. I hopped over Blondie and hunkered in a defensive pose in front of him. Arms raised, roaring, they fell on me as one. I dropped onto my back, drop-kicking a lithe man with the crunch-punch of both feet to his stomach so he flailed through the air, smacking into a tree trunk with a resounding thud.

His guard wrestled under my shoulders, pitting his face into my back and ripping his teeth into my skin. I struggled to my feet with him clamped on and reached behind, rewarded when my fingertips pressed his pulpy pulse points until his bite relaxed and his legs gave out under him.

I heard Blondie's moan. This wasn't the must-have-you-now moan I was used to, but a bleat of pain.

I wasn't killing. I was gonna question these wild men first. That was the plan, until I swung around and saw a Nomad with a hand ax raised to carve out Blondie's chest.

Slinging over him, I readied myself to take the blow meant for him.

Aw shit.

An anguished shout twisted Blondie's voice exactly when the blade sliced into my right shoulder, "Caspar, no!"

The weapon dug in and drew back, my blood flowing from the gash in its wake. I lifted my head in time to see the butt of the weapon dripping with my blood crashing toward my cheek.

Now, that fucking hurt.

I shook off the dizzies enough to stay aware, but I couldn't move for the ringing in my ears. Besides, my feet had migrated to the southernmost Territory. My eyes still worked though, and there was Blondie on his feet, his fists a fury against the man who'd taken me down. He didn't let up until the Nomad dropped to the ground. Then he cracked his forehead to the last savage standing, nutting him three times in quick succession.

His ballistic offensive was awesome to see, and I regretted thinking I needed to protect him from the vicious thugs.

The final fucker capsized, I coughed a laugh, curious at the warm iron taste under my tongue.

Ah, blood. Old familiar.

My weak laughter brought Blondie to my side. He touched my shoulder, and my stomach heaved. "Caspar? Caspar? Stay with me, big man."

I slurred, "Ambidextrous…S'okay…"

He slapped my face. "Wake the fuck up, Caspar!"

"Just a flesh wound," I mumbled, and then…

Lights out.

Chapter Seven

I battled through a suffocating mass of blankets, trying to wake up. My eyelids sealed shut, I pushed my legs out straight and cupped my jaw, rubbing down the unfamiliar scratch of stubble.

Stretching my arms overhead, I halted with my right arm half raised. *"Fuuuck."*

I remembered, my eyes peeling open, blinking in the rays of sun, conducting a furtive inspection. Bell-like sounds tinkled from outside, but the unknown source of the noise was the least of my concerns. I decided I was dead for sure and this was my own personal purgatory.

"Hey, big man." That voice was discordant with concern.

No wonder I'd overlooked Blondie while I'd quickly scanned the room. There was so much shit packed into this little place, he was partly hidden by a heavy drape and a cascade of molting books in the corner of the room. The small wooden chair he perched on didn't look sturdy enough to hold his long frame. His hands between his knees, he sat forward, and his face caught the light falling from a window framed in the arched roof of what had to be less than a two-and-a-half-meter-high ceiling. At the top of his cheek was an angry red cut surrounded by raggedy tissue.

I'd done that to him with my elbow. I focused on his failure to take orders, not my relief at seeing him sitting there in one piece. Hating the way my blow discolored his face, I grunted, "You shoulda stayed in the tent."

He strode toward me, his hands braced on either side of my hips. "Guess I'd better remember that for next time."

From the corners of my eyes, I saw him taking stock of my injuries, while I scanned him the same way, making sure of his welfare. I'd been taught a life-and-death lesson on the importance of protecting my people. Problem was, I hadn't realized how quickly Blondie had slipped inside my superior defenses, putting down stakes. When the hell had he become my people—my man instead of my mission?

I cleared my throat and glimpsed beyond him, tempted to shade my eyes from all the gypsy gimcrack. "What is this anyway?"

The space was jammed with a crazy combo of fabrics overflowing every surface. Mismatched lights hung from the low ceiling, some with the old-fashioned style of bulbs instead of the flo-strips I was used to, a couple holding stalks of candles. It was a treasure trove of shakedown delights for scavenging pack rats. The platform bed I lay on seemed designed for my particular torture. Silks, satins, and velvets draped over my legs, dripping off the edges, hitting me with sensory overload.

Considering this odd abode was small, I should've felt right at home. Instead I felt squeezed in tight, a band around my chest just like the one wrapped around my shoulder.

I sat up. "You gonna answer me?"

"It's called a caravan."

"Where?"

"Forty kilometers farther north of our last camp. Chitamauga Commune."

I'd had my suspicions, but hearing him state the fact so calmly sent a charge of anger through me.

I tossed back the blankets. "Nomads?" Sitting my ass down when I listed to the left, I demanded, "Are we being detained? Because this crib is way too frilly to call itself a jail cell."

He pressed me back to the bed. "Not exactly."

I fought to keep myself upright until he withdrew his hands. "Meaning what?"

He didn't even tug at his ponytail when he said, with direct eye contact, "I made some trades for safekeepin' and safe passage."

Safekeeping, right. From a band of primitive punks one step above animals.

"What kind of trades?"

"Intel." His blue eyes were pinheads, needling me. "But don't worry none. The info wasn't on a need-to-know basis."

He was either a damn good liar or, oh yeah, he was a damn good liar. Another factoid to store in my file of fuckery, making me wonder what kind of pull a Company exec had with a pack of Nomads.

"So your enemies let you stroll around like any old wildling?" I put my good forearm over my face and scoffed, "Good to know I'm not the only one you're double-crossing."

"That's me, all right."

At the skin of anger in his voice, I lifted my arm, cranking my head in his direction.

On his feet, his dimples disappearing inside the terse void of his face, he bit out, "And they're the Company's enemies."

I needed to get out of this abysmal place. I hauled myself to the opposite side of the bed. "Same deal."

Man, if his head tricks had me dizzy, the slash to my shoulder had me swaying. *More shit to hate.* Before I could bat him away, he eased me down. His calloused palms pursed around my ribs.

His lips pursed too. "Stay the hell down, Caspar. You lost a lot of blood."

I grinned. "The pain feels great."

"God, I oughtta punch you. Maybe that'd make you stay still."

"Yeah, but you're more likely to give me a spanking." When his pupils doubled, I doubted the wisdom of my remark and blamed it on the wheelies splitting my vision.

His head lowered until he kissed me. Soft, gentle, hot. The tips of our tongues touched and traced away.

"Seein' you out like that, Caspar." He grasped the back of my neck, groaning. "Asshole, you need more protection than me."

I bit his earlobe inside a pinch of teeth. "The hell I do."

His smile curved against my forehead. "Let me check that dressing." He unwound the bandage, warning, "This is gonna hurt, honey."

The ripping pain roared up to my ears and heated my scalp, but I didn't flinch. "Feels good." This was nothing compared to the psychic agony I'd known inside and out. "Do it again?"

"Shut up."

He prodded the neat black stitches quilting the skin of my shoulder and gathered a warm cloth. With each dab, the cut became clear. It was deep, ugly, and the swollen edges were raised.

He grazed them lightly with his mouth, getting me all good and tongue-tied before saying, "We'll be stayin' on for a few days."

I shoved him away. "No fucking way."

"You think you can hike the remainin' couple hundred kilometers in this condition, you stubborn shitheel?" He threw the stained cloth toward a ceramic basin.

"I told you, I'm ambidextrous. Got full use of my left arm." Seeing the rise and fall of his chest, the expanse of his shaft along the seam of his pants, I seduced, "Be happy to demonstrate."

His laugh was low and shaky. "You gonna use sex to get your way?"

"Only with you."

His face cleared of emotion. *Good, he's learning.* "That's not funny."

"Neither is this situation." Sick of being bedridden for all of the ten-minute duration of my consciousness so far, I got to my feet, holding myself upright against the wall. "You expect me to do what? Sit around in this?" I crushed the lace of a curtain in my fist. "Just fucking wait it out? There's a Revolution, man. I've got a job to do."

His head shaking pissed me off. But worse was the smell making my nose itch. "And what the goddamn hell is that stench?" It clung to my skin. It wasn't Blondie's soap, his scent.

His eyes rose over me, taking a return trip to my groin before landing on my lips. "It's their homespun soap. I gave you a sponge bath." He took a step forward. "Minus the sponge."

Damn it. My face scorched, and so did my need to fuck the man already. Tucking it all down, I returned to glare territory. "Stay here and what? Sing some songs with a bunch of gypsy bandits I loathe and who hate me right back?"

"You don't hate 'em." His voice lost its hard edge.

Mine was just starting up. "Fuck off."

"You wanted to live among 'em, remember?"

"Correction, my sister wanted me to join up. I know jackshit about these people except what I've witnessed, and that has nothing to do with the bogus BS Sis believed." She'd been the dreamer, a woolgatherer of romantic notions that had no place in my systematic don't-screw-with-me makeup. I'd never made fun of her ideas, but I'd never given this way of life the time of day either and I wasn't about to start now.

"You're denyin' the call of fealty, the freedom of choice?"

"Moot point." I shut down his arguments, which ran too close to Erica's for my comfort. "They're not gonna roll out the orgies and garlands for me anyway. I distinctly recall doing a number on three of them."

"That'd be an understatement."

"Besides, even if I was inclined to get my sing-along around the campfire on, I don't know any songs."

He burst out in laughter. "You do know one."

"Yeah, that fucking Brown Eyed ditty you keep whistling. And that's getting old too."

Doing the conscientious routine, I took stock of the painfully overpretty room, coming to a stop when I spotted our gear piled against the far wall. I lurched toward my pack, cursing when my legs got tangled in the mountains of motherfucking covers intent on taking me down.

"Hold up, Caspar. What's your rush?"

I had to get to my D-P, check in. "Liz."

When his hand dropped onto my shoulder, his low, fast words ripped another gash through me, this time an untidy hole in my heart to go with the one on my shoulder. "There's been no word."

"You went through my stuff?"

"Not like you did mine that first night, anyway. I glanced at your screen because I knew you'd be concerned. You got nothing from her."

"How the hell'd you access it?"

"Bein' head of tech has its perks." He waggled his thumb.

"That's great. Got the keys to the Company's kingdom at the tips of your fingers? You had no right." I scrubbed my hand down the back of my neck and peered over. His grin was gone, replaced by some of the self-hate I saw in myself. "Fine. It's okay, but it's not okay, you know?"

"Pretty much sums us up, huh?"

That didn't need an affirmative. "How long have I been out?"

"About twenty-four hours."

"That's not right."

He winced. "I got some drugs to knock you out before I stitched you up."

"Shit." I exhaled. What I really wanted to ask was if he'd been with me the whole time. Instead, I kept my face a stoic shell.

He knew that game too. "Other than organizing our…stay, I've been right here."

"Guess you had to protect our gear."

"'Course. That's exactly why I never left your side."

Bet the smooth fucker was wearing a half smile making way for his dimple. A swift glance in his direction confirmed my suspicion. Reaching across the bedding heaped with pillows, I brushed that dimple. It didn't escape my close attention the way he held in a breath while his cheek clenched. I also noticed that right above my fingers was the cut on the crest of his cheek.

I turned toward him, cupping his face. "I didn't mean to hurt you."

"Yeah, you did." His eyes shut as he leaned in to my touch.

"I'm sorry, Blondie."

I moved my hand to the strong column of his neck and looked at his fists. Both were tight around a hank of lace, like he wanted to strangle it or was trying not to touch me. I smiled, until I saw the crust of blood on his knuckles. "You're not supposed to get hurt on my watch."

"Does it still count if you're the one doing it?"

My breath whooshed out. "I said I was sorry."

"That's not what I'm talkin' 'bout." His breath beat near the side of my mouth, going at the same pace as my heartbeat working itself up to bursting point.

"Then yeah, it counts." Taking a gut check, I realized it counted more than I cared to inspect. After a slow exhale, I got close enough to taste his lips, to lick the bottom one with a light swipe. The air was thick, lashing us as tightly together as the fabric smothering my legs. I pulled back after a slow dive in, our lips parting softly.

"It'll probably scar," I murmured.

"Won't be the only one I get before this thing is over."

Another slammer to the chest. While I was recovering, he stood. "We need some food."

"You and your food. Frigging only thing you ever think about."

Back to form, he bent over and flicked my earlobe with his tongue. "Not the only thing, big man."

I swatted him away, boosting to my feet in search of my clothes. I managed to dress with my usual economy of motions, only slowing when I pushed my right arm into the sleeve.

Looking at the door, I went back and pulled out my weapons. "On second thought, I'm bringing my friends."

"Go for it. They've been discharged."

I strapped the KA-BAR to my thigh and grumbled, "This'll do."

The visual bombardment grew to what-the-fuck proportions outside. I jumped across the rickety three steps to a bright stamp of green grass inside a little fence that surrounded the caravan. Painted a cheery red, the fencing was the innocent younger sister of the badass barbed wire I had lifelong knowledge of.

I stepped back and got a load of our patchwork prison. The wagon was done up in that same red on the bottom half, Blondie blue on top. At various points along the scrollwork eaves hung the wooden and metal noisemakers I'd heard inside. I took a last glance at the caravan, amazed something so small could contain the sprawling bed, the two of us, and a whole lot of eyesore.

The morning sunlight paled next to the colorful contraptions sitting together in neighborly plots. A network of winding narrow pathways created with no grid system in mind converged toward a single unpaved road that widened enough for five men to walk abreast. There was nothing in this helter-skelter that resonated with my Epsilon Territory upbringing or my military training. Outbuildings of wind and rain-lashed boards huddled together in the center of the village, their open doorways providing views inside a trading hall, and next door, a workshop accommodated two different types of old-fashioned, unfamiliar textiles machines. Across from the textiles site was a larger, more carefully constructed building inside which rough-hewn tables were arranged in a circle.

"Schoolhouse," Blondie informed me.

I pointed to the structures farther out from the main road, edging up to the half circle of dense woods whose tall trees guarded the commune. "Those?"

"Munitions."

Great. "And?"

"Medical."

With the forest forming a natural boundary on the far side, fields and meadows to the left, and a lake deep enough to appear black over on the right, I felt a tug of admiration at the situation. Bastards had a sweet deal here.

My sightseeing trip was cut short the farther we went because, of course, this was where the populace liked to hang. And the populace wasn't really looking to chum up to a pair of Territorians like us. The looks I intercepted came from positions to the left, right, front, and back of us and were less *welcome home* and way more *wait till we get our hands on you...again.*

Weapons were raised, their motley crew of agricultural implements rounded out with a hatchet or two, and so were my hackles. Ugly glares drilled holes all over my body, integrating with not-so whispers along the lines of hissed, "Traitor. Corps whore. Sewer rat."

Pushing past the insult to my Corps calling, I concentrated on the fascinating instead of the really fucking irritating. Passels of kids dawdled and giggled, immune to the growing animosity in the way only children could be. They came in all ages, colors, and sizes. *No problem with regeneration here.* Milling animals trotted, pecked, and ran right alongside them, free to range.

When a dog approached me minus the growls of the mob that reverbed all around, I forgot protect-yourself protocol and went down to its level. Scratching behind its ear, I leaned in to the soft fur. Its wet muzzle tunneled in to my palm.

A pair of muddy boots toed up with the polished blacks of mine. The voice that went with them was gritty. "Git yer hands of mah dog, filthy flattop."

That comment could've easily bought doggie's daddy the farm. I did another round of play nice with the natives and backed away as I rose, keeping my hands at my sides, as unthreatening as a hulking, solid mass of one-hundred-plus kilograms of muscle could be. "No harm intended."

"Haven't heard that from your kind before." Decorated with sparse gray whiskers, his face was grizzlier than his mutt's.

As he stomped away to join his compatriots, I told Blondie, "You can stop watching me like you expect me to start gutting these fuckers at any given moment. I'm a professional soldier, not a mercenary."

He didn't comment, just started walking again, head held high, broad shoulders at ease. The perfect image of CO indifference.

In the mess hall, the sun's hazy beams sifted between loose vertical boards. Flags fluttered down from the high, boned rooftop: red, purple, and golden cloths absent of the *Regeneration, Veneration, Salvation* slogo and Territory symbolism. They had their own motto, stitched in glinting threads: *Live in Freedom, Love at Will.*

Their coined phrase was a hell of a lot more welcoming than the CO hardline, but it didn't mesh with the gory stories I'd been told.

The air smelled clean and a little damp. Barrels of hay made round towers in the corners, where groups of kids hunkered over chalk-drawn lines, rolling colored orbs into one another. Tables in the schoolhouse style were decked by benches occupied by Nomads getting their fill of breakfast.

The silence at our arrival lasted ten long-ass seconds before folding back into the din of eating, talking, and a little bit of gawking at us, this time minus the murderous regard. *Fucking weird.*

Since I seemed to be off the chopping block, at least in here, I gathered some intel on them while they sucked back their soup. Their individual coloring told of the introduction of multicultural stock and, since the seething rage outside was missing from this morning meal, some sort of civilization must be at work here.

Blondie asked, "Somethin' wrong?"

"Yeah, where are the rest of the pitchforks? And how did they re-populate like this?"

"Like what, now?" He squatted down and waved at the kids playing games in the corner opposite us. A dark-haired girl and her redhead friend giggled back, a blush rising in her cheeks.

I blushed too, watching him. "Thought they'd be more—"

"Untamed," he said, gaining his feet.

"Was gonna say matchy-matchy." My hands went to my hips, looking to finger my missing pair of Glocks.

He brushed a sweep of hair off his forehead, and my fingers twitched to push it behind his ear so I could get a glimpse of his double-helix piercing. "Well, there's newcomers all the time. Their genetics are pretty diverse."

"So those two girls aren't anomalies, like us?"

"You aren't an anomaly, Caspar."

"No, I'm just gay."

His rich, low laugh tumbled out, hitting me hard, landing with prickling heat in my groin.

Gathering bowls of stew from giant steaming vats, we found a place to park our butts and tucked in. Well, Blondie did. I made like my bowl of meat and veg and stewed. "You sure I don't need a taste tester for this?"

"Not at all, but I'll let you know if you start seizin' and foamin' at the mouth." He winked.

Even though I had a feeling the safe-haven-so-comfy feeling inside the mess was gonna be replaced by suck-the-business-end-of-my-ax soon as we got outside, I chuckled. "Again with the reassurance?"

Quickly hemmed in on all sides, I tensed. What the hell was with this kibbutz shit? I was all for mealtime with my troops, but not a crowd of anti-Territorians. A man needed his space, damn it. When a leg jostled mine, I readied to use my dull spoon as a flesh scooper until I realized it was Blondie, and he was laughing at my unease. *Cunt.*

Seeing he hadn't flopped belly-up yet, I set spoon to stew and kept my head up, my eyes assessing. Talk went on around us, that ménage of chatter that had no words I could decipher. A few even engaged with Blondie when he asked about their harvesting schedule, tapping into his knowledge of the land that always astounded me. Like he was anything but a Company schlep.

My damn spoon clanged against the bowl when out of nowhere his thigh press turned into a thigh squeeze. *Ahhh, shit.* I bit my tongue to keep the groan swallowed down my throat. Amazing, he could make bullshit conversation with anyone and put me at ease with his hand on my leg. I shook my head down at the bowl, then lifted my eyes and very, very slowly slid them away from Blondie to the left, toward a blatant threat.

This dude was taller, broader, and had badass emblazoned on the wide shelf of his brow. Under it, his eyes burned into Blondie's back. Apparently, I didn't like that one bit because the fuck-you-too I'd done so well suppressing surged to the surface with one target.

"Why the fuck's he staring at you like that? He got a deep need to find out how well a pine box will fit him?"

Blondie spared a glance behind him. "Oh, him? He's the one who had me sharpenin' my knittin' needles on your shoulder." The hardened planes of Blondie's face, the instant coil of his body, gave clarification to his next statement. "Had to have an extra chat with him."

I touched the fresh scabs on his knuckles. "An extra chat with your fists on his face?"

"That mighta been what happened."

With that he went back to eating. I went back to scowling. Blondie had bare-knuckled the man until his hands bled and dickhead's face had ink-blotted in blacks and blues. An old quote came back to me, working me so perfectly in that moment of protective possession. *Turnabout, fair play, all that.* "Yeah, well, if he doesn't stow those eyeballs in his back pocket right now, I got new plans for this spoon."

Big Bad took his glare to the next level, and that was all the dare-ya I needed.

"Do you, now?"

"Yeah. Don't like the way he's looking at you," I said.

"This one of your understatements?" Blondie asked.

"Something like that." When the bruised bastard ducked outside, I got to my feet, announcing, "Breakfast's over."

"So it is." Beside me, Blondie excused us with perfect manners. "Ladies, gents, squirts"—he ruffled the little head that barely reached his knee—"if y'all will pardon us."

Before we went outside for a little roughing up, he called to the woman directing the food-filling station, "Might wanna keep the littl'uns inside, ma'am."

Her blue eyes tightened on us before drifting away. "'Course, son."

Outside I found the ugly sonuvabitch waiting for me with a bone to pick. "If you're done takin' advantage of our hospitality"—he jerked his head toward the dining hall, indicated the few scoops of breakfast I'd eaten—"you can pack up and ship out."

I had a bone to pick with him too, seeing as he'd shoved an ax blade in my shoulder. "I really need to brush up on my social skills if I wore out my welcome already."

"Your kind ain't welcome here at all. In fact, I oughta cut out your tongue before I send you back to the Territories, save you squealing on our location, you Corps pig."

Sensing a tussle in the near future, the roaming Nomads in the village square regrouped, forming a ring around us.

My gait loose, my expression damn near amiable, I was ready to get down to some light stress relief. Not quite as casual, the skulking male drew up his fists. He obviously hated me hard-core. *Feeling's mutual, motherfucker.*

I clapped him on the shoulder and toyed with him. "Aw, now, I thought we were just gonna talk it out, man."

He shook off my hand and got in my face, a bad place to be if he wanted his fat nose to stay in the middle instead of shoved past his eye sockets. "We don't like Breeders, whoreson."

"Really? Seems you don't have a problem with that, what with all the kids running around."

When he gave a nasty grin, I got a close-up of his recently chipped tooth. *Way to go, Blondie.* "Out here we do it on our own terms."

"No fault with that." I kept it cool.

"And I got a problem with men who shovel the Company's shit."

Cue the not so cool anymore. "Perfect. 'Cause I got a big problem with you, too." I rolled my shoulders, including the one he'd carved up.

"That hurt?" He gloated.

"You have no idea"—his smile lifted until his mealy eyes disappeared—"how much I like the pain." I pressed my fingertips into the stitches, winding myself into a tight knot of controlled energy.

He blinked once, twice.

Nice.

Tearing his shirt off his arms, he bragged, "Good, then you're gonna love what's comin' next. No weapons, no time-outs. We are warriors. And since I took your man's fists in my face a couple times already, I get some extra players this time."

Blondie made some noise in the background. Filed, ignored, stored…*whatever.*

Terms I could live with. "I always work better with a bigger playing field."

Corps commander I might be, but given the opportunity to kick some ass in hand-to-hand combat, my cement shell of *I don't give a fuck* rapidly disintegrated. I took my time removing my shirt, making sure I didn't pop a wince when the reopening wound in my shoulder sent out a *you-gotta-be-shitting-me* twinge. Tossing the shirt to the ground, I backhanded my knife to Blondie. Clothing was expendable, but my KA-BAR, she was not hitting dirt.

I scanned the small group of fighters from beneath my brows. There were three of them to one of me, so I formulated a plan that included a lot of kicking, punching, headlocks, and all-out fistfighting, starting with the scrappy little shit jumping back and forth on the balls of his feet.

I rolled my neck, cracked my knuckles, took a real deep breath, and shot my fist out to nab a shirt collar, bringing Scrappy off his tiptoes and into my face, where I snarled, "Wanna kick some Corps ass, *Nomad*?"

Before he could answer, I reeled forward, my forehead slamming into his. The impact knocked him off those rocking feet and sent him sailing into the ring of bodies surrounding us.

I was about to spin around when my worst nightmare, aka the grinning village idiot with the chipped tooth, threw his boot tip into my kidney. A sunburst of pain clouded my vision. As I swayed with the blow, the spectators raised their fists in unison, yelling, "Kill, Kill, Kill!"

Hell no. My ears cleared first, enough to figure out the shout was actually his name, "Kale, Kale, Kale!" Then my vision went the pure red of rage at being kicked in the back. Dropping my knees, I swung around on one leg, my other lifted to undercut Kale at his ankles, bringing him down on his back with a boom to rival the tree I'd chopped in half the other day.

TIMBER!

He was down but not for long, and lo and behold, the third of their trio of twats decided to have a go. His uppercut missed my jawbone, glancing off my temple, ringing a few bells that jangled with the same sound as the noisemakers outside the red caravan. This dude's hair hung in clumps down his back. They weren't braids, but knots upon knots in thick separated strands. When he whipped back from my advance, my hand connected with the tail end of his coarse locks. I pulled that shit hand over hand until his neck met the muscle of my ribs and was clenched under by my biceps. He gaped for air, his face turning purple with my crushing stranglehold against his airway.

Scrappy looked a little dizzy off to the left but managed to find balance on the balls of his feet again. He had some long arms tensile with muscle, ready to land a punch anywhere he could. There was no grace in his attack, only the sheer frenzy of *gonna mess you up, Corps whore.*

Just when I thought the scruffy-haired headlocked dude was gonna go night-night, he twisted his face up and took a big bite of my arm. I shoved two free fingers up his nostrils and wrenched him loose, following with a drop kick to his lower stomach as he tried to army crawl away.

This was dirty fighting, and I really got into the bare-chested, bare-knuckled brawling with a side of cheers from the crowd, which had grown to encompass what looked like the whole damn village.

At that thought, the village idiot and Scrappy decided to two-time me.

Thanks, boys, but I already have a date, and I'm a one-man man.

Unloading some serious aggression, I advanced with my fists braced, my stance squat, guarding all the necessary organs by curling in on myself. When I took one on the chin—the metal toe cap of a boot, not the soft touch of knuckles—and only staggered a step, the cheering changed direction. It wasn't "Kale, Kale, Kale," they were calling. It was a mash-up of "Thatta boy. He deserves it! Don't take no guff."

I heard Blondie's low rumble of, "Cannon," amid it all, and my name sparked, leaping back and forth until the scant mix of cheers contained a heartening, "Cannon! Cannon! Cannon!"

Winning the Nomads over from that brutish lug Kale made my brain buzz with excitement.

Chapter Eight

Man, filled with that fuel, I charged. Everything the warriors gave, I sent back with the kiss of fist and a side of lovemaking care of my boot-clad feet. Our bones crunched, faces swelled, skin peeled away, and still we went at it, daring each other for one more round.

Cornered, I was gonna roll under their feet, taking my bruised ribs on a ride when a hand appeared before my face. Not fisted in punishment but open palmed in offer.

That better not be a mercy move.

As blood, theirs and mine, leaked into my mouth, the palm grabbed my elbow and hoisted me up. The hand belonged to an older man whose kind face I really didn't want to mar, so I stowed my punches. "Welcome to Chitamauga Commune, Warrior Cannon. My name is Hills."

I tried to steady my feet, my breath still sawing in and out. "But I was just getting started."

He hooked a sheath of wispy white hair behind an elongated ear. "I believe you've proven yourself. Even gained a few supporters, which is no mean feat, so you've earned a reprieve." Before I could shake the ringing from my ears, Old Man Hills took a moment to bring his quiet advice. "We're an accepting society, Corpsman, but the matter of your allegiance has been alleviated, not relieved."

Holy hell, my brain is a big ball of pain and he's working the tongue twisters?

Such a small person, but his bearing was obviously the compass point of the commune. "Though you've earned some respect, should you stray, I will allow them all to go at you. And I won't step in again."

I struggled only a bit to raise my head. At least my voice was steady. "Affirmative, sir."

"Hills, son. Never call a Freelander *sir* unless you're part of that sort of scene." His wink almost made me go at ease, until he raised a hand, calling my unwelcome committee forth. At least they looked as beat to shit as I felt.

"Shake hands," Hills said.

Can I spit into my palm first? No?

Grudgingly, I clutched each hand in turn, holding extrahard to Village Idiot, hoping to dislocate his pinkie in the process. *No such luck, this time.*

Everyone moved off, fading into the background. Only Blondie remained. He grabbed my shirt off the ground, shook it out, and hung it over his arm. The way he handled it with such care let me know he'd been watching that article of clothing lie in the dirt, wishing he could save it since he couldn't save me.

He handed over my knife, watching me strap it on. It took only three tries with my busted-up hands. *Not bad, all told.*

Sweaty and seeing even more swirlies than earlier, I said, "Thought you might try to stop me."

He scarcely looked at me. "Know better than to get between you and a target."

My grin wasn't returned.

"Anyway, you've passed muster."

"The fuck does that mean?"

"Initiation rites."

"Everyone gotta go through this?"

"Just jerkoffs like you."

Not exactly a gold star on my merit roll. "You got a new problem I need to sort out?"

"Nah. I really love standin' back while a stampede of Nomads hand you your nuts in a bag, babe."

I beat the flat of my hand to the board beside his head. "Worried?"

"Suck it."

His reply, which wasn't quite a denial, added to the warmth infusing my punching-bag face. "You oughtta have more faith in me than that."

"Yeah, it's all about faith, ain't it?"

I dragged my forearm across my bloodied mouth. "So when's your initiation? Because I want the same front-row seat."

He didn't answer, glaring beyond me instead.

"How come you know so much about this Wilderness stuff?"

Another nonanswer.

Our standoff ended when he exhaled and the tension drained from his features. "Let's get you cleaned up, big man."

Bolstered by his arm arranged around my midsection, I prodded my mouth and in the general area of my face. I was sausaged, my face the same consistency as the canned meat back in Alpha.

I made my feet count cadence until a stool was wheeled under my ass inside another kaleidoscope caravan. When a floor-to-ceiling curtain shuffled aside, Ma'am from the mess appeared, gathering vials and snippets of plants from the windowsills as she approached. The bead curtain clattered in her wake, and I scooted over for a closer look. They weren't beads but finger-sized silver buckets strung one upon the other. Since it didn't look like I'd be getting my ammo back anytime soon, I could melt this stuff down to make bullets, once I located their gunpowder cache.

Pushing a fingertip inside, I tinkled them, then yanked a little harder when my pinkie got stuck.

Amused by my predicament, Blondie watched me disentangle myself. "They're thimbles, for sewing."

Ma'am scowled. "No need to laugh at the man just 'cause he's never seen the like."

"Wasn't laughin' at him." He got a sullen look on his face, complete with a pout. "Anyway, here he is. Thought you'd like to do the honors of cleanin' up his mess since I already stitched him back together once."

I don't know what the hell he's bellyaching about. Just another day in the life of the Great Commander Cannon.

The look she shot Blondie was so disapproving, he blushed. That was almost interesting enough to make me not want to pass out from the pain that increased instead of fading, adding some nausea to the mix.

"My apologies for bein' abrupt, ma'am." He even shuffled those big feet.

"Hmmph." Setting her bandages and bottles on the table beside me, she dismissed him. "Since you don't seem to be in a helpin' mood, boy, I believe you'd be better put workin' in the fields than staying here."

He performed another foot shuffle, gaze wavering from her to land on me. "Rather stay here, if that's okay."

I was enjoying the awkward show. *Damn. He's acting like a schoolboy caught cheating on a Company test, the kind that could get him neutered.*

Her voice stern, she replied, "And I said scat."

Letting this hard-nosed little woman get the best of him, Blondie backed out the door, ducking his head. His look remained on me until, with a final nod, he pivoted and stalked away.

Ma'am was laying out her supplies, muttering, "Durn fool boy. Got the sense of a goose."

"Excuse me?"

Her wide-set blue eyes slanted up. "I didn't mean you, son, though by the looks of it, same could apply."

I shifted in my seat, getting the uncomfortable feeling I was being scolded in a roundabout way. While she swabbed the congealed blood from my latest acquisition of cuts and scrapes, I got a load of what was going on around me. The collections of hundreds of tiny plant pots fighting for space inside her home, the radiant colors and sheer gauzy fabrics tenting the place, her demeanor, all of it reminded me of Mrs. Cheramie back in Sector Five.

That led to thinking about Erica, which directed me to Liz, because why not just flay myself open with razor-sharp thoughts about all the women who'd been in my life. The ones I'd lost. Like my mom, for instance.

They weren't the only ghosts chasing me out here in the Wilderness.

The caustic squeeze in my chest had nothing to do with the short gash bisecting my pectoral muscle. Another screw in the works came from all the built-in bullshit I'd been sold about the Nomads. They'd cheered me on, against one of their own. They had schools, healers, their own culture. I couldn't just label them as rabid animals anymore.

Just Kale.

As Ma'am cleaned me up, moving with compassion and precision, the hard knot descended from my chest, zeroing in on the pit of my belly, growing bigger. Liz always tended my battle wounds, and I hers, unless I did it alone.

Unless Blondie did it.

So that was enough thinking for one day.

"You've got a lot of scars."

Or maybe not.

"Hard life, tough knocks." I pushed out a breath.

"Scars on the inside."

Direct hit.

I had a wound that could never be mended, one that might've been avoided had I thought for one second places like this really existed. I stiffened, and her soothing hands slid away from me. "Sorry. I don't like being touched."

I couldn't escape the beam of her eyes when she narrowed them at me. "You don't like being read."

"True."

"Want me to continue?"

A short huff of laughter made my ribs ache. "With the healing or the head tripping?"

"Whichever you prefer."

"Proceed, please…"

"You can call me Miss Eden if you like."

Eden. The Garden of Eden was in the Bible. I remembered that much of religion. It looked like the garden had deployed all over Miss Eden's caravan. Maybe her soul was as fertile as her soil, because she was lit up from the inside. Her feminine features were neither young nor old, and freckles dusted her slim nose and high cheekbones. Her light brown hair was a wavy mass swaying with her movements. Only when she saw me watching her, when her lips cast a pretty smile, did I see the faint wrinkles forming starbursts around her eyes.

"All right, Miss Eden."

"Or ma'am." She winked.

She'd taken care of my shoulder—*again*, Blondie would say—rubbed me with salves and sweet-smelling leaves, and was preparing to add more bandages.

"Don't need any more of those." What I needed was ease of movement. Clean up and clear out, that was my style. Besides, it was just surface damage.

"You might, Cannon, someday."

My clear out went south as I dropped back onto the stool. She wasn't talking about the wounds to my body, again. "Ma'am." I cleared my throat. "Miss Eden, I'm a homosexual." I didn't know where that confession came from. Maybe I'd been punched in the head one too many times today.

"Reckon there're worse things to be."

"Like a Corps commander," I said with a self-disgusted grunt, suddenly seeing myself as the Nomads did. Probably with the same prejudiced blinders I'd had about them.

"That's not what I was implyin' at all." She stood up, hands at her hips, gaining my attention with her crisp voice. "Some here are gay. Others are straight." She ticked off on her fingers. "Then we have the bisexuals, the undecided folk, the subs and Doms, and a few who enjoy both sexes at the same time. We've got families in all varieties, and we don't question anyone's preferences so long as they're consensual." Her hips gave an emphatic thrust. "You are not that original in your wants and needs, Commander Cannon."

The way she said my rank without malice or accusation was a new one coming from a Nomad.

"And you do like to be touched. Only by that boy I sent outta here."

It was my turn to blush.

She ignored my blazing face. "But you don't like to talk. So let's get."

Over the next couple of hours, she led me all around the compound. She showed me the giant open-sided kitchen and the meeting hall, where commune business was dealt with. The livestock barns, granary, and silo were pointed out. Electricity was used sparingly, powered by makeshift sol panels as well as a formation of effective, if clapped together, windmills. Unfortunately, I was not given the guided tour of the munitions unit.

Moving away from the center of the village, I watched the receding buildings. Silvery gray, their wood gave off a shine in the sunlight similar to the alloy sheen of Territory cityscapes, except the commune was enclosed by forests, not trenches and four-meter tall fortifications topped by wire, the coloring organic, not manufactured.

A learned guide, Eden put paid to my preprogrammed misconceptions about Nomads. What they missed in technological devices, they made up for in ingenuity, common purpose, loyalty, and acceptance.

They weren't an untamed people either. But then there was Liz's father, and even though I didn't want to revisit the subject of her dropped coms, I needed to know what she'd intended to tell me about him and the Nomads. Considering what I'd just been through at their hands, anything was possible—and highly probable.

Well, isn't this a circle jerk of gigantic proportions?

The name *Nomads* was considered a misnomer and a slur, Miss Eden informed me as she walked me across the meadow to three squat brick domes. These buildings I was allowed into, even permitted to touch and inspect the contents of the Seed Domes.

"These here seeds are the distant relatives of the ones collected from all over the world by the first settlers decades before the Purge."

Her fingers drifted through a tub of rattling white button-sized seeds. "Yessir, those naturalists and back-to-earthers began a communal way of life long before that catastrophe did its cruel work on the rest of us."

She took my hand and trailed my fingers through the cool contents of another bin. "Imagine you've heard all sorts about us, son. I know what it's like out there, the falsehoods bred. I lived in the Territories, too, for a time."

"Where? When?"

"That's neither here nor there, no more. What's important is this. We are Freelanders, tied to this earth. This here is *our* land. Those who come to us are refugees, fleeing, displaced exiles. Those who stay with us become one with us, as we are one with the land. The land is a miraculous thing, Cannon, when it's treated with respect, just as love is."

I withdrew my hands and brushed them off. "Cultivating the land is one thing. Cultivating love is another, especially where I come from."

"Never said it was easy, did I?" The corners of her mouth slid up as she made a slight *tsk*ing noise. "Takes patience. Sure does. But look at what we got here. And we're not alone, no, sir. All over the Wilderness, heck, all over the world, we share our teachings, trade and take up arms for one another. Help in times of poor harvests and disease. The wealth of the land is freely distributed. Just like love."

Just like love.

And all without the fear of being hounded, hated, hanged because of who you were. Shit, these people had created a stable society with a viable way of life. This wasn't legend or make-believe. It wasn't the stuff my nightmares were made of. They were that something more my sister had always thought.

By the time Eden escorted me to the fields, my think tank was redlining, giving me a headache, which compounded my chest ache. I was happy when she assigned me a work shift. I decided to put my back into it, never mind it was still spasming from the beat down.

"If you wanna eat, you gotta do your share." She gestured over the sea of fields, thigh-high waves of wheat so gold, its color put me in mind of Blondie's hair. People were spaced at wide intervals, and I got my own giant square of work-it-out the old-fashioned way. I studied her wielding the lethal tool to take down the ripe wheat, grasping its feathery plumes and shearing close to the roots for a couple minutes before I relieved her of the weapon.

Turning to leave, she reminded me, "'Sides, you already owe us for breakfast."

I joked, "Thought I'd already paid for that with a pound of flesh."

It was a good thing these people didn't like me, because if they showed one ounce of niceness, I was ready to move in. It was like Corps fellowship, without the lies.

Left with my own plot to mow down, with that sweet handheld scythe I could easily put to more violent uses, I stripped off my shirt, bent over, and went at it with gusto. Dirt embedded under my fingernails, the fresh smell of the wheat lifting to my nose, and the scratchy little fronds sticking to my skin, I razored off stalks and moved at a steady pace. It was a game of my scythe versus the faded green farm machinery threshing wide lanes of wheat on the edge of the field. I really wanted to take that beast for a spin.

These Freelanders had some merits—I'd give 'em that—but I wasn't hanging around. Hope had no place within me, and Blondie wasn't getting a deeper toehold inside my heart either.

For the bulk of the day, I didn't lay eyes on the man. The twinge at that thought was solely caused by my knee-cracking posture, nothing else. The Freelanders didn't go easy on me, and there was more than enough work to keep my mind emptied of most everything but occupation.

Then two things happened. The I'm-being-watched feelers crept up my back and made me look about six meters over to find Blondie fence side as a pair of female water bearers proffered a pail and ladle of the cool stuff to me, as well as a whole lot of eyelash batting punctuated by hip juts and tit jiggles.

The hell? Do I have fresh meat stamped across my chest?

I was trying to do the eye-to-eye thing with Blondie—there was the arched brow, the quirked mouth, and he was accompanied by a threesome of males all motioning with their hands to recapture his attention—but the twin spinsters redoubled their efforts with kissy lips and obvious invitations.

Whoa.

I supposed they were attractive, but all I saw was breasts and full hips, and that totally turned me off. I was an ass man, Blondie's to be specific. By the time I'd shaken them off, he was ambling away, a last look and nod our only goodbyes.

The remainder of the afternoon was productive. A fourth of the field had been cleared, there were no more Blondie sightings, and thankfully, no more women coming onto me.

*   *   *

The work did its thing. I was unwound and loose by the time I returned to what I'd started calling the Love Hovel, Blondie's and my junkyard caravan. I'd rinsed off at the lake and hung my shirt from the waistband of my camos on the way, hurrying to get back. Just outside, I slowed my steps, calming whatever the hell was making my heart clamor. For sure it wasn't a feeling of coming home.

Nope, not that at all.

Performing a peripheral sweep inside, I saw Blondie had beaten me...home. Already stripped to the waist and barefoot, he lounged on that behemoth bed with a spread of food.

I joined him, making the bed bounce him closer to me, and leaned back on my elbows, feeling lazy as hell. "So, you still pissed at me about my fight?"

He popped a chunk of cheese into his mouth and lifted one to mine, making sure to rim my lips with his knuckle. His eyes were deep pools and his voice even deeper as it curled out from his chest. "Think you did the honorable thing."

I laughed. "By honorable, you mean taking and giving a beating?"

"I ain't finished yet. You had to earn your place. That was honorable. And, Caspar"—he shook his head in disbelief—"you are so fuckin' beautiful like that. Powerful and so in control."

His hand moved up my thigh to my stomach. He watched the ripples his touch caused, then splayed his hand flat to still me when he sensed my upward shift for a kiss. "You were beautiful, honey, when I detached myself, but I don't want to see you gettin' hit ever again, knowin' I have to stand by while you suck it up and spit it back out." His hoarse words hit me harder than any uppercut could. "Not bein' allowed to strike alongside you, not havin' your back, yeah, I'm not doing that again."

What was that about toehold and heart earlier? Hell, he might as well have moved in. Covering up the warmth his words caused, I shoveled food into my mouth to keep from blurting ridiculous, flowery, and possibly even romantic crap about the way he made me feel.

After I'd chewed and swallowed, I asked, "What was all that chitchatting about, by the fields?"

"Could ask you the same. Had you a little viewin' gallery goin' on out there, didn't ya?"

I snorted and sent my eyes skyward. "Yeah, because I'm such a boob man."

Blondie's smirk glided up his cheek, then lowered slightly. "What'd you think of Miss Eden?"

I stewed over that for a moment. "Honest and handy with the healing, but she knew too much for my liking."

He tugged back his ponytail, and I rubbed my fingertips on the strips of short hair above his ears, slipping to the nape of his neck, thinking, *Let me do that for you, with my cock slipping up and down your perfect ass cheeks.* His faraway look stopped me just short of going for a Blondie ride.

"Yeah, I thought so, too."

After that, we ate in silence. Being with him felt too damn… homey, which made me horny. Getting to know Blondie, sharing a tent, a room, and a bed with him affected me in a way I'd given up as Old History. Moving the platter aside, I lowered him slowly, getting ready to enjoy the feast of his mouth. "I need to kiss you."

He ducked away. "Uh-uh."

Scrubbing my hand on top of my head, I groaned. "What?"

"First we're gonna check that shoulder."

"I'm getting that kiss afterward." I collapsed to the bed, gritting my teeth when he started poking around.

He concentrated on the gash and grumbled, "You overdid it today."

"Shut it, Nursie."

After he finished, he smacked his hand to my stomach, and I lifted my hips with a hiss. "Said you were gonna be gentle."

He blew out the candlewicks, taking his plump bottom lip between his teeth. "Don't recall that."

In the gloaming darkness, we undressed, our eyes on each other as pants dropped and legs, asses, and hard cocks appeared. I wanted to fuck him.

Under a shitload of covers, he had other ideas, unfortunately for my cock.

Face-to-face, front-to-front so our dicks brushed against each other—thick, hot, and hard—his hand wandered over my chest. "You like it here."

I whispered, "What gave me away?"

With my neck cradled by his biceps, my lips straddling his corded throat, he hummed, "Your smile."

Shit yeah. I'm grinning like a goddamn fool. I made up for it by biting the big tendon between his neck and shoulder, licking it a few times. "Feels weird, babe."

"This?" He pumped against me, the broad shelf of his cock catching the underside of mine, running back and forth in a slick caress.

"Ahhh, no..." My arms around his back, I split his thighs with my knee and got against him, good and tight until the wet sucking thrust of our cocks and the smooth slap of our balls had my hips glued to his and my back arching away.

"This acceptance stuff," I explained, when I could speak again.

He stopped me with his hands gripping my ass and a puff of laughter against my ear. "Acceptance? Pretty sure a few of your new friends wouldn't mind seein' you laid low again."

"Yeah? And how would you like to lay me?"

"Like this, Caspar." Showing me exactly how, he shoved me onto my front and took a lone finger on a sexy journey down my spine to the clasp of my ass.

I pushed against it, dipping with his moves, my erection dripping with come. His finger drilling, circling, exploring, he folded himself over my back. All his muscles, from his chest to his stomach to his legs, pressed against me.

"More fingers, please."

Instead of complying, he pulled out slowly. "We can't do this tonight. You need to rest, 'specially after that macho display today. You lost too much blood."

I pulled him from his knees into my arms. "Funny thing is, a whole lot of blood's rushing south to my cock right now."

He aligned his lips with mine and moaned, "Too temptin', Caspar. Far too fucking temptin.'"

He restrained himself, muscles trembling while he watched me circle my shaft, tightening my fingers around the base to stop myself from shooting all over my stomach from the starving stare he aimed at me.

I blew him a kiss. "Sure it's not my messed-up mug putting you off?"

He straddled me so his cock hung down, a viscous thread connecting with my belly. He stroked himself a couple times, his fist making a slick noise. "*Mmm*. Yeah, that'd be it. I can hardly keep it up for you, big man."

Then it was fucking around, but not fucking, no matter how tightly strung my balls were, and those bastards were practically harnessed to the base of my cock. I was in a real bed with Blondie. Touching, kissing, laughing, and…waiting.

When we slowed down, I hauled him on top of me. Kneading the muscles of his back, I pushed my head up. "Still owe me that other kiss, lover."

So slowly, I dragged him toward me. Slanting his head within my hands, I tapped his mouth with my tongue. He gasped, inviting me inside with twining heat. Sucking the silky insides of his lips, I grabbed his hips and made sure he felt me all over his body. The fast heated fulfillment of our kiss grabbed me from inside my cock until I was ready to burst. I broke off with a gasp, squeezing my eyes shut.

"Fuck." My hips kept thrusting up to him even though I knew we weren't finishing tonight.

His mouth moved to my shoulder, his breath ragged. "*Uhhmm,* Caspar."

I pushed Blondie onto his side and snuggled in behind him. "Better go to sleep, babe, before I decide I don't give a shit about blood loss and whatnot."

"Ain't you a sweetheart?" His hand found my thigh and stayed there.

"Yeah."

'Course my cock had the final word. It wasn't real cool about the lovey-dovey moment going down, because it sure as hell wasn't going down anytime soon.

Let's just see how well he sleeps with my boner stabbing him in the back.

Chapter Nine

The sound of splashing water snuck into my sleep-addled brain. I burrowed my nose into a mound of pillows, the hit of Blondie's masculine scent making me shiver awake. Peering out, I saw him at the washstand. His abs crunching, he bent over the ceramic bowl. He whipped his head up, water dripping down his face, saturating his stubble, his cheeks scrubbed pink.

I sat up to watch the show. "Goddamn, you look good like that."

"Like what?" There was that breathy voice again, warmth rolling through me as he prowled in my direction.

Blondie leaned over me, and my heart knocked a boulder-sized hole in my chest. "Wet. Warm." *Naked.* Jesus, my voice was a little breathless, too.

He inched closer, his arms braced on the bed. I reclined into the cushions, licking my lips. Just when I thought he was gonna kiss me, his mouth slid to the side, landing beside my ear. "Time to get up, lazybones."

Cranking my arm around his neck, I strong-armed him to the mattress. With a kick of my hips, I groaned, "Trust me; I'm up."

His hands moved across my back. "Yeah, I can feel that. Matter of fact, I felt it all night, big man."

"*Mmm.*" I nibbled his stomach, heading south. "Keep you awake?"

"You kept me *up.*" His grin was full of dimples, delight, and desire.

"Still up, I see." My fingertips coasting low, I lifted them away to watch his erect cock levitate toward my hand.

His drawl turned my body inside out. "That's a given where you're concerned, but—"

"Lemme guess. You're hungry?"

The hand that cradled my head became a fist for a furious skull rub. "Yep!"

We started roughhousing in bed. I hadn't done that since the last time a man had ventured into the no-go zone of my heart. On this glorious morning, Blondie was in need of a takedown.

He scrambled away before I could retaliate, but I latched on to his calf and hauled him back. With his wrists restrained, I rose above him. I kept his eyes in my sights as I lowered my lips to his silky nipples. Mouthing them to tight tan peaks, I waited until he started moaning; then I pushed him out of bed.

After a long, back-cracking stretch, I rubbed my bare chest down to my stomach, enjoying the way he looked at me, his mouth parted, eyes blazing blue buttons. "Yeah, I'm hungry, too."

Pulling on my clothes, arming myself, I swatted his ass in the direction of the door. "Let's go."

"You're a tease." He stepped outside.

I slammed him against the Love Hovel, sinking my hips against his. "Not a tease when I offered to fuck you last night, lover." I poured a long, slow kiss over his mouth.

His grip dropped to my ass, driving me to distraction point, and I disengaged our mouths with a final pluck of lips. "Morning, Blondie."

We didn't exchange words while we walked to the mess. Our fingers brushed, but I put a stop to the lovey-dovey crap just shy of hand-holding. I felt relaxed and good, aside from resembling a human punching bag and boasting a prick as hard as a steel pike. Once entering the main thoroughfare, we were given wide berth—except for that dog and those undaunted kids—instead of pitchfork salutes.

Progress.

At breakfast, there were more of the Freelanders making friendly with longtime enemies, us. Seated at the far end of the table, Miss Eden watched me, her observation prickling along my skin as tangible as the spiky herbal leaves she'd massaged me with. When I directed my gaze at her, she broke contact, blending in.

Keeping tabs on Eden, who excused herself back to the cleanup crew, linking fingers with Blondie's out of sight, under the table, I barely had time to shovel the hot food into my mouth before a round of back slaps hit my shoulders, followed by a rugged chorus of, "Back to work, man."

Blondie let me go with a smile, running his fingertips up my thigh. "Yeah, back to work, big man."

I handed my cleared plate to Eden. It was replaced by her hold on my wrist and a square waxy package pressed into my palm. "For your lunch." She held tighter. "Remember to feed your soul, too, Caspar."

I staggered a step when she released me. "Yes, ma'am," I whispered, but she'd already moved on. Her eyes cut a straight line to Blondie's, and at a small nod from him, she urged me, "Git on now, son."

Conscripted to the crops, I briefly wondered what Blondie's work detail entailed when I saw him walking toward the meeting hall. For once, I didn't want to know. Not out here, in the sun with my hands dug into the soil, on my knees. I suddenly understood the meaning of worship.

The simplest things lured me in: working outside under a big sky instead of caged inside a claustrophobic city with a network of spies. Sitting down to eat with a roomful of friendlies. Hell, even the Love Hovel had some merits. Mostly Blondie's big body in my bed, *our* bed.

But then again, the head knocks from yesterday could've caused a concussion.

My muscles blistering, I bounded from track to track, shanking my scythe on repeat. There was a kink in Blondie's plan for my convalescence, though. What with my all-night erection, the heavy petting, and hauling in hectares of wheat, I wasn't getting a whole lot of R & R.

Stopping for a breather, I patted down my face and neck, looking over the wide swath of wheat I'd cut down. Raising my arms, I stretched left and right and looked around again. A feeling swelled in me, something I'd lost along the Corps road I'd taken. Pride without the price of jaded prejudice. That warmed me more than the bright autumn sun.

Sweat beaded on my brow, but I kept at the hand harvesting, not hating it at all. In my periphery, the lone tractor cut closer and closer until it abutted my lanes, taking down four widths to my one. Envy was another new feeling. I wanted to drive that goddamn thing.

The rangy young farmer hopped down beside me and introduced himself. "Micah."

"Cannon." I put my hand in his.

He shoved his cap back, revealing sweat-matted shaggy blond hair. "You're settin' a good pace."

"Trying to keep up with you."

Tossing me a strip of dried savory meat, he praised, "Not bad. Oughtta keep you around for next summer's cotton crop."

I took a bite and chewed vigorously so I wouldn't say something impossible, like how I suddenly wanted a future here so badly I could taste it. And like the frigging spicy meat I chomped on, it tasted a thousand times better than the food I'd dined on in my bare room alone in Alpha, or the CO crap I'd ingested from babyhood.

I was relieved when Micah finished his ration without further comment. He slapped the side of the growling green monster. "Say, you wanna have a go?"

"Fuck yeah!" I jumped up on the rig and sank my ass to the curved iron seat before he could change his mind.

He got on behind me, shouting above the roar as I put her in gear. "You ever been on a tractor?"

"Nope." I loosed the clutch and shifted the round black knob. "But I've commanded a tank before; can't be too different."

"That's right; you're our Corpsman."

I kept a close eye on the furrows I was running down, a flush from more than the morning's exertion spreading on my face.

He slapped my shoulder the same way he had the tractor. "Yessir, we all got a calling."

I zipped my lip, glaring across the golden waves of the wheaten horizon. *Acceptance, acceptance, acceptance.* Where was the accusation? I wasn't a good person. I didn't deserve their confidence.

Two trips around the perimeter, I left a trail of flattened sheaves in our wake. Coming to a stop, I went ground level and started working backward, Micah beside me as we bundled and stacked, bundled and grouped. Eventually a pair of sandal-shod feet attached to slim ankles hopped on top of the bale I was roping.

I followed shapely legs, the flare of tits to the comely face of one of the water bearers. She dipped her fingers into the pail and sprinkled cool water over my face. I straightened up. My discomfort in the presence of the brazen woman grew when I saw her sister in charms accompanied her.

"Ladies." I nodded.

That single word was all it took to start them simpering in my direction. *Damn it.* I didn't want to piss them off, but I was about to inform of my preference when Micah stepped in, smothering a smile.

"Just the water, Jonquil, Lyra." He tipped his head and the dipper, bringing a full scoop to his lips. "Don't think our man's interested in your wares, ladies. And y'all are full aware I got my own bed warmer."

As they traded small talk and we drank our share, I glanced at Micah's finger, the gold band winking.

"You're married?" I asked when the oversweet perfume of desperate female was replaced by the scent of fallen wheat.

"Seven heavenly years. My wife's Kamber. She oversees the education side of things."

"You really have all types of lifestyles out here?"

Scratching behind his ear, he chewed on a stalk of grain. "Guess we're a little bit like that Amphitheater you've got in the Territories. Open-house kinda thing."

"Underground open house," I corrected. "You've heard of the Theater?" I snapped off a stem for myself.

"More than that, been to one."

"What Territory?"

"Gamma."

He referred to the Midwestern Territory, a fertile belt that added up to his profession. "You grow up there?"

"Sure did."

"Why'd you leave?"

He hooked his cap over his forehead, squinted at the sky, and planted his hands on his hips. "Just wanted my freedom, man."

The ache in my gut spread through me as I stood in silence for a long while, wondering why it made sense only now. I'd spent years broadcasting a fuck-you vibe about the idea of freedom. For the first time I wished I'd gone with Sis's fanciful stuff. I could've been here, too. But I wouldn't have met Blondie if I'd traded my path for another.

Point was, I'd been too much of a coward before my family died, and later, too neck-deep up Corps ass to scope out other possibilities. Now it was too late. Wishful thinking and want never got me anywhere good.

I was glad to see an influx of stragglers crossing outside the fields. The odd combo of Freelander scouts ushering unmistakable Territory refugees and rebels—their hairstyles and garments looking worse for wear but still slick and fitted next to the Freelanders' grown-out locks and rustic garb—gave me a great reason to slap the *Closed for Business* sign on my brain.

My thoughts dissembled ever further when I saw Kale. Dressed in mismatched armor, carrying the hand ax he'd surely used to cleaver my shoulder, he halted adjacent to me. He looked like he'd been run down by a tank and reversed over a time or three. That was something I took pride in, too.

I jerked my chin at him. My silent challenge returned by his heavy eyebrows meeting in the middle and his throwing arm raised.

Micah stopped beside me, winding a malleable strip of wheat between his two fists in the manner of a garrote. "You'll wanna stay away from that one. He's a nasty piece of work."

"I don't run from anybody."

"Your murder, my friend."

"Gonna be his." I sneered at Kale's retreating back.

"C'mon."

*   *   *

We leaped the fence and fell in line. All villagers and newcomers were headed in one direction, to the meeting hall. "What's going on?"

"Seems the Elders are presiding."

The meeting hall was a seething press of bodies. Blondie was taller than most, and it took me only a few seconds to pick him up on my radar. He was leaning over Eden, their unheard words fast, their hands moving just as quickly. She finished speaking and raised her palm to his cheek. He didn't recoil until he met my stare. His eyes unreadable, he invisi'd himself into the throng of bodies as she walked up to the stage and sat at a table occupied by the counselors of the Commune: Hills; Darke, who was leader of the militia; Rivers, who oversaw all things related to water resources; Forrest, the head of the foragers; Kamber, the schoolteacher; and Hatch, the resident inventor.

Hills called order, his voice a low register cutting off the whispers and raised questions. "Friends. Friends! There's been a rash of refugees today, escorted by our rangers to safety."

Claps and shouts were quelled by his wrinkly hand slicing the air. "They've come from Alpha Territory."

I broke into a cold sweat, rivulets down my back that had two names: Liz and Leon. I hoped like hell they were among the refugees.

"More are on the move, coming our way. I ask that every one of you extend the hand of welcome."

Cheers drowned my ears.

Darke took over, his charismatic speech inciting the citizens. "Revolutionaries join with us today, too. They will rearm and deploy back to Alpha with as many as we can spare beside them. The Territory is not won, but it's weakening, and we will bring down the Company. We need volunteers to join them. Able-bodied men and women with the cause in their hearts, hear me now. WE FIGHT FOR FREEDOM!"

"Live in freedom! Love at will!"

Hands shot up in the air amid shouts. Mine was one of the first. Rushing to me, Blondie tacked it back to my side. "What the fuck do you think you're doing?"

"The only honest thing I can."

His grip tightened. "You keep your mouth shut, Caspar."

"Fuck off!" I bit out. I wasn't made to idle this way. Hell, if I was good enough to work like a mule, I was good to go, and we should have been laying tracks north or—

He backed me out the open side of the building. "You're so goddamn naive."

I wrested my wrists free and stormed back and forth. "I'm up for ass-kicking detail." I raised a finger. "Don't you tell me what to do, Company man."

"You're really gonna go out there, against your own men and women?"

Fuck. "Fuck!"

Blondie was right in front of me when I wheeled around. "So what do you wanna do?" he asked.

"Go on a shopping spree in the munitions building and follow it up with a killing spree."

He shook the hair from his eyes. "You can't."

"You're not in charge."

He crossed his arms over his chest. "I'm *your* charge."

Goddamn him! He got me again with his Company words.

I paced, blowing off steam until I was deflated. "Well, they need less talk, more action."

"Double that." He clasped his hands behind his neck, a gesture that said the storm was over.

Deep in my bones, I knew it was just beginning. Never mind his breathy words or bedroom eyes. The too-good-to-be-true was gonna end so fucking badly. The sooner, the better. "We're leaving tomorrow, heading north to the Outpost. Enough of this lying low shit."

"Okay." His agreement was way too easy, figured he had to follow through. "Give it one more day."

"Screw that."

"It's smart to see if any other info comes in from Alpha."

"Fine."

The meeting adjourned, the Freelander volunteers and Revolutionaries made for munitions, and I wanted to tag along, grab a new gun, maybe a bayonet. That was a no-go, so I made do with second best. "Can I at least check out their maps?" *Ammo is off-limits, but aerials should be on the table, right?*

"Think I can manage that, so long as you stay put while I arrange it."

I pasted a smile on my face. "Where am I gonna go without you?"

I tore up more ground than the tractor, watching all the comings and goings, waiting for Blondie's return. A few minutes later, he beckoned to me from across the dirt-trodden road.

Inside a damp, dug-out basement lit by flickering outdated lightbulbs, a table was laid with crumbly old maps in pastel colors and bleeding ink. I pulled up a chair, my fingers drawn to the fine paper with jagged edges. This was so much better than the untextured flat screen of my D-P.

I marked our start point in Alpha and followed the circuitous path south and west before our trek had taken the northern route that landed us here. Smoothing out the paper, pinpointing the Outpost, I measured the clicks in my head and memorized the final jag. All the while, Blondie watched me. The back of my neck heated just as sure as his lips had licked a trail to my ear. Because it didn't matter how dire the situation was, with him I always thought with my dick first, heart second, and usually never my head.

Maybe it was how close we were, every day.

Maybe it was the life-and-death thing.

Maybe I didn't give a shit for a change.

The raised formations were bumps beneath my fingertips. I closed my eyes and hung my head, hearing our breaths chug in slow, sexual exhalations. Running my hands over his sculpted body, trailing the pads of my fingers to his sacs, waiting until he asked me to suck him into my mouth, I thought of all the things I wanted to do to him.

My hands shook when I rolled the maps. I shuttled the chair from the table and stood, my back to him. My voice rumbling, I asked, "What do you wanna do now?"

"I got some plans, Caspar."

Jesus Christ. My temperature soared and shivers spiked up and down my spine.

On the walk to our caravan, we didn't talk or touch or intimate anything about the future, our future. We had none, so why bother?

What we did have was at least a couple more weeks.

Tension of a different kind mounted when we stepped inside and I got a load of the claw-footed tub that, besides the giant bed, dominated the scant space.

Wisps of steam from the water whispered damp tendrils around us. I licked my lips. "Plans?"

He tore off his shirt and found a bottle. "Bourbon and a bath, big man."

"Drink first." I held out two cups.

"Before kink?" His eyebrow arched.

I sank the shot and got one more, kicking off my clothes. Lowering myself into the warm water, I hung my arms over the sides. "How'd you manage this?"

My cock filled about double size when he undressed lazily, his thatch of blond curls flashing from between the unzipped panel of his pants. "Flat-out bribery and good old-fashioned coinage." He dropped a kiss to my lips.

I knocked back the rest of my drink and watched him so hard I didn't blink. When his pants hit the floor, so did my mouth. I almost lost my grip on the glass. His shaft rose in a rigid dark pink totem straight to his navel.

He pushed forward on my shoulder blades. "You gonna let me in?"

That's the damn question, isn't it? And how much is letting him in gonna cost me?

I bent my knees and scooted up for his entry into the tub. In the small of my back, his erection arched, and his hands slippery with soap found my chest. I gave my sore muscles and my mind over to his foamy massage.

"Harvest festival tonight," he mentioned

"*Hmm.* They're still gonna celebrate?"

"Gotta give thanks to the earth. You'll like it; won't hurt a bit."

"Heard that before." I drove my ass against his ramrod cock, chuckling when he gasped.

"Comin' with me?"

"This a date?" I asked, my heart halfway up my throat.

"Yeah, I'm askin' you out, Caspar. Come with me."

I tilted my head and scraped his jawline with my teeth, taking a light bite of his chin. "Always."

His eyes slid shut and he sidled back. "You might regret that."

Spilling bathwater all over the floor, I turned around. "Don't mess with me. Not tonight."

A hoarse whisper came from him when I hefted him from the water. "I won't. Fuck. What are you doin' to me?"

I was patting his lower back where the deep dimples mirrored those on his cheeks, brushing his buttocks with one end of the toweling and using the other to stroke his thick cock inside the textured cloth. "Drying you off. Shut up and take it like a man." I rolled the towel and sent it flying against his ass, landing with the lash of a whip.

*   *   *

Since it was a date—likely the first and last I'd ever have—I relented on the whole hand-holding deal on the way to this harvest fest. It was either grab his hand and weave our fingers together, or grab his ass, clothed in a fine old pair of jeans that clung to his form. While he'd reinvented himself again wearing his long hair loose and soft, face stubbly, I'd stuck to my tried-and-true fatigues.

People wandered toward the meadow's call of music and the bonfire beating off the incoming hoarfrost. Night was falling, blackness challenged by the twisting red and orange flames. The late October moon was a huge yellow orb constellated by bright stars.

Makeshift tents had been set up, and inside them floors of straw were strewn with cushions; flags of fabric glowed in the light from stands of candles. A circle of men and women were dancing and singing off to one side; another group had gathered in a tight ring, their conversation punctuated by beats of loud laughter. The Territorian refugees stood alongside them, immediately gathered into the fold. I'd gone out earlier, tracking each one down and asking if anyone knew the whereabouts of a lean youth named Leon or a Corps lieutenant by the name of Liz Grant. No one had any info, and the two had not turned up at the commune.

Drawn into one of the tents, Blondie slid down onto a pillow and settled me inside the V of his wide-open thighs. Jonquil, Lyra, and a few other young women held court, wantonly writhing around each other, their arms raised with tiny finger cymbals, sending a hypnotic ringing over the audience. Their gauzy garb was sheer enough to show the deeper color of their nipples and the sinuous movements of their hips.

Forward as ever, Jonquil beckoned to me with her curled fingers making a seductive tune. Bystanders encouraged me with whistles and hollers. I shook my head to decline her invitation, but she wasn't left wanting.

"I'll dance with you, Jonquil." A slim young man with black hair that dashed across his forehead fell in time with her, and soon other men danced, their musculature offsetting the femininity of the women.

Blondie settled me closer, slipping his palms up and down my forearms, raising goose bumps. Vibrant, exotic, foreign. That's what this place was. Full of life and purpose. My impulse to call the commune hell compared to my usual bare-bones, party-line existence was on the losing side of a civil war with the idea of the Freelanders, their lives out here, and what they stood for.

Blondie's fingers sweeping up and down the back of my neck made it impossible for me to throw my usual guard up. I tilted my head, kissing him deeply while he clutched my arms.

"Is this the singing-around-the-campfire part?"

A grin formed on his lips. "This'd be it."

Jonquil raised her fingers in a bell-like salute when we left, and Blondie asked, "You got a girlfriend now?"

I deflected by pocketing his ass and asking, "Where are the kids?"

His smile went downright sinful. "Oh, they ain't allowed at this type of celebration."

"What's that supposed to mean?"

He winked and backed away. "You'll see. Lemme go get us some drinks. Stay away from that woman, mind."

Before I had time to process being dumped on my first date, Micah ambled over, giving me a hearty handshake. "I wanted you to meet my wife. Kamber, this is Cannon."

The voluptuous red-haired woman greeted me with an easy smile. "Micah's been tellin' me all about you."

Suspicion strolled up my back and settled on my shoulders like an old familiar jacket.

Micah squeezed my arm. "No need to be shittin' your pants or pullin' out your machete, my friend."

Machete? I needed to pick up one of those, too.

"Just told her about your first time out on the tractor and how you didn't drop the clutch, like most Terries." He prodded me forward. "C'mon, let's go get you a tipple or two. Take the rake handle outta your ass." He brought me and his wife across the field, cutting through singers and dancers, talkers, and so many strangers whose only reaction to our intrusion was calls of, "Hey there."

At a brace of casks laid shoulder to shoulder on wide planks, he accepted a glass for his woman, then asked, "What's your pleasure, besides that Rice fella? And where'd your date get to, anyhow?"

The blazing bonfire was well at my rear, so I knew that wasn't what heated my face. I coughed into my hand to cover up the impulse to deny he was my date. Rubbing a palm over the top of my head, I eyed the barrels. "I just call him Blondie."

Micah's laughter boomed and Kamber giggled while I cut loose with a grin.

"Blondie, huh? Guess that suits him. Now, what'll you have?"

While I pressed a tankard to my mouth to stop any other disorderly admissions, he took a glass in one hand and accepted a pipe in the other. Inhaling deeply, he spoke through a cloud of thick, sweet-smelling smoke, "Want a toke?"

"What is it?"

"Just a little homegrown," Kamber said.

The marijuana smelled good, but I needed to keep my eyes peeled, my thoughts straight. I declined.

The press of a tall body behind me made me close my eyes and inhale a different, more welcome scent. "Thought I'd lost you, but I see you've been in good hands." Reaching around me, Blondie clasped Micah's hand and brought Kamber's to his lips. "Micah, Kamber, what do you think?"

"Think it's startin'." Micah's white-blond eyebrow lifted and his chin jerked toward the fire.

Blondie bent his lips to my ear. "'Bout damn time."

Chapter Ten

I followed his gaze and saw why the kids were put to bed early. Inhibitions rendered to intimacy as bodies meshed in a tangle of limbs, searching fingers, and searing kisses. This orgy reminded me of the Theater, except it wasn't contrived by lack of time or threat of capture. It exuded warmth and welcome and was 100 percent tantalizing. Especially the trio who formed the centerpiece of carnality. A large ebony man stood naked with a fair woman and a lean young man writhing against him.

His arms wrapped around me, Blondie mentioned their names. "That's Darke, who had you all fired up at the meetin' earlier. The other man is Wilde, and the woman is Tammerick."

Now I knew what he'd been up to. Getting in good with the people while I'd gotten the lay of the land. "They're all together?"

"Good as married, in the eyes of the commune and their gods."

Wilde's voice was low. "I wanna suck your release from Tam, Darke." His hands were white against the other's brawny black chest.

"Tam." Darke barely managed her name when the slimmer man got to his knees and slithered his tongue up Darke's wide shaft. "Bring our woman to me."

Wilde lifted her against Darke until she coiled her arms behind his neck and her legs around his huge thighs, her pussy spread above his cock. A spear of black flesh working into a tight pink tunnel. Massaging the swollen meat, Wilde helped his lover enter her. Tam moaned, the wet slink of Darke's aroused shaft pushing into her flushed lips.

Blondie's teeth tugged my earlobe. "I want you spread above me, Caspar, your cock in my face."

Tam's breasts thrust up, and Wilde buried his face between his lover's legs, suckling her clit. He slipped lower and slurped her essence from the hard pumping piston, down to Darke's slapping black balls.

I was shaking inside Blondie's hold, shoving my fingers into his hair, when he bit my throat.

Darke grunted, "Yeah, Wildeman, feels so fucking good."

Wilde sat back on his heels, handling his long shaft, tasting Tam's cock-filled cunt and the cock itself.

"You want him?" Tam whimpered down at Wilde.

He pressed his face against Darke's thigh—the pale against dark beautiful—and panted, "Yeah. He feels good in you? Gonna come, baby?"

He pinched her labia together, a slant of a smile spreading over his lips when her pelvis undulated. She orgasmed with a scream, and Wilde went to work on Darke's balls, bathing them in his saliva and her heavy cream.

Darke held Tam up in his arms. "That's right. You want my cock? You want it too, Wildeman?"

Wilde attacked the pulsing veins of the dick before him. "Lemme lick our baby's cream off you, sweetheart."

Tam arched back when Darke withdrew, his cock dripping with her. He kept Tam against his body with one hand and grabbed Wilde's hair with the other, planting his throbbing cockhead between his man's parted lips just as jets of white come propelled out.

I was sweating, my muscles tensed, Blondie swearing behind me.

When I looked back from attacking his lips, Wilde had lined up behind Darke, his hands running over the straining muscles.

Blondie pulled his bottom lip between his teeth and cursed when someone across the field shouted his name. His hands dragged from my chest as he answered the call with, "Comin'!"

No shit, him and me both.

The cold reinforced my loneliness when he pulled away. "Come with me. I gotta do this one thing; then we'll dance."

I was at my breaking point and wasn't sure how far I could walk, dragging my hard dick between my legs. "Don't dance."

He grinned at me. "You will."

I stayed back when he crossed to Miss Eden. He sat on a stool matching hers, their knees almost touching, their fingers plinking the guitars on their laps in time with each other. Firelight danced off his dark blond hair, skimming the guitar strings, striking the ring on his finger.

His hands mesmerized me, fingers tapping out a rhythm before they began singing. Then…Jesus. His voice was like the high-rising birds he sang about, a revelation. I hung on to every word, and he watched me all the while he strummed and let the words flow:

> *These birds are a reminder of who you used to be*
> *Uncaged and unfettered, so wild and so free*
> *See, I know I was your captor and your guilt was the key*
> *But my heart was too heavy for one bird to carry*
>
> *It's like a war here and there are minefields everywhere*
> *And there are no war heroes, only senseless fear*
> *And we're the cowards, doing what we can to survive*
> *And there are no war crimes*
> *'Cause here no one, no one, no one, no one's fine.*

His singing was as vibrant, clear, and strong as the man himself. I snagged a bystander. "What're they singing?"

"I don't reckon I've ever heard this'un before, but Hills might know if you catch up with him."

We put out some papaya to see the best ones fly
Like anything that matters, unbidden you came by
And danced upon my landscape. I hope you don't blame me
For breathing in your goodness and leaving nothing free

It's like a war here and there are minefields everywhere
And there are no war heroes, only senseless fear
And we're the cowards, doing what we can to survive
And there are no war crimes
'Cause here no one, no one, no one, no one's fine.

I hope you don't blame me
For breathing in your goodness and leaving nothing free.

Beautiful and seductive, the words hit so close to home. Their song ended slowly, softly, his sultry eyes mesmerizing mine.

In the cheering crowd, all I saw was a bunch of men and women starting forward to congratulate my man—or ask to suck his cock. One guy in particular was jerking up his pants and making way to center stage. *Not gonna happen in this lifetime.*

The compulsion to get to him first was instinctual. Going rogue on everything I'd ever ascribed to before, I plowed forward, lifted Blondie's guitar from his lap, looped my arms around his hips, and hauled him to his feet. I shut everything down but his words still singing inside me and the feel of him in my arms.

Swaying with Eden's new melody, he drew me closer, hands whispering to my face. "Thought you didn't dance."

"Only with you." We didn't glide so much as grind, and that was fine with me. "Besides, I don't take well to competition."

"That so?"

The bend of his neck was an open call to suck. And suck I did until he crushed his cock against mine.

I took a handful of hair and made love to his luscious mouth. "You remember this: You're *mine*."

"Fuck, Caspar."

"That's right, we're gonna." No Liz, no Erica, no family. No robo-fish or damn dog and not even my Harley. But here, now, with Blondie—*Nathaniel*—I could have him. The sweet rush of realization made me deep voiced. "Let me take you to bed, lover."

We couldn't reach the Love Hovel fast enough for my liking. But once inside, everything slowed. I wanted to do this right. I wanted this to mean more than a one-night stand. I wanted to fuck him beautifully.

The caravan hit me with sensory overload, the sizzling kind when Blondie opened his shirt and unbuttoned his jeans. And that bed? The best sort of sexual torture was gonna happen on it tonight.

I lit a match and the candles illuminated our caravan, no longer claustrophobic but a cozy lovers' den. The walls and ceiling were covered in a hedonistic array of wavering images, our bodies in silhouette. All the textures were sensuous beneath my fingers, none more so than his shirt dragged from his shoulders beneath my hands. I left him shackled in his shirtsleeves and walked around the room, lighting the last tapers.

"What are you doing?"

"There's a bed; let's not waste it. I want to be with you."

His breathing sped. "In the Biblical sense?"

"Depends on whose translation, probably not the CO version."
The sardonic twist of my lips gave way to a lusty smile. "I wanna be
with you in the way a man is with a man."

With his back to my chest, I divested him of his jeans and drew
his shirt all the way off. "Lie down for me?"

While I undressed, he stumbled to the bed, all his grace forgotten. His tone gravelly, he said, "Jesus, Caspar, I never thought—"

"*Sshh*. I never thought you'd make me feel like this." I hunted
along his body until I was on top of him.

His head racked from side to side as I lowered my chest to his, my
abdomen covering his stomach, my shaft curving against his. "Caspar?" My name came out in a wrenched whisper.

His hands held within mine, I scooped away the two tears from
the corners of his eyes with my lips. "You're mine, Nathaniel." I
hadn't realized how important it was to him for me to say it, just his
name, not a nickname or an endearment. To take possession of him
and claim him as mine.

I took possession of him again with my mouth on his for
long sensuous minutes before gliding my lips and tongue down
the center of his body. My fingers drawing along his chest to
his nipples, I sucked the beautiful emblem of his cock inside my
mouth.

His heels slammed onto the bed as he bent forward to watch me.
"I've wanted you from the first time I saw you."

"Me too." I touched the tight rope of skin between his sacs and
his ass, drumming it. "Wanted this so much. Need to be part of you,
inside you."

Painted in a sensual snarl, I lowered my face to the wiry gold
bloom framing his cock. I said his given name again as I lapped the
base of his shaft because when I called him Nathaniel instead of the
usual Blondie, his thighs shook and he groaned louder.

At his breathy moans, I spread his legs and nipped back up to his stomach, ignoring the heathen's song of his erection dancing in front of my face. My fingers slick with lube, I kneeled in the apex of his legs, slicking his shaft and tight sweet hole. Pushing his knees to his chest, I added my lips to my finger work.

Drizzling more oil, I jackknifed his legs closer to his chest. Rounded up, hard globes of perfect male flesh spread for me, his ass taking my tongue and fingertips, he was sex just waiting for me.

I pulled my fingers out, hefted onto one arm, and kissed him hard. "Wanna come?"

The pulsing pink tip of his dick spurted a burst of preejaculate. I gripped him until the come swelled back down and he sweated and shook within my arms.

"Wanna come with you inside me."

Good man. I quickly unrolled a condom over my shaft. He slung his arms around my neck and his muscled legs over my hips, and we both watched the ingress of my cock into him.

Straining to contain my orgasm with every move inside him, I pressed the flat of my palm to Nathaniel's belly. "Too much?"

"Faster!"

I hung my head against his pecs, then swooped up to his ruddy lips. "Don't tell me that, lover."

He buried his face against me. "Love the way you feel."

My cock curved in and out, pumping into his snug channel. A look of awe blanketed his features, and I had to kiss him. Wet, hungry lips met mine, our tongues coiling and our teeth colliding.

Then there was just the blur of my hips pounding, the rapid sound of my balls slapping his bottom, the view of his chest bunching, and the cords of his throat in sharp relief.

His hands running all over me, his mouth slid up my jaw line to my ear. "Feels so good. Your cock's so damn big. Deeper, honey.

Yeah, *yesss.*" He hissed, taking my earlobe and twisting it in his teeth until I yelped. "Gonna make you scream."

Yeah, we'll see about that. At my next hard lunge, he cried out between gritted teeth, "Yeah, fuck me hard!"

"Baby…" I choked on the emotions rolling over me as much as the velvety purchase of his ass. Skating my thumb from the bridge of skin behind his sacs to the engorged head of his cock, I dipped my fingertip into the slit and took a fistful of cock. "Come for me. Come for me, Nathaniel."

The jerk of his hips, his gorgeous ass sinking over me again and again, he reared up, wildly clutching my hair and clinging to my lips. "Jesus, Caspar. Ah goddamn!"

His fingers gouged into my shoulders, setting off the time bomb of both our orgasms. The final rough tugs of my fist at his tip completed the chain reaction. His semen splashed both our stomachs, and his hoarse yell roared like the blood in my ears.

His ass squeezed me, drawing out my orgasm. Beating inside the condom, my cock grew bigger and come burst out of me. I sank my teeth into his throat and sucked hard through moans I couldn't contain. I hugged him against me, shuddering and shouting, "Nathaniel. Fucking beautiful!"

My heart pounded. It wasn't just the exertion of our glorious sex.

On my back, I pulled him down with me. I didn't want to let him go, because motherfucking hell, our lovemaking was supposed to be a beginning, but it felt so damn final, my stomach knotted and I slammed my eyes shut.

"Honey?" He rumbled against me, lazily caressing my side.

I tugged on his hair, then smoothed it down. "How is it you've gotten out of being married so far?"

His chin rested on my chest, eyes dark with sadness. "They haven't found the right Company female for me yet." His index finger had been randomly twiddling along my torso. Now we both watched as he traced around my heart, joining our hands there.

I'd been thinking about Micah's ring all day, the significance of union and a symbol of togetherness.

I reached beneath the bed to retrieve a waxy paper package, placing it in his palm.

Lying against me, he swallowed hard.

The covers pooled in his lap, he sat up, handling the package with such care my words came out gruff. "It's not that I don't think about you, Nathaniel." I scraped my hands across my eyes. "I...yeah. Could you open it before I change my mind and realize what a phenomenal pussy I'm being?"

I pretended I didn't see the way his hands shook when he peeled the paper off the bulky bundle. His eyelashes lowered, the leather cuff was cuddled inside his big palm. Bringing it to his nose, he inhaled the scent of fresh hide.

Plain and sueded on the outside, the softened band was the same dark fawn as his hair. Between two fingers, he felt the engraving on the inner surface. With the wide strap bent inside out, he rubbed his thumb over the words.

Not an assignment. C.C. 2070.

I started talking when a couple tears plopped onto the band, and he held himself rigid, the wet clicking of his throat closing off his words. "Got Hills to do it. Heard he was handy with his swivel knife cuts. I'd seen some of his work in the bartering hall yesterday."

When he stayed silent, I asked, "Gonna put it on?"

After he snapped it over his wrist, he rushed forward, driving his lips to mine. "Never gonna take it off, Caspar."

I'd dropped the last of my guard by calling him Nathaniel instead of Blondie, by giving him a gift that showed I cared for him. That night, what felt like our first and last night together all rolled into one, I kept my own vigil over him, watching him sleep. Later, when he began thrashing in the bed from the deep hold of a nightmare, I gently kissed his forehead and stroked his back. His fists loosened, hands finding me. Pulling him on top of my chest, all the while sending a hand up and down his back, I comforted Nathaniel. His breaths steadying with mine, I closed my eyes, filled with a sense of rightness, wishing this could last forever.

*   *   *

There was no fanfare or hell-yeah feeling in the morning. It was cold, cloudy, and the frost didn't lose its brittleness as the day wore on. Blondie stroked his cuff and sent me a smile over breakfast, but he also spent a lot of time examining his biscuits and gravy. Before I could collect my scythe and head for a final day of fieldwork, the slow leak of stragglers from Alpha became a new flood of bum-rushed refugees.

"Mr. Cannon, Mr. Cannon!" a shrill voice called across the mess.

I rose quickly, in search of the girl shouting my name. Strawberry-blond hair curled over her cheeks, the same child I'd noted a couple days before. Her eyes were earnest when she grabbed my hand with both her tiny ones. "My daddy, Micah, told me to get you."

I tripped over my feet, trying to limit my steps to her small ones. She braided us in and out of the melee just like her father had. "Right over here, Mister."

Fuck me.

There was Leon, holding his mother's hand and wearing a half smirk, not the full grin he used to bear. The fading bruises, the way he hugged the left side of his ribs, and the new maturity to his expression made my shoulders bend with the weight that I hadn't been able to stop his torture by CO tactics.

I'd never been so happy to see the little fuck in my life, probably because I'd never been happy to see him before. Despite his shitty appearance he was alive, and Mrs. Cheramie, too, so my perma-grin battled my scowl.

"What'd you do, boy?" I pulled him inside my arms, patting him down, making sure all his parts were connected by the right pieces.

"*Mais*, I set off dat tornado alarm at the Amphitheater."

"You stupid dickhead." *Understatement.*

He shrugged. "Bought y'all some time, yeah, *cher*?"

"And yourself a trip to the RACE brig. Don't you ever try to play the savior again, hear me?"

His new wisdom lasted only so long. With his hands on his hips, Leon suggested, "Add to my bad-boy appeal. Makes me hot hot, for when you get tired of dat big handsome glaring over there."

Evangeline smacked him with a "*Tête dure.*"

I swiveled my neck and once-overed Blondie. "How'd you break out?"

"Reckon your boyfriend had somethin' to do wid it."

I couldn't stand Blondie hanging back. I took two steps toward him, until we were side by side.

Now that Leon was safe, I had another concern. "Where's my bike?"

"I stored her. She safe in Alpha, waiting for you."

"Yeah, I was thinking you could keep her."

He cocked his head. "Why would you want me to do dat?"

It was a pretty safe bet I'd never return to Alpha, never find out what happened to Liz or her dad. Never water my dead plant or any of that shit. I wasn't going to make it farther than the Outpost, if that far.

"You take care of her for me." By her, I meant all of them. Evangeline, Eden, Kamber…Jonquil. All the children.

My man drew in a sharp inhale, and Leon's brown eyes flipped open in surprise before narrowing with the shrewdness I'd first seen in Alpha when he was beaten black and blue. "*Mais oui bien sûr, mon petit*, do I rate a blow job for my efforts?"

Blondie cut between us. "No way, boy."

"He your mouthpiece now?"

"His name's Nathaniel." I put my arm around his waist.

I could feel Blondie's gaze boring into me, but before I could say anything else, we were swept up in the tide of bodies. What had been a trickle became a waterfall with shouts called overhead.

"Corps!"

"Coming our way!"

After our hang-free-and-easy time, it looked like the shit had finally caught up with us. Everyone was fixed on Darke, who stood beside Micah on the tractor that had throttled from the barn to the middle of the main street. "A division of Corps scouts found the trail from the latest batch of newcomers. My militia is leaving within the hour. We'll cut them off. Rangers and Revolutionaries, we're going to make it to Alpha. We will win this war!

"You all have a job. This is *our* land. The Company will *not* take it from us without a fight. Fortify the meeting hall with food and munitions. Women, children, and elders who are not fighting will regroup there with a contingent of guards. The rest of you warriors take to the forest and guard Chitamauga."

Handing Evangeline over to Miss Eden, I worked our way backward out of the crowd. "This what you were waiting for?"

"Somethin' like that."

"We're gonna head off the Corps troops?"

Blondie gave a grim nod.

For the remainder of the day, we worked beside the Freelanders. Off and on, I caught Blondie having quiet words with Hills, Hatch, or Miss Eden. I wanted to have words with someone, too, and tell them that I didn't know what Blondie had up his sleeve, but we were going to make sure they stayed safe. I wanted to allay the fears of the children and elders, gloss over the realities of war with some reassuring words.

We set up blinds in trees for the scouts, handing weapons out to them. We secured the meeting hall so it would provide protection for the innocents when the time came. I taught offensive moves to a group of able young men and women, many of whom showed tenacity and talent in the tactics of warfare, having been brought up on it. Leon had a flair, too, so I made sure he received a weapon and adequate ammo, although I wasn't afforded that fucking privilege, again.

I got a lesson in explosives made from their homegrown cotton, a little lightweight combustible called guncotton. We laid a perimeter of the projectiles around the entire commune.

Night fell with its own bleak promise.

At the caravan, we packed with the usual precision and stacked our gear by the door. My ammo had been returned, so I spent a fair amount of time cleaning and loading my weapons. The Glocks, my SIG P229s, the beautiful M4 rifle. I polished my brass knuckles and swept a cloth over my knife, keeping the extras out of sight. Sitting beside me, our asses to the floor, Nathaniel did the same, his arms and armament having been freed up intact.

All set and ready to head out, that just left Nathaniel, me, and a few hours of downtime. All day I'd sensed something was afoot. Maybe even since the moment I'd come to in the caravan. Whatever it was, he wasn't as sneaky as he thought. But neither was I as smart as I used to give myself credit for, since using his given name at a time like this played dangerous games with my heart. Calling him Blondie had been my final barrier against intimacy.

I was sick and fucking tired of the fences I put up, the furrows I buried my shit in, the falsehoods we told each other. Tonight I wanted to feel.

I spun him toward the bed, both of us tearing at clothing. We were greedy, sloppy, shoving at each other's arms, legs, and bodies until we were panting and naked.

I fell into bed, reaching for him. When my heels butted his hips, I crashed him down on top of me. "Can you take me now?"

In answer, he turned to his side and lifted his thigh, peering at me through that curtain of hair with wicked eyes. "You. All I need is you."

Scrambling for the lube, I smeared it over my cock, using two fingers to warm and wet him, biting the nape of his neck to hold him still.

He shoved my hands away, spreading himself open for me. "I'm ready. Inside me, now."

Goddamn.

The condom creased inside my shaky fingers, and I almost shouted in frustration. He took it from me, blew into it, and rolled it down my length, pausing to pinch my tip and bundle my balls between his fingertips.

With him lying on his side against me, I took him in one long slide. "Nathaniel."

All day he'd hardly met my eyes, but now that I was pulsing inside him, he arched his neck and dove into my stare. His eyelids shuttered only fleetingly when I sped my thrusts.

So thirsty for him, I lapped his biceps, his back, his throat. I squeezed him against my chest and fucked him so fast I couldn't breathe. I knew he was coming only when he clamped down on my cock, pressuring my own release.

Our climax was loud, lengthy, and unashamed.

The primitive communion didn't end with just one fuck.

"Wanna stay right here." He nestled against me.

I wanted that, too. Damn shame it wasn't gonna happen.

I kept my watch again that night. This time my eyes were shut, but all my other senses were on high alert because I knew he wasn't staying. A few hours into me faking sleep, Blondie was on his feet and slipping out the door with a stealth I admired. Maybe I'd expected him to return, to linger over me, because I stayed deep in the Blondie-smelling blankets for longer than prudent. Guess that's what earlier had been about: goodbye with a good fuck.

The cold bit into me as I left the same way he had—silently, with my backpack on my shoulders and my holsters on full.

I went after him, because that's what I'd been taught. Not by the Corps. Not by the CO, but a place inside me they hadn't warped. When you cared about someone, you protected him until your last dying breath any way you could. Even if he didn't want it, might not deserve it.

Honor.

Duty.

Loyalty.

The forest was asleep, stark in black-and-white shadows. The frost held the imprint of his footsteps. The way they were spaced out and pressed lightly, I knew he ran at a fast, even clip. I stole off to the left of Blondie's path, ducking and weaving past branches trying to tackle me. Doubling up my steps, I veered right again when I figured I'd outrun him.

Six kilometers away from the village, I stopped and waited. When he appeared before me, I strolled from behind the dense arms of a fir tree. The big, cold moon pinpointed the spiny needles of pines. Icy crystals crackled between us.

"What do you think you're doing?" I asked.

He didn't show any surprise as he slowed. He probably had a dozen contingency plans all mapped out about how he was gonna ditch me. "Savin' the commune. Savin' you."

I snorted at that last one. "Well, you're not leaving without me."

"I can see that." Sorrow reached up into his eyes and dropped down over his shoulders.

"You can't get rid of me that easily."

"Not tryin' to."

"It sure stinks like that's what you're doing." Then a miserable thought sideswiped me, the same one that had haunted me for a couple days. Man, I did not want to do this now.

Fuck that. I don't want to do it ever.

I brushed a hand over my hair. My regulation buzz cut served only to remind me that the man wielding the shaver on me last time had been Blondie. And the haircut had ended in hot, wet kisses all over my neck, ears, and chin, finally my mouth.

My jaw clenched. "This about Eden?"

His sharp laughter landed in the pit of my stomach. "No, you idiot. It's about doing what's right and keepin' the soldiers away from the commune." There was no amusement when he stared at me. "It's about you." Closing in on me, he pointed his finger at my chest and shook his head. "You don't need to be jealous of her, Caspar."

My denial of jealousy didn't make it past my mouth, because it was too busy gaping open, probably like my fish in its death throes. I was a schmuck for not putting it together before. Their quiet words, the blue eyes, same as flowers, their love of music and the way they'd played the song so seamlessly together during the harvest celebration, right down to the scathing look Eden had given him the morning he'd delivered me—bloody and beaten—to her healing hands.

Those lingering looks, not of lovers, but bloodline.

"She's your mother!" exploded from me.

"Yeah."

"Your mom's a Freelander." Against the pitch black of predawn, clouds of cold breath came from me faster and faster. "When we were ambushed, you were never in any danger. I took a goddamn blade for you!" That particular wound suddenly hurt worse than any injury I'd suffered in war.

Chapter Eleven

I stalked within decking distance of him, my fists white-knuckle tight.

He must've had balls of iron because he didn't even back up. "I would've done the same for you. I tried to—"

He needed to shut the hell up. I was tempted to make sure he did with my hand wrapped around his windpipe, maybe some fingers pinching his nostrils closed for good measure. I was generous, opting for words before ass-whupping. "Why didn't you tell me?"

"You don't trust me, remember?" His features hardened until the rigid planes looked unbreakable. "Besides, the less you know about me, the better for you in the long run."

And my patience was about to run out. "The fuck's that mean?"

"Look, I already took a risk showing you the commune."

"*Showing* me?"

He exhaled, long and deep, like he was the one getting frustrated.

That's when I let my fingers do the talking. Grabbing him by his jacket, I pulled him in to my face. "I'm fed up with you playing me, *Blondie.*"

His head on recoil, he said, "I'm not goddamn playin' you. I didn't want you to have to go against your own people." He peeled my fingers off him, the muscle in his cheek jumping. "I was only tryin' to protect you."

My hands moved over his chest to his throat. "You better start thinking about protecting yourself right about now."

I went for his neck and squeezed. I got some satisfaction when his eyes widened in shock, then narrowed in hurt. The nimble fucker jerked his knee up between us, connecting with my stomach with such power my fingers released, giving him enough time to dodge aside and raise his hands, hands that were spread toward me when they should have been doubled up in fists. "Caspar," he implored.

"Cannon," I snarled, going at him. This time I got in a fast jab to his sternum that left him gasping.

When he looked up at me, the hurt was gone, replaced by rage. *Excellent.* He flew at me, all feet, fists, kicks, and hits. I feinted; he followed. I threw off my jacket, whipped it around his arms, care of that neat little lassoing trick Micah had so thoughtfully taught me back at the ranch.

Digging his heels in as I dragged him to me—his arms wrenched behind him—he tried twisting away but didn't get far. I hauled Blondie to my chest and pulled back my fist. He was so furious, his lips were a thin white gash.

I simply grinned and asked, "Still not talking?"

We stared each other down, our torsos billowing against each other. Suddenly it was too warm, as if it weren't the dead end of a frosty night. A drop of sweat rolled from his temple toward the corner of his mouth, the same way his flesh had teased me our first day on this goddamned mission.

"Fuck!" My fist that had been raised to pummel his goddamn gorgeous face opened and sank into his hair. "I swore I wouldn't hurt you." *And I won't, not like this, no matter what he has planned for me. Fuck!*

The angry adrenaline rush turned into such fierce arousal, I let him go, steadying him when he stumbled, and tackled the buttons of his pants, flinging the material aside to get to his cock. Blondie gasped. The pain, hurt, and the anger bled from his irises, until all that was left was the same hunger surging through me.

His arms bound behind him, he watched while I traced the ridged contours of his penis stretching up to meet my hand. I palmed the domed head and a sticky drop of come pushed out. I used that slickness to ease the glide of my hand down; my thumb dragged over the softest triangle of skin just under the lip of his cock.

His pelvis swiveled, following the lead of my stroking hand. Hips that hypnotized me with the button points of bone and heavy cliffs of muscle tracking to the base of his thick cock. The honed muscles of his abdomen rippled when I yanked his shirt up.

My breath caught somewhere in my chest, a moan tearing out of my throat. "Goddamn you, Nathaniel."

Shoving him against a tree, I attacked his mouth, biting his lips. Our tongues twisting together, I grabbed his hair and held his head still. I licked up his groan as his erection reared against mine.

With every one of our heartbeats *rat-a-tat-tatt*ing from chest to chest, I felt time speeding up, but there was no time left.

He grunted, struggling with his arms tethered by my jacket. I gave a yank to free him. Clouds of breath short-circuited between us, faster, hotter, harder. We scrabbled to get closer. His kisses scalded my lips, and his moans deafened me to all but the sexy sounds sending shoots of white heat into the base of my spine, through my balls to my unbearably hard cock.

Digging into my pack while I tore my pants down my thighs, I grabbed the first condom I reached. Turning back to Blondie, I ripped it open with my teeth, rolled it on, and grasped the firm rounds of his ass.

Lube. Goddamn lube.

Blondie pushed his bottom into my hands and arched his back. He widened his thighs and planted his feet solidly on the ground.

Fuck the lube.

I spat on my fingers and handled my erection. Rubbing my fingertips together, I dipped down to his hole and pushed inside that hot ring. With my arm around his chest, I guided him back until he was sitting on my thrusting fingers. A quiver raced down his spine and caught fire inside my cock.

"I don't want to hurt you," I whispered.

It always came back to that. I could take any pain thrown at me, so long as it didn't involve my heart. And I didn't want to be the cause of his pain, ever.

"Not hurting me." He mashed his forehead to the tree trunk, his hands roaming to my ass, urging me on. "I need this. Need you."

I wet us both once more and grasped his hips, pulling him onto my cock while I slowly penetrated, hissing as his body took me in. I lowered my cheek to his back, knocked his thighs farther apart, and plowed into him with long, forceful thrusts that came from the soles of my feet all the way through the tip of my dick.

My hand slipped down, enclosing his erection where it beat against his stomach, and his neck arched back. "*Uh*, Caspar!"

Pressing my fingers over his mouth, my voice was shaky against his ear. "*Shhh.*"

His neck cranked aside, he bit his lip and curled forward, jets of come landing on my hand. I had the urge to laugh until the contractions of his wild climax sent a screaming release through my body. Rising onto my toes, lifting Blondie with me, I ground my hips to his ass. I reached low and cupped our testicles in my palm, tugging once. I erupted inside him, bending backward with a howl, leaving me shaking.

Steam rose from our breaths and bodies. Blondie fell against the tree with his chest heaving to tug his pants up.

My hands behind my neck, I paced around the circle of forest. "So, you brought me to Chitamauga to prove what?"

He stared at me, standing stock-still. "Not tryin' to prove anything. You'd be too pigheaded to get it anyway." He gathered his hair—a few tendrils were sweaty from our hot-and-heavy session, his smile just a twist of his lips. "I wanted to show you a different life, a choice." Sure of step, he marched up to me. "We could have that life, together. I know you're holdin' out on me." He crossed his arms while I digested the implications of his words. "Every inroad I make, you throw up another roadblock. I'm not stupid, Caspar."

I massaged my chest.

He watched my hands. "There any room left inside there for me?"

I remained on target. "You meant to leave me behind all along, didn't you? Even before the Corps decided to go hunting for Free-landers."

He shrugged, the appearance of innocence all perfectly packaged in a cunning Company lie. "You got me."

"That day. When I was chopping wood instead of going on a shooting spree on the Land Cruiser. You went off. You—holy fuck—you arranged the ambush."

"You weren't supposed to throw yourself at Kale! Why the hell would you do that?"

Why the hell was right. But I knew now.

"Keeping you alive," was all I admitted.

"Yeah? Well, same here. I wanted to see you safe, for once. Happy."

"You thought a multicolored nightmare of a tripped-out caravan was gonna do it for me?" I sniggered.

"Shut the fuck up." He was the one pacing and pointing then. "I wanted to know you might still be alive after all this is over. I'm not gonna apologize for that."

"I don't need you to look after me."

"I have no idea what hot hell awaits us at the Outpost. Can you understand that?" His brows curled inward. "Not after what we're gonna do to keep the commune off the grid."

"I'm in it all the way. I'm a big boy, baby. Don't try to save me." I pivoted and picked up my backpack. "I'm not worth it."

I heard him mutter, "You are to me."

I focused on straightening my straps, not the shot of warmth his quiet words sent to my heart.

From behind me, came a new whisper. "I wanted you to meet my momma."

I couldn't ignore that. I inhaled against my shoulder, my head half turned toward him. My clothes, my body smelled of him. He pushed his toe cap into the frost. His cheeks pinked.

Fuck me.

Taking in the stars rather than his unsure demeanor, I ate a piece of humble pie and called over, "I like her. I like Miss Eden, Nathaniel. And I'm not going to let her down. You're going nowhere without me."

He stuffed his arms into his pack and joined me, watching me instead of the stars winking out with the wakening dawn. "No surprise there. You're too stubborn and I'm too selfish."

"Fucked?"

"FUBAR."

"Double that."

Blazing our own trail, we took to the tree cover and headed toward imminent danger, care of the Corps recon subunit. Our D-Ps were down, but Blondie could've uplinked us. He didn't want to and I understood that, because I was living in my own state of denial. There was nothing out there I needed to know right now. Every hateful, fateful twist of my life had come down to these final days. The last person to worry about was Liz, but if both of us survived this, she'd find me. If not? We'd meet at grave's end.

Our guidance system came down to the maps I'd memorized while Blondie's eyes had walked all over my body, first in Alpha and then at the commune. The ground softening as the sun rose, the cold crunch of our boot steps became the quiet pounce of running feet.

Hours later we came upon a creek cracking under a thin glaze of ice. Leaning over, I dipped my head into clear water and filled my canteen. Blondie was watching me again.

I backhanded my mouth. "So…Eden's a Freelander?"

"Through and through."

"How's that work for you? You're a CO lifer."

"Not precisely." He topped up his canteen and knocked his knee to mine. "We don't have time to get into that right now."

"But we had time to screw?"

"Didn't think you'd take no for an answer."

A gut punch doubled with guilt. Great. "I was pretty pissed off." I pulled him in so I could brush my lips over his jaw. "But that's no excuse. I'm sorry, babe."

"I'm not complainin." Blinking at the sun topping the rangy forest, he got to his feet and gave me his hand.

But that wasn't enough. Not then. I threw my arm over his shoulder. "Would you have said no?"

He grinned. "No."

For those few peaceful moments, I held him against me.

Our hugging and hand-holding disappeared by midday. We'd be catching up to the troops soon. He asked, "You're willing to turn yourself in?"

"Yes." I'd already run through all the ramifications and was ready to man up.

"For the Freelanders."

"For freedom." I repeated Darke's call to arms. For Kamber, Micah, Hills—not so much for that cunt Kale. "Affirmative. I believe in them."

Blondie's searching ended at my eyes. His were glowing, saying silently what he wouldn't out loud. *For me?*

Even though his question was unvoiced, I assented. "Yeah."

I could admit to one change of heart, just not everything, not yet. Besides, if I really wanted to do the whole introspection thing, which I wasn't a huge frigging fan of, I'd have to admit I half hated, half worshipped the man.

Even with his "Eden's my momma" reveal, I was leaning toward the latter. "And I never said anything about giving up." *I won't give up on you either.*

His eyebrow arched. My cock rose at his daring look, hard as a plank of wood and about as useful in this situation.

I coughed and cleared my vision of repeat scenes of lovemaking. "Just gotta get their attention, then beat them to the Outpost, right? We're gonna snare them."

"They could outflank us."

"They won't. There's only the two of us. Their unit on recon travels with twenty-four soldiers." I swatted his ass. "We're light on our feet, faster. No chance. You know how to maneuver as well as we… as well as they do."

The corners of Blondie's lips lifted, dimples shifting into place briefly before he cupped my shoulders and sank his head to my neck. "I'll make sure you get out of the Outpost. I'll take care of you."

"Just like Leon."

Nodding under my chin, he said, "Just like Leon."

But he didn't sound so convinced.

*   *   *

Late afternoon found us running at full stretch. The sun was a cool orb barred by the thick canopy overhead, but exertion made us sweaty. We went down to T-shirts and then bare chests, jumping over fallen logs and twisting through foliage, heading south and east to cut off the Corps team.

The ricocheting calls of birds sang a shrill *Time's up! Time's up!* Every snap of twig or brush of red, orange, gold leaf told our story. We had no time to cover our tracks. I didn't like that.

With our packs' weight diminished, we racked up the clicks. Most of our gear was left at the commune. We carried the basics: weapons, spare boots, a change of clothes, rations, water. The way I was used to, the way it was supposed to be.

Gnawing on some bread supplied by Eden, we jogged for a length, running through our plan, if by plan I meant knotting the noose around our necks with our own hands.

"Listen, big man, you keep us safe out here, and I'll keep us safe once we reach the Outpost. Do your job." Blondie was back in biz mode.

"And I've been getting the gold standard so far." I nodded to the last small bandage on my shoulder.

"That was an accident."

"Yeah, I accidentally got between you and a friendly hatchet."

He winked. "Said I was sorry."

"Fuck off." I grinned. "You don't get it, man. I rarely get wounded."

"Jesus, your ego's even bigger than your cock, isn't it?"

He had a point.

My laughter joined his, and I sputtered, "Yeah and so's the chip on my shoulder, baby."

My laughter got derailed when we reached higher ground. It took a few seconds to survey the scene below us, a sight I wished we'd never come across. A half-day old, blood had pooled on the ground and congealed. The iron tang of it filled my nose. *Anything but this. Not this.*

He didn't speak. He couldn't. Neither could I.

In the lee below our feet, spread over the burnt-colored autumn grass was a slaughter. Bodies twisted in gruesome shapes, defiled by bullet holes, bludgeoned skulls, and all that blood.

Blondie retched.

While we'd been fighting and fucking in the forest, they'd been massacred at daybreak.

My stomach had ideas of doing the same as Blondie's. I clamped my throat shut, but couldn't cut off my emotions. Not this time.

This wasn't the work of Freelanders.

This *was* the Freelanders.

The scene was grisly and could only be Corps work, a kind even *I* hadn't witnessed before. Giant ugly birds black as sin cackled, cawed. Creatures fought over fingers and eyes, gore dripping from beaks and maws.

I ran at them. "Get off! Get off them!" Both SIGs raised, ready to blast, I stood over a body and ran my sights in a circle, checking the encroaching woods.

Kneeling down, Blondie gently turned a face. "They're ours." His throat bobbed and my weapons wavered.

Then I was with him, among the bodies, checking each one, waiting for a pulse, a cough, a lungful of air. Hoping I didn't know the next person, praying I hadn't sat beside them in the mess or shaken their hand or shared a story or two during the harvest festival.

"From the first wave that left with Darke."

Oh Christ.

My stomach heaved, but I held it down. My hands were red, my vision the same color, swarming with violence to do unto others.

I spied a faded green cap askew on a bed of flax-white hair.

I stumbled across the field of the fallen, going to my knees. I touched the cap and leaned over. *Not Micah, not Micah, not Micah…please.*

It wasn't his blank eyes I saw, but they were familiar nonetheless. Last time I'd seen this man, he was smirking, naked, ready to fuck Darke. Now he was naked, in death.

Wilde.

I pumped my hands to his chest, pinched his nose, and breathed into his mouth, begging him to come back to life. "Breathe, man. Just breathe for me."

His lungs ballooned with air, though his eyes stared at nothing.

I startled when Blondie clasped my shoulder.

"It's Wilde." Closing his eyelids, I dropped my head.

My gaze glided down his arm to the hand he clasped in death. He'd held on to Tam to the end. She was curled on her side facing him, her free hand dug into soil; she'd dragged herself to Wilde. His other hand was thrown out, empty.

"Where the hell is Darke?" I searched frantically.

"He's not here. He's safe. He has to be."

"That's not better for him." I gasped, openmouthed so I wouldn't smell the death.

"Not one bit."

Scanning the surrounds, I asked. "Where would he lead the rest of them?"

His voice was thick with pain, but his chin was held high with pride. "If I know anythin' about Darke, he'll have pulled his militia together. He's tight, a warrior." He stared into my eyes, his thumbs circling my cheeks. "He's like you."

"I don't do this, Nathaniel. I am not this."

"I know."

I didn't know how long we stood there, two men in a gory meadow saturated in blood and bodies.

Picking my way among the bodies, memorizing every face, I pieced it all together, wanting to scrub my brain of each image as it was recorded.

The Freelanders had been busting ass through the woods when their warning signal—a bird call—went up just before the forest came alive with bullets and brush fire. The Freelanders had been flushed into the open, sitting targets for the Corps killers.

A dozen or more would've been mowed down on the spot, the outer ring. Humans, with wild-eyed bleating animals caught in the crossfire, adding to the chaos. Then the real fight had commenced, close-contact combat backed up by sniper rifles. Superior firepower won out over skill and know-how. The Freelanders' familiar terrain had been used against them, and, even overwhelmed and overpowered, Darke's people would've kept at it, no matter what.

Duty, honor, loyalty, freedom.

My allegiance had completely switched now that I knew the truth about the Freelanders—now that I'd seen this violent reality.

Of the forty-seven who'd left the commune a day ago, twenty lay here, slain. Women, men, the returning Revolutionaries, too. In this one area, the Corps and CO didn't discriminate.

I found a double-bladed ax, a short shovel with a broad head, too, and we set to work digging a communal grave. It wasn't what either of us wanted, but time was short.

The last time I'd buried someone, it had been Erica, and I hadn't gotten to say goodbye.

It took a couple hours before we lowered the perished.

Tam beside Wilde. Together beyond the end of life.

Over each man and woman, Blondie placed a wildflower and said their names. *Wilde, Tammerick, Shades, Fen, Lil, Burne...*

Our Alpha people were laid to rest with the same reverence once we'd found their ID tags: *Jez, Amee, Hardy, Gray, Flint...*

With lowered heads and hands held over a circle of death, we stood together.

The lack of Corps casualties was the final riddle easily solved. The Freelanders had put up a fierce fight. I scouted twelve wounded or dead as denoted by the tracks of bodies dragged from scene. Twelve to go.

"I guess that answers the question of retaliation." I led Blondie away from the bloody scourge.

"Yeah."

* * *

We moved on, dragging under the weight of the brutal extermination and what it meant. We stopped. Earlier than we should have. No comfort to be had, at least not from the bulkiest manmade materials we'd ditched at dawn.

No fires, no attention. The trap had to be set. I knew what toys the recon troops were using now. We'd seen their work and we were going to use the same tactics against them tomorrow. But all that mattered in this moment was at least we had each other.

No tent, fighting the cold the old-fashioned way—with body heat—and we were so cold after the day's grief and despair. Bundling up together, I cradled Blondie against me.

"Hey, you okay?" I smoothed his hair back, but I could barely see the side of his face.

He gulped. "Yeah."

"Turn around. I want to look at you, make sure you're all right."

Rolling over, he stared down where I linked our hands, threading my fingers carefully through his. I sighed in anguish at the sight of a couple tears topping his downcast eyelashes. "You're not okay. Don't lie to me." Relinquishing one of his hands, I cupped his strong jaw and angled his head up, damp blue irises making contact with my own troubled eyes.

All pretense of being tough guys capable of handling anything had disappeared the second we'd seen the slaughter. I stroked away the tears, found his mouth softly, slowly.

"Forget about it," I whispered.

He sucked in a breath, pulling me closer. "I can't." His words were warm against my throat, fingers digging into my shirt.

Kissing along his temple to his forehead, I left my lips there, feeling how tautly strung his body was. "Then think about me, because I'm right here with you, baby. Be with me. Stay alive for me."

He collapsed against me in deep, silent sobs, as we held each other as tight as possible. When he slumped against me, I waited until his gaze found mine. We touched each other with barely there, gentle brushes on hair and lips and cheeks, grounding ourselves in the feel of warm flesh and each other.

"Hold on to me."

He nodded, curling around me. "I will. I'm not lettin' you go."

"Because I need you to live," I said.

That night our kisses were long and profound, a deeper exchange than any we'd shared before providing the touch of solace we needed.

*   *   *

The next night, the world was on fire.

We'd scouted throughout the day, coming from behind the Corps subunit. Tailing them deep into the mountains, we waited for them to find a water hole and set up camp. They didn't so much as sniff after Darke's campaign to Alpha; they were gunning for Chitamauga.

We'd gotten north of them, pointed toward the Outpost. In the darkout, my eyes had adjusted to Blondie signaling to me with his fingers. *Thirteen.* There should've been twelve. I was never wrong. An unknown was with them.

Thirteen to two was a suicide mission; shame I wasn't scared. We'd left them to their boisterous plans and big-boy brags about the fun they'd had fragging the humanoids. It seemed like their own casualties should have shaken their shit up a bit.

Half a click from Corps base camp, I laid a ring of fiery pits. We were doing exactly what the fuckwits had, only in reverse order. Using ourselves as bait, inside a flaming ring, we were gonna pull the Corps troops to us, then give 'em a little extra punch.

"Use what the earth gave us," Blondie had advised.

I didn't know how much I liked taking orders from him unless his cock was in my mouth, but I did as told, sharpening rocks until they were lethal shards, shaping thick splinters of wood into spears.

"Excellent. We'll make a Freelander of you yet." He'd approved of my handiwork, his own tasks with ampoules of acids and shredded fabric completed.

Packing for this most-recent vacation, we'd had similar ideas about necessities: bullets and bomb makings. Me with the guns, him with that home-cooked wonder, guncotton.

When I'd compiled a mountain of shrapnel, he'd set me to digging duty. I was a-okay with that, since I had dug enough holes in my lifetime, storing all my thoughts and feelings beneath a stratum of dirt so goddamn deep I hoped to forget where I'd buried them. The thing was, as he praised me, proving himself to be a battle-ready man, those emotions burst through, blinding me with hope.

Our trap ready, after we'd eaten quickly and quietly, we nodded to each other in agreement. Our lips met in a kiss that was deep and soft and something I never wanted to end. In the press of his tongue and the whisper of his stubble, the words went unsaid.

When our lips parted, we'd worked in tandem around the circle of bonfires. The strike of spark, the *whoosh* of fire, a fucking job well done, and one more to accomplish. For damn sure we were gonna pique Corps interest a hell of a lot more than a bunch of *crude, rustic Nomads*. We were going to give the troopers something better to chase, a bigger prize.

"Well, that'll fix 'em." Blondie's beautiful face was lit in reds and oranges.

Walking toward him, I said, "I only want to fix you."

"C'mon then, give it a shot." He hooked a thumb into his waist-band.

I met that challenge with all my passion. Chances were slim to none we'd make it out of this ensnarement intact, and even if we did, our asses would still be swinging in the breeze as long as the CO remained in power. My hand strong on Blondie's neck, I pulled his face to mine. Watching gold eyelashes brush his cheeks and breaths stutter from his chest, I held off from kissing him by a few heartbeats.

Eyes softly smoldering, he looked up. "You just gonna tease me, honey?"

A swipe of my lips, then another. I groaned as his mouth opened, taking him in a kiss that shocked me to my very soul. Pressing away, I was struck by the twist of anguished longing in his expression. I ran my hands through his hair, down his back and to his hips, clasping him against me.

After all the years of being told my desires were abnormal, Blondie felt so natural, I didn't want to let him go. We clutched each other, kissing and touching, aching for one more moment. The life-and-death situation gave rise to such intense arousal, I almost lost control.

When I jerked back, Blondie followed. "Caspar."

I didn't want to talk. Instead I moved my mouth to his ear, kissing the shell up to the doubled piercings at the peak.

"Caspar, I lo—"

I shook my head. I couldn't hear this, not now when his life was on the line.

He shoved me away. "Goddamn you. Goddamn you for making me—"

A metallic whistle shrieked over Blondie's outburst, the part when I thought he'd said he loved me. A crack was followed fast by another low-flying hum. Dirt blew up around us. *Ping-ping-ping.* Stampedes of feet headed our way with no fucking subtlety at all. As a commander, I was unimpressed. As a possible captive, I figured we better get the hell down and get out pronto.

I tried to bunker Blondie from the rain of bullets, throwing my body over him like a human shield when I dragged him out of the line of fire. "Well, that did the trick." I grunted as I made impact with the ground.

Then he was silenced by the stream of ammo shot off in our direction.

"Blondie!"

Chapter Twelve

Blondie, fuck!" I bent over him, bullets ricocheting past my head at a rapid pace.

"Get off." He slithered from under me, hand cupped to his formerly scar-free cheek. *Great.* Add another wound to my tally, this one mirroring my elbow blow the last time this kind of shit went down. Blood dripped between his fingers, red conduits increasing my rage.

He hissed, "Close your goddamn mouth and get the hell outta here."

Easier said than done. I'd gone with his plan, and his plan had us surrounded by Corps. We were caught with our pants down, our emotions bared to the subunit.

Blondie's eyes crackled as he listened to the first round of gay-hate chorusing from the troops, mocking our intimate kiss. I heard them with a hard head, deciding on a new strategy to up the ante. What better way to pump their beef than to serve myself up? A Corps commander proud of his homosexuality. Hell, I had half a mind to kiss Blondie again.

My plan changed in an instant.

Inside the ring of fire, we scrambled toward the trench we'd left, rolling into the dug-out ditch and up the other side. They had their night visors down, their vision crystal clear, but their aim was piss poor. Liz would've sheared my neck clean through from that distance. In spite of their victory over the Freelanders, the bulk of these soldiers seemed to be ninety-day wonders, not precision-trained operators. The Corps casualties in the Territories must've run deep.

I kept one eye on Blondie, the other across the fireworks, maintaining the brick fucking wall of my body between the wet-behind-the-ears battalion and him. They funneled into the hellish pit while I strode forward, providing the biggest, baddest target.

Blondie's voice was a distant plea. "What the hell are you doing?'"

I was already handling the SIGS strapped across my chest, drawing more heat from the troops as well as taunts.

"Hands off the weapons, faggot."

I stopped short of raising my twin buddies. "You might wanna rethink how you address me, soldier."

With my face clear of shadows, I looked every bit the Alpha Elite tactical commander. I was a big badass motherfucker, and I'd been cameoed on the D-P enough so my status and face were known InterNations wide.

Whispers sizzled, shouts formed, my name clear amid a flurry of gay-bashing insults. *Oh yeah, they recognize me.*

Silencing his men, the soldier with the medals addressed me. "Commander Cannon. Stand down."

"Suck my cock, Lieutenant." I spread my arms and beckoned with my fingers, detailing the distance between the homemade minefield and me, figuring I was right on the edge.

Fingers scrabbled around my ankle. I kicked back, hoping I didn't hit Blondie's face this time. My lips didn't move as I said, "You got a job; do it."

Unsure of procedure, the troops shifted their aim to the movement behind me. *Big mistake.* I pulled a Liz move, grabbing my crotch. "Like what you saw, boys?"

Immediately, I was covered in twelve red dots, concentrated on my breastbone and my brain. *Better.*

The lieutenant stepped forward. His ugly one-sided sneer went with his skinny, scarred-up face. "Who's with you?"

"My boyfriend."

He advanced closer, the others in formation behind him. "That wasn't Mr. Rice."

I eased back a step, shrugging my shoulders. "Nah. Just my latest CO clone." I made a show of lewdly licking my lips, tasting Blondie's on my mouth, and casually slung a hand to my hip. "Always had a crush on that man."

"Keep those hands in front of you, ass-drafter."

"You giving me orders, Lieutenant?"

"You a queer, Commander?"

"I could take you in for insulting a superior officer."

"I could take you down for sucking flamer cock, *sir.*"

The beast in me dared him forward. I wanted to see him blown to bits. "Ever take it up the ass?"

"Watch your mouth."

An underling hurried to his side. *"Confirmed. Nathanial Rice, Esquire."*

The smile that split the bastard's face was a furlong wide. "Looks like we got us a two-for-one deal that'll earn us promotions, men."

"You think?" I asked.

"Are you fucking him?"

"What'd it look like?"

"But, sir, Commander Cutler ordered—"

The scrawny-faced lieutenant whirled on his junior officer. "Don't you think I know my orders?"

Great. Looked like we'd just gone from shit list to hit list. I'd heard of my infamous equal up in Beta, CEO Cutler's son. Medals up the ass, but probably not much dick. "You're Beta boys?"

"Affirmative. And you're both coming with us."

To my right, the glint of a barrel was aimed at Blondie. Without turning my head, I whipped my Glock up, swung it over, and fired. One shot broke the youngster's grasp, shattering his phalanges and dropping him to the ground, where he whimpered for his momma. *Now, that was sharp shooting.*

"Stand down!" Lieutenant Cunt ordered through gritted teeth. "You pull another move like that, your transport will be a body bag."

I distracted them by holstering my firearm. "*Ooh.* See how much my hands are shaking?" When I straightened, I blew the fuckchop a kiss with my knife tearing into his ribs. Just enough of a love tap to take him off his feet and down ten pegs.

Man, the resounding lock of bullets loading never sounded so good. All eyes trained on me, I moved out. Just a few more steps with them following hot on my heels, I'd get a firsthand look at Blondie's booby-trap brainchild.

The searing bonfires between the Corps crew cuts and me, their sights locked tight, their advance was hesitant. I knew why they didn't open fire. They didn't want to miss the chance to beat the queer out of me or collect their rewards for bringing in live outlaws for RACE rehab.

Belligerent in my need to keep Blondie from the fray, I opened my arms wide and stood on the balls of my feet, doubling my mass. "COME ON, HOMO HATERS! You too pussy to engage?"

"Pull back, Caspar. Goddamn it!"

Not gonna happen.

They moved forward, breaking ranks, not fucking subtle at all. Not like my company. If I were their commander, I'd have taken them to the brig myself for some strafing. But I wasn't their leader. I was no one's leader anymore. I had a new detail, one I embraced. Get them off the Freelander scent.

True to form, Blondie went with his plan.

The tinny click echoed around me.

I looked at their faces as horror descended over smug Corps veneers. I had enough time to crow with delight at their entrapment before the ground exploded in a guncotton hail of my crafty arrowheads and spears spiraling through the air, piercing skin.

The shock traveled in waves until the impact blew me off my feet. Flailing through the air, I reveled in the amount of force triggered by Blondie's pyrotechnics. Hurtled to the ground, I flinched when a shard gouged my upper thigh. *You gotta be fucking kidding me.* I peeled apart the ugly wound…*only a graze.*

Screams rebounded, barely reaching my ringing ears. Smoke infiltrated the area, smelling of charred flesh and spent charges. Wrenched from my sit-down by Blondie, I was hustled into the woods, his hand pressed to my shoulder. Looking back, I could tell he was shouting at me; his mouth worked at a pace matching our feet while a wrinkle creased his forehead.

I lingered over the last muted shouts. It could've been worse. We should've returned the favor and outright killed them. Coulda, shoulda, woulda were the story of my goddamned life. We collected our packs, and I led northward over untouched land. We'd grabbed the recon troops by their nuts, cluster fucked 'em, and given ourselves a decent head start; now it was race time.

Two kilometers in, I was still hard of hearing, but I lip-read well enough, especially when they were Blondie's lips as he overtook me.

"You dickhead!" He tackled me to the ground, an unusual emotion marking his features.

Hmm, maybe life-threatening situations made him frisky.

"Going out there half-cocked like that, what the hell?"

Unfortunately not.

He jumped up and slammed my backpack into my chest. Yanking on my hand, he pulled me to my feet and threw my pack out of the way so he could grab my face and kiss me hard and fast. He let go with a sharp nip to my bottom lip before he dove at my mouth again, moaning.

When he finally slumped against me, my grin widened against his taut jaw. "Worried, lover?"

"You got a serious hero complex. You're gonna get yourself killed."

I licked the sweet spot beneath his ear until he panted. "You're sexy when you're pissed at me."

His biceps bunched to punch me, but I calmed him, sliding my fingers over his muscles. "You're really hot when you think you can tell me what to do."

"Don't screw with me."

I rocked into him. "I wasn't half-cocked."

He exhaled fast. "You never are."

Freeing himself, he set to work with more wires, his back bent over his deluxe D-P.

"You going online?"

"I'm scramblin' their D-P's so they can't send or receive any coms."

"Smart."

"I had my moments before I hooked up with you."

"Cute."

When he finished fiddling, the bright green screen sent a ghastly glow over the hollow of his cheek, the one decorated in new blood.

"Let me look at you."

"Get off."

"You're bleeding out!"

"Jesus Christ. It's a scrape; that's all."

"So you can take care of me, but I can't see to you?"

"Fine." He sat on a rotting log and lifted his chin.

I foraged around the forest until I came up golden with those pointy-leaved herbs Eden had used on me. Wetting the foliage, I plastered them to his cheekbone. His sigh was worth my trouble.

"Feel good?"

"Yeah. You oughtta be a nurse, big man." He took my hand, linking our fingers. "C'mon. Won't take 'em long to re-form."

"Hope we hobbled a few."

"Would be good if we blinded some too," Blondie said.

I looked over at him, his swelling cheek causing a fresh pulse of anger. "I should've killed a couple point-blank."

"You don't mean that."

My head in my hands, my elbows on my knees, I muttered, "Don't know what I mean anymore."

*   *   *

Several days later, the far-off snow-capped mountains became our latest campground. Straining uphill, we broke through a foggy layer to come out on top. Valleys, lakes, and chains of mountains stretched beyond anything I'd ever imagined. The Wilderness was unengineered. Armies of forests in nature-made formations gained my admiration. Birds looped above, sending out song, not calls of alarm. No roads, no tenement buildings, no Territories, no terrorizing.

Our arms around each other's shoulders, I wondered who else

had the honor to see this majesty. Probably only a handful of Free-landers since the Purge.

It was breathtaking.

And piss freezing cold.

Blondie was majestic, too, silver from the moonlight and so god-damn handsome. "The Appalachian Mountains." His arms opened as if gathering the whole damn vista in an embrace. "That right there's a bird's-eye view, big man."

"Glad I had the chance to see it." With his smirk in my side view, I hugged him closer and whispered into the cool shell of his ear, "With you."

We saw everything below us, including the Corps troops lagging behind by a good three clicks; their fires dotted the distant dark cliffs. Those fuckers weren't scared about being caught.

With the wildlife few and far between the farther we fled into the Wilderness and its onset of winter, hunger set upon me with two different demands. The kind I knew how to deal with—the one that sat in my gut, asking for food and knowing none was forth-coming—and the new painful pangs brought on by Blondie. It had started as straightforward lust but had somehow gotten tangled in-side my heart, the screws tightening the longer we lasted out here on our own. Distrust melted away like the wintry ice from a creek.

We took down a rare doe and dared to start a fire. A little bit of *screw-you-fucksticks* attitude went into the kindling. Venison was dinner that night, the rest of the meat saved for something called brunch, whatever the frig that was.

Blondie's lips were a tasty feast when I leaned over to lick them. He made freezing his sweet ass off look comfortable and too damn tempting for my own good.

"We just gotta keep this up for four more days." He pulled his knees up for an armrest.

Icicles gashed my heart when his words sank in. "That all?"

The Outpost was only the first hurdle. I was banking on Blondie to keep me off the scaffold. I had to believe, and I wasn't much into blind faith.

Later, he returned from a piss break, and I opened the slim shell of my sleeping bag, warming him within my arms. He kept sliding his fingers under the leather cuff.

"That bothering you?" I withdrew my arms. The least he could do was stop acting like it was burning a brand into his wrist. I was the one carrying around a tattoo on my heart.

Bringing me back against him, he rolled his eyes. "You are so quick to jump to conclusions." I opened my mouth, but he strolled a fingertip across my lips before I could speak. "The wrong ones."

He shut his eyes and smiled, running the suede band between his fingers. "Not botherin' me at all, Caspar. I just like feelin' your words."

He opened his eyes, opened my jacket, tugged my shirt up, and flattened his tongue from the brush of black hair escaping my pants to my nipples. It was so fucking cold outside, but he was hot on my skin, lining every muscle. I spread my thighs, dug into his hair, and held him near.

We couldn't sleep; we shouldn't fuck.

Diving into his pants, I palmed his ass, those round globes spilling through my fingers. I spliced him with my fingers. So tight. He bucked in my clasp, his kisses vicious on my mouth, on my cock that he uncovered.

I grabbed him, our bodies striving for more. "Can't get close enough."

Pants at our ankles, legs wrapping, torsos twisting, we fought with this starving need.

"*Shh. Shh.*" He rose over me, the tendons in his arms pulled tight. Our bodies were painted in bites and marks and wetness. Slowly, he lowered. "*Shhh,* honey."

I shouted when his cock turned against mine. "*Aaah.*" Shushing be damned.

Our hips rounded, the columns of our dicks butting from balls to ballast.

His hair sweeping over my face, he straddled me, stroking our cocks together in his fist. Stretching our penises and leaning over to add the sting of his tongue to his hands.

"*Oh yeah.*" Flexible motherfucker. I liked that.

The glide of his fingertips and the suction of his mouth, the turgid thrust of his cock rolled against mine. Our groins swiveled, groans merged.

Come fountained over our abs and chests, hitting my chin.

Nuzzling. Warm. Satisfied…sort of.

In a damn sleeping bag on top of a mountain with the threat of death ready to deepthroat us at the Outpost.

And yet I wanted more of him.

*   *   *

Down the other side, into the valley that had been pretty from above, daybreak was the usual backbreaking full-out run. They weren't slackers, that was for sure. Labored shouts trailed us, heavy boots finally falling away. We'd earned a respite, but not really.

The second night of the last leg, I woke to tickles, my sleep-deprived swollen eyelids parting. In the gloomy light, Blondie sat cross-legged in front of me. Tucked next to my face was a bouquet of winter bulbs, their blooms nodding closed.

I reared back. It was the same stuff we'd laid over Freelander and

Revolutionary graves. I didn't like flowers so much anymore. "They smell like death."

"They didn't die in vain, Caspar. Flowers smell of hope; that's why you like 'em."

"I don't need you to analyze me."

"Don't be so defensive."

"Don't be so annoying."

"Annoying?" Crouching over me, a small smile played on his lips. I brushed the hair off his cheek, rubbing my thumb along the short shaved side above his ear. "Cheerful, whatever."

"You think I'm cheerful?" Nestling in to my hand, he enjoyed my comforting caress.

"Hell of a lot more easygoing than me."

He sat back, eyes twinkling. "Probably a good thing. One moody motherfucker's enough."

Launching into a playful punch, I ended up wearily snuggling him and planted a kiss on top of his head. "I'll watch; you sleep."

An hour later, the stars shrouded in wispy clouds, I heard him mumble my name.

"Mmm?" I burrowed in to his body, taking advantage of his slumbering heat.

"Can't sleep."

With a little smile, I said, "Want me to tell you a bedtime story?"

"Nah, but I've got a story to tell."

I went completely still. If Blondie was gonna talk about his past, I was all ears.

"It ain't a fairy tale, though."

"Tell me, baby." The moonlight lined the frosted grasses in silver, flirting with his hair when he lay down inside my arms. My fingers flickered through his polished locks, cupping his neck.

"Back when my momma came of age, there wasn't the overruling hate for the Company. They were the saviors of our race, the stewards of the earth's resources, you know? My father was sent to decommission her family land, and since the Freelanders and last Landowners weren't yet a threat to Company dominion, it was easier to strike a bargain than a flintlock.

"He'd come knocking down the door of the plantation, acting as if he owned it. But one step inside the foyer, he pulled up short. He fell for a pretty girl." Blondie's face was sketched in hard planes, too much like mine, distancing himself from his past, relegating it to Old History.

"Cut him a deal, he did. Allowin' Granddaddy to keep his land for the privilege of courting his daughter. Beautiful, innocent, different Eden was so unlike the contrived Territory women of his approved matings. She wasn't unaffected either. Infatuation, youth, maybe the idea of adventure, made her agree. My father was a good-lookin' sumbitch. That was all heady stuff for eighteen-year-old Momma, that and the thought she was saving her daddy's land.

"It was just after their Validation of Union that he announced the plantation had been incorporated into InterNations holdings. Helluva wedding present. See, he had no problem breakin' his word. Still doesn't."

Eyes blazing, his drawl turned tight and clipped. "That killed Granddaddy, givin' his daughter to a scumbag like my father. It didn't make a damn dent in my daddy's agenda, although he very generously gave Momma leave to bury Granddaddy in the plot outside Alpha walls."

"Holy shit." *Those grave markers, the ones he took a moment to honor our night at the Amphitheater.* The letters came back to me: HARM.

"Hamme and Harmony Rice, my grandparents. Never did get to meet 'em."

"Baby." I tried to cut in, but he turned away.

"You wanna know the really sick thing? Father loved her. He still loves Momma. I think he would've done anything for her so long as it didn't interfere with his plan for InterNations domination."

I grabbed his hand, softly swiping my thumb over knuckles flexed bony white.

He blew out a breath. "She didn't really have a choice after that, with nowhere to go, especially not with her position so well-known. She was the wife of a hotshot executive and had become pregnant." Drawing his hand from mine, he dragged his hair forward. "Hurts like a bitch, talkin' about this, Caspar."

I remembered how Miss Eden closed down when I'd asked about her Territory past. I cradled Blondie's cheek, already worried about how this would end.

"I mean, there's no way she could love him, not after what he did, right? Who would? But he was oblivious. Maybe because he was away so much cleanin' up Company crap, maybe 'cause he was an obtuse motherfuck, or just plain old wishful thinking. When he was home, he spoiled her, us, anything to win her affection. After a spell, things got ugly. And when the verbal abuse got him no gains, well, it took only one punch in the face to knock her out. He was a pretty big guy, and she's so small. I was eight." He squatted, arms doubled over his knees, keeping himself together through sheer will.

I saw the little boy he must've been, making himself as small as possible, wishing he was big enough to stand up for his mother.

Speaking in a daze, he didn't even notice me rubbing my palms over his shoulders to comfort him. "He was contrite. 'Course he was. *He loved her.* It was disgusting, watchin' him apologize, listenin' to his excuses.

"Once the bruises faded, she told him he wouldn't ever get the chance to hit her again. Damn, it was good to see her stand up for us.

It was goddamn great to watch him cower, fucking coward that he is. For once *he* had no choice. She asked for land, the rightful property stolen from her family. He gave it to her. Rich, fertile acres. Chitamauga Commune."

He shook himself back to the present. "Of course there was a price for leavin'. She would vanish—her death faked so he wouldn't be known as the CO cuckold or, worse, get demoted. She had to disappear and give me up. Give us up."

"Who's us?"

"My twin brother, Linc. He's top-level Corps. We're a little bit"—he grimaced—"estranged. He fell in step with Daddy's new regime once Momma was gone. I found ways to keep in contact with her, but he put her on radio silence."

An itchy feeling of unease crept up my skull.

He jumped up to his feet, pacing with emotions too big to be contained. "Things went a little south then. Linc was always the star pupil; all I had were my skills."

"And your father?"

His face shaded under his arms, he said, "He lost his love, along with any semblance of humanity. Adolescence sucked, man. There were the socials for meeting sponsored CO teens. Dates were monitored, graded for long-term compatibility. You had your equivalent traditions in Epsilon; you told me about it."

Blondie's eyes were far away. "Then there was the Proving Ceremony when we turned eighteen."

Jesus fuck.

Hands up under his armpits, he rocked sideways. "This is what bein' bred into Company means. A debut. I been through my initiation. My brother loved it all."

"You were with a woman." The scratchy discomfort turned up a notch.

"Not a woman, Caspar, a girl my age. So damn pretty—not my type at all."

"You saying I'm not pretty?"

He chuckled and sat beside me. "Farrow was her name. She was as naive as me, so how the hell we were supposed to just get it on in a roomful of our peers and executives, I got no idea."

He pressed the heels of his hands to his eyes. "Nothin' to it; that's what Linc told me. Bastard passed with flyin' colors. No one could doubt his prowess with women. Wasn't like that for me. Farrow was smart and sure, but put anyone in that position and she'd freeze—anyone with any feelin', that is. They let us get into the bed naked before they filed into the room. A cold, sterile room about as sexy as an exam cubicle."

The horrific scenario filled me with rage; my hands balled to punch something.

"We held hands under the blankets. It was a damn miracle there were blankets to begin with. But that wasn't all. Electrodes were attached to us, measurin' heart rate and blood pressure. Keepin' tabs on arousal. Bet mine spiked"—he blinked up at me—"in fear. I couldn't do it. No way in hell could I do it. She was shakin' so hard, her teeth rattled. I made no move on Farrow except to hug her before I slipped out of the bed, the deed not even started, let alone consummated. I faced the frowns of disapproval, the victorious grins of people I'd considered friends. I walked bare-assed outta that room, thinkin' I could just get gone and go to my mom. Shoulda known it wouldn't be that easy."

He dropped his head. Unclenching my fists, I reached for his hands. "What happened?"

"Father caught up before the doors even closed behind me. Linc was waitin' in the hallway, too. It was like we weren't even brothers; the way he glared at me said exactly what Father voiced. 'You're a disappointment, Nathaniel. I should have sent you off to the Nomads with your mother a long time ago.' I wished he had. I'd thought, I'd hoped—Jesus, I'd really hoped—he would. Maybe I'd messed up his image enough he'd have to let me go, declare me dead, too."

"He didn't, did he?"

"Hell no. Mercy was for the weak. I learned that lesson the old-fashioned way." Putting on a tough, cold voice, Blondie said, " 'If you can't get a wife, you'll get me the world. I want the respect of all the Territories. You will not be another black mark against my reputation, boy.' "

I was torn between finding a target to demolish like the tree branch beside us and reaching out to him. "How the *hell* did you get through that without being scarred?"

He turned his face up to me, and it felt like he was showing me his sliced-up heart. "You think I'm not scarred? Trust me. Father made sure I was, maybe not on the outside, like Momma, but on the inside. I got taught a lesson on the many reasons why I couldn't screw up again."

"Your brother, he just let this all go down?"

He threw back his head and sighed. "Let it go down? He helped him out. Made sure I walked the straight and narrow." His blue eyes pierced my soul when they hooked mine. "Survivalist training was in order. I was sent from Alpha into the Wilderness with no supplies. One thing was certain: He wasn't raising pussies. His punishment brought me to starving point, and then I learned the crafts of my people. Momma found me. I was taken in."

I had to take his hand in mine, stopping him from raking his hair back again and again. "You couldn't have gotten away with that long."

"Six months was all. Until word came Linc was out in the Wilderness with a crew of Corps trainees, searchin' for me. I had to be planted away from Chitamauga, away from my mother, away from my true family so I could be squired back to Alpha to take up my position as the esteemed son I was supposed to be. Least those six months were a good ride." His smile was breathtaking. All innocence and hope over the cruel wisdom.

"Rice is a Freelander name, your Landowner family name."

A fainter smile fastened to his lips. "That's right."

"How is it you were able to keep Eden's maiden name?"

"That was my price, for staying in Alpha after they brought me back while I made like the good protégé."

"You don't hate her for deserting you and your brother?"

"In that situation, would you rather your momma took a punch or take the heat yourself?"

I've already done the same thing for Blondie twice. He knew my answer.

"I wasn't gonna watch him suck the soul outta her. I learned how to take care of myself. I earned my place." His fingers skipped across my mouth. "Sound familiar?"

I nodded, bringing him close to me. "Your brother go by Rice?" I didn't know any top brass by that name.

"No. He chose our father's surname."

The creeping misgiving curled its fingers over my scalp and I bit out, "What's Linc's last name?"

Chapter Thirteen

The family name is Cutler."

Holy shit. "Commander Cutler...Beta Commander Cutler is your twin!" I could barely breathe, let alone pronounce the words.

He assented, spreading his hands around my sides as if to hold me in place while the entire goddamn universe toppled to a new axis. Linc Cutler—his goddamn brother—was the man overseeing the recon unit out to get us.

"Your fricking family's got a hard-on for us?"

"It looks like they do now." His chin took on that stubborn tilt.

The double whammy followed so fast, I was glad Blondie's hands kept me solidly on the ground because the bottom of my world fell out.

Nathaniel Cutler, Linc Cutler...and fucking CEO Lysander Cutler.

"Motherfucking hell!" Because it wasn't bad enough the famous commander was his twin brother; the supremacist Alpha CEO just had to be his dear goddamn daddy, too. The man who already had a toe tag picked out just for me.

I almost puked up my left nut, reliving that very first oh-shit moment at CO HQ when I'd been made to stand stone-faced while his cunt of a father promised a demotion for Liz. When I'd been ordered by the head of Alpha Territory to escort *his son* safely to the Outpost.

Goddamn it! When I screwed up, I did it from the top and got ass-fucked from behind. It didn't get much worse than this.

"I'm gonna kill your father."

"Not if I do first."

"Why have you stuck it out with the Company?"

"Linc's a Cutler through and through, but I have to believe I can save him." I recognized his closed-book look when he said the next. "And I got other reasons."

"Jesus, thought I had it bad."

"Oh, you did." Sitting beside me, he shrugged. "We all do, in one way or another. It ain't a competition though, 'specially since you don't like that shit."

It was hard to keep a straight I'm-so-fucked face when he made me laugh. "You remember everything I say?"

Blondie pulled me close, lightly kissing my lips. "Everything you say, honey, and everything you've done since I first saw you."

His statement could've been dangerous to me. Instead it sounded devastatingly romantic. I had to have his lips, his tongue pressing against mine. I needed his body. My hands shaking—for once not from cold—I tugged at his pants, battling the snap and zipper. "I need you inside me."

When my palm found his cock, he ground his forehead against mine, his voice cracking. "What?"

"You. I need you inside of me, Nathaniel. I want you to take me, have me." I stroked up, catching my thumb on the lip of his hard, broad head and slipping slowly all the way back down. His beautiful tumescent cock filling my fist with virile flesh and pulsing veins.

"Oh hell. Caspar." He yanked his pants down his thighs, kicking them off his feet. Moaning into my mouth, he ripped through my clothes until he got to my chest, twirling my nipples, then pulling them between his lips.

A rush of laughter came from me. I'd never seen him move so fast. As my chest rumbled, he peered up and soothed the skin he'd been nibbling.

His voice low and gentle, he asked, "You ever had a man inside you, honey?"

A memory slammed into me—skin the color of the milky coffee I'd had at the commune, brown eyes above me, deep words with a foreign lilt, *Mi corazón, Caspar*—and my head whipped aside.

"Caspar?" His hands stilled, my shaft half revealed to the night. "Did someone hurt you?"

I met his eyes with all the honesty I could muster. "Not like that. Not with intent." Wriggling free of my fatigues, I linked my fingers with Nathaniel's and brought them to my mouth. "I haven't let anyone in for a long time."

Kissing his fingertips, taking one inside for a long, slow suck, I shoved the memory away, concentrating on the man I had right here. "I want you."

"I won't hurt you ever," he whispered.

My lips shifted with a smile, one that fled when his mouth trailed from my earlobe down the middle of my torso, wetting the thick line of hair until he buried his lips at the base of my shaft. Sucking me deep, he loved my cock with his tongue until I rode his lips.

I writhed to go further, shouting when his throat opened and all I knew was the tight cavern of his mouth and tongue. "Oh Christ!"

He went all the way down on me so many times. I fisted his hair and forced my fingers to relax before I hurt him or bludgeoned him to death with my dick.

Finally pulling up, his lips were swollen and my cock was a deep red. *"Mmm,"* he murmured, licking at me, spreading our moisture up and down my shaft.

The click of the lube bottle preceded the glide of a solitary finger slipping over my sacs, running tight circles over my pucker. I jerked when his finger worked inside me, my hips bearing down, my breath coming fast.

"Can I add another, honey?"

I nodded quickly, spreading my thighs. On my elbows, I watched this sexy man between my legs, his mouth drifting up and down my cock and his fingers threading into me. His head moved the same way it did when he kissed me. In and out, up and down, side to side. Counterpoint moves that kept me on edge and so erect tremors racked my entire body.

He slurped my cock with obscene noises and chuckled every time I snuck up for his lips and down for his fingers; his torrential tease made me smack my palms to the ground, groans leaking past my lips.

He licked straight between my cheeks stretched by his hands. "Gonna fuck this sexy ass."

He pulled out a condom, but I grabbed his wrist. "Come in me, please. Fill me, Nathaniel. I need to feel you."

"I've never been with anyone like this before."

I swallowed hard. "Me neither. I've never wanted to." I'd never made love before with no protection, no pretense.

That set him off. On his knees in front of me, his features were stern in sensuality, locks of hair falling forward as he surveyed my body and returned to my face. "I've wanted this. I never thought you'd let—"

"Enough talking, babe. Fuck me."

He was so erotic above me, holding my thighs back, watching the thick ridge of his cock enter me. I groaned when the head disappeared inside me. *Jesus, he's a big boy.*

His fingers found my face. "Okay?" he panted.

"Fuck yeah." I lifted my hips and he slid farther in.

His cheeks flushed, eyes feverish, he hardly spared a look from my ass parting for his cock, but when he did, a sheepish grin flashed over his lips at getting caught staring. His moan was long and low as he sank all the way in.

The feel of him rocking into me made me grunt. His big cap and wide shaft hit me just right. I was stripped down to the essence of being fucked by my lover, his hands at my hips and mine rooted in his hair.

Every kiss, every caress, every endearment and gasped curse was precious.

He hit his stride, chest heaving as he stretched over me. From that angle, he smacked my gland, sending a full-body thrill through me along with a ragged groan.

"Hell yeah. You like that, big man?" Blondie lunged again, and the feel of him was making me insane. His shiny, slippery cock poised at my entrance, he demanded, "Tell me you like it. Tell me you want me to fuck you."

"Ahhh, fuck!" Squirming to get closer, I considered throwing him onto his back and sinking right down on his dick to get him back inside me. "Fuck me. Fuck me like that, babe."

Sweat glistened on his chest, each thrust driving me wild with lust. My balls ratcheted high, cock stretched up from my belly, beating against his abs. When he kept spearing into me, my back snatched off the ground and my head swerved from side to side.

"You gonna come, honey?"

"Yeah!"

He licked his palm with that delicious pink tongue and curled it around my cock, grinning when my erection leaped and I bucked beneath him. "That's right. Come for me, Caspar. Come on my body." He concentrated on the head, strumming it fast, his eyes low-lidded and his piston hips pushing, fucking.

I doused his chest, shoulders, throat as I cried out, laughing because I had no fucking idea how he could still be talking. I was barely breathing, more like moaning.

His mouth ran away with him. "Aw yeah. Feels so good, god-damn tight, honey. Fuck *FUCK!*" My orgasm, my joy squeezed him inside and he practically screamed, coming inside me. "I love you! I LOVE YOU!"

I stopped laughing then.

Dropping onto me, his hands ranged over my face and his lips found mine. He said it again. This time quietly, tenderly. "I love you, Caspar."

Not exactly the way I thought it would go down but...*damn*. My stomach clenched, and my heart crowded my chest. Our mouths met in a soft kiss.

"*Shh,* honey." He swiped under my eyes, staying against me, a jumble of arms and legs. The pounding of our hearts slowed to a gentler pace.

Those words, in his voice, replaced the fear, the huge hole of hate and hurt that always left me hungry and haunted.

Curling around him, I tucked my lips to his neck, blowing away strands of hair until I met his skin. I kissed the little divot there for a long time, listening to his deep breaths, the ones pulling my arms tight across his chest.

I couldn't say it back yet even though I felt the words swelling inside me. All I could do was hold on to his love, hold on to him.

*   *   *

A blast of wind sheared across my face the same time as Blondie said, "We're not gonna make it."

We'd pushed ourselves to the limit, tromping over bleak mountains, splashing through icy streams, staying one step ahead. The love we'd shared two nights ago was the only thing keeping us warm anymore. Lack of food added to hardly sleeping had taken its toll.

"They're gainin' on us."

The cold teeth of a gale-force wind spat fat plops of rain over us. *And fuck you very much, Mother Nature.*

Breaking from the headlong run, I clasped my knees, squinting at him. "What did you say?"

We couldn't outrun anymore. We might outlast, but it was imperative to get to the Outpost, still another two days' travel away, before them, before rumors—or real truths—wrecked our reputations.

"We need a plan."

"Well, you're handy with strategies."

"You're the commander," he volleyed.

As I clasped the back of my head, the steady beat of rain pissed on the very last shred of *Holy fuck. Nathaniel "Blondie" Rice loves me.*

And it wasn't the normal kind of rain we had in Alpha. It was a pelt of ice forming rivulets down my face and into the neck of my jacket. "Odds ain't bad."

His smile cantered, dimples showing. "Ain't?"

"You're growing on me."

"Odds ain't in our favor, either."

I stamped my feet. "It's all in the prep work."

Our hearing split between the incoming storm and the oncoming recon troops, we kept ahead until nightfall, gaining a couple hours.

No plastics, no explosives. Our guns were loaded and we had ample knives. I didn't know if Blondie had any experience slicing and dicing, but I didn't have time to show him the ropes. Maybe during all the *character building* atrocities his fucker of a father had put him through, he'd learned the right grip, stance, and thrust.

I took his direction when he found a deep pool of mud. It was chilly enough my nuts thought about taking a walk off my body and sending me a message on my D-P from warmer climes.

While we slathered up, going dark as night in deep-cover camouflage, he gave me a little lesson in the Freelanders. "They're classic Fifth Column in the Revolution."

"Fifth Column?"

His neat white teeth shone amid the black mud. "It's Old History."

"New history to me."

Sleet painted our black-out clothes to our bodies like a shitty second skin.

Checking his weapons, he said, "Fifth Columnists are saboteurs. Sympathizers."

"With the rebels, the Revolution?"

"Yeah. There's an underground movement goin' on, Caspar. You saw the Freelanders fighting with the rebels in Alpha. The same thing's happening throughout the InterNations; the two sides have joined up against the Company."

"You have anything to do with that?"

He settled against a tree trunk and looked me over top to toe. He didn't say a word.

"We're not gonna report them."

"Nah."

"Ever."

"Nope."

"They're your family," I added.

"Part of it." He slunk forward, only his eyes and lips uncovered. He rounded my waist with his forearm and brought me up sharp. "Half my life. You're the other."

"How'd you get Leon out?"

"I used the 'Cutler's mah daddy' card."

"Why the hell would you take that risk?"

"For you." He bent toward me. "But if I catch that boy askin' to give you a blow job one more time, all bets are off. I'd do the same for you." He held my face in his hands, coming away caked in more mud.

Again with the gut check. "I don't want you saving me."

"You worry too much."

"You don't worry enough."

"So, we gonna stand here until our dicks fall off and fight about it? Or are we gonna do somethin'?"

"You ready?"

"Affirmative."

We doubled back. It took us twenty minutes to catch up with the first crew of Corpsmen, the ones most uninjured by our little TNT tête-à-tête a week ago.

I signaled the numbers—five—and we circled to their rear.

The pouring shitstorm worked in our favor, rendering night visors null and void and noise undetectable. They were spaced out beautifully—at least they'd been taught that much—scoping back and forth through the thick woods.

At the end of the column, I tackled the rear guard without a sound, cold cocking him into oblivion and dragging him into the underbrush.

Blondie leapfrogged ahead and pulled the same number on the next soldier, his actions impressive and dangerously choreographed.

By the time we got to the lookout, we'd left a trail of his four comrades scattered behind. Tapping him on the shoulder, I flashed him a white smile amid the sea of black that was my warrior face, bringing my hand down on his wrist before he could grip his pansy-ass blaster.

Blondie's palm smothered the trooper's mouth while I asked, "We gonna have a problem with you, soldier?"

He shook his head, as much as he could from its position inside Blondie's heavy forearm.

"Good, because I need you breathing and talking."

He went over Blondie's shoulder like a rag doll, and I took one of the knocked-out douche bags on each of mine.

Blondie made our prisoners all nice and comfy with their hands and feet bound, their eyes blindfolded, and their mouths gagged while I fetched the last two twats.

Once everyone was tied to his own deluxe tree trunk, I hunkered in front of soldier number five, pulling a corner of the gag from his mouth. "Name?"

"Rast."

Fitting. Rast had a rat face. He looked exactly like vermin, the kind I had in my apartment, instead of a big blond dog or a goldfish.

"How many approaching, Rast?"

"Seven."

Pulling my KA-BAR along my palm, the metal pearling under freezing drops, I repeated the motion across his cheek. "That wasn't the original number. You need a mathematics lesson?" I flicked my blade over a few body parts he probably wouldn't miss—an ear, his nose, a finger—counting as I went.

He stuttered, "Twenty-five in total, b-b-but now it's twelve. Twelve took a hit. One of them had other orders."

"Twenty-five's an odd number."

"We were joined by a latecomer."

My eyes narrowed, but I didn't have time to question further. His D-P blared, "Need your position, Rast."

My forearm collared his neck and I sank beside him. "You give these coordinates and not one bit more and I won't slit your throat from ear to ear, soldier. You know your numbers now?"

A quick learner—even if he couldn't count for shit—he relayed the position, and I replayed the same move I'd started the night with, a crunching blow to his head sending him to la-la land.

The echo of heavy boots beat toward us. Things worked so well the first time, we went with the same welcome-party greeting.

One, two, and three down.

That's when things got a little hairy. Guns swiveled back, the sheen of wet bayonets showed up ahead, and the remaining four fuckers descended on us. I used my beloved KA-BAR in defense, knocking back gun barrels and slicing aside stabbing attempts.

Hand-to-hand got real fun as Blondie and I stood back-to-back, offering hurt with our hurtling fists and the hard heels of our boots. The sleet didn't roar loud enough to mute the meaty blows. Taking a massive fist to my cheek, I staggered sideways, spinning away from Blondie.

A foot crashing into my chest threw me onto my back and far above a face distorted by rain looked down on me. He wasted no time pulling his firearm, one of those useless plastic blasters. I wasted even less wrapping my arms around his thighs and pitching him over my head like I was tossing a bale of hay onto a pallet. His short flight ended in a disjointed landing, headfirst into a tree. Bonelessly, he dripped down to the forest floor and lay unmoving like a sack of soiled shit.

Jumping to my feet, I whipped the water from my eyes and halted with my hand half across my brow. Right then I rethought our decision to engage but not to kill.

Our old friend the lieutenant held his blade to Blondie's throat, steadily exerting more pressure until a drop of blood welled over the sharp edge, joining the rain in a red-colored river. "You wanna save your boyfriend?"

I focused on Blondie, the knife, and the cunt's intent. I nodded.

"Throw your knife down, kick it away, and lose the weapons."

Done deal.

Only thing was, Lieutenant Unlucky wasn't counting on my left-handed trick. While he pulled Blondie toward my KA-BAR, I lifted the extra strapped behind my back and sent it whizzing toward them. The point made contact, spiking Lieutenant's neck. He gurgled while Blondie ducked from his arms, came up behind him, and jacked my knife clean of the cut to another agonized scream.

Blondie aimed the blood-splattered shaft to his jugular, held my eyes, and sliced another clean line, dropping the man dead.

Cool, in control, and utterly lethal.

Fucking hot.

The rest went down like limp dicks.

Confiscating their supplies and weapons, we sorted through what was usable and secured the rest in a hidden location. Their D-Ps we destroyed. Blondie got his operational long enough to contact Hatch at Chitamauga, sending the details of the prisoners and their whereabouts. Whether or not the soldiers survived the next week or so out here, I didn't give a flying fuck.

His eyes pinched shut between his thumb and forefinger, Blondie shook his head. "Nah. No, not a good idea, man. Just tell her I love her. Yeah. Tell her Cannon's okay."

He ended the transmission, pulling me close, his cold nose against my throat. "We gotta go."

Running again, this time to warm up, I was hoping to outpace the foul weather, maybe find some frigging shelter or sunshine or something other than the howling rain making waterlogged soup inside our boots.

Muscles burning and eyes blinded, I had to take my mind off this hell. "You were good support back there."

I caught the blue tint of his eyes when he winked. "Not bad yourself. Told you I was more than a corporate whore." He panted beside me, feet pounding in time, but his next words were tender as his caresses. "Needed to have your back this time, big man."

Rain matted his hair and ran into his mouth with every word spoken. My heart wheeled in my chest as I slowed down. "How do you come up with that stuff?"

His arms rounded my shoulders, and I walked into his hug. "It's all you, Caspar."

I ducked my head from his intensely personal stare. "I'm not good enough for you."

"Got that right. You're better than me." The brush of his lips along the side of my throat was the only heat to be found in this godforsaken forest. "'Sides, can't believe you threw your precious knife into the mud like that."

"It was either that or watch you get your throat slit."

"Glad you've changed your priorities."

"You got no idea," I whispered into his neck,

We forged through the sleet until it made a dark mane of Blondie's hair. Our clothes were heavy, and we could no longer speak through clattering teeth. Finally, we broke free of the forest and faced a huge, squat building enclosed by two rows of pitchfork iron fences. "Fort Knox," he breathed.

I stopped short, revisited by nightmares.

My teeth started a new rhythm, chattering with more force.

Walking on, Blondie tested the iron barbs, eyeing the fence as if he were about to vault over. "C'mon, big man."

Along the square roofline speakers sat at even two-meter intervals. Rusty with age and disuse, they were the same as the ones that had once rung with the execution announcement. The placement of the dimmed halo lights was similar, too, to those radiating around the Quad in Epsilon. It had been a nighttime event, the Quadrangle opened to the public and filled with the ferocious atmosphere of brainwashed hate.

My knees buckled. "I'm not going in there."

Blondie returned to my side. "Didn't hear you, honey. What?"

Words stuck in my throat. "No. I can't."

"Can't what? Look, you're turnin' blue, for Christ's sake. It's been abandoned for a long time." I filtered out all but a few words. "Safe…shelter…rest…"

Close to passing out from pain, I reeled to the ground. All my running from the past and living with a barricade of razor wire between me and my feelings—me and life—had been pointless. One look at this place brought back a ghost I'd never laid to rest.

All it took was Blondie beside me, shaking me, grabbing my face and shouting at me. He seemed to have a way to make my heart crack apart with the eye opener that this mission, this trek was gonna end down the same heartbreak road as before, despite my best defensive maneuvers.

Here I was, face-to-face with the one damned memory I'd been running from, combined with the fucking thing I had no control over.

My heart.

I gagged. "I *cannot* go in there."

Chapter Fourteen

Blondie wouldn't be stopped. He hoisted me over the fences, chanting, "Just let me get you warm, big man."

He pulled some high-tech shit on the bronze locks of the double doors, making me wonder why he hadn't done the same on the gates instead of heaving me over.

Forty thousand and some odd hectares of former Fort Knox land had been left to Mother Nature after the mass destruction of the Purge, yet the interior of the last intact building—the Gold Depository—was Company clean. This one building, which had safe-housed the first of the Company's bullion and the last of the former United States of America, sat pristine and polished like a lopped-off pyramid amid a scavenged wasteland.

All but a few halos were turned off, and those few stabbed my body just the same as the deep brown of *his* eyes—soft, teasing, and laughing—until they'd become mere slits at the end.

The half-light of the stormy night shaded into the stronghold, lending to its eery atmosphere. I had my own specter keeping me company in the empty tomb.

The rain pounded outside.

Echoes of our boots resonated on marble floors, then silenced.

My heart rate resumed, raced. The way it had with the bass music my last time at the Amphitheater, my first time with Blondie.

I found a corner and sat, shuddering from cold and adrenaline, memories and fear.

A fireplace would have been handy, but I figured there wasn't one. That didn't stop Blondie as he went to work on a stack of Territory newspapers piled on a lone titanium desk. The broadsheets were from before the world went completely digitized. They were crumbling, unread, out of place.

I focused on the innocuous details: Blondie busting the dry slats of a wooden chair across his knee. The way he huffed his hair out of his eyes, eyes that searched for me.

Clapping his hands together, he bounced on his heels and tried to strike a light. "Gonna get you warm, Caspar."

I tried to ignore the pain driving me down with the same piercing pressure as the sleet outside until my neck was squished into the corner and my knees were at my chest.

I couldn't get warm.

I'd never get warm.

On the desk, newspaper relics curled in on themselves. I hadn't seen a broadsheet for such a long time; they'd been banned since the Plague. Lunging for one, I pulled it across my lap, tail ends of phrases coming away in my hands. *Plague! Viral contagion. Stay inside. Breeders unite!*

Rubbing my hand over pages, underlining hateful words, I concentrated on the black mark of ink on my palm and the pads of my fingers spreading to join the stain in my soul.

Blondie blew into the fire he built in the middle of the barren floor, the stigma spreading—sparks, ash, scattered words. When the newspapers burst into flame, a batch of burning headlines caught my eyes: *Thousands Dead. Don't Be One of Them. Embrace the Straight.*

I'd represented all of that knowing I was not a single part convinced, simply because I was weak enough to need some semblance of family after mine died. My stomach churned. The only thing to force down was my empty gut, and I kept swallowing the burning acid.

Blondie wisped his fingertips over my face and hauled me onto his lap. "What's goin' on?"

My throat was dry. "You said *your Leon.*"

"Did I? I don't recall."

"That day, when Leon was taken to the brig in Alpha, right after I was assigned to you, that's when you said it."

"It's just a figure of speech. I don't see what that's got to do with anything." He turned a confused expression on me.

The slush of foul weather outside and the fire hissing at our feet were the only sounds around us until I made myself speak. "What you said, what you implied was belonging with someone, caring for someone. Before you, I'd spent too much time alone, making sure none of that shit happened to me again." The fort surrounding us made all the memories rush back at me. "I was in Epsilon, at a training camp. I'd never wanted to return to that Territory. In my head, Erica lived on, but once there I couldn't escape the fact she was dead. Then I met someone."

His jaw tightened; the comforting caress of his hands up and down my arms ceased.

"I never had Leon, never wanted him that way. He wasn't mine, but Alejandro was."

Blondie dipped his eyes, but not before I saw the pain scuttling across the deep blue of his irises. "Alejandro?"

The possessive, painful feelings dredged up from my past bore down on me. "*My Alejandro.* My lover. My first love."

He took his hands from me, first from my shoulders, then from my chest where breaths cranked out of me. His hands slipping down my thighs, he stood up and withdrew to the opposite wall. A look of twisted hurt made mealtime of his handsome face.

"You wanted to know this," I said.

He shook his head, planting his feet in front of himself. His hair streamed wetly down to his shoulders, his big body steaming from the fierce fire beside him. "Don't think I do anymore."

I wouldn't be shut down. "Alejandro was beautiful and brave in a way I'd never seen. He had no allegiance. Not him." I spared a look at Blondie. I wished I hadn't. He looked as sick as I felt.

Yet I couldn't stop my smile. "He wasn't a Corpsman. He had ties only to himself and then me. He was half rebel, half Freelander, and completely mine."

"Caspar, please don't—"

I couldn't stop my confession, no matter his plea. "I met him during my off time. He lived on the edge of poverty, same as Leon and Evangeline. But hardship didn't touch him. He was tall, true, and hard bargaining. I'd been in need of a pick-me-up." I curled my fist in a stroking motion. "My hand wasn't cutting it anymore. I just went trawling for a toy, a cock sleeve or something. Hell, I didn't know. It was my first time going to one of those gigs. I never imagined I'd come away with a man." I chuckled. "He overheard me haggling and stopped me from taking out my money, saying, 'Think we can get you something better than that, *Papi?*'

"One look and I was a goner. His eyes dark brown, his skin deeply tanned, he damn near glowed. I was a couple years older, but when he invited me back to his place, I felt so fucking unschooled.

"It was a squat, pretty much like mine but overflowing with stuff. Every corner, every table piled with crap—and a lot of damn tables. I was always knocking into one of them, making a mess of his collections of old photographs and his formations of film canisters and ancient cameras. He'd always grin and say, *'No mas.'*

"A photographer, he used cameras going by the names of Pentax and—he really laughed when he showed me these others—Canon. His thing wasn't landscapes but men. Pornography, the Company labeled his artwork. That first day he kissed me stupid, then asked to take my picture—not to sell, but to keep. I was so fucking into him, I said yes. Being with Alejandro, naked while he snapped my shots, was one of the most erotic experiences of my life."

I closed my eyes but didn't miss Blondie's agitated groan. I wouldn't torture him. I wouldn't tell him all of it. I thought of lying with Alejandro in my arms, his short black hair silky against my chest, his head always resting over my heart so when he talked to me in low Spanish words, they were imparted on my skin, seeping into my spirit.

"Man, I was such a fucking romantic with him." A short laugh escaped me. "Sappy as hell." The time I made him stay still for hours so I could map his body, his muscles, his scent like those spices, Blondie's spices. When I was done loving him, I'd washed and covered him carefully before bringing us the forbidden street food he loved, little cakes called *magdalenas,* empanadas, olives, tapas of all kinds. I fed him one by one.

Rubbing my hand down my face, I stayed in that memory, just for a minute. It was better than the ones to come. "We laughed so much, pretending the risk to our lives didn't exist. We loved so hard. He called me *dulce.*" I'd blushed all the way to my hairline when he told me what that meant; for him I was sweet.

I risked a glance at Blondie. He was rigid, his lips clamped together, breathing fast through his nostrils. "We wanted more. I wanted more. I was green back then. It's unbelievable, the shit I pulled to see him, how fast I fell in love with Alejandro."

At Blondie's choking noise, I threw out my hand. "Come here."

"No." He backed further against the wall. "No. I'm all right, Caspar. It's okay."

Obviously it wasn't fucking hunky-dory, but I couldn't stop the onslaught. "I had more freedom of movement in those days. For almost a year and a half, I took every detail I could to Epsilon; Command helpfully chalked it up to administrative closure with my family's deaths. It wasn't ideal, seeing him only every few months, and we didn't dare communicate by any other means. Shit. I was pretty sure I'd go knocking on his door one day and he'd be gone." I shook my head, a head swarming with happy memories.

"He was always waiting." His bronzed skin, his bright smile, his arms around me as soon as the door shut. "He wasn't perfect, though, not by a long shot. Some of the stunts he pulled plain pissed me off. Like taking a gamble with his life every time he did his illegal wheeling and dealing. Not that he had a choice. No way was he Corps or CO material."

I pushed a finger against the grin working at my lips. "The other things, they were irritating but so endearing. All his goddamn crap, all over his tiny two-roomer. You know how I like my shit, Nathaniel."

His head popped up when his given name slipped through my lips. Rocking forward, he nearly reached out to me, nodding. "Neat. Spare. Tidy."

Yeah, he knows me.

"Alejandro was anything but. Dishes, pictures, books, up to my eyeballs, his rooms full of so much stuff that one time I just blew. Alejandro came right back at me. Man, he had a hot temper. *'What you wan' me to do? Throw eet out? Like thees'* He started to rip through a photograph, and I just laughed and stopped him. All it took was one touch to cool his anger, to heat him in another way.

"I was being careful. Yeah." I snorted. "I'm still trying to convince myself of that one. It didn't ring true then, and it sure as hell doesn't now." My voice grew harsh. "Just because I wore civilian clothes so I wouldn't be recognized, what the fuck kind of half-assed precaution was that? Someone caught on. Two men spending a lot of alone time hit a homophobic radar. Probably should've been thankful it hadn't happened sooner."

His lips pursed, Blondie's face leeched of all color.

"*Mi corazón*, Alejandro called me." On my heels in front of Blondie, I gave it all up. "The hard rap on his door was so loud, he pushed me off his lap. He punched me, mouthing, 'Get the fuck out, *malparido!*'

"Not *corazón*, not his heart, but *malparido*, bastard." I retched on the huge dry sobs clogging my throat. "He threw me out the back door. *Cholo. Gringo.*"

Blondie squatted down with me. "You don't have to say it, honey."

"Yeah, I do." My heart was breaking, but I had to get it all out. "I hid across the street. He was taken into custody, cursing all the way, earning Christ only knows what torture for his hot Spanish temper. I should never have left him! I should've given myself up."

I punched the wall until the skin on my knuckles broke and blood joined the stains inside me, fighting off Blondie's arms. "No one's ever taking the fall for me again. No one."

That tic in Blondie's jaw twitched like he was about to argue with me. I shouldn't have let Alejandro do it, and no way hell would I ever let Blondie. A man could live with only so many hateful regrets.

I cut him off before he could even start. "I don't know what they did to him. I only knew what was gonna happen when I saw it on my D-P the next morning." Gripping Blondie's face in my hands, I asked, "Don't you see? He turned himself in. For me!

"This place"—I slashed through the air—"out there." I pointed beyond the walls to the courtyard. "Those spotlights and speakers and the setup. It's exactly like the Quad in Epsilon Territory."

He pushed himself right against me, taking me in his arms. "Stop. Please stop, Caspar."

"I can't. I can't. Not until it's over." I shivered inside my clothes, wishing there was enough heat to reach my bones, to deliver me from this pain. "When the curfew was lifted, hundreds of people crushed into the square, hungry for a spectacle, anything to break up the daily grind. Street vendors brought their wares and fare; there was the stink of meat and the smell of too many bodies. It was downright festive like the CO meant it to be."

I still tasted the stench behind my teeth. "Sensationalism at its best, right? The big wide-screen D-Ps panning the mob, focusing on raised fists and shouting mouths."

Blondie brought me between his legs, holding me close.

"Yeah, they wanted to make an example of him. They did it well. Alejandro was marched through the throng, and at one point he was so close I could've touched him." Openly crying, I dug around for my voice. "I could've touched him one last time."

Next to me, Blondie cursed, quiet and fierce.

"He forewent the trial. For me. I will not be put in that spot again, so don't you goddamn ask me to love you. Don't protect me. Stupid fucking—" Heaving into Blondie's neck, I bit out, "Alejandro. Before they covered his face in the black hood, his goddamn beautiful face, his eyes found mine, his mouth moved. '*Caspar, te amo, mi corazón.*'"

Blondie's face was stormy as the night outside. I figured I looked the same, with a healthy dose of guilt mixed in. The kind that always kept me company.

"When the countdown began—a countdown for fuck's sake—the

whole crowd chimed in. The speakers weren't even necessary because everyone was just so fucking keen to see him do the hanging dance." The words were forced from me, heinous things hollowing me out, leaving me the shell I'd been before I started this journey with Blondie.

"His nose covered, finally his lips. His head held so high." Tears wet my face. "The last thing I did for Alejandro was bear witness to his execution."

I'd watched his murder until his feet stopped twitching. Until he stilled, his voice never to be heard again, his heart no longer beating in time with mine. Trembling all over, I put the lid back on all the visions that had made my sleep a recipe for night terrors unless I was wrapped around Blondie.

Some cruelties couldn't bear the light of day.

Drops of sleet had melted on Blondie's face, glistening in his stubble, reflecting the orange firelight. But his eyes held no life. They were bleak blue stones. He was gonna talk, and I didn't want to hear it, whatever he had to say. Not yet.

"He's the reason I opted out of life. Want to know the most fucked-up thing? Alejandro would've loved the commune, man. That was his scene. He should've been there, not me. He's the reason I started getting it."

His hand slid up my arm to my shoulder; his fingertips ghosted my chin and fell away. "He must've been a good man for you to love him so much." He struggled, his face torqued in torment. "I...ah, damn it all. I envy your love for him."

I studied my palms, the smearing black ink surface damage only. I took a hit of air, then another. The dark blemish in my heart lifted, taking with it the hidden scars that had numbed my emotions for so long. I felt lighter for telling someone about Alejandro, for letting go of our brutal fate, for remembering the moments when we were so right together.

I drew Blondie to me, my arm around his back. His shoulders shook, his whole body was quaking. "Hey."

He didn't respond, his face turned in the opposite direction.

"Hey, baby." I touched his cheek.

He jerked away.

"Nathaniel, what's wrong?"

He staggered to his feet. Face red, he admitted, "Jesus Christ, Caspar. You still love him." He raked his hair forward. "That's why you couldn't say it to me the other night. You love Alejandro."

With his hair pulled over his face, he tried to close a curtain between me and his emotions.

Not gonna happen, baby.

I laughed in a way I'd forgotten. Loud and from my stomach that was suddenly unknotted. "You're really a stupid shit sometimes, aren't you?"

He sputtered, "Cannon—"

Stalking forward, I was filled with intent. "Caspar. My name's Caspar."

The kiss I gave him shot straight to my toes and right through the roof of my head. Deep into his mouth, my tongue was all over his. I tried not to whine when he slicked the insides of my lips.

He pushed me back, pivoting away.

Like that was gonna put me off. His heartbeat sped beneath my forearms crossing over his chest from behind. His damp tendrils brushing my neck, I sniffed at his throat, licked a throbbing vein. "'Course I love him. I always will." Still as a tree caught in that breathless moment between standing and falling, he made no noise. "He taught me to love."

His attempts to wrangle away stopped when I nuzzled his jaw. "Losing him, that's why I couldn't feel anymore. That's why I didn't want to love you."

"I see."

"No, you don't. You know, you're not as smart as you think."

Swiveling in my arms, his eyelashes swept across flushed cheeks. "Caspar…"

I pulled his hand to my heart, where the beats thundered for him. "Doesn't mean I can't love another. I love *you*, Nathaniel."

He froze for maybe an instant, but it felt like hours. Maybe I'd misheard him the other night. Was I a fling to him? Had I gotten this all messed up in my head? *Aw shit.* "Think you could say something here?"

His lips were parted, his hair messy, his expression challenging. *Here we go.*

I grinned.

"You just told me not to ask you to love me, you fuck."

"Yeah, I'm not so good with words." I uncurled his fingers from the fist balled at his hip. "Not real good with emotions, either." I pulled; he pulled away harder.

So not happening.

He strained from me. "You're just figuring that out?"

I kissed the corner of his lips. "Nah. Just thought you should know, babe."

He yanked again to free his hand. "What are ya' sayin'?"

I'm not going anywhere, baby.

"I might be a big dumb asshole." I shrugged when he muttered something that sounded like agreement under his breath. "But I love you, Nathaniel. *Blondie.* And I'm pretty sure you love me, too." When he opened that luscious mouth again, it was to bend down and slam it onto mine. His kiss was better than words. Breaking away for a second, he skipped his lips to my ear. "I never thought I'd hear you say that, Caspar."

"Get used to it."

That quiet unsure interlude lasted another few seconds, and then we were all about the kissing. Wild kisses where our noses bumped, our teeth scraped against tongues, and our mouths bruised. Blinded by those intense kisses and his intimate moans, I thrust my hands between us and scrabbled with the button of my pants.

The wet cloth was a bitch to work with. Stuck to my groin, suctioned onto my thighs.

Elegantly stripping down in front of me, he raised an eyebrow as I hopped on one foot. "Need a hand there, big man?"

"Fuck you." My boots banged against the wall when I threw them, echoing across the empty room.

"Please do."

I couldn't get at him fast enough. Tackling him to the floor, I strained above him, so erect my cock danced against his in midair.

"I'm gonna make love to you, Blondie."

"Oh, are ya?" That damned arched eyebrow of his daring me.

"Damn right," I growled, rolling him onto his hands and knees.

He moved so sensually, his ass raised in my hands, my cock dividing his tight buttocks and running along the seam. I drew my hand up the musculature of his back, rubbing his shoulders, using them for leverage while I rode outside on the crease of his ass.

I needed lube, wanted him sleek and ready, and to hear that wet slurp when I entered him. With a kiss to his spine, I whispered, "Just getting us wet, sweetheart."

"*Mmm,*" he hummed, my fingertip dipping inside.

Adding more drops, I massaged my fingers together inside him and gasped when he squeezed around me. "So good, baby. You're gonna take me so good tonight."

Sucking in a breath when I massaged his swollen gland, he exhaled with a hiss, "*Yes,* I'm ready for you."

"Yeah, you are." I breathed into his ear. "But I gotta make this hard cock nice and slick for you."

"Fuck."

"Soon. And once I start, I'm not gonna stop." I smiled while he squirmed beneath me, making sure he heard the cap opening and the slippery sounds of me jerking off behind him, my harsh breaths on his neck.

He arched below me and I patted his ass with my cock. I leaned over and interlaced our fingers. "I'm right here with you, babe."

"Okay," he rasped.

Not good enough.

I flipped him onto his back and cupped his face. "Nathaniel, I am right here, only with you." I watched his eyes as they opened and blinked slowly. "Every time we've been together, it's been you."

His hands wandered from my hair to my ass to my thighs; then he opened the taut curves of his bottom to me.

Teasing his rosy star with the crown of my cock, I vowed, "I love you, Nathaniel fucking Blondie Rice."

He rose to capture my lips. "You say the sweetest things."

I slapped his sweet ass. "Now you say it."

"Already did." He smirked.

Painting his ass in precome and wedging a finger deep inside, I demanded, "Again. Before I make love to you."

"*Ahhh*, I love you, Caspar! You cocky motherfucker."

I took my time reacquainting myself inside his warm clasp. "So tight, babe. Gonna have my tongue inside you tonight, too."

Fully sheathed, I stopped. His was a burning grip surrounding my dick and making my nads tingle. With every thrust, I bit him lightly. Nipping his shoulder, his wide ribs, the underside of his biceps. I pinched his nipples and his hole seized around me.

I thrust to the hilt, circling my hips inside his warmth, waiting for his welcome gasp before pulling out all the way. Watching his bottom close, I opened it again, spellbound by the sight of him spreading around the head of my cock and sucking me in. Over and over again until my preejaculate squished in his ass and foamed at my base and a sheen of sweat covered our muscles.

He was shaking and gritting his teeth, thrashing with each thrust. "Feel so good like this."

Lowering until I was completely on top of him, I held his head off the floor and kissed him with slow, soft tastes. "You make me good."

Faster, harder, I drove him across the floor until he braced his hands against the wall, shoving back onto my cock and wrenching grunts from me. His gorgeous dick rammed into my stomach every time his ass hit my hips. His pubes rasped my groin, and mine scoured his full pink balls.

"You gonna come like this?" I spoke in a rumble that came from so deep within me.

He didn't answer, frantically forcing his body up to mine. I slowed down.

"Ahh, Jesus! Don't stop. Faster. Fuck me fast, honey!"

I pounded into him and held still. "Answer me."

"Yes!" That affirmative led to a litany of others when I resumed a furious pace. "Yes, yes, yes."

I found his mouth and sucked on his lips. His shaft grew, his testicles compacting, and I followed suit, my orgasm called by his. Eruptions of come coiled between us. We were sticky all over with seed and sweat. After I licked him clean, he kissed me, making his body the bed I fell asleep on, his arms and legs the blanket keeping me warm.

Sometime during the night the sleet tapered off and with its diminishing patters we stopped worrying. We started feeling safe for the first time since we'd left Chitamauga. We talked in whispers about our future but not how we were gonna make it happen. We traded hopes about how our lives were going to be when we returned to the commune, with friends and family. I didn't believe it for a second, but I could do that make-believe thing, for one night, for him.

"After I find Liz."

"After we find Liz." He pulled me into a sleepy embrace.

Chapter Fifteen

Quitting the fort the next morning, we dragged ass on purpose. After our lovemaking, after admitting my love for him, I could've run all day, I was so refreshed, but I preferred to dally. So did he.

The weather, flowers, and wildlife—none of it registered on that final day. All that mattered was a series of moments, flashes of what could be that I wanted to record on my D-P, preserve in color, savor forever.

Walking across a meadow that never woke from its frosty slumber, we held hands. His fingers tightening around mine, Blondie closed the gap between us. Our footsteps crunching to a stop, we turned together, not to face a new danger, but each other. I ran my fingertips over his whiskers so bright in the sunlight, warm to my touch. When I kissed his jaw, the rasp of his stubble stung my lips as it had the first time I'd kissed him. His mouth held the freshness of blossoms and something so much more sensual. I hummed when our tongues danced and groaned when his arched to the top of my mouth.

We walked on, his head on my shoulder and my arm around his waist, our thighs brushing, smiles permanent on our faces.

At midday he was whistling. Van Morrison, I assumed. It was light and lilting like birdsong.

"I regret the time I spent hating you, baby."

His whistling ceased.

"We had it so easy, those first couple of weeks, didn't we?"

He blew the hair from his eyes. "Well, I wouldn't say easy, big man."

"But it could've been, if I hadn't been so suspicious. I wasted so much time with you." I blinked quickly to rid myself of visions of what-if.

Plucking a twist of grass, he chewed on the stem, regarding me. "I don't regret it. You wouldn't be Caspar otherwise, if you'd just hopped into the sack with me."

He ambled on, song on his lips and his hand reaching back, waiting for mine.

Lunch was gruel, aka canned crap, that we'd picked up from the soldiers to replenish our supplies. Our table was a cool carpet of moss, my seat Blondie's lap, and the view a little stream beside us.

He was less than impressed. "Tastes like a bag of nasty after a tank's backed over it."

I took another big mouthful of the nondescript shit. "Yup."

"How can you stomach it?"

I moved to sit in front of him, my knees bent over his, my feet planted beside his hips. "Reckon it was all I knew before you. I didn't really care much about food or other pleasures at the time." I shrugged, chewed, swallowed. "Only enough to survive on."

"You're not just surviving now." He replaced my raised spoon with his warm lips.

"Not with you."

Too few hours later, dusk threatened.

"Your hair is getting shaggy," he mentioned.

"So's yours."

"You like it."

I grinned, not about to deny that.

"And you need a shave," he added.

"You gonna tell me I smell like shit next, Blondie?"

Sniffing along my collarbone, he licked the hollow there. "You smell so good. All man. Musky, natural, you always smell fresh from a good fuck."

Well, that made me horny. I dropped my pack and pushed his off, too, ready to march him to the next solid tree trunk and take him. He shook his head, holding up a hand to ward me off. I halted when he squatted over my pack, purely because his ass was my wet dream come to life not because he'd ordered me to.

He pushed stuff around, digging deeper. Coming up with my shaving soap and straight blade, he launched a smile. "Can't do anything about your hair right now, but you don't like not being clean shaven. Let me."

Making a fire, warming water, layering my throat, cheeks, and chin in foam, he straddled me. "Now, keep your hands to yourself. You get me worked up, I'm liable to slip."

I bit my lip to keep from laughing and bit my tongue to keep from groaning when he cupped the nape of my neck and dragged the blade through lather until it hit the corner of my mouth.

My lips tilted; my hips swiveled.

He sat back. "Like to live dangerously, do ya?"

"Wouldn't be here otherwise." I positioned his blade at my throat.

"Good thing I love you, then, ain't it?"

Oh, man, it really is.

He shaved me, taking his sweet time, kissing my clean skin, making it tingle.

"That's nice."

"What is?"

"Being taken care of."

"Hmm."

He mopped up the last of the lather, laying a warm cloth over my face. "I'll always take care of you, you know?"

"A few more hours and we'll be at the Outpost."

"Uh-huh," he agreed, "and there could still be one other operator out here. Anonymous number thirteen."

"Yeah." I wiped my chin and looked around for my shirt.

Blondie wet his lips. "We can spare one more night."

Hell yeah.

*   *   *

"What's that?" I eyed the present he set in front of me.

"Why don't you open it and find out instead of watchin' like you think it's one of my bombs set to go off in your face?"

We hadn't moved from the copse beside the stream where he'd shaved me. The night fell around us, a bright pattern of cold-weather stars turned into crystals high above.

"Well, it's too small to be a flower."

Heaving a long sigh, Blondie rested the back of his head on the ground. "You could just open it, Caspar."

I remembered how anxious I'd been over the cuff I'd given him. I was equally nervous now. My stomach ranging through dips and rolls, I fingered the newsprint he'd wrapped the gift in. He must've taken it from Fort Knox.

"Is there a message here?" I peeled back the paper, letters swimming before my eyes.

He peered at me. "Yeah, there's a damn message. Fuckin' open it already."

The thing rolled out into my hand. Heavy, metal, round. A ring. It warmed in my palm.

"You gonna look at it?"

I'd seen it on his forefinger. A thick band that was worn and rounded on the edges. It broadened to the Rice family's Landowner crest, a spray of grain engraved inside the oval. I held it up, admiring the workmanship, unable to slip it on. When a glint of firelight hit the inside of the band, I blew a fine line of breath between my lips.

Everything.

In simple script, inside the ring. No initials, no date. No beginning, no end. Just me and him, endlessly.

Holy shit.

"That there was my granddaddy's. He'd have wanted you to have it."

I couldn't fathom that. What Territorian in his right mind would want his grandson to hook up with the likes of me? But he hadn't been a citizen, hadn't even had the chance to become a Freelander. Hamme Rice had been the last of a massacred breed, the Landowners.

I closed my fist around the ring, bringing it to my chest.

"Now it's yours, same as me."

"I can't." I put it on the ground between us.

A small smile etched the corner of his mouth. He didn't pick up the ring. "What was all that before, huh?"

"Guess I'm not as graceful at accepting gifts as you."

"Ya don't say."

My heart hammering in my chest, I snatched the ring back and sat on my heels. It looked so light, but it was heavy with meaning. I slipped it onto the first finger of my right hand; the band didn't make it past my knuckle.

"Try your left hand." He'd come closer and his knees butted mine.

"What?"

Sitting up real straight and real still, he tugged on my fingertip. "Ring finger, left hand."

"A promise ring." The words scraped my throat.

"An engagement, if you'll have me." He slipped the ring over my fingertip and stopped there, a question in that one small gesture.

In answer, I rolled the band all the way down, my heart banging.

There should've been celebrations. Instead, after a long kiss, he ducked his head. "We're contracted now."

I pushed up his chin. "Don't say it like that."

"Like what?"

"Like you want to shake my hand to seal the deal instead of *asking* for my hand." I wondered when I'd exchanged my manhood for girly worries. "Like I'm a business transaction." My short thumbnail already catching on the ring in a motion I could easily see becoming habitual, I frowned. "If the only reason you're giving me this is because you know we're screwed, then you can take it back."

I started twisting off the ring, but he stopped me.

"I want you to be mine, Caspar. You know that. But I need you safe first."

"So this is how you propose?"

"No. This is how I make sure you stay alive, so I can be with you again."

Frustration and futility overrode the joy I'd felt when he'd made it clear he wanted me long term. "So you think I'm gonna do what you tell me because of this piece of metal?"

I just want a minute to kiss him. I want this cracked-up thing between us to be a sacred union, not a commodity for safe-keeps.

"Let me go in alone."

I shot that idea right down. "Not gonna happen."

"Please."

"No fucking way."

"Fine." He rubbed his eyes. "You finish your escort detail; then you're gonna turn right back around after debrief and disappear. You hear me?"

"No."

"Why are you so pigheaded? I have to fight you on everything?"

"Yeah, maybe you do, baby." I sank back to my ass and tinkered with the ring. "So what does this really mean, then?"

"It means you'll remember me."

"I don't want to remember you, and I'm not very good at waiting. I want to have you."

"Don't be a stubborn ass. I can't do my job if I'm worrying about you." His words were a shock of cold water thrown in my face.

"Funny. Worrying about you *is* my job," I scathed.

At loggerheads over nothing we could control, we went to our separate corners—or trees—boxing with our own demons. Me with a ring and a promise, him with a leather cuff and my heart.

Eventually we came together for one last mealtime. We didn't talk, but touched, apologies in our fingers as we ate from each other.

The fire smoldered to glowing ashes, but the one inside me remained ignited, burning high. Our backs against a fallen log, I had my arm around his waist, and his was draped over my shoulder. Our boots tapped together and the November stars shone like jewels.

I couldn't keep my mouth shut. "Well, this was a nice vacation."

He rolled his head to the side, squinting at me until I squirmed.

His fingers finding mine, his boots stilled and he made me look at him. "You know we're more than that."

I remained silent, kicking over the ember of a log.

We'd been together through bitterness, suspicion, battle, and into something like bliss.

It didn't goddamn matter. "You're fucking Company, man."

"What if I wasn't?"

"Quit dicking me around."

"I'm not." Exasperation tinged his voice.

Strapping my arms around myself so I wouldn't touch him, I glared at the sparks dying out in front of us.

"So, you think this is our last night together, huh?" he asked.

"I think our outcome at the Outpost looks pretty frigging grim."

"You just gonna waste it glarin' at me?" He stood, stripping down. "Or are you gonna fuck me?"

At his call to action, I shed my clothes and wrapped my arms around his thighs, tumbling him on top of me.

Our lovemaking was a passionate mixture of motions and emotions.

My tongue flattened up his shaft until I hit his round head. Wrapping my mouth over him, my deep suck was punctuated by his sharp groan. "Not goin' anywhere, honey."

I danced down his erection, grunting when he positioned my thighs next to his head. Rough hands guided my hips over his face until my cock parted his lips. He held my butt firmly apart and let me fuck his sweet pink mouth.

Rubbing my cheek against his saliva-wet cock, I managed, "I'm not gonna lose you, Nathaniel."

Lifting my head, I looked underneath me, along his body. The head of my cock perched at his mouth, his tongue snaking around me. I pushed off of him and spun around, replacing my mouth with my fingertips, slick and ready to open him.

His head shake sent strands of dark blond hair into my eyes. "Not goin'"—he ran his lips up my jaw until he found my mouth—"anywhere."

I took his nipples, his belly button, the trail of fine hair between my teeth, slithering between his legs. My tongue joining my fingers, I dipped inside, moaning at his taste and tight hole. Two fingers, my tongue thrusting, his channel dilated.

As he pulled me up his body, we joined. In heat, in need, and…*oh fuck,* in love.

I slanted all the way inside, my hands tangled in his hair, our breath shared. His lips and tongue spoke a language that needed no translation. *Pure desire.* His words inside my head, his big body spread below me, his slick hole taking me harder.

Not leavin' you. Ever.

His arms curled around my back, fingers pressing into my muscles. Our chests strived together while our bodies writhed, hips, bellies, thighs, and cocks. The flat slick slide of tongues tasting, flicking, sucking.

I squeezed and stroked him, his cock bolting in and out of my fist and his voice cracked like it always did when he was ready to come. "Anything, I'll give you anything, Caspar!" He grabbed my biceps and tilted up to take the full force of my rapid thrusts.

"Anything?" I sucked his nipple until he cranked his pelvis higher, grinding into me.

"Everything, Caspar."

Oh fuck, fuck!

His ass bore down on me as he came with a surge of power bending him near in half.

A few sharp thrusts later, I yelled, "Yeah, yeah!" rocketing off inside of him. "Oh fuck yeah, baby." I blindly smoothed the sweaty strands of hair from his temples. "Everything."

"Nothin' wrong with us, honey," he said softly.

The moon drowsed above us. I no longer heard the soft padding feet of nighttime foragers, and the birds went to sleep, too, but we stayed awake. The roughened pads of his fingertips rubbed the back of my neck, and I almost goddamn purred.

"Tell me what you wish for, honey."

On my elbow, I traced the sexy curve of his bottom lip. "As in birthday wish?"

"Mmm-hmm."

Rolling onto my back, I crossed my arms behind my head and looked up. *Stars. Sky. Freedom.* I looked at him. Blondie. Nathaniel. My lover. My heart expanded with hope I couldn't afford now and that I'd never fathomed seven weeks ago at the Amphitheater.

"A life I can be proud of. It doesn't have to be peaceful or easy." I turned sideways and whispered, "I want to remember this feeling. I want to *feel*." Pursing my lips over his quickly, I added, "I want to be allowed to love you."

His throat moved, but nothing came out.

"I wish for the same thing I wanted the night of my birthday. You. More of you. Endless days and nights with you." My mouth trembled, the ring on my finger a watery vision.

I watched those steadfast stars and knew they were in my eyes right then. "I love you, Blondie."

That seemed to be good enough for him, because after our days of running, nights of loving, he fell asleep with a smile on his lips.

Having no fondness for sleep myself, I stayed awake just to watch him, touching him with the most loving light caresses so he wouldn't wake. Dawn would come. It always did, and I'd already forfeited too much time with him.

*   *   *

Morning started out shitty with snow. It could've been pretty—all the white fluffy flakes falling into pristine mounds, unmarred by the touch of people—if I didn't feel like I was walking toward the type of hell even the Love Hovel with all its garish delights couldn't compare with.

We were so close to the Outpost, I could taste hate and distrust in the air. Or maybe that was just me being a bitch about the snow on my tongue and coating my eyelashes.

The closer we got, the further me and Blondie distanced ourselves.

Seven fateful weeks. Eight hundred kilometers. From Alpha Territory in the southeastern block of the former United States, through the Wilderness on a winding path. Our pit stop at the commune felt like years ago. The Outpost wasn't situated in any of the Territories, yet it belonged to the InterNations. To the Company. Northwest of that magnificent mountain range people three generations ago called the Appalachians.

Eventually, the path we trod turned into a narrow road cleared of fallen snow. It must've been the work of Outpost people, so recent only a thin dusting of the white stuff puffed under our boots, drilling together, *Left, left, left right, left…*

Underbrush and rubble had long since been bush-hogged. This pathway was well maintained, pointing toward civilization. The kind I now hated, the type I'd have to mold myself into once more.

In about half an hour.

We walked forward, hands linked across the space separating us until the walkway turned into a narrow paved road, salted against ice. Our fingers slipped away, hands falling to our sides. Clinking my Glock, the ring on my finger rang clear as a bell through the drifting white hush.

We approached wicked steel gates looming five meters high. Regulation razor wire, speakers, gun towers, halo lights—all the usual tricked-out accessories—emphasized their evil presence.

My breaths came faster; my feet slowed to a halt. "Thank you for the ring, baby."

His smile was so pure. "Promise ring. Remember that." Shaking the snow from his hair, he started toward me. "Caspar, I—"

The gates groaning inward cut him off.

The sixteen Territory flags all flapping in the wind was the sight I focused on as the gates opened. I didn't know why they bothered. It was a waste of fabric, if you asked me. They were all the same from the insignia, colors, and of course, the slogo: *Regeneration, Veneration, Salvation.*

Close-circuit cameras dotted around the compound homed in for our close-ups displayed on the massive data screen bolted to the front of the Outpost building. Even out here in the heart of the Wilderness, you needed your daily mind-feed.

More of a mansion than a bunker, the Outpost itself was a bit too fucking swank for my liking. The building looked white, clean, and corrupt. The centerpiece was a big fat rotunda for big fat CO fuckers to preach their prohibitive publicity from, no doubt. On either side, two wings came forward in blocky marble shoulders, adding to the imposing atmosphere of the building. The architectural crap was kept to a bare minimum and the windows were one-way eyes, always on the lookout.

It had been called Greenbrier Bunker in Old History. Seeing as they'd pretty much bulldozed the green part into the ground, preferring cold concrete to nature, the new name for this secret locale was simply the Brier, as befitted the sweet-ass rumble-wire decorating the barricade. Aka the Outpost, or as I liked to call it—especially seeing all the weapons raised, locked, and loaded—Screwedville.

I finally dropped my sights to the semicircle of soldiers and higher-ups. They represented an odd mix for a firing squad from crisp fatigues to pressed suits to—*Jesus Christ*——that thorn in my side, the blade to my shoulder, and now the noose around my neck.

Goddamn fucking Kale.

He just had to be unlucky number thirteen, the missing party from the recon unit.

Click, click, click.

That was all the pieces of this cunt of a puzzle coming together. Oh, and the sound of hammers cocked. I scanned over the guns pointed at us. *Correction.* They were all aimed at me. Turned out I was right to hold on to that last little splinter of suspicion.

Seeming at best like it was bunking it in the garrison for me as opposed to the CO suites for Blondie, I chanced a look at him. Suddenly he was unrecognizable, appearing to be all those things I'd thought about him up in Alpha CO HQ. Cold Company Blondie.

I didn't even think I could call him Blondie anymore. Maybe I'd change his nickname to Backstabbing Two-Faced Son of a Bitch. Or BTS for short.

When the pair of cuffs came out and five guards approached me, I definitely settled on his new name. My wrists were cinched so tightly inside the metal rings, my circulation went south and cuts opened immediately.

I couldn't decide whether to puke or laugh.

Maybe I'd just pass out until we got to the rope around my throat part.

"Commander Caspar Cannon of the Elite Tactical Unit, Alpha Territory, you are hereby charged with homosexual acts and wanton corruption of a Company officer."

Chapter Sixteen

Didn't that charge just lend a whole new level of hopelessness to this brand-new snafu?

I didn't even want to think about that motherfucking canary, Kale. I was waiting for him to break out in hoots and hollers; instead he settled on that chipped-tooth grin. And Jesus Christ, even the stupid notch in Kale's tooth made me think of Bl—Backstabber.

Man, this is gonna be a fun ride. Wonder if I can disembark early, if I cause enough trouble. Bypass the rest of the hell headed my way.

Snuggled between two soldiers, with one more in the lead and two at my rear, making my hackles rise, I was marched off. On the way to my dungeon-style digs, I caught a glimpse in one of those blacked-out windows. That shit was as reflective as a mirror. And who did I see? Blondie. With something skittering over his features—that formerly beloved face—something more human, less mask.

Probably just a trick of the light.

What wasn't an illusion at all was my appearance. I'd seen myself only through Blondie's eyes recently and figured I was still pretty handsome. Now I didn't look so hot. Face pale as snow.

Eyes empty in sockets dug deep in my skull. Though I would bet my appearance, reminiscent of being gutted by my own knife, was recent fallout care of Blondie's nonreaction to my arrest. But what are you gonna do?

Copying his stoicism, I gave away none of the turmoil inside.

Like how, behind my back, the ring was a brand of his betrayal, no longer a betrothal, weighing me down more than the heavy shackles cinching through the skin of my wrists. It was an effort to walk ramrod straight when my knees were halfway to buckling. In fact, it was an effort to move at all when my heart would rather just stop beating.

I imagined opulent halls inside the Brier, bursting with rich furnishings done up in those velvety fabrics from our caravan. Fragile chairs and long tables brimming with delicacies, vases overflowing with flowers. The bastards presented an austere exterior, cut from stone, grafted in hate, but they lived it up once out of the public eye. I had only to think of Blondie's taste for finery, his lavish spread in the heart of Alpha to know that.

What I got was a long walk around the compound to the brig. The garrison was low to the earth, as if it had been caught with its pants down and was unsuccessfully trying to pull them up. Built of rough-hewn granite blocks, crystal flakes shined amid the maudlin gray stone.

I learned it was so low because the bulk of the jail was a maze of underground tunnels going farther and farther south until it really did feel like I was walking into the mouth of hell itself. The halos skipped off; red lights flashed on, showing tunnels devoid of decoration, nothing to distract from the overwhelming sense of desolation. Cells were partitioned by thick walls slick with cool moisture and fungus spreading green fingers into the grout. Iron bars in narrow slats separated the units from the corridor.

How frigging quaint.

There were no seamless steel doors, no motion sensors, no retinal scans, only skeleton keys, iron bars, and the putrid stink of death.

Classic.

I wasn't motioned into my two-by-three-meter cell. I was shoved by a hand between my shoulder blades so I ate the cake of concrete. Spitting a glob of saliva and dirt at the soldiers' feet, I was hammered in the stomach before I could even think of the pain.

Boots beat the shit out of my belly and ribs, ramming into me one after the other, until I knew bearing bruises was gonna become as fundamental as breathing. But even when my kidneys were burning and my liver crying for mercy, I gritted my teeth and rode it out.

Always with the insults: *Homo! You like it up the ass. How'd you like this boot up your ass, faggot?*

I was "liberated" of my clothes, but that didn't concern me. It was only when they catalogued my weapons that I felt like hyperventilating. Standing naked, I watched them empty my guns, unsheathe and inspect my knives, and find the special hidden in my pocket. I sent a smile with that one, instead of the bullet I wanted to fire at their brains.

"That it?"

"You wanna check my asshole for anything else?" I stole a Blondie move, lifting one eyebrow.

"You'd like that too much, slut."

"Doubt that."

Scraping along my jaw, my fingers itched for a gun. The motion highlighted my ring.

Blondie's ring. Ripping the ring from my finger, they left me naked, cold, and unburdened, adding theft to my charges. With the promise ring gone, the sight of my bare finger shook me from my suspicious thoughts. It burned like a bitch to lose that token. Minutes before I'd been whining about its weight. Now I was desperate for its return.

Blondie always had a plan.

He couldn't have set me up. We'd been through too much together. Of course they wouldn't send him down here with common riffraff like me. He was just being questioned in plusher surrounds. I ought to be thankful about that. He'd find a way to wipe off whatever mud Kale slung at him. He was a smooth talker.

I gave up skewering myself with any more thoughts, concentrating on the cell, marking out the space instead. Not bad. I'd seen worse. A bit different having an inside view of the bars.

At least they'd uncuffed me. I wasn't hog-tied anymore. That turn of phrase came from Micah, and I wasn't spending any head time on him or the commune either.

Shutting it all down, I put my bare ass to the cold floor.

I didn't even have my arsenal that used to keep me warm at night, before Blondie, who was looking more and more like Old History.

*   *   *

Wakey-wakey time around here obviously meant breaky-breaky time.

A fist lancing off my temple shifted me into blaring awareness from a dream of Blondie. I was overcome by punches that didn't do a good enough job dulling the buzzards pecking my brain. *Was it all a lie, or was everything he said the truth?*

Coming off the contact high of my dream—a colorful landscape through which our fireside moments and waterfall interlude had spun, so unlike my grim, gray surrounds—my heart thumped with recognition. I was looking down the barrel, and just like so many times before, I wanted to save Blondie at all costs. A bleak end to a heavenly beginning, but I was gonna do my duty until my very last breath. I'd be the other man. I'd take Alejandro's place on the gallows.

I'd die with honor, hoping Blondie still had some.

Thank fuck the knuckles collapsing my cheek ended that train of thought. Physical pain, I could deal with. A good thing, too, because my guards made our mean Alpha devices look like a day at the ranch.

"Lover boy's sitting up in his dee-luxe digs. What you got to say about that then?" A whip of spittle flew across my chin, dripping down my neck. I didn't move, didn't wipe it off.

"Seems the least he could do was visit his nut-Nancy, don'tcha think?"

Since I didn't know the names of my twin torturers, I generously handed 'em out. Spitter couldn't rein in his saliva as it leaked from the corners of his mouth, a mouth bent out of shape with hate, a tiny twisted thing to match his mind. His broad, flat head sat on the plinth of square shoulders with no neck to speak of.

Hitter liked to giggle. His clenched fists felt like cement blocks, all knuckles and meat. He boxed around behind Spitter, his boyish pink cheeks oh so out of place. He shoved his pal excitedly. "You know what? You know what?"

"Back off, fuckface. I'm questioning here."

Face falling, Hitter looked like a crushed little boy. "Was just gonna say Rice is probably too busy with his lady friend up there topside."

I made a point not to hear that. Instead I was all about Blondie saying to me, *I won't hurt you, ever.*

"So, so, so he can't think too much of Commander Suck-Cock here, can he? Ain't seen those two leave his office since he arrived. Guess he's got his hand shoved so far up that blonde's skirt, he ain't got no time to visit his own prisoner, ya know?"

"You got a fine point." Spitter congratulated his pal with a slap on the shoulder.

I would not let their dumb fucking two-for-one show affect me.

"Got nothin' to say to that, you big bastard?" Spit landed on my shoulder.

Lifting my hand, I flicked off the offending wetness just as I deflected their comments that were missiles assaulting my heart.

When those goads didn't faze me, they conferred in the corner. I stood stock-still, head high, hands down, my fingers twitching for my KA-BAR. Throwing a punch would only mean more honky hijinks from the pair, so I kept my lips sealed so fucking tight I doubted I'd ever say a word again.

Which was for the best.

After a protracted discussion about how to proceed with my questioning, Hitter deferred to Spitter. It didn't take a genius to figure out who'd be the topper in that relationship.

"That'll get him good, won't it? Won't it?" He clapped his hands.

"Just upload the scans." The guard in charge splatted another round of goo to the floor.

To make sure I saw exactly what they wanted, Hitter dropped me down and held my palms flat to the ground, his knees digging into my calves and his hand grabbing hold of my neck in a classic doggie-style position, although I hadn't gotten the impression he was interested in me that way.

He kept me bent over until I had no choice but to look at the D-P peep show they were so keen for me to see.

Images rolled over the screen showing Blondie Betrayer Backstabber holding hands with a slim young woman whose fair hair was tightly drawn from her face in a bun.

Next the woman was making big pretty eyes at him, clasping his cheek in one hand, rubbing that dimple I'd tasted. Her other hand met his, on her waist.

In another frame their lips were touching. The passion I recognized had his hips tilted toward hers. A desk in the background was cluttered with papers, gadgets, wires, and crap. *Blondie's office here.*

I'd thought earlier he was just being questioned in more comfy surrounds. Yeah, he looked comfy, all right, with his hand on her ass. I was pretty damn certain now Blondie's plan had always been to send me down.

"S'her name again?" Hitter asked, pushing my face closer to the pictures that made my stomach curdle, my brain seize, my arms shake as I tried to duck away.

"Eh, just call her Nate's Jailbate—his new one, that is."

Laughing it up, Hitter made me look some more, his forearm digging into my windpipe until my breaths gasped and I closed my eyes.

Spitter leaned in and peeled my lids back between his thumb and forefinger. "That hurt yet? 'Cause I promise you, it's gonna get a whole lot worse."

Right then, his buddy had a revelation. "Farrow! Name's Farrow. Right? Right?"

"Yeah, fucking Farrow. She was betrothed to Rice in Alpha before he backed out of it. Looks like Farrow the female done brought him to his senses."

He was with Farrow *right now?*

An endless screen of photographs, an endless scream inside me. Fingers twined, lips touching, smiles exchanged. My hold on his vow slipped. *I love you, Caspar.*

I should've known better than to hold on to those last shreds of hope, but I guess I was just a stupid lovesick fuck. Every moment caught between the two was so convincing, it could've been captioned by the announcement of their Validation of Union. I spiraled right into my home away from home, shutting down the leaky valve of my emotions.

When Spitter pulled the D-P away, his bottom boy let me go, and I huddled over, my brow to the cold floor.

"Well, that there did it."

"Yup, but now we gotta know the truth. Allegations can't be standing if Rice returned his faggoty favors."

Their voices spun over me, meaningless.

All of my time with Nathaniel, meaningless.

"Because where there's smoke—"

"There's fire! I got that one right, didn't I?"

"Sure did. So we need water to put it out."

I was wrestled to the wooden board they brought in, my arms and legs tied down and my face covered by cloth dark enough to blind me.

My world narrowed to the gush of water poured over my face. *I had to breathe.*

I wouldn't scream, goddammit.

I didn't beg.

I struggled so much, my arms wrenched in their shoulder sockets. The pop of joints hit my ears. I was gonna black out.

I had to breathe.

Jets of water rushed in, drenching my face, my pulse pounding in my ears, fresh flashbacks drowning me just as hard and fast.

Alejandro on the scaffold, his nose covered and then his lips.

Liquid pounded into my nostrils, filled my mouth.

He held his head so high those final moments. I'd wanted to shout at them to stop. I'd bitten my lip, drawing blood, hot as the tears I'd swallowed back.

The water kept pouring over me, into me. My back arched off the board and I thumped my head, trying to twist aside because my lungs were getting blocked up. I was gonna—

The pounding stream let off.

This was not condoned. Only the highest-ranking Company officer could order waterboarding.

I gasped for breath, water running out of my mouth and over my chest.

"Did Executive Nathaniel Rice accept your advances?"

I choked out, "No."

Another round. Liters of icy water beating inside my mouth, down my throat, chugging out through my lips and nostrils. I still couldn't inhale.

I'd reached out and stumbled forward, but I was shoved back. When that coiled knot had slid over Alejandro's neck, when it tightened enough the muscles of his throat bulged and turned purple, I cried out.

I wanted to claw at my neck, puke, turn on my side, but I was strapped down.

My mouth foamed, every one of my sluggish exhales sounded wet.

I tried to focus, but their words swam in my ears.

"What do you know about the whereabouts of First Lieutenant Grant?"

Liz is missing? "Nothing." Razor blades cut all through my lungs every time I inhaled. I didn't talk because I'd never give Liz up, even if I did know where the fuck she was.

The water grew colder, icy rivers slicing down my throat. I jerked inside the restraints. I couldn't turn my head.

They hadn't used the long-drop technique. The torque wasn't calibrated to bless Alejandro with the quick reprieve of unconsciousness. They'd wanted him to dance.

I had to open my mouth. I had to breathe.

The water cascaded over my tongue. One of them held my mouth open, aiming the tube into my throat, forgoing the pitcher technique.

I blacked out.

I came around, retching, gagging on the watery soup swamping my lungs.

"Rice. He's your fuck-buddy, yeah?" A hand pried my lips open, so I knew what was coming next. "He ask you to fuck him?"

"No." For all the liquid sloshing inside me, my mouth was dry. "Innocent."

"Well, good. Now that that's over, we can take you for a nice long swim, Commander."

Other than their questions that came at untimed intervals, they were silent. Blood rushed to my ears…no time to recover, drowning.

Suffocating.

I'd rather be hanged. I just wanted to hang.

I'd watched Alejandro's brutal murder until his body stopped moving.

When I had a second amid the water chugging, craning my body for freedom, in my heart of hearts I wanted Blondie to be the man I'd come to know—

I'd touched my heart where it raced in my chest and whispered back, "I love you, Alejandro."

Crashing my heels to the board, I thrashed as water coursed into my esophagus, giving me no chance to swallow.

My head rang; my lungs were full. There was no air to be had.

Not a single breath left.

Only resolve. Despite the hurt, I wanted Blondie to be safe when all was said and done.

*   *   *

I came to from another dream.

Ring finger, left hand. His words had been formed in his husky drawl. *An engagement, if you'll have me.*

I balled into myself and breathed, hurting all over. I hadn't said a bad word about him. I wouldn't.

The wet suck of my breaths was loud in my ears but not loud enough to dim the roar of my heart when I thought about his promise. The ring. *It wasn't all a dream, was it?*

My thoughts splintered into a million fragments, followed by my heart, when I touched my bare finger where I still felt the kiss of metal on my skin. *Everything,* it said. Everything included a little jail time, too. How frigging thoughtful of him.

Rolling painfully to my feet, I grabbed a handhold of cement and inspected my body. The highest marks I could give my physical condition were that I was still breathing, still standing, mostly, and still one step away from death. His promise ring took on a whole new meaning: a "promise to get you lynched" ring. He really shouldn't have gone to the trouble.

Look at me, getting fucking poetic. Well, someone had to laugh at this FUBAR situation, and since it was just me and my cell rat, it had to be me.

I wondered if Blondie had given his family ring to Farrow.

Since I could barely stand and breathing hurt like hell, I decided sitting would do me good. I wondered if dry drowning might be an option.

*   *   *

The passage of time was hard to make out what with no windows or D-Ps. Just a routine of banging my head against the wall to build my pain tolerance and regularly timed beatings to prove I hadn't reached my limit.

The thing about being cell bound, there was no choice in visitors.

I'd had fuck-all to eat all day—or however many days it had been—not that my stomach could take a meal anyway. It was enough that I stood on my feet when the bars slid back, revealing my best fucking mate, Kale.

While he overshadowed the faint light from the hall, I crouched on the balls of my feet. His chipped tooth was a jagged edge under-cutting his nasty grin. I steeled myself against the quick jolt of pride and possessiveness over Blondie that snuck up on me. I watched as Kale locked us in.

The graceless bull he was, he overturned the bare mattress, the water bowl. He kicked the shit pail and came at me with his dense, dark hate. "Didn't like you from the start."

"Surprise."

Energy massed in his muscles; he didn't move. Neither did I. "Wasn't about to step aside to let a Corps clown and CO man set up camp in the commune. Don't give two shits if Rice is Eden's kid."

"Obviously." I folded my arms over my chest.

"Figured givin' you two up was the safest bet to saving the commune. Y'all did me a favor when I heard you were aiming to be heroes. I wasn't gonna let you get all the glory."

I shrugged, fully aware my stoicism over what he obviously thought was his excellent master plan was pissing him right off.

His brow beetling, nostrils flaring, he stomped in front of me. Pointing his finger, chest pumping, he chewed out the words like raw meat. "I saw what y'all did with that guncotton. Shame Rice is such a traitorous bastard, 'cause we need people like him."

"The only traitor is you."

He gave me a maggoty smile. "Yeah, I went to the Corps recon troops. I was the one let 'em know there was bigger fish for the takin' than a commune full of *Nomad* peasants."

I bristled when he insulted his own people.

"While y'all were busy trapping those ignorant Corps bastards, I beat feet north." He came closer until his face filled my sight. "Beat you to it, didn't I?"

Guess he hadn't gotten the accolades he'd wanted up above if he was down here asking me to validate his bald-faced snitching. All he got in return was a blank look, the one that fit so well on my face. I'd forgotten how good it felt to go with zero emotion.

"So, you're gonna be the fall guy? Fuckin' pussy." *Bastard better not spit at me.* He tweaked his hairy brows in blunt fingers. "I wasn't able to implicate Rice. He's too far up the food chain, but I figured you'd squeal on him and get him that way."

While I waited for him to break out in high-pitched pig snorts, I kept up my mute routine. Pissing him off gave me almost as much satisfaction as knowing I'd put a wrench in his scheming plot to off us both.

Apparently my silence didn't cut it for him. Narrowing his eyes, he jerked his chin. "Maybe this'll change your mind. You think Rice was ever true to you? It might be Farrow right now, but who do ya think kept him occupied while you were out there in the fields with Micah? He had his pick of the bitches and used 'em well. He's quite the lady-killer; now he's gonna get you killed."

He inspected me for a response.

I showed nothing. That story had run endless versions in my head already, adding to the bonfire incinerating my heart that had sparked off with the thought of Blondie fucking Farrow.

"Got somethin' you want me to pass on to him, *big man*?" He winked.

I wasn't about to react to that, either. No fucking way. I didn't even breathe, although I wanted to scream hearing Blondie's pet name for me come from his fetid mouth.

I blinked once.

He wasn't such a village idiot after all. He read that tic for what it was and pounced all over it. "Yeah, that's right. You should hear him talkin' about you. He can be pretty funny when he wants to be, *Blondie* can." Clapping his hands, he launched into a new tale. "To hear tell, you're a bad fuck and a crybaby to boot. Goin' on and on about that other fag you got killed. What was his name again, starts with 'A', right?" He rubbed his skull right where I wanted to punch it. "Huh. Not as talkative as you used to be. That's okay. 'Cause I got my own message for you."

I wasn't gonna spare one single word on him, but inside I reeled. It wasn't enough Blondie set me up, probably fucked around on the farm per Kale, who was sounding a lot more trustworthy than him at the moment. He'd shacked up with his chickie and beaten my good faith into the ground by bad-mouthing Alejandro?

Since I couldn't get to Blondie—and I'd made a damn vow not to harm him, one I'd keep if only to prove I was more noble than him—I'd let my fists do the talking with Kale. They always had just the right sentiment.

"See you already had your pretty face busted up. Maybe we could do something about your ribs."

"Aw, now. You think I'm pretty?" I taunted the crazy asshole.

He recoiled as if I'd put the moves on him. I could practically see him clenching his ass cheeks. That made me laugh. "Don't worry. Wouldn't bugger you if you were the last man standing in the InterNations."

That earned me an uppercut. So much for leaving my face out of this.

Without Hills to step in, we let fly.

In much better physical shape than me, considering I'd had only water rations, liters and liters of water, Kale had the upper hand. But that didn't matter, because I'd been waiting for the chance to beat something.

Pummeling, punishing, pounding never hurt so good. Maybe if I pushed him hard enough, he'd end me right then.

After a few bouts that left our mouths bleeding and knuckles bruised, Kale cracked my back against the wall and then floundered to the floor when my knee took a bite out of his crotch.

Sliding backward, he climbed to his feet at the gate.

"Guess I shouldn't kill you right here. Gotta leave that for the CO, ya know?" He panted, "Wouldn't wanna spoil the show."

Now look who's getting all poetic. My breath winching in and out, I flexed my fingers and glared at him.

And then he frigging spat on me. As if I hadn't been spit on and shit on enough already. Just for good measure, he left with this clincher, "Almost forgot. Your trial's been expedited, thanks to your ex-boyfriend."

After I got over my beating, I sought out the next-best mental torture, because why the hell not? My trial had been expedited by Blondie.

Good. Let's get on with the main event already.

*   *   *

The next time the bars groaned open, I stayed right where I was. Head down, knees up, making a nice comfy cornerstone of myself. "Visiting hours are over." My gut lurched from hunger, hurt, and whatever else I was feeling. It was all the same, which was why I'd trained myself against that shit a long time ago.

Footsteps and silence greeting me, I peered over my forearms and shot to my feet.

Blondie.

My heart dropped, my head spun, and my knees noodled before I wedged myself back up.

I won't hurt you ever, he'd whispered. His sentiments kept eating a hole through my gaping chest. I wanted to ask him about that nice little lie. But I wouldn't.

Blondie being here now hurt me. I had no time for more mind games or, god-fucking-forbid, sympathy. And fuck me if that wasn't pity in his forget-me-not blue eyes.

"Get out of my cell."

His voice was even, his eyes all over me. "Had to make sure you were okay."

I almost waited for him to tack on *big man.* It wasn't coming, now or ever.

"Yeah, fucking peachy." Punching my hands to my hips, I remembered belatedly I was naked. For the first time I was nude with him and not sporting a boner. "This place has all the comforts of home. Now"—I put the steel edge into my voice—"get the fuck outta my sight."

He approached me until he stood too close. I could smell the spicy scent that clung to him. My body reacted with a visceral twist of longing that made me shut my eyes.

"What the hell did they do to you, Caspar?"

"What you ordered, I imagine."

Reaching for me, he pulled back when I flinched. He had the goddamn audacity to look hurt. "I'd never allow this treatment. You know that."

That got a laugh out of me. "I don't know a damn thing about you."

"It wasn't me," he repeated.

Like it goddamn mattered. Then my eyes flipped to his as they went wide. "Your dear daddy?"

"Jesus." His hands swept back over his hair. "Or my brother."

"Either one here?"

"No. My father carried on to Beta to be with Linc. But that wouldn't stop him, once he caught word of—"

"My crimes? My capture? My wicked, salacious deeds against his precious son?"

His mouth pruned inward. "I'm assignin' new guards."

"Very fucking magnanimous of you. Now I can break their fists in with my face too. Thanks."

"There won't be any more beatings. That was unconscionable." He looked livid, but appearances were deceiving.

I snorted. "Says the duplicitous bastard."

He cringed as if I'd slapped him. His hand came forward again, stopping on the wall beside my shoulder. Flattening myself away from him, I tried to ignore his eyes, the damp blue of flowers and dew.

I also tried to tune out his soft words. "Why didn't you give me up if they tortured you? They wanted to know about me, about my role in all this, right?"

I sidled away. "Don't go thinking you're the end all. They wanted details on Liz, too."

Palms pressed to the wall where my shoulders had been, he turned his head to me. "Why didn't you tell 'em?"

I met his eyes dead-on. "Momentary lapse of judgment."

It hadn't exactly been a moment of stupidity, but I wasn't gonna tell him the truth. The last time Spitter had let me come up for air, when I was hoping for nothing other than a quick death, I managed a croak before delirium towed me under.

They'd wanted an accusation against Nathaniel, but instead I'd given them a confession.

Guess my lies had worked, because here he was, all polished, pressed, suited. His credibility assured.

He came to the same conclusion real quick. He always was a smart boy. "You lied for me, didn't you?" He grabbed my face and brought me within kissing—or spitting—distance, hovering with his mouth so damn close to mine, I could taste him.

Oh, Jesus. I want to taste him one more time.

Leaning toward my ear, he hissed, "Don't be such a goddamn hero, Caspar. It's gonna get you killed."

"Yeah? I thought that was your job."

He stomped out of the cell, reappearing with some fancy domed platter covering food so hot, tendrils of steam licked his fingertips. "And make sure you eat this so you don't drop dead before your trial."

He started walking away from me, but I called out, "You know what?" He stopped and my voice dropped to a rough whisper. "I do have something to say to you." I wouldn't say his name, wouldn't call him Blondie, wouldn't even think it. This wasn't about me, *us*, or this InterNations mess.

Wooden as the beam that would soon bear my weight, he turned, and I could've sworn I saw a wick of hope in those blues, blearier than I'd ever seen them. He looked as if I were gonna pledge my undying love to him at this final hour.

"I don't trust you for an instant. But maybe there's still a heart beating inside you. I doubt it, but I got no choice."

He gave a stiff nod.

"Liz." I aimed my finger at him. "Find her, free her, and don't fuck her over. Not like you have me. That's my dying request. Now leave, Company whore."

His throat bobbed, and his eyes screwed tight. Then his features went placid as the lake at the commune.

I had to add a last rushed whisper. "I hope Miss Eden can forgive you after this."

The auditory illusions must've made a return because I surely misheard his mumbled parting shot. "Only need *your* forgiveness, big man."

*　　*　　*

After Blondie's visit, the food kept coming, fast as I could digest it. The beatings abated. I even managed to rest and exercise, but all that refueling afforded me was ticking minutes during which I played mental games with myself.

What I couldn't figure out was why he'd tried to ditch me all along our trek. Maybe Blondie had grown a conscience somewhere between Alpha and Chitamauga, knowing what downfall awaited me. Whatever. That good intent certainly wasn't evident now.

It felt like I'd done this before. *Oh yeah, that's because I have.* Only the roles were reversed this time because it wasn't Alejandro on the chopping block but me. If I thought about it, I ought to be thankful it was my turn with the fancy neck-tying in my near future and not Blondie's.

The ring, again, came back with precise pain sitting solidly in the middle of my chest. I wished I had it in my hand, on my finger, where it belonged. With Nathaniel, I'd belonged. Possessed by him and likewise getting that happy hit of *you are mine* in return.

Love.

Ah shit.

Cracking open, I gave in, just for a little while. Those Company fuckers couldn't confiscate my memories, and goddamn it, I was keeping them. It was probably my last night in this godforsaken life, and I was gonna spend it remembering every single moment with him from the times we fought to the times we flirted. From waking up in his arms and holding his hand. Blondie, Nathaniel. My lover.

My love.

Dancing at the celebration. Him singing to me with his wicked eyes and lusty ideas. Letting him inside me, my body, my soul.

The flowers.

The cuff.

The ring.

My fucking ring.

The promise of the two of us.

No one was gonna take that shit away from me.

Passing my hands through my hair and down my face, I rubbed over the wetness on my cheeks. *Christ, I love him.*

What a fucking schmuck.

Shaking my head, I understood why Alejandro did what he did. One hundred percent.

Clasping my arms around myself for warmth, I waited for sleep. At least there would be more dreams to ease this ache.

At least death meant no more wondering what might have been, what almost was, or any of that other fairy-tale made-up crap.

*   *   *

Sure enough, my RACE trial was moved forward. I was granted a few more days to heal up and clean up, and true to his word—this time—there were no more go-arounds.

They took me to shit, shower, and shave in a real bathroom and had a brand-spanking-new uniform for me with full regalia for extra shock value. I could see the byline on the D-Ps now: *Commander Caspar Cannon on Trial for Being a Deviant Homo.*

Decked out in dark blues, bars, stars, and a few new scars, too, I was escorted aboveground, up the marble stairs, and straight to face my fate.

My head was screwed on tight, my heart put back in its locker, where it would never be unearthed again. I wouldn't break. I was ready to see this final mission through, maybe cause a little ruckus in the process. *Fuck yeah.*

The room was enormous, the ceiling shaped like the silver domes used to keep my food warm. Dark polished wood, plush velvet seats. I blinked at the streams of sunlight slanting through the windows.

Heavily guarded, I marched forward. The shackles at my ankles and wrists didn't slow my military gait. Rows of seating circled me. Stemming up the walls, tiers of balconies were at the sides and back of me. *I hate that.*

Every single seat was taken. There had to be hundreds of Company here, waiting for my punishment to be meted out.

Traversing the aisle, my newly minted black lace-ups rang a sure tune in the hushed silence thickening around me. Facing the head honchos of the RACE Tribunal, I raised my chin another notch… and almost faltered.

There it was, the final kick to my gonads.

Presiding over my trial was Nathaniel Goddamn Rice. Suave, sharp-suited, sporting expressionless features I immediately replicated, he was accompanied by fifteen of his peer group of pussies, one for every Territory.

Hemmed in on all sides. I was going nowhere.

Liz's no-nonsense voice came to me. *Taking it up the twat, Commander.*

Otherwise known as thoroughly fucked.

Chapter Seventeen

Not only was Backstabbing Blondie part of my one-sided jury—sitting up there in the middle of the raised platform behind a bank of transparent D-P screens—he had a nosegay or bouquet or some such shit of those bastard forget-me-nots in the lapel of his suit instead of a handkerchief monogrammed with MHF. Major Head Fuck, reverting to the asshole I'd come across in his dickhead daddy's office.

I was still hocking up my nuts when head honcho the hangman mentioned to Blondie, "We all set, Foreman Rice?"

Foreman Rice. Wasn't he proving to be a jack-off-of-all-trades?

"Ready to start, if you please, Judge."

Speaking into an invisible mic, the master of ceremonies, aka the head honcho, announced, "We are online."

Oh, bliss. My trial was being mainlined via live feed, care of MHF.

Talk about fanfare. The room erupted. I should've felt honored, except, of course, the crowd of CO men and women weren't cheering for me. They were jeering at me.

"HANG THE SODOMITE SOLDIER!"

"Fuck him with his own gun!"

"KILL THE QUEER COMMANDER!"

The room had the kind of acoustics Blondie appreciated, the insults raised in volume and venom. His head dipping briefly to his hands so the sun glanced off the high double-helix piercing, he didn't appear to love the growing noise so much now.

I thought I was in for a good old-fashioned gangbanging. Masculine and feminine voices mixed alike until the slew of slander slapped against my upright back and slid straight off.

My eyes remained fixed on Blondie.

My fingers relaxed and my breathing steadied.

I am a brick fucking fortress.

A phlegmy chuckle spurted from the head honcho whose name I hadn't caught, what with the catcalls. "Indeed. We'll get to that, my fellow officers of the InterNations Council. However, as deemed by the statutes, we must commence with the proceedings. I call for order!"

The wave of silence spread outward, leaving only the near-death buzz in my brain.

Head Honcho began. "On this day, November the twenty-third, year 2070, we convene over the case of Commander Caspar Cannon of the Elite Tactical Unit, Alpha Territory. By the bylaws of the Company, which governs from the Sixteen Founding Territories of the InterNations, it is stated that sexuality of immoral description shall not be abided. As such, the accused will be allowed the opportunity for reparation and rehabilitation as afforded by the approved methods of the Repopulation and Civil Enforcement Program."

He halted for a breath and peered out over the gathered gung-ho officers. "Our work in the trial of Commander Cannon is facilitated by his confession, which was signed by an authorized proxy on his behalf."

Nothing said fair like a CO paper pusher simply signing your life away on your own behalf.

For a sickening moment, I wondered if they'd done a fix up on my confession, managed to play my words against Blondie.

Turning to Blondie, he said, "Feed link twelve."

Oh, they'd worked it over, all right, that declaration I'd omitted to reveal during Blondie's welfare visit to my cell. The recording was edited to wash away entire sections where I was fighting for words after the watery confinement. My voice ranging across the room sounded as sure as I felt. "Rice hates me. He fought me, and I forced myself on him, raping him repeatedly. Company bitch is what he is. He deserved every ass-pounding I gave him. And I reveled in his screams."

Relieved my part went off without a hitch, I aimed a pleasant smile at Head Honcho and his fellow fuckwits, keeping my eyes off Blondie, who'd gone ash white.

While the crowd craned forward in their chairs, Head Honcho began his recitation. "The charges against Commander Cannon stand as thus."

I focused on the visuals. The giant D-P's showed scenes of me in combat, comforting families of victims, up-to-my-eyeballs covered in muck, with guns slung across my chest and a Corpswoman over my shoulder running for safety. Every single image screamed of the once-honorable soldier now utterly debased. Every byline underlined the CO message that anyone was culpable of illegal behavior if upstanding Commander Cannon was.

Good soldier gone bad.

I'd provided them with the opportunity to fine-tune their anti-homo message. I'd given them the ammo to breed more hate, inject more suspicion, to boost the remaining civilians who had sworn their allegiance to the Company and against acceptance.

Rage spiked inside of me while I watched my own personal video and listened to the charges.

"Accused of uncondoned oral copulation."

My head fell back with a laugh. "Uncondoned oral copulation? Shit, it was straight-up forced blow jobs, a lot of 'em. No need to mince words, right, Blondie?" I winked at him just before the butt end of a sidearm whipped across my cheek, ending my hilarity.

Blondie put me in this coffin, and I'd make sure it was nailed shut. Backhanding the blood from my mouth, I sent him a gruesome grin. The pistol-happy guard snapped a second blow to the back of my skull. I reeled, my chains clanked, and the crowd cheered it all on because a good show was a good show.

"That's for your insolence, slut."

I let the rest get recorded in whatever verbiage they wanted, certain my mission was complete.

Rape.

Sodomy.

Wanton corruption of a Company officer. *Always a crowd pleaser.*

Homosexual acts of depraved measures—that is, *making love.*

Theft. *That fucking ring was mine.*

Assault on numerous accounts. *Bonus points.*

Per the CO policies, there wouldn't be a defense. This was merely a promotional event of this highest order. Only the verdict remained.

Clear-cut, right down the line. Each representative's ruling rang clear. "Guilty. Guilty. Guilty…"

Times fourteen, until it was Blondie's turn.

Waiting for his say, my blunt nails dug into my palms. I willed him not to do anything stupid because I'd put a lot of work into my setup for his own good, and I hated leaving shit undone.

To my relief, he added his opinion in a low voice. "Guilty."

With Head Honcho's vote, I was branded a homosexual deviant thief with a tendency to battery and causing bodily harm…who liked blow jobs. I had to hand it to them. They made short work of this short rope. My trial had ranged through confession, charges, guilty, going down in less than twenty minutes.

Needless to say, I was shocked when the judge asked if I had anything to declare for myself. Maybe he was expecting me to cower or beg, which was so not my style.

"Sure, why the hell not?" I'd go out swinging, give them something they couldn't spin before it went out live to the masses.

The bloodthirsty mob was just like the one at Alejandro's hanging. Barely staying in their seats, they raised their fists, snarling taunts. I spoke low, going unheard at first, but as my voice grew in volume, theirs fell away, replaced by narrowed stares stabbing all over my body.

I dug deep, determined to speak for everyone who'd been silenced. For the Freelanders. For Alejandro. For my sister. For Blondie, if he still had the ears to hear it. For me. "I've got something to say, all right. In defense of homosexuals. In defense of freedom!"

I jerked my chin toward a young woman polished and pressed until her personality had disappeared. "You ever thought about having sex with someone because it was your choice instead of an ordained match?"

Eyes wide, lips thin, she shook her head.

"You there." I looked at a middle-aged man whose face appeared chipped from the same granite as the garrison. "You remember your Proving Ceremony? What about the young woman brought to you? Did she get off on it? Being watched by your elders and the executives so you could show just how dedicated you were to the Company cause?"

His hands curled over the arms of his chair, nostrils flaring.

"Was she excited to be on public display? Did she come?" Given enough lead to shake off my armed guards, I bent down in his face, which was beginning to show fissures. "Or was she scared, ashamed, and so fucking alone?"

He warned, "Back off, now."

I stepped away, into the arms of my security detail. "The decades of upholding rules that discriminate against one faction of our society while championing another, hasn't that affected anyone here?" Nodding toward Blondie, the man broadcasting this abomination, I repeated, "Not a goddamn one of you?

"This regime, these decrees for what? To recoup the world's population? That's bullshit!" I stomped my foot, a futile physical outlet. "I've been to a commune. I've spent time with the Freelanders. Nomads, you call them? They aren't the savages the Company's banged on about. Not animals whose only goal is to kill and screw. They are *Freelanders* because they live in freedom. They love at their own will, and they are *thriving*; their children are plentiful and healthy.

"You have a chance to change this world! You just gonna sit there and wait for the shitstorm to destroy the Company and you with it?"

In the ensuing silence, no one moved to join me.

Surprise.

"You're just cogs in the Company machine, pieces of InterNations inner workings. They bred you to maintain their rule." I tried to pull my hands forward, the interlocking chains holding me back. "Where the fuck are your balls?"

I turned to Blondie with his flushed cheeks and drawn lips, a feverish light to his eyes. "I can goddamn guarantee you the Revolutionaries joined by the Freelanders are going to win this war. They have courage." I wanted to pound my chest, pound their heads together. "Passion! They have honor. Theirs is the righteous fight."

My balls jumped when a few eyes rose to mine, and the mouths on a handful of onlookers worked as if they had something to say.

In the upper reaches of the balcony, a woman shot to her feet, shouting, "He speaks the truth!"

It was goddamn spiritual, until Head Honcho leaped up, smacking his fist to the table. "Enough! Silence!"

What is he gonna do if I don't shut up? Kill me? My death warrant is already signed.

That small show of support put a hot coal under his ass. Enraged, the veins in his face lit up in a florid network. "This traitor is not a RACE rehabilitation option."

"Got that right. I'd rather fuck a goat than be told who to do." As if I'd ever have sex with a woman. Dumbfucks. My chin shot up higher. Courage, bravery, honor. That was how I was gonna die.

After treason was added to my rap sheet, Blondie spoke up, keeping his eyes on a spot behind my back. "Petition for immediate execution of Commander Cannon, Judge."

I swallowed my heart right then. I must've kept breathing. At least I didn't pass out from lack of oxygen, even though it felt like I was in an airless chamber.

"I see no harm in this. We have plenty of footage. All of which will prove useful in dispelling future atrocities of this nature."

I swallowed again, kept up that breathing thing. *No harm at all, only to my person, my heart.*

"Permission granted."

From out of nowhere came the image of Nathaniel below me, the tears in his eyes the first time we made love, his gasps and soft mewls.

I love you, Caspar! You cocky motherfucker.

Maybe I had fallen, hit my head or something, because the next thing I heard wasn't Blondie proclaiming his love but his smooth drawl asking, "Request special dispensation to carry out the sentence myself."

Surely my heart would quit now, spare me the details of all this twisted bullshit.

Amid the dissent drowning my ears, Blondie's voice rose. "Commander Cannon is Elite OPS. I know his MO and his weaknesses."

Got that right.

More opposition found him standing, his sultry accent replaced by cold, clipped words. "It is my right to kill him! He ruined my reputation. He raped me. If you disagree, I will go straight to CEO Cutler for permission. I want to put the bullet in his brain." His brow peaked, he demanded, "You dare deny me this?"

"Order! Order!" Head Honcho intervened. "Have you all forgotten we're waging a war against the likes of Commander Cannon? Let us rid ourselves of one more carrier of this plague in our midst. Permission granted, Nathaniel." Clapping him on the back, he ordered, "Take him to the woods. Shoot him clean. Bring back his body. You can air the evidence tonight."

At Blondie's nod, Head Honcho's head lowered in his direction. "Well done for bringing him in and tying up the loose ends. I'll report to your father immediately. He'll be so proud."

"Thank you, sir."

My spine was rigid as an iron bar, my heart destroyed, and all the loving memories of Blondie were finally erased from my head.

Good, let the Company executive execute me.

*   *   *

Escorted outside, I marched. *Left, right, left, right, left.* This day in the life was gonna end with me dead.

My cadence was matched by the three men riding my ass. Blondie plus the muscle backing him up because a prisoner of my magnitude couldn't be trusted. The guards were surplus to requirements. I knew Blondie could cold-bloodedly cut a throat just as easily as he'd become a turncoat.

No words passed between him and me, only the puffs of our cold breaths commingled. Me in shirtsleeves—stripped of my military honors. He swathed in an overcoat that brushed his calves as he strode.

Beyond the perimeter of the compound and through the gate, the sun washed over my face and the wind bit my skin. Shutting my eyes, I smelled the air. Untouched, the scent of forest filled my lungs. A branch heavy with snow creaked overhead, a plop of slush hitting my shoulder.

Into the woods where no path had been trod, our boots punched through the crust of old stuff underneath. My head was high, shoulders back, muscles stiff against the drag of the metal cuffs as we headed forest-deep, where feathery dark greens were topped by pristine white drifts.

Tension rolled off Blondie, reaching toward me, putting a stumble in my step for a second. I was glad the man I loved would survive. I was tired of living with this hate inside of me. I chanced a look behind me. His jaw was locked in place, his mouth firm, his eyes clapped on my face.

Stopping in a near-perfect circle broken only by scant animal prints and one lone tree soldiering on its own, his overcoat passed to one of the guards, he lowered me to my knees.

The snow melted fast beneath my legs, slush seeping through my pants.

I twined my hands together, giving one last rub to my naked finger.

In my periphery, the two guards unholstered their sidearms, their bodies blocking any escape.

Before me, the bare branches of the single tree danced in a swift breeze, the same way I listed sideways for a moment.

I wouldn't spend my last moments angry. I'd wasted too much time.

My head bowed, I thought about Liz.

I was glad I'd be with Erica soon, unless the CO controlled heaven and hell too.

Tasting a drop of salt in the corner of my mouth, I held in a smile, grateful Leon had made it...with my bike.

Alejandro came to mind. My hot-tempered lover with his passion for life, his truth in death.

The tears rained faster when I thought about Blondie, the man standing right behind me. It was a goddamn good thing I was gonna die because I would never be able to live through the agony of his actions.

Forty seconds or so of that sniffling was more than enough. Wiping my face against my shoulder since my hands were still fucking bound, I cleared my throat. "I'm ready."

His voice was ghostly as a thin cloud racing across a midnight sky. "Last words?"

Oh yeah, I had a lot of those. Starting with Fuck and ending with You. But I wasn't doing that. I squared my shoulders and opted for a different FU. "I forgive you."

He was so silent, I wondered if he was just gonna plug me with no warning. Shooting my head around, I had to look at the man one last time. My gaze landed on his lapel overflowing with the nodding flowers he'd first given me and then his eyes, so glittery blue they put those frigging blooms to shame. "Forget me not, Nathaniel."

I turned my eyes to the tree ahead.

The brush of metal from leather sounded, his weapon readied.

A loud *click* as his gun was cocked.

Its discharge deafened me, two blasts in quick succession.

Blondie. Nathaniel! LizEricaLeonAlejandro. Blondie!

I was slammed into the ground.

Heavy breaths sped against my neck.

A broad chest covered my back.

Blondie.

"You stupid fuck. Caspar!"

Not a bullet. Blondie. Tackling me to the ground inside the cage of his arms.

Turning me over.

Touching me everywhere.

There was wet warmth between my shoulder blades, but it wasn't blood. It was his tears, the ones coursing down his face and in between his lips.

The only blood spilled was on both sides of the clearing, not mine. Red rivers melted snow, forming puddles. The guards were flat-out with neat bullet holes in their foreheads.

I hunched over and croaked, "Nice shooting." He'd shot his own people, Company people, and covered me with his body in case he'd missed his mark.

"How could you believe it?" Undoing the handcuffs, rubbing my wrists until circulation pierced my fingertips, he was shouting. "How the fuck could you believe I'd kill you? You idiot!"

I grabbed his face and hauled him on top of me. I brought his mouth to mine between gasps. Our tongues swooped inside and out, tasting, feasting.

I went at his throat, nipping, biting, hungry, greedy. Alive.

Relief, disbelief, and rage all fought for airtime within me. I didn't know where to start first.

"Brought it down to the wire, didn't you?" I shoved him off me.

I'd vowed not to hurt him. *Fuck that.* This time I was gonna put a world of hurt on him. An entire goddamn universe.

"You didn't leave me with a whole lotta options." His voice was low and rough.

"I thought you meant it."

He walked toward me. The sun reflected off the snow, working through his hair and soft stubble, his beautiful lips, setting off the sorrow in his eyes.

"You believed I'd kill you?"

"Sure."

"Sweet Jesus, Caspar." He leaned down with his cheek against mine and his mouth near my ear, the sad truth coming out in a pained whisper. "You could believe all those lies but not the truth?"

I made full-body contact with Blondie, folding my arms around him. It felt so good, so right. I wanted to give in to the love flooding me, but I couldn't. "The truth?"

"I love you so much it hurts, Caspar. Knowin' you were beaten…" He sucked in a breath, impaling me with his blues awash with all the emotion he'd hidden from Company eyes. "That they convinced you I was playin' you. I don't ever wanna know. I don't think I can take it, honey. I'm sorry. I'm sorry. I tried to get you out sooner."

"I convinced myself of it all." I felt only deeper sadness for all the words we were saying.

"Why?"

"I don't think I deserve love." I let him hold me, my face in the nook of his neck. "I don't deserve your love."

He exhaled on a curse but wouldn't let me go. "Well, you got it. You got all of me."

My throat grew tight.

His lips left damp marks over my face. "I love you."

I burrowed into him, willing my heart to stop its pounding, trying to break free of imprisonment.

My head playing catch up with this great big mess, I disengaged from his arms. The warmth of his body replaced by the cold liquid of distrust, which was always so much easier to go with. "You love me so much, the only way you could get me off was by letting me sit in my own shit without a stitch of clothing while I was drowned, starved, and browbeaten by images of—" I gulped down the choking sensation of jealousy, which was fresh as the water that had damn near killed me.

"Images of what?"

I shook my head.

"Goddamn you, Caspar!" His voice broke, and he opened his eyes wide to the sky, blinking, blinking, blinking. Balling his fists, he poured his words over me. "Everything you told me about Alejandro was in here." He pointed at his temple. "His sacrifice for you. Just like him, I knew there was no way in hell you'd go through with rehabilitation. I knew you'd be an unrepentant, stubborn sumbitch, and if I could just get you out here, I could save your life."

The corner of his lips twitched up and he wiped the tears from his eyes. The cuff of his shirtsleeve slipping, I caught a glimpse of suede at his wrist.

My heart flew around some more. Frigging thing must've grown wings in there.

"I cut the live feed as soon as the trial started."

"You did?"

"'Course I did, big man."

I inhaled sharply. Last time I'd heard those words, Kale had been taunting me.

"What?" he asked.

I wouldn't let Kale corrupt my feelings. I was too good at that myself.

"Hooked it back up when you gave your speech, though." The other side of his lips perked up.

"Yeah?"

"Hell yeah! That was a call to arms, Caspar. Do you have any idea what you did?" Energy pinged off him as he paced a wide circle, punching his fist to the air. "You gave purpose to our cause. Shit, you're the badass darlin' of the Revolution." His approach tentative, he came close enough to touch my shoulder and no farther. "I'm so proud of you, honey."

I took a step back.

He stalked forward. "Aw, hell, Caspar. You're willin' to let it all go? What we had, what we could have?"

"What you did, that was a helluva gamble."

"You think I was screwin' around in there this whole time? I was goin' insane while you were down in the dungeons. Everyone was breathin' down my neck. My father, the executives, hell, even the guards were keepin' tabs on me. I'd just been plannin' to blow the Brier sky high. That shit all went haywire as soon as you were hauled in. I had to figure out how to get you off, honey, and the whole time, I couldn't get you outta my head."

Pulling my hands from under my armpits, he slammed them against his chest. "This was dead! Don't you get it?"

Softly, he touched my chin, cupping my jaw. "I don't want this life without you." His lips brushed over mine. "I can't let you go."

I returned his kiss, relearning the plump contours of his mouth. I touched the bow of his lips, the corners, caressing all that sweet skin with my tongue before drawing away.

"I want to believe you."

He nodded.

"Not sure I can take the risk."

The corner of his jaw pulsed. "I'm not a risk."

I waved him away. "The worst torture was thinking you'd planned this all along."

"Caspar, don't do this."

Plowing ahead, I voiced all the fears that had eaten away my happy-ending dreams, leaving me with a head full of nightmares. "You always seemed so guilty."

"Goddamn you. I couldn't tell you about my father. I didn't know how you'd react to the Freelanders until I got you to the commune." He growled, "Only thing I'm guilty of is lovin' you, tryin' to protect you."

"Did you know Kale was gonna be here?"

"No."

"Did you know this was gonna happen?"

"No way. But I had to think ahead. Why do you think I wanted you far away from this place? I've been stewed in the Company's ways for so long. It's true. I did have plans—"

My laugh was spiteful. "Always the man with the plan. Did you plan to tell Kale about Alejandro, or was that just a slipup?"

"I never spoke to him about Alejandro. I never spoke to him at all. He must've overheard me talking to—"

"Lemme guess," I cut in. "You were having a nice little chitchat about your banged-up ex-lover with your new-old flame, Farrow."

"You know? What did they say to you?"

"Guilty now, aren't you?"

His cheeks turned red. "It's not like that."

"I saw the pictures."

"She's here to help us."

"From what I saw, she helped herself to you." I stood above him as he bent over, gripping his knees, his breath chugging out of his chest in short, sharp shots.

"Sitting on my jury? Prancing me out here with a weapon in your hand? How do you think I felt about that?"

"That's why I wore the flowers," he groaned. "To signal you."

"I thought you were just tormenting me."

He was on his knees before me. "I don't know why I bothered." His chuckle was a short-lived burst. "What do you want from me?"

On his knees, just as I'd been, with his Glock to my head.

On his knees, beseeching me to believe him.

What the fuck am I doing?

I didn't ever want Blondie in that position. He'd taken out two of his own people for me—nothing said love like that—and this was how I repaid the man? When was I gonna fight for what I wanted?

"Get up." I hauled him to his feet. When he swayed, I caught him in my arms. Turning my lips to his ear, I blew his hair aside. "I do."

"What?" He trembled in my touch.

"I know now." I pulled his face to mine. "I'm sorry. God, I'm sorry."

"Caspar?"

Tenderly roaming down his back, my hands slid to his ass, and I couldn't resist pulling him against me.

He gasped. "Caspar?"

"You saved my life because you fucking love me." Nipping his earlobe, his chin, his bottom lip, I said against his mouth, "And I love you."

A mountain of emotion grew between us, too great to withstand. We went down into the snow, rocking together. We kissed like it was our first time. Slips of tongues and sips from mouths, sighs becoming moans.

There was no more knocking in my chest. My heart was soaring free.

No more beating in my head. I'd finally figured my crap out.

Sneaking down to suck on his throat, I whispered, "I'm sorry, baby."

"*Sshh*. You went through hell because of me."

"Thanks for getting me out of there, even if you took a round-about route doing it."

"Okay, now you're pushin' it." His eyes were bright, his cheeks pink, his lips swollen from mine. "You decided I'm worth the risk?"

"You're not a risk." I dipped close. "You're mine."

With suspicion, my death sentence, and all that other shit out of the way, I was of the same mind as my cock, especially when Blondie reclined to his elbows—in the fucking snow—inviting me on top of his body for a fierce, forgiving kiss.

Just a romantic interlude, with two dead bodies on ice.

I was getting ready to break it up when he gave a long whimper interrupted by the very near sound of a low laugh.

"Well, well, well, quite the pair of lovebirds, aren't ya?"

Chapter Eighteen

I knew that voice, thought I'd heard the last of it. *Caught in the goddamn act again.* Coming to my feet, I couldn't believe my eyes when a figure emerged from the surrounding trees.

Beside me, Blondie leaped up, wrapping his arm around my waist.

"Seeing as there's a war going on, maybe you could save the ass groping for later?"

Marching forward, I ate my grin. "Lieutenant Grant."

She saluted. "Commander Cannon."

I crushed her to me, covering a blast of emotion with my gruff tone. "Goddamn you, girl."

In my arms, her rigid stance faltered, but her smart mouth didn't. "Not going soft on me, sir, are you?"

I just clutched her harder until she squealed. Probably a first for First Lieutenant Liz Grant.

Eventually, I let her loose. "What are you doing here?"

She looked good. Orderly. Unhurt. Jerking her chin aside, she joked, "Heard there was a party. Didn't want to miss it. Hey, Nate."

Nate? Scanning between her and my lover, I reeled back. This was my right-hand woman, who'd never been anything but levelheaded. "Did he coerce you?"

The man in question crossed his arms and glared at me while Liz rolled her eyes. "Sure. If by coerce you mean contacting spies, searching the Territories for me and sending an escort, salvaging plans, saving your sorry ass...I gotta go on?"

I looked at the ground instead of the pair of them, unsure of what to make of the situation.

She knocked me on the arm with one of her famous motherfucking punches. "Did I forget to mention your man sweetened the coercion with promises of bombs, raids, and turning our guns on the bad guys? All my favorites." She hit my other arm. "Don't be such a dickhead. Jesus, Nate, what do you see in him?"

"He has his moments." He looked at me with that arched eyebrow.

"I'm sure. And I don't wanna be privy to those."

So this is my fucking life now? My best friend and my boyfriend doing the one-two hits on me?

I cleared my throat and stared into the mirror of her eyes. "You understand the implications of joining us?"

"Fuck's sake, Caspar. I thought getting something up your ass besides that ax handle you usually walk around with would loosen you up some." Strutting back a couple steps, she raised her hands, flicking her fingers. "I look stupid to you?"

Amid Blondie's stifled laughs, I said, "No."

Grabbing her crotch, Liz said, "I'm a big girl. I can handle this."

A soft voice reached us. "Ah can attest to that."

Oh, look. A cunting reunion.

Where was the peace, the joy?

"What the hell's she doing here?" I ground out.

"You really are an ungrateful bastard, aren't you?" Liz casually remarked, both of us watching while Farrow and Blondie exchanged some kind of fancy-pants, double-cheek, air-kiss crap. Whatever. At least it wasn't full mouth-to-mouth contact.

"She helped Nate keep up appearances since you couldn't keep your hands off him."

I took offense to that. "Wait a frigging minute. He's the one who pursued me."

The tilt of her head was cocky. "Yeah, I'm sure you played real hard to get. You can save the whole romance story to tell to your grandkids."

Lieutenant Grant was looking a demotion right in the eye if she kept up the insubordination. Then she swept her arm open, welcoming the petite woman to her side. "She helped Nate, and then I helped her." Her harsh, beautiful features smoothing over, Liz dropped to Farrow's ear and was rewarded with a peal of feminine laughter.

I scowled at the striking pair—the small curvy blonde next to Liz who looked so formidable with her short razored locks—my world turning upside down again.

"And you can stow that glare while you're at it, Commander, preferably in your ass, if you've got extra room back there." Hugging the newcomer close, she added, "She's the spy who located me. She's with me, not Nate."

The dainty creature, who happened to be a goddamn spy, strolled up to me, her hand outstretched. "Commander Cannon, Ah've heard a lot about you."

I harrumphed. Blondie pushed me forward. When my big paw engulfed hers, she beckoned me down. "Ah'm sorry for the misunderstandin'. Ah've spent a lot of time with Nathaniel over the years, Caspar, and Ah've never seen him as distraught as he's been this week, just beside himself about you." Quieting her voice to a low lilt, she said, "Nathaniel was nevah mine to have. He was nevah available to anyone, before you."

I squeezed her hand, and she took the opportunity to dig her nails in. My eyes flicked to hers, their soft appeal compacting to harsh green nuggets. "Liz is your family just as Nathaniel's mine. You have my word Ah'll look after her as long as she'll let me."

The idea of the little woman taking care of Liz was laughable until I re-focused on the flinty eyes and biting grip of this double agent.

"I can count on you to do the same for Nathaniel?"

I grinned at her hardball methods. "We have an understanding, Farrow."

Blondie entered the conversation, rubbing his hand over my shoulder. "I needed all the help I could get for you, honey. Farrow here took the heat off. Sometimes it takes a"—he paused, glancing at the D-P positioned in his hand, silently ticking off seconds before finishing—"village."

A series of thunderous explosions rent the air, rocking the ground underfoot. I steadied myself while the rest of them looked unfazed. He nodded in satisfaction and carried on. "She's a sister in the Revolution. You are my only lover."

"Yeah, yeah, I get it." I brushed him off. "Never mind that stuff." Another shock wave rolled over ground and through the sky, bringing big black clouds with it. "What the hell was that?" I pointed.

"TNT," Liz responded.

Farrow watched dense gray smoke cruise across the treetops. "Some tear gas."

"Bunch more hillbilly dynamite," Blondie said.

"But who—?" I asked.

"As I was sayin', sometimes it takes a village." He started guiding me from the clearing.

Liz piped up from behind, "Freelanders, Revolutionaries."

Farrow fell in step. "Don't forget the spies."

Their words beat a good rhythm to our retreat.

Jogging in the opposite direction of the Brier, I heard Farrow again. "A little technique perfected on the water plants."

"What?" I halted.

"We'll get into that later, big man. We gotta hustle."

I stood my ground. "Oh, we're gonna get into a lot later." My suggestive smirk faltered with the echoing *pop-pop* of pistols, the *rat-a-tat* of automatics. "We have to help!"

Blondie blocked my retreat. "No more playin' the hero."

"The casualties—"

"There won't be any. We've taken out the Outpost. Stragglers will be shot on sight."

I cranked my hands to the back of my neck. "This changes everything."

"For good."

Knowing what I was committing to, being an outlaw, a Revolutionary, I nodded. "For the good of the people."

* * *

Running at a fast clip in the direction of Fort Knox, we maintained a close huddle, sticking to the dark woods. As much as I was glad to see Liz, relieved she was alive and safe, I was desperate to get Blondie alone. Every step sent a painful bounce through my cock and a muttered curse from my lips.

He hung back. "You okay, big man?"

He knew I wasn't peachy fucking keen. His eyes dancing, he wet his lips.

I jerked him to me by his collar. "I need to get my hands on you."

"You're not gonna hurt me, are ya?"

Sucking on the muscled cords of his throat, I stroked his ass and swatted it. "No. I have to touch you. I need to make love to you, baby."

In a husky drawl, he called out to the women. "You two go on ahead. We'll meet you at the fort."

So far gone I didn't hear their teasing volleys, I scooped him up in my arms, tearing open his jacket, shoving his shirt up to his shoulders. "Yes."

All that flesh, for me. Chills ran across his torso, and I chased them with my tongue. He was heavy in my arms, but I wasn't gonna drop him, and I'd be damned if he was going back down into that cold snow.

His back arched and the muscles of his chest and abdomen clenched. I muffled my face in his armpit, laughing when he chuckled. Sucking down the virile scent of him, I licked the padded line of his ribs, carving every indent and jut of muscle. I made him lean back over my arm, yanking his pants low on his hips so I could get to his groin, the dusting of dark gold hair leading to the fabric-covered bulge of his crotch.

He caught my eye while I dipped my tongue under his waistband, landing unerringly on the tip of his cock as a fat drop of preejaculate emerged. *"Mmm."* I murmured my appreciation.

Blondie stiffened, watching something behind me.

I went on full alert.

All he did was squint, but I got his message.

I shifted him with no sudden motions, my hand landing on the pistol hanging from his shoulder holster. His fingers brushed my hip as he palmed his second weapon.

I swung Blondie to his feet, and at the same time, we raised our guns, standing side by side as a wounded, bellowing Kale barreled toward us. He must've taken a hit during the explosions at the Outpost, because blood spread up and down his left side.

The recoils sent our shoulders together as we fired at him, my bullet buried in his heart, Blondie's dead center in his forehead. I wanted to empty an entire cartridge into him, but that'd be a waste of good ammo.

Placing the gun in the back of my pants, I made sure Kale stayed down while I settled Blondie's shirt back over his chest and buttoned his jacket. "You okay?"

"Yeah. I'm sick of the close calls though." He kept his piece pointed at the ground and we approached the dead bastard.

"Me too. Sure could do with some R & R."

Using the toe of his boot, he rolled Kale over, nodding at our clean kill. "That'd be nice."

I couldn't resist a final kick to Kale's ribs and a couple words instead of RIP. "Stay. Dead."

If Liz's appearance had been a mere interruption, Kale's attack was a goddamn mood killer. Hours later, half a day away from the Outpost, Blondie dug around behind a giant old oak tree, swiping a fat layer of snow from a tarp to unearth the backpacks he'd hiked out for our escape. Mine was the same damn thing I'd left Alpha with eight weeks ago. A lifetime ago. Checking the contents, nice and neat the way I liked it, I closed my eyes when his lips landed on the nape of my neck.

"I got somethin' for you."

I spun around, only to smother my disappointment. It was my D-P. I looked at the thing like it was bugged, curling my fingers into my palm.

"G'on. It ain't gonna bite you."

"I don't want any links to my past as a Corpsman."

He stroked my face and spoke just like Eden. "You might, someday. Besides, I disabled the coms, unless you want it back on." He waved it at me. "It has all your naturalist notes and pictures on it, remember?"

I took it reluctantly, touching the screen but not turning it on. I pocketed the thing and bent back over my pack.

"You expectin' somethin' else?"

I shook my head. "No."

"Huh."

When I strained around, he looked genuinely perplexed, rubbing his jaw, the rasp of his softwhiskers carrying over to me.

Standing in front of him, I narrowed my eyes. "Yeah, actually, I was waiting for something else. And you know exactly what it is."

"I do?" He stepped back.

I strode forward. "I want my ring back, baby."

His smile breaking free, his face lit up. "That's more like it."

Mine went dark when he dropped to his knees again.

One knee, to be precise.

Bewildered, hating him down there below me, I reached for him. "Get up. I can tie my own damn bootlaces."

That brought an even wider smile to his face, and holy shit, he was gorgeous. The uncaring mask completely dissolved, his emotions shining clear and true. "Ain't tryin' to tie your laces, honey. Talkin' about tying a different kind of knot."

His hand went to his breast pocket and reappeared with the ring sitting in his palm. "This is how they used to do it, Caspar. How a man would propose."

I didn't mind my heart pounding, or my ears ringing, or the way my lungs constricted this time. My hands shook and my eyes swam. "You asking for my hand?"

"Not yet. Give me a second." He tried to keep up that smile, but it was hard with his lips trembling. Opening my hand, he stroked each of my fingers, fitting our palms together.

He poised the ring at my fingertip. "Will you marry me, Caspar Cannon?"

This time he didn't wait for an answer. He slid the band home. I reeled him up, stating between kisses that started with his jaw and ended at his mouth, "Yes, yes. 'Course I will. You know I will. I love you, Nathaniel."

Right then, with our arms around each other and our mouths meeting chastely with brushes of lips and murmured words of hope and future, there were a lot more important things than a victory fuck.

We just stood there, being together in the cold, but it couldn't get ahold of us. Not this time. Not after what we'd been through, what we'd fought for.

Each other.

Our lives.

Freedom.

Love.

Tilting my face up, he kissed me with sweet, moist presses from one corner to the other. "Feel better?"

"Mmm-hmm."

I nuzzled his neck, working down to the big tendons of his shoulder. "Think we might wanna get a move on, though."

"You scared your delicate parts are gonna get frostbitten?" He smirked.

"No, I'm afraid your dick might freeze and fall off; then what would I do?" I winked.

Not content to be out in the cold, and definitely not thrilled about remaining within spitting distance of the Outpost, we didn't slow down until Fort Knox loomed ahead. Its boxy night-black bulk illuminated from within, fires and candles lit by Liz and Farrow holed up inside.

Jumping the fences, we landed on a thinning patch of hard-packed snow.

A new standard flew from the flagpole, its colors flapping brightly, its message clear. *Live in Freedom. Love at Will.*

The hopelessness that had dragged me under last time we'd parked it here was a thing of the past, a past I'd finally let myself remember—and let go.

I tugged Blondie's hand. "C'mon, baby. Let's join the Revolution."

*   *   *

On a cold, clear December morning, Blondie and I and Liz and Farrow returned to the commune.

The daily hustle and bustle was just beginning. Kids were on their way to the schoolhouse, workers to the munitions or greenhouse gardens, the medic center or the tannery. Weary to our bones, we walked through it all, my arm slung around Blondie's waist and his about my shoulders, Liz and Farrow taking point.

The whisper of our quiet return spread from boy to woman, from the farmers to the healers, from the mess to the armory. Fences were vaulted, doors flung open, the schoolhouse emptied until it felt like the entire damn village surrounded us with cheers and congrats led by Hills.

I didn't want to let Blondie go. There were too many people swarming around us. Well-wishers all, but it was overwhelming, and I was worried about him. He'd been through the shit-mill, brave-facing it for the Company, taking on the responsibility of freeing me, locating Liz, organizing the takedown of the Outpost. Not to mention my prissy bitch routine when, instead of putting a bullet in the back of my head, he'd bared his heart and soul to me.

I had to admit loving me wasn't exactly a vacation.

I had to wonder if my love was enough.

So when we were welcomed back to the Chitamauga Commune, I didn't know where the hell I fit.

The swag of his eyelashes brushing the gold skin of his cheeks, he clamped his hand on my shoulder when I started moving away. "You got a pressin' appointment I don't know about?"

"I just wanted to give you some space with your people." I bluffed.

His hand sliding down my back, he gripped my hip. "Our people." That y'all-don't-wanna-fuck-with-me look fired up on his face.

I took the back slaps and handshakes and returned them tenfold. The feeling of belonging taking flight in my heart soared when a path parted in front of us.

Flyaway hair in a tumbling bun, freckles magnified by drops of tears. Frantic blue eyes searching for us. For him.

As Eden ran at Blondie, the grizzly man with his friendly mutt sidled up. "Y'all done good."

Mother and son crashed together.

I focused on the dog's damp muzzle in my palm, scratching until his hind leg hitched up and down.

His white whiskers twitching, the old man pushed me away. "You're needed."

Eden was waiting. "Get on over here, son."

Awed by her embrace, I was held beside Blondie as Eden's shoulders shook beneath our arms.

"I thought I'd lost both you boys, just like Lincoln."

"Linc isn't gone, Momma. We'll get him back."

Patting a handkerchief to her eyes, she pushed up into our faces. "Now, that may be, Nathaniel. I wish it so. However"—she swapped the hanky for the hitting hand she used on both our skulls—"y'all

ever do anythin' like that again—servin' yourselves up to the
Company—I'm like to wring both yer necks!"

"Ow, Momma!"

"Quit your complainin'. Go on. Git cleaned up. Caravan's been
waitin' on ya."

The Love Hovel had been spiffed up some since the last time we'd
left it, fresh candlesticks, another layer of lace I was sure, and that big
bed all made up. The toxically overdecorated two rooms still held
some of the best memories of my life, but no memory could compare with the present.

As that realization slammed into me, I didn't shut my eyes or wait for
the bottom to drop out of my gut. Hell, I didn't even worry. Instead, I
led my lover to the edge of the bed and watched him stretch onto it. All
the coiled grace of a predator, the dark sensuality of a satyr.

"Hey, you okay?" His eyes gleamed, a light grin teasing me with
the barest dip of his dimples.

I leaned in and flicked his earring, nuzzling my nose into the
soft razor-cut sides of his hair. When I lifted his hand, I kissed each
knuckle in turn, loving the hardness of his flesh, the all-man flavor
of his skin. "Yeah. I'm just breathing in your goodness, baby." I remembered the song he'd sung to me during the harvest festival.

"You gonna serenade me next?"

"Don't push your luck." Those dimples damn near delighting me,
I swooped in to linger over one, then the other, laughter rumbling
while he knocked me to my side.

We angled for just the right fit, mouths flitting together, tongues
flirting shyly. "Reckon I already did that." His rich, low drawl
sounded against my ear. "Love you, Caspar."

"I love you, too, Nathaniel."

For the first time I had the best of both worlds—a mission to live
for and a man to love.

Chapter Nineteen

That sweet first taste of rebirth continued as I grew into my place as part of the Freelander commune. When I wasn't in a tête-à-tête in the town hall, fielding questions about Corps makeup and the demands on the Revolutionaries and Freelanders as far ranging as all the InterNation Territories, I took every work detail thrown at me. I spent most of the time in the barn with the animals. I had an affinity with the big furry bastards. They couldn't talk. I liked to shovel shit. It was a win-win.

I wasn't strategizing in top-level talks or manhandling manure the late-December evening Blondie caught me hopping on one foot. Some damn thing Micah's daughter Callie—one of the marble-playing kids in the mess hall my first morning in Chitamauga—roped me into called *hopscotch*. She twisted a light red lock of hair around her fingers, her eyes fastened on my feet while Dauphine, Callie's sister and the bolder of the twins, squatted beside me.

"Cain't clear the square, can ya, Caspar?" Dauphine teased.

Tossing the pebble over the hard-packed earth behind the schoolhouse, I felt Blondie's stare at my back. He was the only man who made my prick perk up with nothing but his presence.

I dropped both feet to the ground, shaking my head when Dauphine shouted, "I win!"

I pivoted around. Blondie's hands were loose on his hips, a smile wide on his lips. "Not as easy as it looks, so you can wipe that grin off your mouth."

"You learnin' new games on me?" He winked, letting me back him against the rough boards of the building.

I slipped my fingers into his waistband, pushing the hair from his neck to make space for my mouth on the soft stubble that became denser under his jaw.

"Best not get up to anything naughty, big man. The kids are watchin.'"

On cue, the girls butted into our legs, worse than the billy goats I tended. Blondie swung Dauphine across his shoulders, and after I pulled her sister onto mine, I leaned over for a quick peck to his cheek, unable to resist.

He rubbed his hand over the spot. "That was sweet."

I just smiled foolishly at him until Callie twisted my hair into painful knots, shouting, "Race, race, Uncle Caspar!"

A shot pierced right through my gut. She'd taken to calling me Uncle Caspar, not Mr. Cannon. A lot of the kids had. My big bad rep was getting a bad rap. Instead of racing through a storm of whizzing bullets, I was playing chicken at sundown, the tips of my ears and nose going cold and the smile on my face huge. That December evening we ran the length of the schoolhouse and back again, the girls giggling so hard I almost lost my grip on Calliope.

On our next circuit, Kamber straddled the raceway. "Girls, y'all behavin' out here?"

"Yes, ma'am." They nodded furiously.

"*Hmmph.*" Her fierce maternal expression softened. "Looks like you have a way with the littl'uns."

Blondie shuffled his feet and sputtered, "Thank ya kindly, Kamber."

She set him straight in record time. "I was talkin' 'bout your Cannon there."

Barking a laugh, I knocked him on the shoulder, which made Callie giggle and wriggle more on her precarious perch, earning them another stern address.

"Dinnertime, and don't be forgettin' y'all's manners none."

When the girls gained firm footing on the ground, they peered up at us with the same solemn brown eyes. It was with very serious expressions that they said, "Thank you, Uncle Caspar, Uncle Nathaniel, for playin' with us."

I coughed behind my hand to cover the brusqueness of my voice. "No problem."

Blondie ruffled their hair and sent them packing. Skipping away, they bent their heads together in whispers, stopping once or twice to wave.

Later that night, after we'd taken our meal in the mess and messed around in the big bathtub, we cuddled under the blankets. Candlelight cast shadows across his face, his damp hair making wet blots on the pillows. "Linc and I used to switch places, tryin' to trick Momma up. She got so steamin' mad when she couldn't tell us apart. I had to brush my hair just so, make sure my tie was straight and my shirt tucked in. Linc razzed me about my sloppy appearance, but he made the switch just the same. We placed bets on how long we could get away with it. One time we made it two days, foolin' Momma, Father, our instructors. Hell, even Farrow couldn't tell us apart."

"You miss him."

"Half the time we didn't get along, and then he went on over to Father's side, believing all those goddamn lies. But it doesn't matter. I'll never be rid of that missin' part of myself." Rolling to his back, he ran his fingertips up and down my thigh in an unconscious caress. "Those sisters, Callie and Dauphine, made me think of it."

Man, seeing him with the kids, the idea of him as a father supplanted the hundreds of other fantasies in my head. "I want children," I blurted.

"I want yours."

"How?" It didn't take a damn doctor to know neither one of us had the right receptacle for growing babies.

"Well, no one's sayin' we can't, for starters."

"Yeah, but—"

Rising above me, he kissed me into silence. "There's adoption, surrogacy."

"Out here?"

"*Mmm-hmm*. Even here. Not everyone's cut out to be parents, ya know."

I spread my hands over the muscles fanning his back, lifting my lips to his ear. "You are."

"Think we could get married first?" He encircled the ring shining on my finger.

"I'm ready now." I growled against his throat, throwing him onto his back.

His guttural laugh coiled a hot ball of need in my groin. "Soon, big man, soon."

*   *   *

"You know the drill, *beb*?"

"Roger that." I hauled up my pants, trading my fatigues for sleek new leathers Liz had picked up for me along the way, adding them to a stash of ammo, C4, and other fun treats. I shot a look at Leon and caught him checking out my ass. I couldn't wait to tell Blondie about that. "No, actually. Not sure I do."

The only drills I knew came with shouted orders and moving targets. This handfasting malarkey was something else entirely. When I got no response from Leon, I cut around to him again. He lounged against the Love Hovel's narrow doorway, his gaze fixed on my shirtless torso. "Boy, you better stick those eyes back in their sockets. Blondie won't take kindly to you ogling me, you know?" I smacked him on the back of the head, trying to pop his peepers back in and the lust out. "Besides, what's this I hear about you and Darke?"

Darke's battle-weary warriors had returned to the commune a few weeks after us. The winning combo of Freelanders and insurgents had worked its magic in campaign after campaign, coming up goddamn golden when Alpha finally fell. But triumph in war was cold comfort against the haunting of their dead brothers and sisters who'd been ambushed by the Corps recon soldiers, not to mention the casualties of later combat.

Breaking from the disquiet around me, I'd stepped beside Darke as he hung back from the villagers' subdued welcome. "I'm sorry."

The movement of his mouth was the grimace of a cadaver. "You're not responsible."

"I'm Corps. I'm responsible."

"Then you understand this is how they would've wanted to die. My Tammerick, my Wilde." He'd grabbed my shoulders, wide brown eyes sketched in sad acceptance. "Weapons in hand. Righteous of heart. Together."

Flushing a swarthy shade of pink, Leon curved his lanky frame from the door and pulled his fingers over his lips. "Ain't nothin'." Poised with one boot tip over the other, his sharp chin ducked to his chest. "I'm not sure he's ever gonna get over Wilde and Tammerick.

Just wanna be there for him. Plus, you can't blame me for looking.
I'd sure like to have all that dark meat."

"Fuck, boy. You sure know how to pick 'em."

"What I'm gon' do?" Tonguing the corner of his mouth, he surveyed me again. "Like dem big and hard."

I had to hand it to the kid. He still thought with his dick, but he'd
manned up while I was having my whirlwind vacation at the Outpost. The word in the village was he'd pulled every shift he could
pick up. On the blackest nights, when they weren't sure if the fight
was headed their way, he'd entertained the children, cared for the
elders, and kept the hand-me-down Colt on his hip at all times. A
babysitter with a handgun.

"What am I supposed to do now?" After I pulled on a blazing
white shirt, I inspected my appearance in the mirror as much as
I could. The frigging thing was framed in curlicues and plastered
in flower cutouts. I reached for my tie. I didn't really like anything
around my neck anymore, but I'd wear it for Blondie.

"*Gawd*, Caspar. Just tell 'im you love him. And if dat don't work,
get on your knees. Does it for me." Leon handed me a shot of liquor
and set to work on the throat-choker. "Wearin' cologne?"

"Shut it."

"You talk to your man like dat?" He tied the knot, yanked the
ends together, and knocked a glass to mine.

"No. It's all romance and flowers."

The strong woodsy flavor burning him, he choked out a laugh.
"Your hands are shakin'."

"I got the DTs." I sank my shot and took more time than usual
putting the glass down on one of the gaudy little tables.

Leon held the black leather blazer open. "Jacket."

I punched my arms through and inhaled. Exhaled. I checked the
time like an addict waiting for his next hit. Ten more minutes. We'd

been kept apart all damn day, and I needed to see Blondie so badly I couldn't concentrate on anything other than my heart thumping along with the minutes, trying to rush them along.

Satisfied I didn't look like a total schmuck, I quelled my stomach and pushed Leon out the door. "Let's go."

At the gate to the meadow, I stopped and stared, a smile curling up my lips. It was a damn pretty sight, festooned with ribbons in red, fat bows and bells of all sizes clanging together when we entered. A trail of red berries scattered over the wintry walkway showed us the way to the altar.

"You're shivering. You scared?"

It was January and cold as a CO heart. Not the Beltane ceremony Hills and Eden had pushed for—a time of rebirth for the natural world—but Blondie and I had agreed. Two months of courtship was time aplenty, and I was so eager to become his husband my heart was ready to leap out of my chest.

The shivers were from excitement, pure undiluted emotion.

"No, I'm cold," I lied.

When we crested the small hill, there was no stopping the chills coursing up and down my spine. *Nope.* This sure as hell wasn't a Joining Ceremony, a cold affair specializing in the commerce of two people, or even a Validation of Union, the same deal for CO higher-ups. This was a gathering of people invested in our love. Arranged in circles, their hands joined, I estimated about five hundred villagers to be looking up at me.

"Just don't let me cry, Leon."

"*Mais,* cryin's good."

"I'm not into public displays of weepies." I started down the far side of the hillock, knowing I was gonna get hit by a heavy case of blubbering pretty damn soon.

"You seen your man yet?"

Holy shit.

Tendrils of dark green ivy worked their way between white blooms on the bower arching above Nathaniel's handsome head. *Nathaniel.*

I might know jack shit about handfasting or tying the knot, but when I wove down the aisle toward him, I was tongue-tied. And even though there was a crowd of people around us, it felt like we were the only two men in the world.

All my bluster faded, just like that.

His suede jacket hugged his shoulders, the flaps flipped up over his ass in a dovetailas he leaned toward little Calliope. She held on to his hand, listening with the all-consuming attention of a four-year-old.

I knew exactly how she felt. Nathaniel was worth the attention. He'd commanded mine from day one, and his hold over me had only ramped up since we'd returned to Chitamauga.

On the verge of getting hitched, I thought back to my squat with its bare cot and the plant I'd let die. The robo-fish that'd gone belly-up before I named it, the dog I'd never had. I had more now than I could ever quantify, starting with a family made up of so many more relatives than I ever thought possible. They were all waiting in this snowy meadow, watching me get closer and closer to Nathaniel.

When he straightened from bending Callie's ear, he saw me. His throat flushed up to his ears, pink captured inside the open collar of his white shirt. No tie.

Narrowing my eyes, I loosened mine.

I never thought myself one for commitment. Hell, I was never even given the chance to consider it before, let alone dream about it. Now I wanted to punch the air, sprint to him, make out with him for hours on end. I held it all together by a tight wire, winding through the throng of Freelanders. In muted wool and multicolored layers of lace or satin or velvet, they'd come out in their best finery. Old, rich leather, collars and cuffs in fur, hats and delicate woven, woody crowns.

The Rivers and the Fieldings.

Fischer and Forrest and Hatch.

Darke clapped my back when I passed by, and Leon stayed behind with him.

Traitor.

The inner ring held Liz and Farrow, their linked hands not nearly as noticeable as their standout Territory garb. Tall and lean as a hairpin trigger, Liz was dressed head to toe in motorcycle black, holstered and booted. Tiny and blonde, Farrow wore a fine lady's gown.

Micah and Kamber were right there with Calliope and Dauphine.

All but buried in petals, the altar held a simple wooden table bearing the sacred tools for our ritual. I hated to crush those delicate petals on the ground where Nathaniel stood, but they were in my way. Barely noting Hills and Eden behind Nathaniel, I walked to him, his look sending shock waves all the way to my toes.

"Goddamn." Grasping his neck, I fingered through the loose strands of his hair until I had a good hold. Too impatient to wait until the *I do*'s, I crushed him to me as his mouth parted for my tongue. Our kiss was hungry; it heated me from within.

Hoots and hollers of the best kind swirled around, followed by Liz's throaty call. "Doncha think you should exchange rings before spit?"

Turning in to his throat, I groaned.

His hands on my arms, my lover wore a happy, dazed look. "You're blushing."

"It's frostbite." I stomped my feet in the flowers and snow. I still couldn't get used to making out with him in front of other people, having the freedom to touch him when I wanted to. I never wanted to get used to it; it felt too good.

Our fingers twined together as we faced Hills and Eden. Beyond the altar, the beautiful meadow was an icy landscape of misty ghosts giving way to love.

Hills the priest was a much better master of ceremonies than Head Honcho the whoreson. Even with his long ears and the crown of fat berries titled on his head, his demeanor was that of a beneficent sage. He gave us each a searching look before proclaiming, "There are two men among us seeking the bond of handfasting."

Eden held a gnarly wand in one hand, a slim dagger in the other. "They shall be named."

My eyes brimming, I held on to Nathaniel's hand, bringing him forward. I didn't dare look at him, only squeezed his hand harder and rubbed my thumb over his bare finger, which would soon wear my ring.

"Nathaniel Rice unto Caspar Cannon." A perpetual smile dented the white whiskers on Hills's face.

Eden wiped her eyes and spoke to her son. "Are you Nathaniel Rice?"

"I am." The heat of his stare landed on the side of my face.

"Why do you stand before us today?"

He took one step closer to me until I turned toward him. His voice resonated with his pronouncement. "To vow my life and love to Caspar Cannon. Before the people of the Chitamauga Commune, and for all the world to see."

Hills planted himself next to me and asked. "Would you forgo this man in one year and one day, as is your right by the ceremony?"

"Screw that. I don't need an escape clause," I answered.

"No?"

"Never." Lifting Blondie's hand, I kissed his knuckles. When his lashes fluttered down, I smiled and brushed my mouth over them again.

"What is your desire, Caspar?"

"This man right here." Fuck yeah. He felt so good. This was the most right thing I'd ever done.

"Anything else?"

"I love him. I want him always. And ditto what he said." I needed to recite poetry about how much I loved him? I could tell he knew by the way his chest rose, filling with the force of my emotion.

Placing the priapic wand between our joined palms, Eden bade us to hold it firmly. I stroked the soft skin of his inner wrist, watching while his lips parted and his breaths came as fast as mine.

A long red ribbon trailed through Eden's hands, its color a carnal shock in the white-on-white landscape. This was the kind of bondage I could get behind. The wide red sash trapping our right wrists together stretched up our forearms with our arms crossed between us. I had plans for that ribbon later, maybe tie Blondie up, have my way with him for hours, days. Hell, I was gonna have him all to myself forever.

Lifting a teardrop from his cheek, I cupped his beloved face. It was hard to smile through all the emotions churning inside me, and when I managed it, I tasted the warm saltiness from my own tears.

The ribbon tethering us as one, Eden quietly blessed us in a bond I never wanted to be freed from.

"Caspar, I love you so much."

Heat like I'd never felt before lit up every single nerve in my body. "I can't wait to make you mine, Nathaniel," I whispered for him alone.

Eden's voice rose to encompass the commune. "People of Chitamauga Commune, Nathaniel Rice and Caspar Cannon ask that you bear witness to their vows."

When she passed the athame to Nathaniel, I didn't waste any time admiring the craftsmanship of the fine dagger. My attention was solely directed on the man before me.

Turning the point to the inner flesh of my free wrist, he hesitated. "You ready?"

"More than ready, baby."

He lifted my wrist, kissing the pleasure point before driving the tip into my flesh. He watched my face the entire time he said his pledge to me. "I, Nathaniel Rice, bind myself to Caspar Cannon. I commit to him my heart, my honor, and my strength, for I will cherish him always.

"I will watch over him, stand beside him, and guard the love he has given me."

Mesmerized by his voice and his vows, I couldn't stop caressing his wrist.

His timbre deepened as he held the knife aloft between us. "May this athame be used against me if my love does not hold true." Glowing blue eyes tore in to mine. "All this I swear to you, Caspar. So may it be."

The athame went from Nathaniel to Eden and over to me.

This was the first time I handled a weapon to profess my love instead of do harm. Small rivers of my blood stained my shirt as I continued the blood rite. Cutting a line across Nathaniel's vein, I focused on him. "I, Caspar Cannon, give myself to Nathaniel Rice." I tugged him closer, sealing my lips over the red trail.

His moan was rich and low.

"Through war and combat, in times of peace, I will be beside you. My love, my heart, my soul is yours, Nathaniel."

"Caspar..."

"Not done yet," I said. Breaths slid between us. Parted lips a centimeter away. "There is no place I'd rather be than at your side. You have brought me solace. You have shown me honor. You are so deep inside of me, Nathaniel."

His fingers caressed mine, his eyes a brighter blue, shining with unshed tears.

"With *everything* I am, I commit myself to you. All this I swear in the name of liberty, life, and our love. So may it be."

We closed the last bit of space between us, pressing the shallow cuts on our left wrists together. The red ribbon was mirrored in the crimson drops, and we were linked by both hands in an infinite chain.

There was nothing more beautiful than that.

Except for Blondie's pink cheeks and gorgeous forget-me-not eyes.

Hills's deep bass married Eden's soft lilt as they spoke together. "From this meadow to the forest, from your hearts to your souls, you will be blessed. Hold on to each other. Be true. Be brave. Know that life and love are a journey you will undertake as one."

As one. I inhaled against Nathaniel's cheek.

Hills and Eden encircled us. "Nathaniel Rice, Caspar Cannon, you are one before this commune, unto each other, for all time."

"So may it be." The chorus surrounded us.

Our rings were placed into our palms, and I curled my fingers against Nathaniel's, enclosing my token.

We'd both been down to the forge, giving our orders to Smitty. He'd inspected my castoffs, ruminating, the corner of his sandy mustache dipping into his mouth. I'd offered silver from a necklace Farrow had given me as well as a rose-gold pin that had belonged to Liz's mother.

"Think I can do somethin' with these." He'd pushed his smeared glasses up on his nose. "That Nathaniel of yours already been down here, just as keen as y'are, I'd say."

Nathaniel's lips moved against my ear. "Love you, husband."

My hand shook in his firm grip as he eased a new ring on my finger. The wide band was dark as the insides of an old oak, capped in silver, and scrolled with tiny tree limbs. It sat perfectly on my finger, the metal warming as quickly as my heart.

I didn't think I had enough breath to even speak the words welling up inside when I gave him my ring. Smitty had done a fine job, smelting down the metal and twisting it into lean lines of silver barred by a few rose-gold nuggets, the same color as Nathaniel's lips.

"There's no token on this planet that could ever signify how much I feel for you. I love you so much, baby."

His throat bobbed as the wedding band slid home. His fingers clasped mine as he pulled me into a searing kiss. His tongue coiled against mine, a slow licking motion making me roll my hips into his.

He lifted his head. "Ceremony. People."

"Fuck 'em." I bent to him again.

"Only one I wanna fuck is you, so we gotta get through the rest of this thing."

I covered my groan, turning with him to face the Freelanders who were already ringed around us, six deep. We worked sunwise, accepting hugs from people with broad smiles and teary eyes.

The same path I'd come down earlier was now strewn with waxy white petals and lit by votives eclipsing the early evening. I wasn't walking alone. Blondie's hand was in mine when all around flares of red bloomed against the sky. The snapping release of hundreds of ribbons joined chants of *Live in freedom! Love at will!*

"Holy shit. That's beautiful." I stood stunned by the sight.

Some of the ribbons were more pink than red. Some were old things with frayed edges. Satin, cotton, the simplest strings waved from the hands of every person in the village.

"Yeah, it is."

Captured by the crowd, our path through the snowy fields was a celebratory stroll under the dusky sky awash in a wild rash of red. Reaching the mess hall, we were rushed inside to a view of the rafters rigged with more white flowers and bright banners.

Casks of homebrew were opened. Cider went the rounds again and again. Music swilled up to the ceiling. Fiddles and banjos, guitars and harmonicas, and voices signing songs I didn't know.

I propped up the corner of the makeshift bar, talking with Micah, but really I was watching Blondie work the crowd. He fucking glowed, and his eyes, whenever they sought me—which was approximately every twenty seconds—suffused me with their passion, starting a tight tingling that ran from my toes to my stomach.

"You gonna ask him to dance?"

"Nah. I don't want to interrupt him."

Micah drained his tankard and leaned away for a refill. "Seems to me that's exactly what you're s'posed to do."

"Really?" I peered around again but couldn't locate him. I turned back to Micah just as a pair of rough hands guided me into a well-built body.

While my eyes slid closed and my mouth parted with a low groan, I heard Micah strolling away. "That's what I'm talkin' about."

"*Mmm.*" Blondie purred in my ear. "What were y'all talkin' about, now?"

"Dancing."

"Gonna dance with him?" He shifted right up to me, his cock a long line against my ass.

"No. I'm gonna dance with you." His fingers twined with mine, I led him to the center of the room as a slow song started and the floor emptied for us.

His cheeks were pink, his eyes merry, and his lips lush. I brought our hands together between our chests, and our rings clinked softly.

Reaching behind him, I caressed his shoulders, sighing when his arms wrapped around my waist.

The silky stubble on his jaw moved over my cheek. "I wanna feel like this forever, honey."

As we moved in a series of loose circles, I gripped him tighter, our bodies perfectly aligned. "Like what?"

"So in love with you. The way you feel in my arms makes me wanna kiss you all night long just because I can." Leaning back, he stared at my mouth. "When you look at me, Caspar, those brown eyes so full of love and passion for me, that hot damn mouth." He enclosed me in both his arms to whisper in a voice that was near breaking, "Can't believe you're mine."

Pushing my voice over the lump in my throat, I cradled his face against my neck. "Double that, baby. Double that."

Then we danced, just like that. Eventually others returned to the floor, filling in around us. The songs changed, but the music, the other people, everything else was background noise shut out from our close embrace.

"Can I cut in?" I opened my eyes at the sound of Liz's smoky voice.

A kiss dragged down my throat. Blondie touched his tongue to my leaping pulse and pulled away. "'Course you can, Lizbeth."

I watched him saunter off, grabbing small Dauphine under her arms to spin her about the floor, his deep laugh joining her squeals.

Liz's fingers snapped in front of my face. Cutting my eyes to her, I narrowed them at the sight of her smug grin. "What?"

"You done good, Commander."

"Yeah, I did." I went back to watch detail, admiring Blondie's sweet ass. Then I remembered. "Wait. You let him call you Lizbeth?'

She shrugged. First Lieutenant Grant never let anyone call her that, not even me. "*Mmm-hmm*, and Farrow too." She waggled her eyebrows. "We gonna do this dancing thing?"

"I suppose."

"You afraid I won't rate as well as Nate?"

"No." I caught hold of her whipcord hips and moved with her. "I'm afraid you're gonna step on my feet."

"Ass."

We didn't share a lover's embrace, but we didn't fumble too much either. We kept looking at each other, our expressions probably the same. A little quizzical, a little surprised by all the new shit we were both experiencing. She'd been my right hand for so long, but now I had a lover, a husband. A new compatriot in all things.

We'd had word from abroad. Casualties, victories, intrigues. The very first steps being taken toward democracy and rule by the people in Alpha. The Company had been booted from Kappa on the continent of Europa and the Free-folk and Revolutionaries in FarAsian Nu Territory were kicking some serious ass.

Blondie had started it. He wasn't just a desk driver; he was the catalyst. The son of CEO Cutler, the head of technological acquisitions, he'd hot-wired the purifiers all over the world to release a bogus contaminant into the water supplies at the same time, throwing the CO into immediate InterNations chaos.

He'd been groomed for takeover, just not the kind he'd served up. Like millions of us, he wanted something more. First and foremost, the freedom to love whoever he wanted.

Blondie wants me.

There was still a hell of a fight ahead of us, and no doubt it was gonna get real dirty, but we were gonna hang tight for a while. Take advantage of this thing called the honeymoon period.

"So…" I started, peering at Liz as we swiveled around the floor. Her head tilted. "So?"

No matter Blondie was going to be by my side from now on, I still had a healthy dose of protective instinct where Liz was concerned, especially since while I was planning on honeymooning, she was prepping to go headhunting.

During our trek back to the commune, I finally found out what she'd wanted to tell me the day her D-P fritzed out. She'd been under attack during a fierce Wilderness battle between our Corps and a band of Freelanders from another commune on the road to Beta. After the fight settled, she and the others were interrogated, and she'd had her own questions for her captors. The intel she got did a massive head number on her, so much it forced her to see the tribe of people in a whole new light.

Her father, Robie Grant—a high-ranking Corps medical officer and chief geneticist—was killed while treating wounded in the Wilderness. *By Nomads.* At least that had been the official story. Now there was a possibility it had all been a Company cover-up, and she needed to get to the truth. A truth that could be found only in Beta Territory, where Grant had last been based.

My face turned sour. "You're going to Beta. I don't like it."

"The war needs me there, Caspar. Don't go all fucking big brother on me."

"You're not just going for the war."

"I have to find out about my dad. Wouldn't you want to know?" She stepped away, knee cocked and fingers resting on the butt of her Desert Eagle, where they felt most at home, no doubt.

"I'm going with you."

She rolled her eyes, and I thought about breaking her neck for her to save her the trouble of getting eyeball deep in Corps and CO espionage up in Beta. "You are staying here, with your man." She took a step forward, fingers now curled over her sidearm. "Why the hell'd you think I let you get hitched anyway? Nate keeps you out of my hair."

Anger tightened my throat. "You're a real piece of work, you know that? I'm still your superior officer, Lieutenant."

"And you're a real sumbitch, sir." She gave a smart-assed salute. *And* she'd picked up the local lingo. Nice.

It was fucking impossible to love her, yet it was unimaginable how much I did. I rolled my shoulders and blew out a stream of air. "Fine. For now."

"Thanks for your blessing, Big Papa." Getting back into my arms, she jerked her chin over to Farrow. "Besides, I got backup. Farrow knows Linc. He just doesn't know she's in the underground. It's fricking perfect. She can get me close to him and the info I need."

"Foolhardy *and* stupid." I gave my strategic assessment.

"You ever know me to go off without my head on tight?"

I hugged her close. "No."

"Not going to start now, sir. Besides, I'm sticking around here a bit longer."

She'd gotten caught up in the spirit of the place just as I had. The commune with its colors and liveliness reminded me of her bedroom back in Alpha, the sanctuary she had decorated in such a pretty fashion, that she'd kept hidden from everyone. The village may have been shabbier than her paintings and feminine treasures, but this was someplace to share in the fabric of life instead of shying away from desires in fear.

Motioning to Farrow, I asked, "How's that working out for you?"

"Digging for some dirty details to spice up your love life already?"

I turned red right to my hairline. "I want to know if she's treating you right."

At that, she threw her head back and hooted, like a goddamned owl. "Oh yeah. That's one way of putting it." Her hair a black ruff on her head, her slim body swayed away from mine. "But I still like dick, and since yours is not now—nor was it ever—an option, I'm gonna go find a new partner."

I figured that was enough socializing and tried to get back to Blondie, but people kept getting in my way. Every damn time I got close, he was spirited off or I was waylaid. Man, I wished I could wipe them all from the face of the earth, or at least wind the revelers down and send them to bed, so we could get to ours.

I'd just planted my ass on a bench and was keeping an eye on Leon with Darke when Blondie's arm slid over my shoulders.

"Ain't he always falling for the wrong fella?"

Darke leaned down to listen to Leon, locking Leon's hand inside his big brown paw. After Leon pushed up to say something in his ear, the huge man pulled back, a smile glistening on his lips and a hint of russet under the deep ebony of his cheeks.

"Huh." I sat up straighter.

"Or maybe not." Blondie knocked against my shoulder. "You sort things out with Lizbeth?"

"Don't know about sorted out. She's going off to Beta, and I'm not thrilled about that."

Propping his head on his hand, he smiled. "You are such a protector."

I grumbled some more. Probably damn blushed too.

"*Mmm-hmm.*" His hand spread around the back of my neck and he drew me near. "Don't get me wrong. I like it."

Against his lips, I said, "Of course you do. Got me into your bed, didn't it?"

Blondie's slow perusal of my body added a whole lot of pressure in my leathers as my cock hardened. "Sure did. And that's exactly where I wanna be right now."

"Hell, yes." I hopped up, grabbed his hand, and dragged him out of the wide doors before anyone could stop us with more annoying stories about when they got hitched.

"Slow down!"

Slow down? Not frigging likely. I picked him up in my arms instead.

By the time Blondie figured out I was heading in the opposite direction of the Love Hovel, I was already two thirds of the way to our destination. Dazed from the kisses I'd been laying on his neck and against his ear, he asked, "Not taking me back to the Wilderness, are ya?"

"Just a little farther."

Rounding a big stand of bushy pines, I stopped when I saw it. Our caravan, lit up like a harlot's den in a far corner of the meadow where we could still see the votives trailing toward our altar.

"What the—? How did you—? Caspar?"

I laughed, tightening my hold on him as I bounded up the rickety steps.

"You gonna put me down sometime?"

"Not yet." I nipped his bottom lip. "Did some research of my own, and it's traditional for the groom to carry his beloved over their threshold."

After stooping a lot and turning to make it through the skinny doorway, I slid him down my body.

"When'd you do all this?" He fell back against me.

All this was having the fire in the cast-iron stove lit hours in advance. Pillows and food, flowers and fine bourbon all at the ready. As well as a fucking thousand little silver tinker's bells I definitely hadn't added laced all over the outside of the caravan. The mind-boggling bullshit the villagers had put up was gonna make me think twice about fucking him hard and fast in case I set off alarms.

"Got some of it sorted this morning, during all those hellish hours when no one would let me near you. Then Micah hitched it up to the tractor and hauled it out here." I walked across the room burnished in candlelight and smelling of sweet blossoms. "Wanted some privacy."

Giving me a slow, burning smile, he stalked toward me. *"Hmm."*

I suddenly felt nervy with his seductive approach. I scrubbed my hand over my hair. "Uh, Evangeline helped with the flowers."

He didn't spare a glance at the bouquets bursting with colorful winter blooms. "I like 'em." He had me backed up against the dresser. My hands flew back. I knocked over the whiskey tumblers. "Know what else I like?"

"No." My breath was trapped in my chest, my chest billowing in and out so fast I cried out when his midriff met mine.

"You." His lips were hot, his kiss tender, inviting. His tongue a succulent treat stroking into my mouth.

I clasped his face, my cock throbbing when he groaned.

"So damn gorgeous, honey. Can I undress you?"

Nodding like an idiot, I watched every slow move he made. His fingertip trailing from my waist up the middle of my chest, he slid the tie from my neck, whipping it aside. "I'm gonna make you feel so good, so cherished."

Spending our first night as married—handfasted—men, I already felt cherished. But his hands unbuttoning my shirt and then tickling through the hairs on my chest took that good feeling to a mind-blowing level.

"Love your chest." He nuzzled against my pecs, his tongue swiping a nipple. A thrill shot down my body and my hips jolted forward at the sensation of his mouth closing over the nub.

"Oh fuck." Felt like the only solid thing in my body was my dick, and I was about to fall over.

His fingers scratched over my nipples as he spread my shirt and jacket wide. Backing up, he left me like that. "You look good in a suit."

"Don't get used to it."

"Oh, I won't. 'Cause you look a thousand times better without a stitch on." He jerked the buttons on my leathers and I gasped. With the placket open and my cock leaping against my stomach, he slid the shirt and jacket down my arms, returning to caress the heavy muscles of my shoulders. He breathed deeply against my neck before working that pink mouth down my body, nibbling muscles, licking into my belly button, sucking the side of my cock with his hands stuffed down my pants.

"Jesus Christ, baby, please."

"Mmm." The smirk on his face totally erotic, he cast his eyes to mine while he lowered my pants, ridding me of everything below.

Up and down my thighs his fingertips teased, his eyes on my shaft. I was getting close to whining when he leaned forward and rubbed his bristly shadow through my pubic hair to my cock. The groan that came out of me broke off when he sucked the head into his mouth. Leaning on my hands against the dresser, I shifted onto my tiptoes and watched him take me deep.

When my cock was wet all over, when I couldn't breathe anymore through my moans and my entire body was straining, he lifted up to suckle. Just my cockhead between those lips, his eyes closed, he drifted his tongue around and around and into the slit welling with liquid.

So hot I was sweating, so overcome with lust I was swearing and panting, I pressed him off, my hands in his hair.

"Your turn, before I come all down your throat, baby." I hauled him up my body, and goddamn it was sexy feeling his clothes rasping against my naked skin. I kissed his luscious lips before setting to work on his coat, making my way through his shirt in record time just so I could get to his strong shoulders and lean chiseled chest.

He wasn't talking anymore, but I was. "Jesus, look at you." I sent kisses all over his abdomen, sucking his skin into my mouth to feel his muscles tense against my lips. He gasped when I reached down for his foot, resting it on my thigh as I kneeled before him. Nuzzling my face against his thick shaft inside his pants, I traced the ridge of his head clearly defined against the tight fabric.

His hips jutted out and he grabbed my shoulders, nails biting into my skin.

My tongue wrapped around the indecent length of his penis, I made his pants so nice and wet I could even see the veins standing out against his stiff cock.

"Fuck yes," I growled, tearing off his boots and socks.

Planting his feet on the floor, I sent his pants buttons flying. His back arched when I squeezed my hands inside against his hard, flexed ass, going at his bared cock, grinding my nose in the soft blond crown curling at the base of his beautiful shaft.

I jerked him nice and slow, running my tongue all around his balls and underneath. The tip of my tongue swirled along the tiny bridge of skin just there until he whimpered above me.

Finishing off his trousers, I stood. "Bed, now."

I followed, placed him on his knees, and faced him in the same position. Our hands wandered over the landscape of each other's bodies, our mouths never leaving the other. Overheating, grabbing hair and muscles and cocks, we moaned together.

I placed my palm on his chest and retreated, catching my breath. Retrieving the lube, I snapped it open and poured it into his palm and onto my fingertips. "Lie down, Nathaniel."

"Like this?" His breathy voice was a massive turn-on, and so was he. On his back, his legs spread for me.

I admired his wide-open body, my hand running up his thigh. "Just like that."

His cock jumped against my mouth when I snuck down to linger over him with long, moist kisses, and then I straightened over him on my knees. "Get me wet?"

His hand wrapped around me, slick and hot, the sensation of his strong touch ripping through me. I gently kneaded his sacs and dipped below, easing a finger into his passage, smothering his groan with my mouth on his.

Both of us ready, I sat on my heels, shaking to be inside him, but there was one thing I had to do first. "I did some other research." I pistoned my hand up and down both our cocks in a torturous fist fuck.

"Did ya?"

After a deep kiss, I rubbed my mouth over his. "Found this other ritual I like. Let me show you?"

He plucked my bottom lip between his and let go with a growl. "I'll do any damn thing you want, anytime you want."

"That's dangerous." My kiss rough, my tongue searched his teeth, the roof of his mouth, devouring his groans. "I'll be taking you up on that offer."

I pulled his wrist to my lips, licking the neat pink scar from our earlier rites. "Nathaniel Rice. Blondie." I kissed that sweet flesh. "Blood of my blood, you honor me with the gift of your heart."

I smeared the tear from his cheek and leaned over to kiss him again, lying fully on top of him.

He captured my hand and turned it over, meeting my eyes to swear, "Caspar Cannon. Bone of my bone, blood of my blood, I take you into my heart. I give mine in return."

I let the emotions flow. This moment above all others felt so right and true. "My mate, my match, my love and lover."

I hovered just outside his entrance, letting him accept me into him.

With a small press toward me, he whispered, "I take you into my body."

I thrust into him, tipping my pelvis, hitting him wide and deep and long, groaning, "God, yes, you do, baby."

His laugh was snuffed out when his hips rose to mine. I held his neck in one hand, his ass in the other, and we moved together, one writhing motion, one endless wave. His thighs circled my waist and his arms wound around my back, and we kissed through every lunge and each pulsing withdrawal.

The urge to come hit me hard and fast when his hand moved to my thigh, pulling me forcefully in to him. Locked within Nathaniel, I roared with the release that came from my heart and soul, pouring out, pouring into him.

He reared off the bed in his orgasm, face straining, biting down on his lip and moaning, "Love you. Oh God! I love you."

Rolling against each other, I pushed the hair off his brow and held him.

Although the red ribbon had been folded and placed in a cushy carved box on the dresser, our hands were bound together. Our hearts tied to each other, linked in love.

We stayed that way for a long time, until he rubbed his hand across my chest. "What do you wish for now?"

I could wish for a million things, but none of it mattered then. Not with my husband in my arms and his head on my shoulder, his love filling my soul. "Not a goddamn thing. I got it all with you, Blondie."

"Me too, Caspar. Me too."

Look for the next sizzling novel in the Don't Tell series!

See the next page for a preview of

On Her Watch.

Chapter One

February, 2071, Chitamauga Commune

Liz Grant, are you the daughter of Robie Grant?"

I held the polished doorknob in my hand, straining to see the young trooper's eyes hidden beneath the low brim of his cap. I nodded, my heartbeat knocking around my chest.

"Your father, First Class Medical Officer and Chief Geneticist Robie Grant, is dead." He sped through the details of a gruesome killing at the hands of Nomads, speaking like an automaton, no emotion on his face, no inflection in his voice.

I stared at the badge on his chest until my vision swam and what was left of my heart sank to my knees, knees that buckled. The gleaming metal of his insignia winked when he turned toward the corridor. I stood in the open doorway, watching his retreat, tears spilling down my face.

"Lizbeth?" Mom called from behind me.

Bending in two, I retched, shoving an arm out to ward her off as her cautious footsteps came closer.

"Lizbeth?" She hurried forward, pulling my face around. "Lizbeth, what's happened?"

Vomit stained the carpet, curdled under my tongue. I spoke the words I never thought we'd hear. "Dad's gone."

"Your father's—" A tall woman with black hair, so elegant and refined she could sweet-talk any Company stuffed suit, Mom backed away from me, her hand shaking, her finger pointing. "Don't you dare say that."

"Mom?" I rose to my feet, and my stomach heaved again. "Mom!"

Stopping halfway down the hallway, she crumpled to the floor, wails breaking from her as she beat her head against the wall. "No, no, no, no. He said we'd be safe! He said he'd make sure. Rob told me not to worry."

I crawled to her, sliding her head into my lap, my world falling apart with each of her fragmented cries. "Mommy?"

Jesus and Christ! A litany of swears sped past my lips as I jumped off the bed, hefting one of my Desert Eagles in a shaky grip. The sensation of all-seeing eyes watching my every move didn't stop just because I was in the Freelanders' Chitamauga Commune, somewhat safe from immediate danger. Scanning the moon-saturated surrounds of my borrowed caravan and coming up clear, I put the safety on, rubbing the barrel against my cheek. Sweat-soaked sheets pooled around my hips. My thin top clung to me, and perspiration slid in icy trickles between my breasts, brought on by the habitual nightmare of my dad's slaughter.

I was a hard-ass. The Revolution, the deaths I'd witnessed, and the kills I'd caused, not even the Company itself, with its aggressive worldwide lockdown on so-called aberrant sexual behaviors, could break me. The only thing that terrorized me each and every night was my dad's murder. He'd been mutilated, the blame placed on a Wilderness Nomad tribe, people we'd been brainwashed to believe were bloodthirsty savages. I didn't buy that particular feed anymore either, not after I'd ended up in Chitamauga, where the people had proved themselves to be exactly what they purported: Freelanders, not vicious, ignorant Nomads.

I lay down on the bed, snuggling my pair of pistols under a pillow, close at hand, just in case. I kept my hand on the butt of a gun instead of the firm bottom of a petite blond spy who'd become my playful pastime and a fond friend far too quickly for my liking. Rolling onto my back, the smile gathered from remembrances of Farrow was replaced by a grimace when I shut my eyes, thoughts of my father spinning back to me.

Sleep off the roster for a second night running, I tossed the pillow aside and lit one of the old-fashioned lanterns, its warm glow nothing like the cool halos powered by Territory electricity. I ripped several pages from some ledger Farrow had left behind and located a stilo-pen. After my dad's death, I'd ransacked the condo searching for his personal digi-diary, coming up empty. This was one connection I still had with him. Distilling my thoughts and fears into mere words on a page I'd later destroy meant I didn't have to truly face them. Some hard-ass I was, all right. I gave a dry laugh and set the pen to paper, scribbling quickly.

Heading up to Beta in a couple days. My mind hasn't been on straight since finding out about the cover-up on Dad. Eleven years and it feels like yesterday I answered that knock on the door in Beta. I expected a mandatory quarantine order because of the spread of the Gay Plague or another CO soiree invite for my folks. Judging from the sharpness of the knock, I should've known it was neither. The trooper outside couldn't have been much older than me. The cap he wore shaded his eyes from view until he pushed it up, revealing scathing snapdragon-blue irises.

Looking down at the paper clenched in my hand, I saw the wet blotch of a tear making an even bigger mess of my words. That my father had been sent into the field should've been my first tip-off something wasn't right with the bullshit palaver my mom and I had been force-fed. He was high ranking and a scientist, not a frontline medic. But I'd been only eighteen at the time, and watching my mom fall to pieces with the news hadn't left me with a whole lot of thinking space.

The Company, the CO—the Cunts—remain oppressive to the core. Pumping us with a dawn-to-dusk spin for the good of mankind during day-long doses of pro-CO promos filtered in on our handheld, government issued Data-Paks for two generations running. The thing is, I used to believe in them. It was how I'd been raised, all I'd had left. Now I feel sick about all I've done to keep them in power. This regime with their so-simple manifesto: Maintain order, recoup the InterNations population, and execute anyone who stands in the way of their brainless breeder politics.

Maintain order; that's one thing I'm good at.

Too fucking bad for the CO a few million civilians teamed up with a massive wave of Freelanders from every InterNations Territory and the surrounding pockets of Wilderness to finally lay some beat-ass on their homophobic, homogenous hate-filled regime.

Too bad for them, but good for me, for us. I'd finally done the right thing, something I could be proud of, and I hoped my dad would've been, too. I'd dropped my first lieutenant rank, dropped out altogether from the Corps—the military branch of the CO—and skipped off their grid, joining up with the Revolution that had begun only seven months ago.

Blindly searching the bed where Farrow usually slept, I flattened my palm to nothing but a bunched-up pillow. She'd left two days ago, a spook for the Revolutionaries and the best babe around, care of her CO connections and the way she made me come, finger-tips traipsing over my clit, her puckered lips slipping up and down my slit. I shut my eyes, my body pulsing with memories, far better memories than deaths dropped on my doorstep or bullet holes I'd plugged into possibly innocent tangos on both sides of the war. I should've been worried about Farrow, but she could take care of herself and so could I.

Shaking my head, smiling, I started writing again.

I've been taking care of myself since the minute that knock sounded on our door. Took care of myself in other ways, too, hardly lingering over a handful of infrequent lovers. Hitting It and Heading Out: a little insider Corps motto, and we're not just talking about sorties. I've never been sweet to anyone but Farrow and she knows it.

My first affair with a woman and probably my last, since I'd figured I was incomplete in a way even she hadn't satisfied. I'd never had the time or wherewithal to explore my femininity, my sexuality, and Farrow's nightlong erotic escapades hadn't filled the aching hole.

Jesus, if Cannon could see me now. I remember one afternoon in Alpha, the two of us sitting side by side on the pavement, tinkering with our motorcycles, spending silent hours on the endless maintenance he called "twat to tit." He popped me on the shoulder. "Beats journaling, right?" Because we'd never be caught dead doing that. I came back with, "Maybe, but not as good as getting laid." He turned so red, for a minute I thought he took my remark as a come-on. Nah, I was only digging for a little truth about the commander, even back then.

Ah, fuck this. Maybe I should blame my mental masturbation on him. Cannon's infected me with his lovefest. It's no joke he and Nate go at it like rabbits. I knew about his illegal activities long

before he made a clean cut from the Corps, but I never let on until
he gave me the send-off last September. Pulled from his duties as
commander of the Elite Tactical Unit in Alpha, ordered to escort
Nathaniel Rice, the Company head of technological acquisitions,
to the Outpost, he didn't deny my suggestions then, but he didn't
affirm them either.

I pressed the slim stilo against my temple as I had the barrel of my gun earlier. A grin tugged my lips. Cannon would murder me if he ever read this.

Nathaniel Rice, known to his lover as Blondie…I'm not even call-
ing him Nate anymore, preferring Cannon's fuck bunny. He's
proven himself a worthy asset, and more than that, the major mas-
termind behind the Revolution, setting off InterNations-wide as-
saults on the global water plants so the regime ran around with their
asses to the wind, giving rebellious civilians a reason to incite war.

Cannon's love for Blondie makes sense. He never had any women
around, just his boyfriend, the Fist. It doesn't matter to me which
way he swings his club. But I wish they'd left their caravan—called
the Love Hovel by Cannon, me, and everyone else within hearing
distance—in its honeymoon position on the edge of the Chitamauga
meadow because Blondie the Fuck Bunny is a screamer.

Eyeing the pages in my hand, I placed the stilo on a stand beside the bed. The potbellied woodstove in the corner burped out faint gusts of smoke as fire ate through wood, warming the one-room caravan. The small door whined when I opened it, ash blazing blue. I shoved in the papers, waiting for the edges to curl and combust. I burned the evidence of my late-night weakness. *Leave no trail behind.*

My head slightly clearer, I returned to bed. I checked my rounds, hilled a few quilts to buffer my body, and closed my eyes. This lying-low-and-hiding-out gig had gotten old. It wasn't my style. I had some work to do, in the name of freedom... and for my father.

*   *   *

Leaving my caravan behind the next morning, I hastened through the snowy network of the wagoneer neighborhood. The caravan it-self was another surprise I liked more than I cared to admit. Its brightly patterned fabrics put me in mind of the Alpha digs I'd filled with colorful, luxurious black-market finds. Works of art, books that were banned, the feminine touches had been more than decorations to me. They'd been cherished treasures speaking to a side of myself I tended to ignore and kept hidden from all others, except for that nosy sumbitch Cannon.

Once freed of the forest, I crossed onto the commune's main street, crunching snow beneath my high-laced boots, securing my Corps cap to my head. I passed the mess hall, the trade stands, and the schoolhouse. Inside every silver-wooded structure, fires blazed and men, women, children, and animals milled, working off the winter's cold in this thriving back-to-the-earth community.

The usual undaunted mutt hightailed it after me, his owner's gray bleak face and growly voice the same as his dog's when he snapped an order to the mongrel and a slightly less irate G'mornin' to me.

Brought up a Corps brat, I preferred the war room—aka the meeting hall—to the women's hour that took place every morning, noon, and night within the open-air kitchens. Stepping into the town hall proper, I was greeted by a round table filled by the usual group of down-home councilors including Hills, Hatch, Darke, Eden, and Fuck Bunnies one and two.

Maps were splayed on the table, real paper things we could touch and handle. Before exploring the commune's well-maintained archives, I'd never seen a nondigital representation of the Territories, thanks to the CO destroying our history and replacing it with neat and tidy readouts easily digested from our D-Ps. Around the table, Hills and Eden carried on a murmured conversation while Nate winked at me and Cannon perfected his fear-inducing glare from deep brown eyes. One day before I departed for Beta Territory, he wasn't happy. *Surprise.*

Cannon's finger struck the green landmass at the upper-right quadrant of the InterNations map of the former United States, an area just outside Beta. He didn't even wait for me to take a seat before high-handing me. "Tell me what happened again."

Fuck. I mutely went about making myself a cup of coffee from the fixings in the center of the table, ignoring the hulking giant across from me.

"I won't stand for your insubordination, Grant." Cannon addressed me with a growl in his voice.

Holy hell. Clearly someone woke up on the wrong side of the caravan this morning.

"I don't think you have the brass to tell me what to do anymore, Caspar." Smiling sweetly, I took him down a notch by refusing to address him as Commander, Cannon, or sir. I loved Caspar Cannon like a brother, but sometimes he needed to be slapped, and Nate was probably too soft on him to do it.

Leader of the commune's well-organized militia, Darke matched Cannon's size kilo for kilo and came in a couple years older at an even thirty. From down the table he didn't seem too fond of listening to us spar. "Now, I know y'all two don't need to fuck it out—pardon me, Miss Eden." He apologized to the fair-haired healer, Nate's mom. "You need a fighter's ring to square your pube hairs away, we can sort that out right quick. I'm sure Micah would be more than happy to call our people in from the fields for a little Corps entertainment this morning."

I guessed he'd rather watch us duke it out.

"Jesus." Cannon pressed his knuckles to his temples.

"Christ." I sank into the last open chair.

We grinned at each other.

"I'm not shitting you, Liz," Cannon said as his grin evaporated and his expression became troubled.

"I know. I get it. Have my back, I'll have yours. I just didn't think you'd be riding my ass the whole way, too." Mug of hot coffee in hand, I took a sip before launching into an abbreviated version of what went down during my evacuee-escort detail from Alpha to Beta at the outbreak of the Revolution for the umpteenth time.

Still a hundred and sixty kilometers from Beta with a ragtag group of refugees, our supplies rapidly dwindling as winter approached and our trucks' fuel cells funneling low, I'd been all about hustling. "We were on Alpha-Beta Route Two, pushing the numbers, hoping to make it to Beta before we became frozen vulture food when either our supplies or gas tanks ran out. We were cutting it real close to those mountains." I nodded to the map.

"That's the home of the Catskills Commune," Hills commented, the presiding Elder of this democratic society.

"Right. Our fleet was engaged at nightfall. A freak early winter snowstorm had wiped out any hope of further travel during the afternoon, and we'd hunkered down inside the trucks, using body heat to keep out the cold. I must've dropped off. I shouldn't have fallen asleep. My tits were practically iced over, so I'm not even sure how I managed it. I was woken by the screaming whistle of bullets tin-canning our trucks."

Darke leaned forward. "They gotta have superior firepower and a lot of warriors to go at a Corps convoy."

"I can attest to their resources and resourcefulness. We were engaged with no warning. I shouted for the civilians to stay inside the trucks and take cover while the unit and I took the heat and sent it back. I knew how close we were to Beta. I *knew* this was the commune my dad's attackers came from. Taking down a Corps medical officer would've been big news. One of them had to remember." I glanced at Cannon, his face grim. "I lost my lid a little."

Lost my lid was an understatement. When I got close enough to a group of them, I'd ditched my guns and gone for hand-to-hand, nothing as satisfying as bloodying my knuckles. I must've been screaming the whole time. I'd never been so crazed before. I remember laughing, half hysterical, thinking I was as wild as the Nomads who'd murdered my dad.

Cannon nodded, pressing me on.

"I was restrained eventually, all of us detained, those who had survived the hail of bullets. They went for the big fish first, the full lieutenant of the operation, questioning me. I had a few questions of my own." I backhanded my eyes, blinking away from the sympathetic stares around the table. "I didn't believe them at first. Why would I? Corps to the end. Right, Cannon?"

"Shit." His hands scrubbed down his face.

"Yeah, a steaming load is what it was. Their elders gathered, and surprise, surprise, no one had heard of Robie Grant. None of them recalled a murder of that magnitude. He hadn't been sent to the front. It was all a wash job." I peered around. "Not a single one of them was lying. I've been lied to enough. I can smell it a kilometer away."

Taking a long drink of coffee, I swallowed down the anger and sadness that had been my constant buddies for more than a decade. "They let us go. I thought it was damned foolhardy. But they were Freelanders. What are you gonna do, huh?"

His long ears peeping through clouds of white hair, Hills imparted a nugget of his wisdom. "We don't believe in taking innocent lives."

"Should've told them that before they opened fire in the first place. Besides, no one's innocent in a war." That included me.

Cannon's voice echoed around the room, "You could've taken a bullet."

"I'd take a rain of them to know the truth."

"Liz."

"Cannon." I grasped his hand. I knew he thought I was headed on a reckless mission. "For once, don't be a pigheaded shitheel."

Nate took his hand from me, clasping Cannon's white knuckles in a gentle hold. "What happened then, Lizbeth?"

Lizbeth was the name only my mother and father had called me before him...and Farrow. Popping my knuckles and rolling my neck, I sat back, letting a grin slide across my mouth. "Then your friend Farrow showed up, right about the time we were approaching Beta, when I was pretty damn sure I'd be put into action for your brother Linc and his Beta Corps. That was a close one. I thought I'd have to kill Revolutionaries and Nomads—Freelanders—whose vision I was starting to share." I nodded to Cannon. "The rest is good as Old History, sir."

Cannon was no longer officially my commander and would never be part of the Corps again, not after blowing his cover sky high about his sexuality, which was as good as a death sentence in the eyes of the CO. But old habits die hard.

Nate turned to Hatch, the resident inventor who monitored transmissions to the commune. "Any word from Farrow?"

"Not yet. It's too early," Hatch replied.

Farrow was a family friend to Nate and his estranged brother, Linc, working all sides of this FUBAR situation with a feminine aplomb no one could pull off but her. She was to be my eyes and ears once I reached Beta. "My rendezvous is set up with her anyway."

Cannon snorted.

"You got a problem over there?" I asked.

"Yeah, I've got a problem. In fact, I have issues with the whole stinking thing. For starters, I don't see how a forty-five-kilo woman is gonna keep you walking the straight and narrow."

I gave a snort of my own. "I'm surprised you'd know anything about being straight, lover boy." Cannon blushed, making his hard and handsome visage appear sweet and boyish. I plowed on before he could stutter his way through his only vulnerability...Nate. "She's not tasked with being my damn babysitter."

Cannon's face cooled with his tone. "Someone needs to keep a leash on you."

My sidelong smirk slid to Darke. "The only one who'd know about the proper way to handle a leash is Darke. Let's leave that to him and Leon."

That was a direct hit, too. The brawny man's crush on Leon was as obvious as the telltale russet flush under his smooth brown skin. I couldn't even make another quip about their flirtation because his longing for the pretty-faced, twenty-year-old street hustler and his self-enforced denial was too painful to be comical. The man had lost his two life partners last autumn, casualties of this brutal war. I could only assume Darke had willfully decided not to put his heart on the line again, although it looked like he wasn't being too successful with his emotional lockdown.

A few days before Farrow had left, Leon moseyed up to us, saying he was ready to sign on and join us in Beta. The sweet, sexy boy was getting his heart beat up and broken every day from Darke's hot and cold emotions.

I figured that wouldn't go down well between the overprotective pair of Darke and Cannon, both of whom had a vested interest in Leon, but I listened with mild amusement as he tried to con his way into our operation. Idling on the edges of our discussion, Darke appeared not to be listening, but his big shoulders had turned rigid as rock.

Farrow had smiled gently at Leon. "You're gonna have to let me think about this now, Leon, but you might-could prove useful." I had to agree. The kid was wily as hell as well as easy on the eye. "Ah reckon you'd be good company for mah brother."

That comment had sparked Darke into action. Making the barest of excuses, he'd pulled Leon away from us, parked him against one of the outbuildings, and proceeded to kiss him with such heat, his hands running along Leon's lean waist to settle on his hips, it was a wonder the building didn't go up in flames. We'd walked away when Leon arched into the embrace, his loud groan carrying across to us.

Now, as then, Darke mumbled a few excuses and strode out of the meeting hall. Tipping my chair back, I looked out the window and, sure enough, he'd snagged Leon by the hand and was leading him down the dirt road.

Hills tugged on one of his long earlobes and cleared his throat. "Let's talk strategy."

I didn't know what the old goat knew about strategy, but I'd go with it. "We're planning a three-prong, long-term attack."

Nate pulled his chair forward. "Infiltration first."

"I've got that covered. Then I need to dig out the missing intel on my father, convince Linc to give up everything he's ever worked to attain, and take Beta down." All without letting on that I knew Beta Commander Linc Cutler's identical twin and his mother closely, or that I was on friendly terms with the Freelanders and a Revolution sympathizer. In the civil war of the Rice/Cutler family, Linc had followed in his notorious father's footsteps while Nate had finally freed himself from that man's reins to return to his mother's roots.

I couldn't let any cracks show from the time I landed in Beta to the time I left, hopefully in a blaze of glory instead of with my carcass carried out in a body bag.

I decided to play it down even more when Cannon's glower reformed on his face. He didn't need to know that I was feeling a few nerves, or that I hadn't been sleeping, or that I was scared the truth would turn out to be uglier than the lies I'd been eating all these years.

I was a soldier after all.

"Just a day in the life, Big Papa." I played his familiar line about our messed-up situation back at him.

Fist pounding the table in front of him, Cannon got ready to let loose when Eden cut in. "I want Lincoln out of there."

I joined Cannon in grumbling under my breath while I thought, *No added pressure or anything.*

Rubbing his mom's hand for a moment, Nate swiveled to his man, calming the beast with a few quiet words and a quick brush of his lips until Cannon's shoulders relaxed from their punched-up place near his ears.

Brushing his finger along Nate's jaw, Cannon whispered, "I know, baby."

Their apparent affection for one another would've given me another round of the sweats, except, if any two people deserved to be together, in love, it was them. They'd been through hell and back a few more times than anyone rightly deserved. Hounded on their trek from Alpha to the secure Outpost bunker, working through attraction, suspicion, sabotage, betrayal—you name it—just to end up with Cannon being arrested for wanton corruption of a Company officer. Not to mention finding out Nate was Alpha CEO Cutler's son must've been a big kick to Cannon's nuts.

But they'd come through it.

Aside from his blatant snit about my self-imposed assignment,

I'd never seen Cannon so happy. A day in the life was never gonna be the same for him, nor should it be. He'd found contentment, joy. Hell, seeing Cannon like this made me wonder just how much pain he'd been in, hiding his sexuality all those years and fighting to maintain rigid laws that went against his very nature. It also made me wonder what I was missing out on. After my mom committed suicide, unable to cope with the fallout of a family torn apart, the Corps and Cannon had become my family by choice. I'd since given up on one and watched another move on while my past was littered with those *hitting-it-hard* hookups. I envied Cannon and Nate's intimacy, craving companionship born of enduring emotion.

But thinking was for pussies, and I wasn't one of those, even if I had one.

Cannon jerked his seat back from the table to loom over me. "It's too risky."

I stood up, too, forcing him back a step. "You've made your objections clear, sir." I tacked on the *sir* just to placate his stubborn ass. He'd made his point clear, all right, about a hundred times in the past few weeks since finding out my plan to vacate and infiltrate. But no way in hell would I let Cannon risk his life fielding this operation. He had too much at stake. Displaced, transient, I didn't have anyone waiting up for me at the end of the day, so it made perfect sense to go in alone.

"Fuck's sake, Liz. You're going in there with your balls hanging out."

I looked down my body and back up his. "Good to know you think Linc will be more distracted by my hard-core gonads than by my feminine charms." Charms I'd only just discovered.

Commander Linc Cutler was my starting point in Beta, my only link to the Corps. I hoped to get close enough to either him or his father, CEO Cunt Cutler, to hack into their high-clearance D-Ps, where I could search out info on my dad and the InterNations plans for the Revolution. *Linc, well, his name is fitting anyway. He just doesn't know it yet.*

Letting me pass before him out of the building with a wry twist of his lips, half fond smile and half simmering sneer, Cannon caught up to me in two strides. We walked down the single road cutting through Chitamauga Commune side by side, falling into an easy, companionable march. Just like old times.

It was cold as a bitch out here, and Cannon's ears, nose, and cheeks quickly turned pink. The Freelanders were preparing for their midday meal in the mess hall, and we stepped to. It was a large, brightly lit wooden structure with long tables sided by benches, where all the families and newcomers, refugees and Revolutionary stragglers, ate together. Most mealtimes were so noisy with chatter and laughter it was hard to hear myself think, which was always a good thing.

"Fucking hell." Cannon grunted.

Peering past his shoulder, I looked into the open barn door of Smitty's iron forge. The insides were as red as fire. It must've been hot, too, because Leon and Darke were stripped down to their pants, glistening male chests on show.

"What's going on in there?"

"Darke's getting a tribute to Tammerick and Wilde. What they used to call a moko, a skin tattoo made with a bone awl and black dye." Hands running across his short black crew cut, he said, "It's a testament of his love for them."

"And he's making Leon do it? Jesus. I didn't think he was cruel."

"Leon's done it before on others, and he wouldn't let anyone else. He's too fucking headstrong for his own good. Maybe we should've let him rot in the brig back in Alpha when he was arrested."

Darke tenderly cupped Leon's face, giving him a long, slow kiss.

They were so beautiful together, Leon's sinewy build and tawny gold skin against Darke's rich brown body. Bits of their conversation drifted across to us, Darke's rumbling voice counterpoint to Leon's higher-pitched accent marking him for what used to be the Cajun people.

Darke pulled away. "You don't have to, angel."

"*Mais*, I wan' to, *cher*. Let me do dis for you."

When Darke lay down with his face buried in the muscle of his biceps, tears stood out on Leon's lashes, glittering in the hot red light.

A sharp spear of sympathy for the two men twisted through me. "Leon's getting his heart slayed over there."

"Doesn't have enough smarts to put that tattoo tool down and walk away." Cannon turned his brown eyes to mine. "Which is why I'd prefer him to stay out of the Revolution."

It was too intimate a scene to watch. One man devoted to his lost lovers, the other determined to give whatever he could. Their plight reinforced what this Revolution was about. Lives were not the only thing at stake but the freedom to choose whom you loved, how you loved no matter what gender. *Freelanders*, their very name was a call to arms.

Ambling on, Cannon asked, "Getting an early start in the morning?"

"Sure as the cock crows." I winked at him.

He barked out a laugh before getting his serious face on again. "Blondie and I are flanking you, at least part of the way."

I started to interrupt when he shut me up, pulling me into his arms, and through his strong embrace I felt him shaking. A giant tower of power and strength, he'd always been my steadfast comrade. Now I was getting ready to go it solo.

"Caspar."

"Keep that damn mouth shut and let me hug you for once." His gruff voice ruffled the short tufts of my black hair.

Surprised by the suddenness of his emotion, tears burned the back of my throat.

He leaned back and attempted a grin. "There. Now when Blondie and I have to turn you loose, no goodbyes."

"No goodbyes, Caspar." I kissed his cheek and spun away.

*　　*　　*

Still in the grip of winter, March's icy wind ripped through my flak jacket, eating through any warmth the torn material had afforded me. I'd made it through Beta's four-meter-high walls fortified by bayonet-sharp razor wire, sneaking in through the west gate Farrow had promised would be open. I owed her some flowers or something when this was all over.

The northeastern gale howling in my ears, I'd hustled to Sector One without any mishap. This was one time I was thankful for the Company's strict adherence to homogeneity. Each of the sixteen InterNations Territories was gridded the same, so I didn't need my decommissioned D-P's navigation system to lead the way. I'd lived here before, too, and not much had changed except from the destructive forces of war. The poorer sectors hugged the outskirts so the select didn't have to hobnob with their poverty-stricken citizens. Closer in, tenements for civilian and Corps grunts alike transformed into shiny high-rises and affluent businesses toward City Center and the heart of operations, the Quadrangle.

I'd gone rogue, been reported MIA, and was presumably wanted. Now I was getting ready to walk back into a Corps stronghold. *Maybe I am a little reckless.*

Clusters of soldiers roved the streets like packs of hungry dogs. It seemed like the curfew was well in effect and the fighting held at bay, at least on this night, but the ragged war-torn evidence was everywhere. Rubble lining formerly pristine streets, buildings with blast holes, sandbagged trenches, and armies of tanks screamed the Revolution was alive and well. On the other hand, the barred gates, the impenetrable fortress of the Quad, the wire, watchtowers, and giant building-wide Data-Paks spewing the latest CO promos all looked like an unstoppable iron fist.

After the commune with its colorful glory even in the dead of winter, with its celebration of life even when they'd suffered harsh losses of their own, Beta was freezing cold, not just because of the minus-zero temperature. I might've been raised a city girl, but I'd been shaken and taken by the Freelanders ideas, and I wouldn't ever be the same.

Keeping my head down, I fell in step with a patrol, laughing along when they traded jokes about the shit-smelling wildling Nomads and too-dumb-to-fuck Revolutionary rejects. I didn't let my hands shake or my shoulders stoop, thankful they must've thought my less-than-stellar uniform was due to a hard day slogging it out on the warfront. I'd spent most of my career learning how to blend in and stay off the radar, shining only in my role as first lieutenant.

Anonymity was second nature, but damn, I was feeling twitchy.

It'd taken two weeks to cross the Wilderness—land left to Mother Nature's hands and husbanded to fresh fertility by the Free-landers—from Chitamauga located in the lower Appalachians to this northeastern colony. We deviated from Alpha-Beta Route Two, and it would've taken a lot longer had it not been for the bitchin' snowmobiles Farrow had delivered for me, Cannon, and Nate, thanks to her family's scrip, which she siphoned off to help fund the insurgency. That ride was as sweet as my motorcycle left behind months ago in Alpha.

Seemed I'd left just about everything by the wayside since this war started, perhaps long before that. Family, friends, thoughts of a fulfilling life…

Caspar Cannon. True to his word, he and Nate had kept pace with me, our snowmobiles running on fancy fuel cells only the elite could afford. Turning back three days ago, Cannon had maintained his "no goodbyes" policy while Nate gripped me in a long hug.

"I want you to know, Lizbeth, you're not obligated to bring my brother back."

"Nate, I'll—"

He'd rocked me side to side, his gentle arms and gentle drawl quieting me. "Hush up now. You have a mission of your own and a duty to the Revolution. If anythin' happens, you make sure to get yourself out. You are priority number one, darlin.'"

"Fuck."

"Now, now, none of that language. You know what my momma would say." Pressing away from me, he'd swiped a tear clinging to my cheek before Cannon could see it.

"Take care of that big bastard for me, will you?" I'd asked.

He'd nodded and stepped back, linking hands with his husband, whose somber features were too familiar for me to look at. I'd raised my hand, a salute me and Cannon shared, before speeding away through the snowy nation.

The commune—Nate, Cannon, and Darke—had become Central Ops for the entire Revolution, but only Darke could answer my call for help henceforth. Cannon and Nate had been branded enemy number one. They'd be killed on sight. In addition to the cool warrior who would be my point man when shit got ugly in Beta, I had Farrow as my liaison to the commune and the other side of the war, because I was about to go deep cover. My rendezvous with the woman was scheduled for tomorrow night, and I was cutting it close, especially if Commander Cutler decided to stick me in the brig for being AWOL. I had to make sure he bought my story.

By now I was downright itchy.

The double-reinforced steel gate in the sky-high barricade of the

Quad opened before me and the other soldiers. My pulse pounded as I squared off with the four cornerstone buildings where InterNations business was beaten out: Company HQ, the hospital, the Tribunal—home to RACE, *Repopulation and Civilization Enforcement,* the court, jail, and killing grounds for those who committed homosexual crimes—and my former home away from home, Corps Command.

Walking into another one of CEO Lysander Cutler's lion's dens, the flat titanium heels of my lace-ups rang on the polished marble floor. My cap in place if a little filthy, an unemotional mask on my bruised face, I canvassed Beta Corps Command, waiting for my retinal scan from the outer doors to send up the expected alarms. Wearing a shredded uniform more dirty than dark blue, my first lieutenant insignia smudged and hanging off the breast of my shirt, I looked like I'd had an orgy with about a dozen dynamite sticks.

I'd figured the surest way to get Commander Cutler's attention was to serve myself up. It might not have been the smartest move in my arsenal, but I waited for my latest date with disaster without a nervous tic on my body.

Not until the rapid-blast guns—pathetic pieces of shit compared to my pair of Desert Eagles—of the five troopers I'd clocked lounging against the black pillars locked on my location. I strived not to flinch when their sights found me. Cannon may have been my commander in the Elite Tactical Unit, but he was the hothead while I'd been his cool, severely controlled second in command. Unless my mouth ran away with me.

Gun muzzles met my temples, their cold barrels promising chambers of pain if I so much as twitched as I was marched wordlessly through the halls into a soundproof gymnasium. I knew immediately what the strategy was. Lock her up; then make her sing for her momma.

Steeling myself for the blows, I sucked in a breath as I was disarmed. The breath exhaled with a whoosh when the first fist hit my stomach. Doubling over, I bit my lip, just stupid enough to stand tall, meeting the second and third knocks with my face.

What with the unending lashings from five pairs of hands and boots, I didn't get a good look at my assailants. Their questions came on repeat, ringing in my ears with no rhyme or reason. *What's your name, slut? You got a rank, soldier girl? Who are you working for?* Where had I been for five months? My answer to every accusation was a gob of blood splatted at the closest beater-upper.

They obviously hadn't been trained in the fine art of interrogation, or fighting, by Commander Cutler, or if they had, it'd been a slapdash operation. But that didn't matter. A punch was still a punch. And that shit was starting to hurt, especially since I'd made sure Cannon had roughed me up so I looked like I'd been done-over recently so my cover would be airtight before he sent me on my merry way. He'd probably enjoyed it too.

Not as much as these untrained shit stains, though. Except when the door crashed open and one tall wall of barely leashed man strode into the room. They all dropped their punching-bag fists before he said a single word.

"Who gave you the order to interrogate this prisoner?"

"The c-command came from CEO Cutler, s-sir," the little rat bait with the truncheon fists stuttered.

"The CEO is not in charge of this or any other Corps operation. They fall under my jurisdiction." Crackling blue eyes leveled every rookie in the room until the smell of fresh sweat coming off his soldiers joined the iron tang of my spilled blood. "Does it look like she was anywhere near snitching to you?"

The dumb nuts stupid enough to answer in the first place replied, "No, sir." His red hair was a total match for his red face.

"Where are you from that you learned such sloppy tactics, soldier?" Sir asked. His back to me, shoulders stretching his uniform, he grilled his insubordinate.

When no answer came from any of the troops, Sir pivoted toward me. His jaw snapped as he scanned me top to bottom. I made sure the beat-ass didn't show in my precise military bearing, unlike the unlucky mugs who answered to him.

With his finger pointed in my face, he gazed around the room, settling on the jar-faced cunt who'd commandeered my beating.

"I didn't hear your answer, soldier." His words were drawn out like silk over the edge of a sword. He waited long enough for the trooper to start flapping his gums; then, before he had a chance to get any more irate, he simply whipped out his fist, flattening the redheaded blunder boy.

He galvanized the rest of them with, "Have I been sent any other *ninety-day wonders?*"

"NO, COMMANDER, SIR!" went up the deep chorus.

Fucking Linc Cutler. I should've known it. I'd never seen anyone control a room of fuckwits like that except Cannon. I sized him up while he seemed to mull over whose ass to kick next.

He didn't look like Nate apart from their irises, but Linc's were storm-ridden blue, not fresh as fucking flowers. And like a thunderstorm, his earlier look had hit me with lightning force. He was built slightly larger, a fresh shave clearing every single whisker that dared to appear on the straight line of his clenching jaw. His dark blond hair was shorter, his shoulders wider.

Linc's powerful presence caused a delicious spiral of heat between my legs, and beneath my ripped shirt, my nipples tightened. Thoughts of his big body against mine pressed the air from my lungs. My immediate attraction to him was unexpected, and worse, unsettling as the sensual line of his mouth became a single neat slash while he watched my perusal. One eyebrow cocked—in interest or disdain, I couldn't tell. I inhaled silently and slowly, training my sights on my Eagles spun out across the floor.

"Good, clean up this mess. And bring Lieutenant Grant to my office." Neither did Linc speak like Nate, whose southern patois was a soft and passionate song. He hadn't once raised his voice or broken a sweat.

And he sure as hell didn't worry about getting his hands dirty.

"Sir, yes, sir!"

Unimpressed by their late show of rank and file, he swept a steely appraisal over me a second time, springing a new leak in my formidable armor. This time it was derision paired with a hint of admiration, or maybe I was just headed for a concussion. Dizzies from getting my face punched in would be easier to brush off than feeling breathless and kneeless because Linc had found me interesting enough for a twice-over.

He kicked my twin Eagles to me, saying, "Make sure those stay on safety, and get her a goddamn clean uniform. She looks like someone pissed all over her welcome-home parade."

Stalking from the room, he jammed the elevator button, his gaze swinging to mine and holding for several pounding heartbeats before the doors closed between us.

Everything about him denoted coiled power, and I made no mistake about it: Commander Linc Cutler was a man made of deadly detachment. I got the distinct impression he was gonna blister my ass from one end of Beta to the other, and if I thought Cannon was bad, Linc was about to introduce me to a brand-new level of suck.

I'd wanted to get his attention. Mission accomplished.

About the Author

A Yankee transplant via the UK and other wild journeys, Rie happily landed in Charleston, South Carolina, with her English artisan husband and their two small daughters—one an aspiring diva, the other a future punk rocker. They've put down roots in the beautiful area, raising children who meld the southern "y'all" with a British accent, claiming it's a comical combination.

After earning her degree in fine arts, Rie promptly gave up paintbrushes and canvas for paper and pen (because she decided being a writer was equally as good an idea as being an artist; of course it was). That was fifteen years ago that her writing career started. With a manuscript of super epic proportions! Safely stored under a lace doily in a filing cabinet. Possibly in England…

Since then she's done this and that, here and there, usually in the nonprofit arena, until she returned to her dream of being a writer. Even though Rie basks in the glorious southern sunshine as often as she can, she's mostly a nocturnal creature, adjourning to her writer's atelier (spare bedroom) in search of her next devious plot twist or delicious passionate tryst.

No matter what genre or gender pairing she's writing, she combines a sexy southern edge with humor and heart—and a taste of darkness. Enjoy!

www.riewarren.com

Twitter: @RieWrites

Facebook: https://www.facebook.com/RieWarrenRomance

CPSIA information can be obtained at www.ICGtesting.com
Printed in the USA
LVOW05s2024060813

346497LV00001B/2/P